Geraldine Penrose Fitzgerald

The silver Whistle

Vol. I

Geraldine Penrose Fitzgerald

The silver Whistle
Vol. I

ISBN/EAN: 9783337065959

Printed in Europe, USA, Canada, Australia, Japan

Cover: Foto ©Andreas Hilbeck / pixelio.de

More available books at **www.hansebooks.com**

THE SILVER WHISTLE.

A Novel.

BY

"NASEBY."

Author of "Oaks and Birches;" "Only Three Weeks," &c., &c.

VOL. I.

LONDON:

W. H. ALLEN & Co., 13, WATERLOO PLACE, S.W.

1890.

PRINTED BY
THOS. SCOTT AND CO., WARWICK COURT, HOLBORN.
LONDON.

THE SILVER WHISTLE.

CHAPTER I.

THERE is one view of the phonograph which I have not as yet seen in print, and that is that it has been made as a quiet satire on the modern higher educated child. It is, as we know, a mere machine for storing up, bottling with care and reproducing words. The resemblance does not altogether cease with modern childhood. A breath of the satire rustles the leaves of the creepers which cling round the walls of our universities.

As, in the middle ages, men who stayed up at Oxford after they had attained the degree of bachelor of arts attended the ordinary lectures of a regent master and plodded steadily, stolidly on with that eternal old phonograph, Aristotle, so, now-a-days, they let loose their words and suffocate their ideas in a perpetual round of history and philosophy, psychology and metaphysics, and if their minds retain one original chord of music, then comes the great and final Thug —logic.

The best tutor at Oxford generally asks his pupils who go up to him in a state of fuss about the honour school of *Literæ Humaniores:* " Do you want really to learn any philosophy, or do you want simply to know enough of it not to spoil your class in history?" In other words: " Do you wish to be a real phonograph or a sham one?"

B

There is, however, one institution at Oxford which is not only distinctly non-phonographic, but whose influence runs directly athwart phonographism. This is the Union. The debates at the Union are carried on on the principle that the best way of learning to say what you think is to say what you think. In order to say it you must think it first. This implies some sort of thought. Hence the dethroning of the phonograph—for the time being, at any rate.

It was a short time before the Union debating was to begin at Oxford, and an undergraduate was sauntering along, dropping in, first to one shop and then to another, buying some little thing he did not want a bit here, and something he wanted still less there, and burying in sweet oblivion the day when his "little account" would come in, with a polite intimation as to immediate settlement. He was standing with his hat rather on one side and his hands in his trowsers pockets, surveying some gaudy neckties in a shop window, when two other undergraduates joined him.

The taller of the two slipped his arm through his and said : "Why, how many neckties do you want? I saw about fifty in your rooms yesterday. Let me lead you out of temptation to the Union, or else —or else—perhaps you may find yourself in another union."

The speaker was Edgar Sydney, a tall, athletic, very active-looking, rather spare young man. Leaning on his right arm was a fair, delicate, small-featured youth, very tiny, and with the air of a choice toy from the Rue Rivoli.

He was, in fact, French. He was a young French Royalist nobleman, the Vicomte de Laboulaye. He was a great friend of Sydney's, and had come up to stay with him for a few days, and see Oxford. Sydney had spent a great deal of his youth in Paris, and had made many friends there.

"Let me introduce my friend, Mr. Lucas—the Vicomte de Laboulaye."

The young men bowed. Then Lucas shook hands in an informal, rough-and-ready, good natured manner, and welcomed him to Oxford.

"Go on with what you were saying, Laboulaye."

Laboulaye was giving an account of a Skye terrier he had which could walk on his head, with his hind paws in the air. There was something irresistably comical in the way he described how "Ze leetle beeste, him stike ze leges up high in ze air, and pat, pat, pat, on ze front paw."

Lucas laughed immoderately, which pleased the Vicomte, who enjoyed feeling his wit tickled English intellects, and he ended up by inviting Lucas to go and stay with him at his château at St. Cloud. And so the three young men sauntered on towards the Union. They arrived about one minute before the president. They had scarcely sat down when a thin, wavy-haired boy, in gown and cap, strode in, and taking huge steps seemed almost to fly into the president's chair.

The first speech was from a fat, curly haired young man, who stood up and said, before the important business of the evening began, he wanted to remark that the coffee cups at the Union were a great deal too small. He had to stop drinking before his thirst was half satisfied.

"I'd rather pay double," he declared emphatically, waving his arm, "and have my drink out, than be baulked in that way."

This caused a good deal of laughing and much sympathetic applause. The president promised the matter should be attended to.

Then a dull-looking youth, without one atom of fire or enthusiasm, stood up and made a speech. As plainly as the tough and perfectly idiotic old hen—for all hens are perfect idiots—can be discerned in the bewildered-looking chick which maunders out of the incubator in Regent Street, so could the future bore be discerned in him. The man who at the bar, in the pulpit, on the select committee, or in the unfortunate House of Commons, would drive the more alert minded and fidgetty of his fellow men to the very gates of Bedlam. But now, as in the days of Wolsey, the undergrads. will not stand much boring. This boy was soon reduced to a state of silent quiescence.

Then up stood a rather remarkable looking fellow. He was extremely broad shouldered and ungainly. His brow was heavy and overhanging; his eyebrows were black and bushy; his jaw was huge, out of all proportion to the rest of his face; his lips were thick, curled outwards, and shook when he spoke; his expression was that of a *blasé* London club haunter of fifty.

"Vel, zat ese an ugely man," remarked Laboulaye. He thought he must have been sent to college for the sole object to *développer la force physique*. As to intelligence, the light ethereal Gaul thought he could not have any.

Sydney surprised him by saying in his ear : " Listen; you'll hear a lot of things from him, whether true or not, said in a way that will make you think about them."

" Yes," assented Lucas, who was sitting on the other side of Sydney. " That is Maxton, the most unpopular man at Oxford. He has not much real intellectual power, and not one faintest grain of heart; but, somehow, he makes you follow what he is saying."

The discussion that evening was about perfect liberty of expression for every thought and feeling in the life of the modern man of the day—Query: Could it be allowed or not? Maxton argued that it could and should.

" Do we not see the mischief which has arisen from the contrary view in the pages of the history, not only of our own country, but of all surrounding nations?"

" This is a fine opportunity for him to air his history," muttered Lucas. " He came out at the top in history. Why is it that history students are always the most hateful prigs on the face of the earth ? "

" I don't think they are, Lucas," said Sydney, smiling. " I know one or two capital fellows amongst them."

" Well, your experience is more fortunate than mine, then."

" We see," continued Maxton, whose hard, harsh voice was, perhaps, the thing most against his power as an orator, " that in studying history, there must be a fundamental classification of influences. It may be briefly put as those influences which make for liberty, and those which make against it. We have, in history, a passive copy of what things have to say of themselves even more than of what people have to say of the things; and we shall find, as we traverse up the long line of history, that on every side we are met by the inarticulate cry for liberty; and if inanimate things seem to cry for liberty, and if animals really do cry for liberty, how much more must it be necessary to man. Nature herself has had perfect liberty in selection, and on that foundation rests the whole of the magnificent doctrine of development; and unless we reconstruct the whole system of creation, and substitute illusory distinctions for real differences, we must come to and cling to the inevitable conclusion that every created man should have perfect and absolute liberty for every thought of his mind, word of his lips, or action of his body."

There was a flash in Sydney's eyes as he threw himself back in his seat with his arms folded, a flash of strange depth and earnestness, which greatly enhanced the interest of his speaking face.

" The attempt to restrain this legitimate liberty, this fundamental law of liberty," continued Maxton, " has always led to disastrous results. We have evidence of this in the few unfortunate mistakes which an infinitesimal minority of men, who happened not to be possessed by an adequate conception of the relation of ideas to things, perpetrated during the crisis of that grandest movement the world has ever seen, the grea French Revolution."

Some of the audience seemed to sympathise with this, but the majority frowned, and put on that stolid, rather sulky look, which stands with Englishmen for what a shrug does to Frenchmen.

"The French Revolution has taught us grand lessons. It was the most vigorous attempt man ever made towards the discovery of an alkahest, or universal menstruum—a panacea, or grand universal remedy. The leaders of that Revolution were the true alchemists of the world. And how have they been treated by those kings who have ever been the bitterest foes of true liberty? How have they been treated by those historians who are but the paid lackeys of kings? Why, just as the Roman Emperor, Diocletian, true to the traditions of his caste, treated the old alchemists. The earliest mention we find of alchemy is an edict of his ordering all books which treat of the art of making gold and silver to be burned. Thus, in the same spirit, have kings, and an effete and tyrannical aristocracy, endeavoured to crush down, when living, and to malign when dead, all those true pioneers of liberty, like Robespierre, Voltaire, Danton, and Maillard, who are the glory of mankind, the bulwarks of freedom, and the crown of intellectual revolt."

"Nice this for a French Royalist visitor to hear," muttered Lucas. But Laboulaye looked quite composed and even amused.

The remainder of Maxton's speech was merely an enlargement of his original propositions; he wound up with rather a bombastic period, then he sat down.

Amidst loud murmurs of applause, Sydney stood up.
The most popular man in Oxford pitted against the most
unpopular. Here was an interesting evening. Sydney
had masses of soft brown hair, which hung somewhat
over his forehead, and brilliant dark grey eyes, full of
life, spirit and intelligence.

"It appears to me," he said, in a voice full of
enthusiasm and vivacity, "that the matter resolves
itself into one, and one only, most simple question :
Which men are to have perfect liberty? All men cannot
have it, for that is a contradiction in terms. If one man
is to rob and murder another, he may have liberty, but
his victim has not. There are ghosts who could rise and
say Maillard had not given them their idea of liberty.
The only question, then, for society in the present day to
settle is, who shall be the tyrants, and who their slaves?
Who shall be the liberty men, or libertines, and who their
martyrs. Everything else is beside the mark, and so
much wasted breath. Let all the civilized world call
one huge convention, and in it decide for ever, and
have done with it, who shall be up and who shall be
down."

Either the logic of this argument, or the personal
popularity of the speaker at this moment, seemed to
strike the assembly with singular force, for a storm of
applause for an instant drowned Sydney's voice, and
prevented him from going on.

Seeing plainly that, as usual, everything he said
would probably be greeted with the most encouraging
approbation, he was too utterly unbumptious, and too
thoroughly a good fellow, to take advantage of such
leniency; so, after a few more remarks he sat down.
During these remarks he said it seemed to him that
Louis XVI. and Marie Antoinette and their children,
and Madame Elizabeth had been allowed a very
microscopic portion of individual liberty, and Lucas
interpolated, quite loudly, they had certainly not been
given their heads.

Sydney sat down amidst great applause.

Laboulaye chided him for not speaking more, but he only said the fellows were too kind, and he did not like to take advantage of it; and added, he was really nothing of a speaker, and knew very little about anything but horses, and ended by suggesting they should go and have some coffee out of the little coffee cups, which they did, and quite agreed with the speaker who had suggested their enlargement.

As they were walking home, Laboulaye again expressed his regret that Sydney had not spoken more.

"The fellows are so awfully good natured, you see." said Sydney, humbly, "I don't like to take advantage of them. I know I'm nothing of a speaker; I go blundering on, taking up any word that suits at the moment, and why should they be bored because they are good natured? I wish Lucas would have spoken; he has 'the gift,' if you like it! He'll do great things at the Bar yet, you'll see." And Sydney ran his arm kindly through Lucas's.

Lucas shook his head.

"Yes, yes, you will, old fellow," insisted Sydney warmly. "When we both reach the seventh age of man I shall be tottering off with my two sticks to try a little change of air for the gout, by a visit to my old friend Lord Lucas, Lord Chancellor of England."

Again Lucas shook his head

" Let us hope for ze beste," said Laboulaye, earnestly.

This made Lucas laugh immoderately

"Of course, I feel all that might have been said on the side of true liberty," said Sydney. " I wish you could have spoken, Laboulaye; not a man amongst us could have told them the truths you know."

"Thanks; a zousand thanks. I would like greatly to have spoke, but I know not ze English well enough."

" That which in the history of liberty appeals most deeply to one's imagination is the way those who most madly seek most cruelly slaughter her," said Lucas, throwing out his arm, with an oratorical and slightly bombastic gesture.

This delighted Laboulaye, who said : " Bien oui ! Bien oui ! Bien oui ! " over and over again most emphatically.

And so they sauntered on through the quiet moonlit air.

CHAPTER II.

SEVERAL years have passed since the events narrated in the last chapter. A young lady was reading the notices posted up on the door of a fashionable church at Turnham Green. With the assistance of her eye-glass she read:

> " *You are requested to kneel at the more solemn parts of the service. Kneelers are hung on iron hooks down each side of the church.*"

After studying this ecclesiastical document for several minutes, she took out her pencil and wrote at the bottom of the paper: " Surely, with this appalling martrydom in prospect, even the most enthusiastic devotee will be deterred from adopting the position of devotion alluded to." Then she put up her silver pencil-case in her pocket, and hurried to the railway as fast as she could; for (she had come down to pay a visit to a friend in the suburbs) she spied an ascetic-looking curate approaching in the distance.

As soon as she reached home, she took off her things, and went down to the drawing room as fast as possible. An old gentleman looked up from his newspaper as she entered.

" Well! did you tell the cook she had perfectly spoiled the soup last night by putting nearly the whole salt cellar into it?"

" I did."

" What did she say?"

" She said: ' Indeed!'"

" Did she seem sorry?"

"She looked as if I was giving an account of a journey I had taken to Jerusalem in the night; as surprised, and as personally unconcerned."

The speakers were Captain O'Neill Sheil, a fat man, with grey hair, and his daughter, Miss Bridget Sheil, a girl of seventeen, with red hair and blue eyes.

"I cannot think why it is that cookery seems as much a lost art as the Italian opera," he sighed. "They went out together. How different things were in my young days!"

"What more did you say to the cook?"

Proportionate to a man's interest in his dinner is his interest in his cook's temper.

"Well, I thought I would manage very diplomatically, so I said: 'Cook! Cookie! I've got a secret to tell you,'" and Bridget's voice fell, and she adopted the mysterious air she had apparently put on when speaking to the cook.

"Well; and what did she do?"

"She began to roll some dough with the kitchen roller, and said, abruptly: 'Secrets is like measles; they take easy, and spread easy.'"

Captain Sheil, or, as he was called at his home in Ireland, "The Captain," for he was captain in the navy, sighed.

"I fear the case is hopeless! And we got such a flaming character with her! Curry equal to any in India; turtle soup superior to Mansion House dinners! Life is full of disappointments!"

"When I went into the kitchen, I found her with her arms akimbo, a position I have told her never to stand in; so I said to her, anxiously: 'I'm afraid you have a bad pain in your sides.'"

The captain laughed. "Well; and what did she say?"

"'There's some mistresses would give pains to a broadside of servants.' She is engaged to a sailor, you know, which accounts for her familiarity with nautical expressions."

At that moment some visitors were announced.

Bridget had lost her mother when she was only three years old. Captain O'Neill Sheil had tried, with tolerable success, to supply the place of both parents to his daughter. He had been a captain in the navy, but on inheriting a property in Ireland from his uncle, he left the service, and went to live in his native land. A year or two before this story opens Bridget had taken it into her head that she was not being sufficiently well educated by the old governess her father had provided for her. She had, therefore, seen fit to go to Newnham for a year, to give the finishing polish to brains which, faulty in many particulars, at no time could have been considered rusty.

During the time she was at Newnham Captain Sheil had been cruising with a friend in his yacht. He had yielded to her desire to go to Newnham instantly, as he yielded to all her wishes. Her word was law to him, down to the smallest minutiæ of everyday life. She was his only child, and his spare thoughts were occupied in planning to make her happy; except such thoughts as were necessarily absorbed in how to bring the ever more and more obstreperous cook into subjection, and to coax some rent out of his tenants.

On Bridget's return from Newnham she exhibited a knowledge of the technical terms of different sciences such as to lead Captain Sheil to the gratifying conclusion that she had obtained the full value of her college fees.

CHAPTER III.

BRIDGET and her father, who had taken a small house in London for the season, had received an invitation to be present at a grand Elizabethan pageant, which was to take place at a Mrs. Beesting's country seat, Beeswing Park. "Twelfth Night" was to be acted, and the whole entertainment was to wind up with a fancy dress ball. All the spectators of the play, therefore, would be in fancy dress. They left town early so as to arrive in good time for dinner. Soon after dinner the guests began to pour in, and the ball room was crammed with spectators in every sort of attire that ever came into the head of man, and still more of woman, to put upon his back. There was a good deal of pushing and squeezing to get good places for *seeing*. The chairs were all tied together in long rows, about the most uncomfortable arrangement for sitting down that civilization has produced.

Bridget and her father, as they were staying in the house, had tolerably good seats, in the second row from the front. A temporary stage had been erected at one end of the ball room, and when the curtain drew up it disclosed a tableau, with Queen Elizabeth sitting in the middle of the stage, surrounded by her courtiers. Presently, Mary, Queen of Scots, attended by Darnley, and with several Highlanders playing bagpipes in the rear, walked across the stage. She stopped exactly in the centre, and looked Queen Elizabeth full in the face for three minutes; Queen Elizabeth rose to her feet and looked at her in silence. This produced a striking effect Then, in silence, Mary passed off the stage.

After the applause had subsided, Queen Elizabeth ordered the play of " Twelfth Night " to begin in her presence, which it did. She remained seated at the back of the stage on a throne.

It was well acted, though Bridget thought a little less dignity and more vivacity would have enhanced its merits. Still, it was decidedly well acted, and Captain Sheil, who was a great admirer of dignity, was delighted with it. Bridget's attention from the first had been captivated by one of Queen Elizabeth's courtiers, a tall, active-looking young man, in a splendid dress of marone-coloured velvet and gold, cut and slashed with satin of the same colour. He had a broad forehead, on which his hair grew low, or rather, his head rose considerably under his hair, which he wore parted down the middle. His features were well shaped, and he had a slight soft beard and moustache, which just shaded round his cheeks and mouth and chin. But his eyes were what riveted Bridget's too wandering fancy. They were dark eyes, with a look beaming from them of earnestness and thoughtful reflection, unusual in so young a man.

Bridget's eyes could not have been accused, by her most ardent admirer, of earnestness; this may have been why she admired earnestness so much in others. The whole pageant was one of luxurious splendour. A great part of the walls of the room and the sides of the stage were covered with exotic flowers, set off at intervals by huge drooping ferns and palm trees, which reached almost to the ceiling. Draperies of crimson and gold hung round the back of Queen Elizabeth's throne; in fact, truth obliges us to confess that the accessories surpassed the acting. The Queen's dress, and the dresses of all her ladies and courtiers were correct to the smallest particular, as a gentleman, celebrated for his study of old costumes, had designed them. They were made of rich materials, and, in many instances, partly covered with precious stones.

"I wonder who that young man is, papa?" Bridget said, in a stage whisper.

"Don't know, my dear, I'm sure."

"I can tell you," said a good-humoured looking old dowager, who was sitting next to Bridget, "He is a Mr. Sydney—Edgar Sydney—and he is acting the part of Sir Philip Sydney; but he is certainly not a descendant of his," she added, with a sarcastic little laugh.

"Really?" said Bridget.

"No, no;" and the old lady shook her head and laughed again.

Bridget found out afterwards that the old lady had a daughter to whom Sydney steadily refused to pay any attention, though his property joined hers.

As soon as the play was over the chairs were cleared away, and the dancing began.

Bridget waltzed lightly. She was small, with a tiny head and small features, and a little, quick, short manner, which irritated some ladies, but which had about it a mysterious element that fascinated some men. As a rule, ladies did not admire her; they thought her insignificant, and some of the elderly ones considered her pert. But some gentlemen thought her passable-looking, and many liked talking to her, in spite of her freckled cheeks.

This evening she was dressed as Erin, in white nun's cloth, with wreaths of shamrock worked on it in raised green silk, and an old Tara harp brooch on her shoulder. She danced a great deal, but never with the one partner she wished for.

At last, escaping from a tiresome heavy man, who pounded round on his heels, and pushed her persistently in the opposite direction to the one he was going in himself, she stole up to her father and whispered, " Papa, dear papa, do get me an introduction to Mr. Sydney."

" Eh ? eh ? " he said, looking puzzled, " How's that to be done, eh ? "

" Get introduced to him yourself, and then, after a few minutes, you can bring him up to me."

Bridget turned away.

Poor Captain Sheil was a submissive man, and he took a look around him to see how his daughter's commands could be best obeyed. That they must be obeyed, sooner or later, he was well aware, if he wished for a quiet life, a thing which, of all others, he desired.

In his difficulty he applied to his hostess, a good-natured woman, who herself took Sydney up and introduced him to Bridget.

" Sir Phillip Sydney dancing with Erin ! Curious combination ? " remarked some of the bystanders.

" Have you ever been in Ireland, Mr. Sydney ? " asked Bridget, between the rounds of the valse.

" No. I have a great desire to go ; but, somehow or other, something has always happened, just as I was on the point of starting, to prevent me."

" You must not let it happen the next time, and you must come and visit our part of the country."

" I should like it immensely. I feel as if every Englishman ought to try and become personally acquainted with Ireland just now ; her wrongs and her rights have got the entrée, and go in at the side door, before any other subject, in Parliament, literature and conversation, at the present hour."

" And likely to be the question of a good many hours," said Bridget.

" Too true, indeed," he said, thoughtfully. " I fear we English have much to reproach ourselves with in regard to your country ; but tell me what you think is the real cause of all the disquiet."

" That the peasants have not amusement enough,"
she answered decidedly. " I intend, as soon as I go
back, to try and find some more for them."

" A good idea," he said. " But what amusements
would you suggest ? "

" Theatricals of all kinds. Only those who know
the Irish know how they take to the theatre."

Bridget had never enjoyed a dance as she did this
one, and when he asked her for another, she accepted
with an almost too transparent pleasure.

CHAPTER IV.

IT was somewhat early on Cup Day at Ascot. A white haze, like rolls of cotton wool, hid the lower part of the wooded heights. Now and then the faintest whisper of a breeze, like a troublesome acquaintance who has forgotten us for a moment, but soon remembers to come back and tease us, stirred the golden blossoms of the gorse. It was a cold, piercing wind when it came, due east, and blighted the good of the sun.

The three-horsed omnibuses, with their freights of Londoners, were beginning to arrive from Windsor. The driver of one of these had just flung his reins on to the backs of his horses, and was rubbing his hands, preparatory to having a glass of "hot and strong," when a man in a black coat, with a scarlet jersey under it, and a scarlet band round his cap, came up and offered him a tract. The driver looked at the young enthusiast for a moment, then at the tract, then said politely, as he handed it back, " No, thank yer; I hattends to hall them matters of a Sunday, not of a Cup Day."

A jockey, who was taking a turn on the famous Berkshire heath, and renewing his acquaintance with its odd and unsuspected ups and downs, heard this remark, and laughed heartily.

Just at that moment a policeman came up, in that state of fume and fuss which always precedes the royal procession amongst the constabulary.

" Clear the course ! Clear the course."

Our friend, the jockey, had sauntered out on to the centre of the course, and was investigating it with those peculiar perceptions which none but jockeys possess.

"Clear the course! Clear the course!" And the policeman roughly pushed him out of the way. He used a naughty, such a naughty, word, and reluctantly bent his slight figure under the iron rail. At that instant a crow flew, only about twenty feet from the ground, squalling in a rude and defiant voice just over the heads of the spectators. The policeman looked up in a haughty and injured manner.

"Aha! You can't keep 'im in order, my fine fellow," said the jockey, triumphantly. The constable's face grew red. He scowled, but scorned to reply. It was a remark that was bad to beat for causticity. The jockey laughed loudly, and the bystanders joined with him.

This jockey was not a perfect character, but he had many redeeming qualities. His name was Baltimore. He could tell in one glance when a horse which had done well on other courses must be classed at Ascot amongst the helpless division. And this because he knew the course at Ascot as well as the letters of his own name. At this moment he wore a loose grey suit of dittoes, a black hat, and a very polished pair of elastic sided boots. He looked like a pious choir boy slowly sinking into a consumption. He was silent during the next ten minutes, while he was taking his walk, and appeared to be ruminating deeply. Who shall divine his meditations? Sydney always said that the knife to open the oyster of a jockey's private thoughts has not yet left Sheffield, and may not be expected to leave it to-morrow.

The coaching enclosures were beginning to get crowded. After the wearying, hateful debates, or rather wrangles, of the past few weeks, many M.P.'s. felt that the only thing which stood between them and Bedlam was a breezy spin through the rhododendrons and under the laburnums which make the road to Ascot the prettiest in the county.

Drags full of hereditary legislators were drawing up, moment after moment. Specimens of that shy, skittish animal, of such curious and solitary habits—the Filius Maximus—having been pursued, and harried on the drags by diligent students of " mama's own book," were seeking a " campo pulito," where they could escape to. Many of them found welcome cover in the paddock. The grand stand was, to their peculiar vision, all hung round with red flags of danger, the royal enclosure little better, the paddock *safish*, but not altogether safe.

Some of them found the merry-go-rounds at the lower end of the course the most absolutely impregnable shelter, and were feign to put up with a certain sea-sick motion, and with the still more certain reproach of, " He has such low tastes." " Beer and skittles fancy !" rather than hazard the perils of squashed strawberry satins and green seaweed hats.

Meantime, that charming, wholly delightful, though somewhat gregarious ground game, " The Frater Junius," was to be found heroically facing every point of danger. In spite of frowns from matronly brows, mutterings of " Two negative younger sons make one positive nuisance," etc., he unblushingly smiled blandly on; put his round smiling face entirely under the shadow of Duchess of Devonshire hats; squeezed little hands, which had been practising the scales of precedence for weeks, so genially that sometimes even French kid gave way. His feet were equally at home on the sacred soil of the royal enclosure as on the steps of his elder brother's drag. Profane creature ! He did, indeed, dare to rush in where angels feared to tread, as dear mamma so often thought, and sometimes remarked to her daughters. Luncheon was the peculiar swarming hour of the genus; *salmon à la mayonnaise*, etc., etc, washed down by dear brother's Moselle of '78, was not only partaken of by themselves, but, far worse, handed by them to those little mouths which were never made to receive libations from an orsedew (which is what some matrons called these detrimentals). [An orsedew is an inferior kind of gold-leaf, or rather *brass-leaf,* prepared from a sort of fine brass]. These mouths, to the disgust of chaperones, did not disdain to smile upon their boldness.

In the meantime, the Filius Maximus was in some instances consoling his disconsolate interior with such husks as stale penny buns, short bread, made with rancid butter, and flat lemonade, near to where Aunt Sally was being played, while eminent daughticulturalists were wondering where he had transplanted himself.

A great crowd had gone down to see the arrival of the royal procession. They were standing chattering in parterres of many colours behind the walk and under the overshadowing trees of Miss Thacker's charming demense. They listened to the music of their own voices, but failed to notice that of the whispering breeze stirring amongst the sharp spires of the firs. Clouds hung heavily over Windsor Forest, but the chill wind kept the sun dogs so far at bay in the neighbourhood of Ascot that the new mile was bathed in a flood of delicious sunshine just as the royal procession turned in to it from Swinley Bottom.

The crimson and gold liveries of the royal huntsmen danced about like a drop of vermilion in the middle distance. Sweeping up the long undulating vista of soft sward, at an easy trot, came the dark Lincoln Green of the rangers, showing the master of the buck-hounds his way to the winning-post; then that showy livery, which England, the most unshowy country in the world, is so proud of; then the open carriage, with the fat, good humoured face by the side of the sweet lovely one which England is still more proud of. As they approached the grand stand, a perfect roar, like a salute from a line of battle ships greeted them. Not a voice was silent.

The Vicomte de Laboulaye, who had come down with Sydney on his drag, was greatly struck by the burst of universal enthusiasm. He observed the cheers came from the poorest tramps with greater vigour than from the curled darlings of the grand stand. He sighed as he thought of the sort of reception the King of France would be likely to receive from the blue bloused workmen at Longchamps.

A dark blue drag, called by the ladies "spick-and-span," and by the gentlemen "tidy-looking," was drawn up almost opposite the winning post. The luncheon board of the first and earliest luncheon had been pushed somewhat in the back-ground, and the champagne bottles, corkless and half empty, seemed to invite gipsies to help themselves.

On the front seat was a lady, in crushed strawberry muslin, with white work on it and parasol to match. She was fair-haired and blue-eyed, handsome, with a good-tempered, easy-going face and manner. All the people on the surrounding drags seemed to know her, and she appeared popular. Everyone came to her for help in their troubles.

A young man on one of the other drags had cut his finger with a bit of broken glass. He climbed up and sat down by her. He was a cousin.

" Dear Gracie " (everyone called her that), " have you got a bit of sticking plaster ? "

And she quickly produced from her pocket a nice little case full of plaster. She washed his wound, and then put the plaster on so nicely that he could not resist bending down and pressing his lips lightly on her soft, plump cheeks.

" Dear Gracie, there's no one like you."

She smiled; and in another minute he was gone. Hardly had his shadow grown faint, when a girl pulled herself up and sat down by Gracie. She had torn a bit of frilling off the edge of her dress, and she knew Gracie would mend it. And Gracie took out a little rolled leather needle and thread holder, and mended it quickly. And then the girl kissed her, called her " dear old Gracie ;" said she did not know what anyone would do without her, and went back to her drag and her flirting, and Gracie had a few moments to herself to enjoy the races. Only a few, for a young man who had driven one of the drags down had just given a slit to his whip. He and Gracie were cousins and old friends, friends from childhood. To her he flew at once. She immediately brought forth from the depth of that " Universal Provider " of a pocket, a nice little bit of thin whip-cord, and with a splinter, wielded by her deft fingers, soon set the whip to rights. The young Jehu was delighted, and for a minute or two gazed first at his whip and then at her.

" Dearest Gracie " (this was a refreshing change from the usual formula), " Darling Gracie " (this was still more refreshing); then, as there was a row going on on the race course, which absorbed everyone's attention, he took her right hand and pressed it to his lips. She smiled in such a nice, good-tempered way, and looked as if she was not at all angry, to say the least. Just then the move came for the second and important luncheon. This is how Gracie went to the guard's tent. A young man who, about half-an-hour before, had twisted his ankle, leaned somewhat heavily on her right arm, though making pretence she was leaning on him. In front of her went a middle-aged man carrying two shawls. Behind her came a girl, who kept pulling the back of her dress, and saying, " Wait, Gracie ; wait for Mabel," and she turned her head, " she will be here directly."

" Yes ; when she's done flirting with Hollands," said the young man who was leaning on her, impatiently. " Don't stop, Gracie," he added, as he urged her forward with his arm.

" Do what you like, Gracie, just for once in your life, by way of a change," said the middle-aged man with the shawls.

" Dear Gracie," said the invalid, " it's awfully good of you to let me lean on you. Of course, I could have asked any of the fellows : they're awfully obligin', and all that ; but it would have bored them."

" Yes, dear ; I know ; and I like to have you. Lean as heavily as you like." He was an old, old friend.

When they reached the tent, as she carefully lowered her invalid into his chair, he said :

" Dear Gracie, why are not all women like you ? By Jove ! he'll be a lucky fellow who gets you."

He had no intention of asking her himself, however. His heart was at that moment captivated by a pert, sharp little minx, the exact opposite of Gracie in everything, whose exquisitely-fitting dress concealed no heart under its smooth surface. Now, Gracie's dresses did conceal a heart, but never seemed quite to fit her. No matter how handsome her clothes, she never looked well dressed. Always untidy, and her hat or bonnet a little crooked.

Luncheon over, she supported her invalid back to his drag, then climbed up on her own, and was, as usual, surrounded by friends. Suddenly a gipsy, in an old red shawl, and a black bonnet falling off the back of her head, stopped opposite the drag, and asked if she might be allowed to tell the fair-haired lady's fortune.

" Yes ; come along," she said, good humouredly.

Up climbed the gipsy on to the wheel, looking not a little elated at having obtained a permission she had been vainly seeking for all the morning from the other fair occupants of carriages. All the ladies on the other drags now became alert and interested. They leaned forward, and called out to know what was going on.

" Gracie's having her fortune told," passed from lip to lip.

"What fun!" exclaimed everyone, laughing.

"Any good shots, Gracie?"

"Not yet," she said, shaking her head.

A great deal of crossing of the hand with half-crowns and two-shilling bits had to take place. These were supplied by a tall young man, in the regulation full-dress square cut coat, with a huge pink carnation in his buttonhole, who was sitting just behind Gracie on the drag.

"Your fate will overtake you this year," said the gipsy.

"No, no; not this year," said Gracie, shaking her head. "Next year; not this year."

"Any good shots yet, Gracie?" called out the girls from the other drags.

"No," said Gracie, shortly.

"You must wish now, m'am," said the gipsy, once more claiming half-a-crown for crossing her palm.

"I've wished," said Gracie.

"You must tell me now," said the old woman.

"Tell you what?" said Gracie. "Tell you my wish?" and she looked full into the old woman's face. "Not quite!"

The old woman pretended that she did not want to know what she had wished.

Here the gentlemen leaned over and listened, with great interest and anxiety.

"Shall I marry the man I love?" Gracie's voice was low, and her face very pink.

Just at this juncture a policeman came up, and seizing hold of the gipsy by the shoulder, ordered her to get down at once.

"These ladies asked me to come here," said the gipsy, with much dignity, "and I shall not go away till I've finished telling them their fortunes, for which I'm paid."

"Yes," said Gracie, leaning forward and speaking decidedly, "I told her to come."

“O, you did, did you?” said the constable. “I suppose you think you’ll get told something nice?” And he turned away with a shrug. “Another five minutes and you’ll be a wantin’ me to interfere to take ’er away;” and he walked off with a sulky face.

At that moment a race was being won, and while everyone turned to look at the horses, Gracie bent down and whispered again, “Shall I marry the man I love?”

The gipsy looked puzzled. She examined and re-examined each line on the plump pink hand; she crossed the palm repeatedly with a two shilling bit; she wrinkled her bronzed brow, until it looked like a fir cone.

The girl watched her with an anxiety which she did not try to conceal, because no one was at that moment watching her.

At length the old woman said, “Not for many years.”

“What matters years?” exclaimed the girl impetuously. “I *do* marry him in the end?”

“Yes; you do in the end.”

While everyone was still staring at the race she slipped half-a-sovereign out of her purse and transferred it to the gipsy’s hand.

It so happened that for two years Gracie had been attached to Sydney, and had gone so near to proposing for him, once or twice, that he had found some difficulty in making his escape with becoming gallantry.

Why he should have made his escape he wondered afterwards, for Gracie was well off, good looking, and quite marvellously good tempered. He knew he must marry some day. It would have pleased his mother if he could have married her; but it did not seem to him that he was in love with her, and that was the whole thing in a nut-shell.

She was the only daughter of a marquis, whose property joined his. Like everybody, he was fond of her ; but though he had never been in love, he thought that he *could* be more in love than he was with her.

Meantime the tears came into Gracie's eyes. The horses finished the race, and, laden with many half-crowns, the gipsy climbed down from off the wheel, and made her way through the crowd as fast as she could.

Two hours later luncheon, in general, was over, as far as it ever is over at Ascot. The paddock was crowded. A very interesting race was to come off shortly. Sydney was going to run a young Irish horse, called Clauricaune—a new horse, who had his spurs to win. Pitted against him were horses with splendid pedigrees, and some of the most renowned racing blood in Europe in them : horses which had made big bids for a place before now.

Lord Hashtheboy was the owner of a formidable rival in the shape of a filly ; a magnificent—apparently magnificent—youngster, called La Tosca, for which he had given a sum worthy of his fortune and his gullibility, but which he was not aware had been fattened for sale. However, even Baltimore, Sydney's jockey, allowed that she " looked dangerous."

There are some men who strut about the paddock at Ascot in a manner which gives you the idea that they think the whole thing was got up entirely for them—races, royal procession and all. Such a man was Hashtheboy. He was fat, thick necked, apoplectic-looking. When first he fixed his eyes upon you, their expression seemed always to be saying, " Pause, inferior lump of clay ; I'll give you until next week for reflection as to whether you will fall down and worship me ; if not, I'll make you regret it the week after." He had taken a great interest in, and been present at, many a curious race and many a false run one ; but he had not lost in the estimation of the world by that. What he had lost by was his passion for boasting. Some men bluster and swagger in life's game to such an extent that their ace of trumps is shaken from their hand, and drops, unperceived, at their feet; then they trample it into the dust with their heel, boasting all the time of their knowledge of cards, while every one is laughing at them.

Hashtheboy had several times lost much that he valued by his bluster, but he was not aware of it. He liked also to make those he was pleased to consider beneath him in position feel his power over them. The result was, he saw nothing but melancholy faces round him; for no one is in good spirits when they are conscious of being the slaves of a bully's caprices. But he liked those melancholy faces. Just as every Italian gentlemen tries to have cypress trees round his villa, so did he evidently consider that every English gentleman ought to have sad faces round his hall. It proved the owner's power to make inferiors subservient to his will in mind as well as body. But, to give every man his due, he was not altogether devoid of personal bravery; and, in spite of his taste for racing, was, in some respects, better suited to the ring than the hippodrome Much as he avoided bodily pain, and disliked a scratch on his own skin, provided his antagonist was a lighter weight than himself, and was in bad condition, he would not have objected to a three-round contest. Under such conditions pugilism becomes brutality, and brutality had been second nature to him since his schoolboy days. The fact was, he was fond of boxing and beating another person, either mentally or physically; otherwise, where personal danger was apparent, he gave signs of belonging to the Prudential Assurance Association.

At the present moment he was talking to his jockey, Bill Mathers, with an expression of genuine tyranny and assumed politeness. Every now and then he put on a look of cunning; the reason he did this was because he wanted Bill to think that he was up to his tricks. Now, Bill would have thought that without his putting

on the look ; in fact, Bill's feeling was, that he was
not quite up to *his* tricks. As a matter of practical
experience—everyday experience—Sydney had caught
him out in so many lies that he usually called him
" Lord Cram de la Cram." It is, therefore, not to be
wondered at that a poor, innocent little jockey should
feel that he might unconsciously become the victim of
deviations from the truth which his unsuspecting
nature could not have fathomed. Many a young
masher who had suffered from Hashtheboy's over-
bearing, dictatorial bluster, eagerly caught up the idea
of " Lord Cram de la Cram." He was particularly
fond of treading on mashers' polished Tory toes. The
name seemed singularly appropriate, for he thought
himself, in spite of the most singular and essential
vulgarity of mind and manner, such as is to be found
nowhere as it occasionally is in the peerage, the very
cream of the whole aristocracy.

As the mashers aged a little in years, and a great,
great deal in experience, they came to question—though
they kept the question to themselves—whether there
was not more than one peer of the realm by whom the
quaint old legend, " Cram de la Cram," might not
have been adopted as a family motto.

Mathers was a clever jockey and a very good
sort of a fellow. At present he looked sulky, and as if
he had the toothache. His cap was pulled down over
his eyes, and his straw-coloured bristles stuck out
angrily from under it. His full, girlish lips, in the
shape of Cupid's bow, were pouted out, and his fair
brow knit. It was easy for an intellect like his to read
between the lines of the bland balderdash Hashtheboy
considered it judicious to bestow on his servant on
the eve of the most important race of the day. The
snobbishness of that nobleman's manner, as he half
patronized, half bullied, looked as if he longed to
thrash, yet fawned before, the boy in whose hands the
fate of many thousands of his pounds lay ; the boy

he considered his inferior, but who was so vastly his
superior, tickled Sydney's fancy immensely.

He was standing, leaning his shoulders against the
rails, his right knee was bent, and the heel of his boot
was caught on the low ground rail. His hat was
cocked forward until its rim reached his eyebrows, for
the sun was shining full in his face. He was watching
the movements of Hashtheboy, and there was a twinkle
in the corner of his eye, as if he was having fun in the
recesses of his soul.

There was something in his lordship's appearance
which added a zest to bucolic manners. His moustaches
were in round, heavy rolls, like German sausages. His
whiskers were large, straggling, and three-cornered in
shape. Short, stubbly hair grew in a continuous ridge
from one whisker to the other, underneath his second
double chin.

He considered himself, both in appearance, manner
and character, like Julius Cæsar. But the great man's
mantel had lost somewhat in transit.

Laboulaye was standing, smoking a Spanish cigarette,
on Sydney's right.

"What do you think of that specimen of our insular
aristocracy?"

"He looks horriblement fagotée," answered the
Frenchman, gazing, with a very odd expression, at
Hashtheboy. Laboulaye's English was now, in
consequence of much practice, almost as good as an
Englishman's.

"Well, he's trying to be civil, and no doubt that
unusual amusement would fagotée him within an inch
of his life."

At that moment, Baltimore was seen approaching
across the paddock. He was now in his best temper;
but he had developed a cold in his head, or hay fever,
or some such thing, during the last hour or two, and
was buttoned up in a thick brown ulster, with a red
worsted comforter round his throat.

As he passed Bill, he pinched the back of his elbow, and gave him a knowing little wink, as much as to say, "I sympathise with you." He did whisper, low and rapidly as he passed on into his ear: "Keep up your spirits. You know how to pay him out." Bill's severe tension of expression relaxed for a minute; but as he continued to listen to his temporary master, soon the frown gathered again. "My deaw boy," Hashtheboy said, constantly. In fact, this was the formula in which he addressed numbers of his friends.

Meantime Baltimore had reached Sydney's side. He looked up at him, saw the direction of his eyes, and let his follow them. He shrugged his shoulders.

"'E's only fit for leather flappin' meetins, w'ere 'e could give 'is blessin' to rowdyism and questinibble practises of all sorts."

Sydney smiled. He knew a jockey could not say a more severe thing.

"His reel mates is spivs and sharps."

Bill must have said something pert, for at that instant, Hashtheboy brought the point of his silver-headed stick down with a bang on the earth, and stamped his foot, while he used a word not to be found in any dictionary; not knowing that his revered political leader, in whose sight he ever wished to appear as the blameless knight of Tintagel, was passing close behind him. Thus are the best of us, now and then, caught tripping by our idols. Meantime, his thinly-disguised passion continued to break bounds.

"Behold!" exclaimed Sydney, flinging out his arm, "Radical Aristocracy, out of Humour, by Bluster."

"Eh! indeed," assented Baltimore, "or Snobbery out of Jobbery, by Trickery, 'ud do 'im as well."

"Or Socialism, by Incendiary, out of Communism," muttered Sydney, reflecting on his political opinions.

At that moment, Hashtheboy's great political leader, swinging his field glasses, and his lips moving, as if holding sweet converse with his inmost soul, passed close to them.

"Ah—a!" said Baltimore, with a long-drawn note of admiration. He was a strongly pronounced Liberal of the most advanced school. "Ah—a, there goes a 'eaven born genius for yer."

"Well, if he is," remarked Sydney, laconically, "all I can say is, I hope the heavens won't be in the family-way again in my lifetime."

Laboulaye knew English well enough to catch the fun of this, and laughed with that peculiar lightness and gaiety belonging to his nation.

By this time Hashtheboy's voice was rising, so as to attract attention in those near him.

"By Jove!" said Sydney, whose eyes returned to him with irresistible attraction, "I do believe he thinks he will bully the paddock into accepting his starting prices, and rule the settling."

"There's a few Hinglishmen left in the paddock yet," said Baltimore, dryly.

After sneezing several times, he fell to watching the growing irritation on Sydney's face with much interest.

"'Twill soon be Mr. Sydney, out of Patience, by Bloated Aristocrat."

Baltimore was a wag in a quiet way. Had he happened to have lived in the days of Sydney Smith, and been born of a family which disliked horses, there is no knowing the position he might have occupied in the social circle.

Sydney smiled. "True," he answered. "But, upon my word, it's extraordinary what a number of members of the present House of Lords are 'a distance' from being gentlemen."

Laboulaye had been listening intently to the sporting conversation, hoping to pick up an expression here and there.

"A distance!" he exclaimed, caught by the word used

in its present position, " Quel est, that is, what is, then, a distance ? "

" Two hundred and forty yards, my lord," replied Baltimore, promptly. He had been told that Laboulaye was a viscount.

" A long way that, Laboulaye, for a nobleman to be off a gentleman," said Sydney.

" A breather," said Baltimore. Laboulaye did not quite grasp the position of affairs.

" If he could get on Clauricaune's back, now," continued Baltimore, " which he can't, for Clauri. would shoot such rubbish ; but if he could, he would soon cover the ground, for Clauri. takes twenty-four feet in a bound when galloping."

" Does he ? " said Sydney. " So you've turned into a literary character, Master Baltimore, and been taking foot notes, eh ? "

Baltimore laughed and looked pleased.

Pleasant as Sydney was to everyone, it was in his intercourse with his dependents that the perfection of his manners came out. Without losing his own dignity, he put them at their case immediately. I do not mean to say that Sydney never fell out with his jockey, for he did.

In spite of his cherub-like appearance, Baltimore's temper was anything but angelic. He occasionally flew into furies with saddles and girths, and used naughty, naughty words. And then, if Sydney attempted to interfere, he turned on him, and was frightfully disrespectful. A few big D——s, however, on both sides, usually tided over the difficulty, and united what threatened to be a breach. A good ringing cement is dammar, as every chemist knows.

At that moment a horse in his stable clothes passed slowly, led by a groom. He was one of the future antagonists of Clauricaune.

" Good looking and fit," said Sydney, eying him carefully. " Moves well."

" Yes," assented Baltimore, with a sarcastic smile.
" I'm told the commission agent was given thirty to six
for a limit."

" By Jove !" said Sydney, laughing. " The stable
followers can't be called cormorants this time."

Laboulaye had an intense admiration for English sport
of all sorts, but especially English racing. Sydney was
his *beau ideal* of an English sportsman ; and, truly, he
could not have made his *début* on a racecourse under
more favourable auspices. No one was better " up " to
the heterogeneous elements of which the turf is
composed. Few knew the ins and outs of its
complicated machinery with such a practical knowledge.

Laboulaye never doubted for an instant that
Clauricaune would win. He had a great deal of
the simple trust and confidingness which so many
Royalists have found to be devoid of speculative
insight. " When Clauricaune win," he said, eagerly,
" I telegram to my brothere, who is at my chateau at
St. Cloud. He get it immejitely, and have ze news
before anyone else in Paris. That make heme ver'
proud."

Sydney smiled. " I fear you may be disappointed,
Paris may know it sooner than you think. It is said
that when Iroquois won the Derby, it was known in
New York twenty-five seconds after the horse passed
the winning post.

" Ese possible !" exclaimed Laboulaye, " Well, could
not be quikere than that. You English do do things
quike.

" We telegram our victories quick, but are not quite
so quick to pay."

" Once I see Clauricaune fly past ze post, I telegram
ze victory, then collect all my bets at once."

Sydney and Baltimore looked at each other.

" First-past-the-post style of thing !" said Baltimore,
with a knowing smile. Sydney smiled back upon him,
then said kindly to Laboulaye : " You are not allowed

to bet on first past the post; that is to say, a backer in
the ring can't get his money the moment his horse
is first past the post, and the number is hoisted; the
Jockey Club won't allow it."

"Not allow you to get your monie when your horse
he win?" exclaimed Laboulaye, in amazement.

Baltimore turned away, and dragged up his red
worsted comforter over his mouth to hide the impolite
merriment which the expression of the Frenchman's
face caused him.

"I told you England was not altogether such a
delightful place as you thought," said Sydney, biting
his lips, because no gravity of politeness could long
have withstood the dismay on the vicomte's fair, boyish
face.

"You will have to wait till Clauricaune weighs in
' all right,' before you see the shine of a sixpence, me
lord," said Baltimore.

"Too true," said Sydney, shaking his head, and
looking quizzically out of his kind blue eyes at his
young friend; "and, if an objection is raised, you
will have to wait until the breeze blows over, and
they fight it out to the bitter end; perhaps for
months."

"Mais! Mon Dieu!" exclaimed Laboulaye, looking
aghast.

"I tell you, Laboulaye, the slowest thing Englishmen
do is parting with their money."

"And dem slow it is, too!" muttered Baltimore,
with a sigh.

At that instant two very smart young mashers, who
were sauntering about, arm in arm, with cigarettes in
their mouths, came and shook hands with Sydney.
They shook hands with a cordiality foreign to their
temporary nature—for their nature is temporary; they
change it after forty. With that natural selection
which exists even amongst mashers, each masher chose
Sydney as his first favourite, and, though hating to

show cordiality, each one was betrayed out of his correct judgment by Sydney's manner.

At a certain fashionable club, it sometimes happened that a row of a dozen mashers stood in the windows. There were four windows, and three stood in each window, each one sucking a tooth-pick. Occasionally, one went out of the room for a moment to drink barley-water; then he came back and stood just where he had done before, having put the tooth-pick back into its previous position. Not one spoke to the other. The fundamental conception of a masher is a cold, still, scornful thing, in the presence of males of his own age and class. Mashers are a distinct race. They seem to have been established *per saltum*, and to have bred true from some primeval egg; for, under one name or another, they are to be found in the most remote ages of history; indeed, implements have been recently discovered which might place their origin even higher up. It is not possible to point out any obvious reason for the appearance of the variety. No doubt there were determining causes for it, as for all other phenomena, but they are not given in any scientific work which is offered to the ordinary student at either of the universities.

In the case of the twelve mashers in the four windows, to which I have alluded, their particular silence arose from a well defined reason. Each masher thought himself so grand that it would be out of the question he could speak to any other masher.

They stood with an austere but somewhat wrapt expression on their countenances. To look at them, they might have been listening to some strains of the music of the future, not audible to other ears. Or perhaps another view might be taken: each one might have been carrying a private jubilee musical cigar case, which, instead of playing the National Anthem, rolled on incessantly with "See, the Conquering Hero Comes!" adding, with a burst of trumpets, " He is here, he is here; I am the man, I am the man!" So there they all twelve stood, and thanked the great unknown cause of all other things except themselves that they were not as these eleven mashers here.

This was interesting, so far as it went; but an indefinite prolongation of unlimited contempt is apt to lead to a total eclipse of almost every other pleasureable sensation. Now, the mashers were, in point of years, young; therefore a personification of Mephistopheles in his sterner moods palled after a time.

When Sydney appeared, with his fresh, open-air, sportsman-like look, his gentle but genial manners, and his apparent indifference as to whether he was spoken to or not, it was found impossible to resist the setting in of a slight thaw.

Sydney was so evidently not going to think he was insulted if spoken to, and still less so if he was not spoken to, that the more courageous spirits, after a hem and a haw or two, took the plunge. And Sydney answered and enjoyed himself. He usually did enjoy himself; his sense of humour was one of the most engrained of his characteristics. He managed to get a good deal of fun out of his intercourse with human nature; his fascinating sympathy of tone and manner put the vainest men completely off their guard; his eyes, too, were so truthful, clear and sympathetic-looking, that the most touchy and bumptious swaggerer could not fail to trust them. It was odd that that quiet twinkle in their remotest corner always seemed to escape observation; the fact was, every masher and almost every man who knew him, except his few enemies, was pleased and not a little proud when Sydney voluntarily addressed him. His reputation as the keenest sportsman in England, to do the mashers justice—and they have their good points—went not a little way in breaking down the monotony of the gigantic fetish worship which was perpetually going on in each one's soul. It enabled him to see, if only for a moment, that a man might live for other things than the perpetual worship of self's unexampled position in the social world. Also, the contrast Sydney presented was in itself attractive. Each masher might affirm for ever that the masher style of man was the grandest ever known ; but, apart from negation, pure affirmation has no meaning.

These two mashers were respectively the eldest son of a well-known and deeply religious baronet, and the youngest son of an equally well-known, but not so religious, North of England horse-breeder. Sydney greeted them with his usual politeness, but without implying that he considered his position a preposterously fortunate one in being honoured by their notice.

Laboulaye became much interested in watching them, and in taking notes about the cut of his own future shirt-collars, and of the way to put a huge carnation into his buttonhole without its getting top-heavy and tumbling out. While they were talking, two or three noblemen who kept racers came up and joined the group. They all liked to have a word with Sydney; he, poor fellow, never could have a quiet five minutes anywhere. The human nature in everyone he met came out towards him, and people who once found themselves in his company liked to remain and bask there. It was like going from a London fog to sit under the orange groves at Monte Carlo; to go from the thoughts of the ordinary society mind to sit under the shadow of his thoughts. That exhaustive scrutiny of their own perfections which many men delight in, could be carried on under his eye without any danger of a drop of cold water falling on it, or a fog obscuring it. After all, the really popular man with men is the one who knows how to play second fiddle to a large assortment of firsts. To listen to other men's bump without bumping himself. Nowhere is bump more predominant than in a paddock. If you listen you will hear I, I, I; *my* horse, *my* jockey, *my* judgment of a horse, over and over again, like the few notes of air in a fugue of Bach's.

The burden of many paddock men's conversation might be summed up in the one dramatic line: "See how we pippins swim." A micrometer, of comparatively small range, could usually decide the question; but this is not what they want. What their soul really desires to find is a listener who will say, " My word, how you do!" A listener of weight in the political, official or social world, who will say it heartily, is what makes life worth living. Now, women, as a rule, will say it ten times as quickly and fifty times as heartily as men. This is why men vary the monotony of existence by occasionally talking to women when men can be had; but, then, it is an unfortunate fact in conversational economy that one man's, " My word, how you do !" is worth five hundred women's : no, five million ! Now, Sydney was always ready to say gently, but in a very charming voice, " My word, my word, *my word*, how you do! what a swell you are ! Why, you can afford to keep a wet coachman for rainy nights !" Like Melchior Anderegg, the great Meiringer guide, he could listen with a calm, unmoved face, while Eton boys and Oxford undergrads. described their marvellous feats of prowess in mountaineering, and merely put in a note of admiration now and then.

This is the sort of fellow who is your man's favourite. The grand, heroic fashion, or in the Queen's English, the bumptious, black-haired, blusterer is your woman's. Had Hashtheboy been about a foot and a half taller and adorned with coal-black hair and moustache, and sooty eyes, with gleaming whites, he would have been the idol of every lady in the country. Women always take men at their own valuation.

While they were all talking, a quiet, shy-looking young man, with a pale face and somewhat starved expression, sauntered by, glancing nervously out of the sides of his eyes to see whether Sydney meant to

speak to him or not. His coat was old and worn, and
his shirt-collar was in a state in which the fundamental
texture of linen could be conveniently studied.

The moment Sydney saw him, he started forward
with an eager, genuine exclamation of pleasure.

"Massinger, old fellow! Delighted to see you!"
and he wrung his hand heartily.

The young man's face brightened. It was worth a
nugget of gold to see the change which came over his
whole manner and expression. He had been at the
Bar for some years; but he was not a clever fellow;
he had no interest, and had a straightforward way of
speaking his mind which is only to be endured from a
man who can give good dinners as a panacea. He had
one or two fast friends and many enemies. He had
never as yet held a brief. The small private fortune
which had enabled him so far to hold his head above
water was derived from land in Ireland. He had not
got a penny for two years. He had been obliged
entirely to renounce society, and had retired to a garret
in the east end, where he lived on bread, salt butter
and bloaters. He could not have lived at all upon
anything, had it not been that Sydney persistently
sought him out, and every now and then pressed a
twenty pound note into his hand. The mashers inspected his threadbare coat with their eye-glasses.

"I'm so awfully glad to see you, old fellow!" said
Sydney, linking his arm in his. "I was wondering,
only this morning, what on earth had become of you.
I shan't lose sight of you, now that once I've caught
you. You must come home to dinner," and he looked
down with his sunny smile into Massinger's careworn
face. "Come along; now we'll go and have a final
inspection of the hope of the house of Sydney" (he
meant Clauricaune).

Nodding to the other members of the group, he and
Massinger and Laboulaye walked away, pioneered by
Baltimore, towards the stables.

The moment of the start drew near. A heavy shower of cold rain, which had fallen about half-an-hour before, made the ground in rather a staying condition, which was bad for Clauricaune. When he was brought out and stripped, Hashtheboy got redder than usual.

Sydney, Laboulaye and Massinger did not go down to see the start. They took up a good position on a friend's drag, where, with field glasses, they could obtain the best view, taken all round, of the race

Hashtheboy was on an American speculator's drag next to them. He was employed tearing a cigar to pieces with his fingers, and throwing the bits on to the heads of the rural spectators who were clustered round the drag. One old gipsy, who happened to be looking up, got a bit into her eye. In return she used some language which was altogether unsectarian and even secular. For once those curses which many had, out of fear, kept to themselves in his presence, got a good airing.

Baltimore, sitting Clauricaune like a glove to the hand, cantered down the course with the other horses. La Tosca did not look her best. Bill Mathers was thoroughly out of temper, and stooped forwards painfully, as if subject, from his earliest years, to imperfect ossification of the vertebral column. Presently, however, in an evident fit of crossness, he teased La Tosca into a canter, and soon put daylight between her and Clauricaune.

At last they reached the starting post, and were all drawn up in line. Sydney, who was watching intently through his field glasses, was irritated at the absurd number of false starts. But he was not half so much irritated as Baltimore.

Just as Clauricaune was making a splendid bound forward, he had to be torn ruthlessly back, destroying his mouth, and taking all the spirit out of him.

At last Lord Marcus told the jockeys that he would stand no more of it. After this the flag fell in good earnest, and off they went. Up they came, breasting the rise in a somewhat uneven fashion, Clauricaune not doing so well as might have been expected, in consequence of the numerous dragging-backs he had gone through. There could be no doubt La Tosca was leading. Just as Clauricaune was drawing up to him, Vulcan, a black horse, belonging to a friend of Hashtheboy's, rolled on to him and knocked him out of his stride, and then gave him such a squeezing against The Bloomer, another horse, that Baltimore afterwards said: "'E felt as if 'e was decidedly ' a day's march nearer home,' for Clauricaune was carried off his legs."

However, when the horses passed the grand stand they were all pretty close together, La Tosca leading by about two feet. Hashtheboy turned his yellow eyes on Sydney, and there was a gleam of most trying triumph in them. At that very instant Baltimore, by some invisible magic, made Clauricaune swerve slightly so as to be clear of La Tosca, and bound forward at such a rate that he passed the winning post full half a length ahead.

Laboulaye and Massinger waved their hats, and shouted with delight, the Celtic blood manifesting itself with singular uniformity of action.

Hashtheboy scowled in many directions now. Extinguished blusterers lie about the tomb of every race, like strangled snakes round the cradle of Hercules.

When Sydney stood smoothing Clauricaune down, and looking up at Baltimore, as he talked to him, he little thought what a race he would one day ride upon the trusty horse; a race, not against a mortal horse, but against death on his black horse.

Afterwards, with his arm tightly linked in Massinger's, and followed like his shadow by Laboulaye, he made his way through a host of congratulating friends. It was odd that, at that moment the thought occured to him, " I wonder, if I ever put that horse upon his mettle, in a matter upon which life and death depended, if he would stand me in good stead ? "

He remembered, later on in life, that he had thought this, and could only account for it as one of those strange presentiments which visit us, apparently without reason, from time to time ; the way a doctor sometimes looks in when we are quite well.

CHAPTER V.

THREE months have passed since the events related
in the last chapter. Bridget and her father have
returned to their home in Ireland, and Bridget,
true to her determination to introduce a little amusement
into the monotonous life of the Irish peasant, had
determined on getting up an Elizabethan pageant.
Several English guests were coming to stay in the
house, amongst others, to her immense delight and
gratification, Edgar Sydney. Her energies were now
strained to provide a spectacle worthy of such a critical
assemblage. She determined to enrol in her service, a
family of Hegartys, some respectable tenants of her
father's, who lived about a mile from Sheil Castle, or
Hall, as it was indifferently called.

The position of the Hegartys was a difficulty in the
social life of the neighbourhood. Mr. Hegarty belonged
to one of the oldest families in Ireland. He was
descended in a direct line from kings, and was, at the
present moment, connected with several families of
the aristocracy. As far as Sir Bernard Burke's table of
precedent went, he ought to have walked into dinner at
the Castle before the greater part of the guests assembled
there at a state dinner party. But, then, a long series
of reverses and misfortunes had brought his great
grandfather, his grandfather, and his father so down
in the world that he now occupied the position of a
struggling, hard-working farmer, and mixed only with
his brother farmers. He had received no education
beyond the village school.

Bridget was always trying to drag them up to their proper rung on the social ladder. The old people did not like being dragged, the young ones took more kindly to the process; but their whole past life and surroundings made them feel strange when Bridget tried to treat them as equals. Times had been bad lately, and they were very poor. The two daughters had only three pairs of stockings between them, and these required constant mending. It therefore became a matter of honour to wear them as little as possible.

It was a balmy afternoon at the Blue House, as Hegarty's Farm was called, because it was one of the very few red-brick farmhouses in Ireland. There were plenty of blue houses, but they were mostly called red. Moyrah Hegarty, the eldest daughter, was sitting out on a wall near the house. She was reposing upon one foot, while the other hung down lazily over the wall in front of her. It was a pretty leg and foot, clean, snow-white and well-shaped. The palm of her right hand rested on the top of the wall; with her left hand she shaded her eyes from the sun, which was shining brightly this morning, as she looked away into the distance.

" Shure, that's one av Dolen's sheep grazin' on our land," said Timothy Hegarty, aged seven years, who, in an old caubeen of his father's, placed considerably on the back of his head, a tail coat with one tail off, a large boot on one foot, and a small shoe on the other, was leaning against the wall, with his elbows resting on it.

" Well, can't ye lave the baste alone? Sure it's ate all the grass on Dolen's contemptible scrap av ground, and now, 'twill have a dacent bit off ours."

Moyrah was very fond of animals, and could not bear to see their legitimate pleasures interfered with.

Suddenly, a boy a year older, and rather more fashionably attired than Tim, approached from behind, and hit him a smart blow on his back.

“What are ye doin’ here, ye pup ? ” he said.

“As much as ye’re doin’ there,” replied Tim, laconically, without turning round.

“Kape yer manners now, Dan, me boy; I’ll have none of yer low fightin’ here,” said Moyrah.

“I’ll *suet* mesilf,” replied Dan shortly.

“Ye will not do that same while I’m here; I’ll lerrun ye how to behave before ladies.”

“Faix, ’tis Daniel in the lion’s den I am.”

“If it is, then, ye’re the lion, an’ ’tis yer den we’re in.”

Dan had an old leather strap in his hand; he put it round Tim’s waist, and began to strap him up as he might a portmanteau. Tim howled.

“Now, look here, Dan, I’ll have none of yer riotin’ here. Ye lave Tim alone this moment, or I’ll box yer ears on ye.”

Dan desisted.

“Ye two bates a fair for the noise in yez, any day ! ” soliloquised Moyrah, as she turned to look dreamingly away in the distance again.

“Where did ye get that shoe ye’ve on yer ? ” said Dan, in a peremptory stage whisper, regarding suspiciously the small shoe on Tim’s right foot.

“Faked it out av Moyrah’s top left-hand drawer,” whispered Tim.

“Ye little divile av a thief,” said Dan, angrily.

“Conduct yersilf now, Master Dan; I hear ye. I won’t have that langige used in my presince,” said Moyrah, sternly.

Dan now devoted his attention to scooping lumps of mortar out of the wall with a pointed bit of stick, so as to loosen the stones, possibly with the hope of eventually bringing down the wall.

“Big-tare-an-ouns ! can’t ye lave the wall alone,” said Tim, who got sundry pushes and pokes during the process.

“Silence, ye pup ! ”

Moyrah's eyes were straining anxiously towards the distant valley which lay beneath the Blue House.

It was August; and already the woods, which had remained insensible to the wooing of the brightest rays of the sun in his June and July splendour, were breaking forth into rainbows and jewels under his parting smile. The vivid crimson of the lowest faded leaves of the St. John's wort and the wild field-sorrel strewed the fields. The trees were just moving through the balmy air, and the little flowers which grew at their feet were dancing slowly like minuet dancers in the breeze. The rocks in the distance were dashed with russet and yellow, and coming out in masses amongst the moss and ferns so purple, and with such a soft, trembling blue haze over them, that you could scarcely tell at first what was rock and what was heather.

The ripple of a distant river in the valley—a river which had small waterfalls in it—came stealing softly through the sweet-briar hedge round the garden.

Lower down the river Moyrah could see—over a knoll, and at one side of a thicket of mountain ash and alder—the green and brown turf roofs of two or three hovels, built on the edge of a morass. Her eyes were fixed on these. A half dreamy, half anxious look was in them. Beautiful eyes, which reflected every feeling of her heart the moment it was felt—eyes once seen never to be forgotten.

Lower down the river was a little old mill, by a waterfall. Tufts of grass and trailing weeds waved from the cracked walls, and caught the sparkling drops dashed upon them by the foam. It was to this mill Moyrah's father had gone.

"Troth, an' I wundhur is he safe wid that skit av a red filly he's taken out? She'd joult the life out av anny Christian man, lepping up and down like a crazy lobster."

Moyrah was thinking of her father, for whom she

had an extraordinary devotion, and who had taken a young chestnut filly out to exercise.

"It's leppin' about on her I'd like to be," sighed Dan.

"Troth, an' so would I," echoed Tim, plaintively.

"Here! I say! Heh! Tim! Dan! come in here, I say, wid ye, ye lazy little beggars! Ye must take all that dirty straw out av the hay-loft, and make haste wid it, now!" It was Mrs. Hegarty who spoke. Her voice was never long silent, and was shrill and piercing.

Moyrah had not been left long alone on the wall before she heard a rustling in the shrubs, and in another minute she saw Bridget, in her straw hat, with its bright ribbons, and her fashionably-made cotton London dress, coming towards her over the grass plot at the edge of the little strip of garden.

Moyrah slipped quickly off the wall and dropped a pretty little curtsey.

When first Bridget saw Moyrah after an absence, she always indulged herself by looking at her for a minute or two before she spoke to her. Bridget was a great admirer of female beauty in all ranks of life but her own. She was a great admirer of male beauty in all ranks of life—much greater than she was of female beauty in any rank. Still, she considered Moyrah did credit to her county.

Even without her shoes or stockings Moyrah was rather above middle height. Her figure was light and agile. She was perfectly proportioned, and her movements had a grace, and a sort of wild dignity, which struck a stranger directly, but which her own family never noticed, and which those who were tolerably well acquainted with her soon forgot, as they became absorbed in the interest of watching her face. She was like a typical portrait by a great artist; everyone who looked at her found what they wanted in her. The thinker found thought; the colourist, colour,

and the idealist—were he the most critical that modern
æstheticism has developed—found his ideal. To bring
her before one who never saw her, all that can be said
is that her features were, all except her mouth, faultless.
If her mouth was a trifle too large, and distinctly weak,
there were a thousand strange movements about it,
expressions of tender feeling continually passing over
it, which more than compensated for such defects.
Her eyes were large, and of a deep violet, with black
eyelashes above and below. Her throat was like a
magnolia blossom, as soft and stately; her hair of a
sunny golden brown, sometimes darkish and sometimes
fairish, hung far below her waist in a huge plait.
Sometimes this plait was tied with smart ribbons, and
sometimes it was not tied at all, but hung loose, with
glossy waves of hair escaping from it at various points.
Such was the case to-day. Moyrah was annoyed to
be caught *en demi toilette*. Except in the warm
weather, and then only quite *en famile*, she wore shoes
and stockings.

"This is your seventeenth birthday, Moyrah! I
congratulate you! See, I did not forget it. I have
brought you a present from London," and Bridget
shook out of a bit of silver paper a smart rose-coloured
silk neckerchief.

"Long life to yer honour!" and Moyrah, dropped a
curtsey. "Arra, me darlin' Miss Bridget! if I'm not
glad to see ye home again!"

"Are you very glad to see me?" and Bridget looked
as if she expected a flattering answer.

"Shure, an' it warms the cockles of me heart!" said
Moyrah, with enthusiasm.

Bridget drew her head up with a gratified air. She
liked affection, and it greatly pleased her to think how
popular she was with her father's tenantry. After
some little time had been spent in greetings and
admiration of the neckerchief, Bridget said, "Who's
in the house?"

" Marthur and the bhoys."

" Well, we'll sit here on the wall for a few minutes," said Bridget, who had a strong *dis*-relish for Mrs. Hegarty's tongue. " Do you know, Moyrah," and she climbed into a comfortable sitting position on the wall, " I've been thinking over a great many things since I've been in England, this time, and I've come to the conclusion that the Irish peasantry haven't got enough amusement."

" That's a grand idea, enthirely," said Moyrah, with the heartiest possible concurrence.

" Well, I am determined to try and remedy it."

" May the hivins be yer bed!" said Moyrah, fervently.

" They're pretty sure to be that," said Bridget, complacently. " I hope they'll be equal to the task. Well, now listen, Moyrah. I'm going to get up a grand Elizabethan pageant up at the house. I want you to come up and help. I think I shall make you Mary, Queen of Scots."

Moyrah looked extremely pleased. The idea of stepping into regal dignities with such rapidity, and such an absence of exertion, captivated her.

" A quane, och! dear heart! to think av the loikes av that," she said, with a slightly shy look in the corner of her eye, and a little blush, as she began to plait the end of her hair, but a deep undertone of delight in her voice.

" Yes. You may, perhaps, never have heard of her. She was beautiful; and she perished on the scaffold."

" May the Lord have mercy on her soul!" said Moyrah, devoutly crossing herself.

" Oh, it's long ago," said Bridget.

" An' what vagabone kilt her?"

" I!" exclaimed Bridget, "I, Queen Elizabeth. I am going to act the part of Queen Elizabeth, and she killed her."

" This day's Teusday. God betwixt us and harm ! " said Moyrah, again crossing herself.

" Well, Moyrah, you must bring Michael, too. I must have him ; he is such a spruce, clean, smart-looking lad. I'm going to make him Marquis of Dorset."

" Faith, his head will be turned enthirely, now," said Moyrah, with not quite such a pleased expression as when she heard she was going to be queen.

" And Moyrah, Miss Moyrah," and a very saucy look came into Bridget's face, as she took one of Moyrah's hands and looked up into her liquid dark eyes, " there's someone else who must come, aye, Miss Moyrah ? "

A blush rose to Moyrah's cheeks. Her skin was so soft and fair that the slighest blush showed on it, as the small pink spot shows so vividly on the white horse chestnut blossom ; not because the spot is so pink, because it is not, but because the blossom is so white.

" Aye, Moyrah, if the road is in good repair enough, you must bring the jaunting car, and you and Cormac must come on one side, and Michael and Eileen on the other."

Moyrah did not speak.

" Moyrah," said Bridget, severely, looking intently into her face, " you haven't been treating him badly ? "

" Faith, I thrated him well enough."

" Oh Moyrah! Moyrah, you'll be driving him to ruin. That road's always in repair. Those who travel on it see to that," and she sighed a little.

" Shure, when he axed me, six months ago, I tould him I was over young to be gettin' marrid awhile, yet ; but if he liked to be lookin' me up agin, whin I was seventeen, I'd enter into considurayshin av the mattur."

" Then, if I know anything of him, he'll be here some time to-day," said Bridget decidedly.

" He's off now, havin' great sport at the stations," said Moyrah, meditatively smoothing down the back of her hair with the palm of her hand.

" He'll be back before the moon rises this evening."

" Faith, I'm not a grayit match at all," said Moyrah, humbly; " but, 'tis somethin' to have a jauntin' car in the family," she added, in a low tone.

" He doesn't care for anything of that sort," said Bridget, warmly; " he's a real good fellow. My father says he is prouder of him than of any young man on the estate. I am going to give you the wedding breakfast out of my own private pocket, and in return you must let me come and dance at the wedding; eh, Moyrah ?"

" The prayers will be before yer honour; long life to ye all the same for that."

" And may I live to see the day, Moyrah, when, in a fine house of your own, the bouchaleens and the colleens are all round you."

Moyrah blushed and looked down at her white feet, with the blades of grass curling over them.

" And I hope it will be a fine day, Miss Moyrah," continued Bridget mischievously, greatly enjoying Moyrah's blushes; " that same wedding-day, at any rate, the bride's part of it." (Up till noon, in Ireland, is called the bride's part of the wedding-day, and it is considered unlucky for rain to fall during those hours.)

" The blessin' of hivin rest on yer honour for yer goodness."

" O, blessings don't bother me much."

She was going on to have said something stronger on the subject, but a soft light in Moyrah's suddenly raised eyes stopped her. There was a great deal of mystery about Moyrah; her character was all below the surface; her affections were so deep, so clinging, that even at her early age, and in her unsophisticated life she had learned it was better to conceal where she could not control them. Her love for her father and for her little sister, Eileen, was so unusually powerful that it would have been a great bore to them had she not vigourously smothered down the outward demonstrations of it. She was absurdly sensitive to a slight or a severe word from one she loved, or even a look which she was pleased to consider harsh. She would brood over such signs for days and weeks. She had none of Bridget's boisterous, high spirits and self-assured complacency; none of her pugnacity or power of caustic speech. A sarcastic reply never came into Moyrah's head, and had it done so, she would have died rather than utter it. She knew so well the long brooding torture which such speeches from others had cost her, that no power could have induced her to inflict the same on another. She had a vivid sympathy with every form of pain, either of mind or body, in others, and sometimes dwelt on their troubles to a morbid degree; for, when Eileen or her father had some quiet little unimportant ailment or misfortune, she took it so to heart that it affected her long after they had forgotten all about it.

Now, with Bridget it was just the reverse; she forgot her own sufferings and other people's with equal rapidity. She had a springing elastic " inner man," which, coupled with a bold independence of nature, would enable her to pass through life without feeling, with much acuteness, the blows which must fall to the share of all before the pilgrimage is ended. Bridget was thoroughly of the opinion that learners owe to their masters only a temporary belief and a suspension of their own judgment until they are instructed, and not an absolute resignation and captivity.

Now, Moyrah would have liked to resign her judgment, her reason, all her faculties into perpetual slavery to one she loved. Her power of loving was something quite out of the ordinary; but that which is quite out of the ordinary from some specific difference distinguishing it from other species of the same thing, is carelessly observed if it be but familiar. No one noticed Moyrah's love.

After sitting on for some time longer, Bridget said she must be going.   She first went into the house to pay her respects to Mrs. Hegarty.   Mrs. Hegarty was a fine specimen of an Irish woman, five feet eleven, thirty-nine inches round the waist, with cheeks which spoke either of the extreme healthiness of the water in that neighbourhood, or else of its great unhealthiness, so as to oblige resort to less innocent liquids.   She was delighted to see Bridget.

Eileen, aged thirteen, was rather untidy at that moment, as she had been helping her mother to clean up.   She was a gentle looking girl, and would have been considered pretty in any other family; but, having so lovely a sister as Moyrah, she was thrown into the shade.   After a few kindly words of greeting on each side, Bridget went home.

———————————

CHAPTER VI.

THERE was a little sort of familiar gathering that
night, in honour of Moyrah's birthday, at the
Blue House. In the middle of one of the jigs,
when the floor was bounding up and down, and the
dust flying right and left, in walked Cormac.

"So here ye are at last, Cormac," said old Mr.
Hegarty, advancing to meet him, "The top of the
mornin' to ye, me boy."

"He'll be a cliver boy to catch that at ate o'clock at
night," said Michael Hegarty, shaking his hand.

Moyrah was dancing, with a hand on each hip, and
her head thrown back, when he came in, and she did
not stop until she had finished the figure. He stood,
with an expression of intense admiration, watching her.
It would be absurd to pretend she did not see him.
Moyrah was an Irishwoman through and through. She
had that fineness of structure of the body which made it
capable of the most delicate sensations, and of structure
of the mind which made it capable of the most delicate
sympathies. She knew Cormac's character well, and
she knew he would be feeling shy and awkward; so,
when the dance stopped, she went straight up to him
and gave him a half shy, but wholly sweet and cordial
greeting. The look of gratitude and delight in his
face recompensed her. Yes; she knew his worth.
She knew he was as innocent and good as St. Louis of
Gonzague. The priest said he was the best boy in his
parish. He had served mass in Latin from the age of
seven upwards. He was never absent from the "stations"; and no one had ever seen him with "the drop
taken" in his life.

" Come, jintlemin," said Michael Hegarty, who always liked to lead everything, and to keep the ball rolling, " the next sport is in the milintary line ; white cockades, jintlemin and ladies."

The game of white cockades, as played in Ireland, is this :—The leader of the sports puts everyone in their seats. He then gets a white handkerchief from one of the girls, which he wreaths in a festoon round his hat ; after this he walks round the company two or three times singing

> " Will you list and come with me, fair maid ?
> An' folly the lad with the white cockade."

While he is singing this he takes off his hat and puts it on to the head of the girl who is to him the girl of girls. She rises and puts her arm round him. Then they both go about in the same way singing those charming white cockade words. She then puts the hat on to some young man, who gets up and goes round with them, singing as before. He next puts it on his girl of girls, who, after singing and going round in the same manner, puts it on another, and he on his sweetheart, and so on. When every young man has pitched on the girl he likes to be his sweetheart, they all sit down and sing songs, for once which do not treat of politics, except of that family political economy which is the same in all nations.

Now, this game suited Cormac well. He borrowed a white handkerchief from Moyrah, and tied it round his caubeen ; then he began to sing in a marked way, and with his eyes fixed on Moyrah,

> " Will you list and come with me, fair maid ?
> An' folly the lad with the white cockade."

Suddenly, as he passed Moyrah, he turned, and with a quick movement, and a deepening colour in his honest face, he snapped his caubeen off his own head, and popped it on to hers. Then, as she rose and slipped her arm round him, he looked down at her with a rather bashful, but very winning smile.

After the White Cockade, while the elders, and a good many of the youngers, were refreshing themselves with whiskey punch, cold ham, porter and potatoes, a few of the youngers sauntered out into the open air. Amongst these were Cormac and Moyrah, arm in arm. They went and sat in the moonlight, on the wall where Bridget and Moyrah had sat in the morning.

"This is a happy kailee. Ah! Moyrah dheelish! Shure, an' from the veins of me heart I'm glad to see ye again. Ye said, Moyrah, whin ye was seventeen I should come again; an' shure it's struck this mornin'. Faith, an' ye've put yer comedher on me, and I feel I can't live widout ye at all, at all." He looked at her. "Why, then, Moyrah, manim asthee hu (my soul is within you). Tell me, darlin', what do ye feel for me?"

"How can I tell ye, Cormac, but that I think I like ye very much?" she said gently, and somewhat placidly, aye, somewhat placidly.

He seemed satisfied. As his arm stole round her, and she felt his first kiss on her cheek, and leaned her head on his shoulder, she was peaceful and happy. But if the whole exact truth must be told, she did not feel quite so happy as she had expected to be when she was engaged. She felt secure. But, at the age of seventeen, security does not represent the sum total of human bliss.

As for Cormac, he felt as if Paradise had already begun. He was certain that the brightest smiles the human face had ever worn were but a mockery of interpretation of the joy which now possessed him.

The moon shone down on the trees, giving them a shadowy and ghost-like appearance, and then went on to touch with silver the distant river. Every now and then the low murmur of the stream broke the stillness of the balmy air. It was a calm night, the air close and somewhat sultry, as if before a storm, and not a breath stirring.

As Cormac looked down upon Moyrah, he felt that

around her was thrown a halo of poetry, which, to the vivid imagination of his race and the chivalry of his nature, raised her to the dignity of a being who, if not herself more than human, had something more than human about her—a divine breath somewhere.

Chivalry did not raise woman from her lowly position. Christianity raised her, and chivalry paid her that honour and reverence with which it found her invested.

Now, Moyrah, in spite of her faults, was a true Christian, and Cormac was as chivalrous as any knight in the middle ages. To be sure, he was not like what we are accustomed to fancy knights were. He was not above the middle height, with a round, plump, homely figure, a fat rosy face, reddish hair and whiskers, and a freckled skin ; but the kindness of his expression, and the genial look in his honest blue eyes, more than compensated for the absence of romance in his general appearance. He was twenty-five years old, and Captain Sheil had promised to let him have a nice little farm at a very low rent, the day he married. He had saved some money, too, and did not come to Moyrah by any means empty handed.

"Do ye know, Cormac, ye're to come up to the big house wid me to-morrer? Miss Bridget herself came down to-day to ax me and ye ; so ye'll have to be puttin' yer company manners on. How will ye like that, me boy ?" and she looked up roguishly into his face.

"Shure, anny where I wint wid ye, was it to the bog of Allan, would be loike the gates of heavin! Moyrah, avourneen, give, or let me steal, another slewsther—a sweet one, now, alanna dhas ! "

Moyrah smiled as he kissed her, placidly and happily. She felt a great sense of security, consolation, and of fortifying support. Henceforth there was some-one she could always look up to as better than herself, someone whom she could lean on in every trouble, and feel he was leading her feet each day more securely into the narrow path.

CHAPTER VII.

A WEEK before the grand performance was to take place, a few English guests arrived to stay at the Hall, and one or two families from neighbouring houses. Amongst others, Edgar Sydney arrived, and his cousin, Mr. Lucas, a barrister, who had never been in Ireland before, and wished to study the question of the hour on the spot.

Sydney had been on the verge of starting for a tour on the Continent with his mother, and had engaged a courier to accompany them, so that his mother might be saved all trouble travelling; but, at the last moment she had been taken ill, and they were obliged to postpone the trip indefinitely. Having engaged the courier for a month, and being obliged to pay him, he thought he might as well take him to Ireland to valet him, and to look after his luggage travelling. He proposed going for a little tour to Killarney and Glengariffe afterwards; and the man, whose name was Alphonse Lenoir, said he knew Ireland, and could direct him to the best routes and the best hotels. Indeed, after he conversed with him several times about Ireland, Sydney discovered that his knowledge of the country and the people was quite unique—sometimes he was inclined to call it uncanny. How could he, a Frenchman, come to know all this? True, Lenoir spoke English just like an Englishman, and gave one the idea of a man who had either lived in England or amongst Englishmen the greater part of his life. There was something in his manner, too, which gave Sydney the impression that he had not always been in the position of life which he at present occupied. He was a tall man, with large, black moustaches, much curled at the points—indeed, so much curled that they almost seemed as if they dragged up the ends of his mouth with them. Really of dark brown, his eyes had such a strong, yellowy tinge, that some people declared they were yellow. They were long and narrow, and his brows were so clearly pencilled as to lead to the supposition that he had pencilled them with brown paint and a camel's hair brush. He had as much hair as a hairdresser's model, brushed in peculiar sort of curly queues all round his head, and covered with a strongly scented hair wash.

Bridget was delighted to welcome Sydney. She had given him the very best room in the house, and that in spite of having two married ladies amongst her guests, both with small but decided titles. Some titles are not decided now-a-days. She had taken into this room all her most interesting and best bound books, and ranged them in bookcases on the wall, and had even gone to the trouble of taking down one or two beautiful pictures out of other rooms and hanging them in good lights in this one. She had picked a bouquet of the choicest flowers, and put it in a small Sèvres china bowl on his dressing table. She felt that she had never seen any man in the world who gave her the impression of so thoroughly deserving the best of everything as Sydney.

CHAPTER VIII.

ONE bright, sunny morning with an occasional cloud or two, Sydney, Captain Shiel, Lucas, Bridget, and Mr. and Mrs. Massinger set off to make a three days' pic-nicing tour at the lakes of Killarney. The journey there was only about an hour by express train. They took their tents and cooking materials with them, and determined to give houses in general, and hotels in particular, a wide berth.

Though thinking much of her theatricals, Bridget had felt she must show Sydney Killarney. She was in great force. She did the cooking, assisted by Lucas. She talked Irish to the carmen and boatmen and women who came out to sell milk and mountain dew from the shebeens. She chaffed everyone all round.

Sydney thought her more noisy, queer and disagreeable than ever, and devoted his attentions to Mrs. Massinger. She united the happiest characteristics of the Irish nature. She was genial, courteous, full of fun, and without those sharp points and irritating bristles which marred Bridget's wit.

An Englishman of the most touchy susceptibilities could argue out the Irish question with her without coming to any of those unhappy collisions which engender so much heat and so little light. Proud of her country, and devoted to its poorer inhabitants, she could yet acknowledge, without flying into a tantrum, that they were a people easy to deceive. That they seemed doomed to occupy amongst the nations the position of Tantalus—thirsting to find political truth, and baffled at every point by their teachers. She was the wife of a landlord whose place joined the captain's.

Sydney found, to his great pleasure, that her brother-in-law was his friend, the poorish looking man he had met at Ascot. Their house used to be one of the pleasantest and most hospitable in the county. But latterly things had altered.

With that charming polish of manner Mr. Mathew Arnold has so admirably described, their tenants told them they were very sorry for them, and even offered to lend them money; but rent they could not pay. They had suddenly become, like the Merino, a Spanish variety of sheep, remarkable for the fineness of its fleece. Because they were so polite and nice over it all, that it was impossible not to like them, and to recognise, even in their fleecing, the fineness of inborn gentlemen. Had they only not been so fusible to the agitator's heat, and in their fusion retained their opacity to his tricks, life might have been so comfortable amongst them.

Well, for some time the Massingers had got no rents, and had been obliged to give up entertaining. They had a family of young children, and no rich relations to help them, as they had always been looked on as the rich ones of the family.

But not entertaining did not prevent their being entertained; and there was no one in the neighbourhood Bridget delighted so much to honour as Mrs. Massinger. She was a woman it was impossible not to admire. She had never been absorbed in her entertainments, but had devoted a good share of her time to visiting the poor, teaching them different kinds of needlework, and establishing reading classes amongst them. Besides, she regularly kept open house for them, and they walked in and out of her kitchen like their own parlour, and even cut slices of the ham and bacon to take home to the village. Massinger was the captain's greatest friend. They sat side by side on local boards; used, before hunting was stopped, to ride to the hounds together; and every first of September saw them stumping away on the same leafy path, gun in hand.

In spite of Bridget's occasional failures in temper, and general quirkiness, they managed to have great fun. They trotted up and down hill on wild mountain ponies. They sang melodies as they laid back in the boats, rowing slowly over the calm water on moonlight evenings. They waked the echo by the eagle's nest with a variety of political and social remarks, which would have frightened the cow out of her traditional three acres, if she had them. They bought three little, tiny, black Kerry cows from a little weather-beaten old man, the father of a charming and lovely dairymaid, who scorned shoes and stockings, and wore a plaid shawl over her head. As they were all standing in a large, distinctly sunburnt party before this girl one day, having just bought a good supply of butter for their *al fresco* breakfast, Sydney asked her if she had any new laid eggs for sale.

"No, yer honour," she said; "the cows in Kerry don't lay manny eggs, an' ours haven't laid anny to-day."

Lucas was pleased; and Sydney laughed as he seldom did since the cares of life were gathering over him. But Bridget told her she was saucy, and would give the English strangers a nice impression of Irish manners.

Although they had decided to cut civilized society, still, as a brother of Mr. Massinger's was living at a small though comfortable country house in the neighbourhood, they could not ignore his existence.

Mr. Septimus Massinger was a land agent. They declined his hospitable entreaties that they would come and stay with him, and even refused his invitation to dinner; but Sydney could not resist when he asked them if they would care to see a unique specimen of the inner life of the country, as exhibited on the local board of guardians.

Accordingly, one morning saw Sydney, Captain Shiel and the two Massingers entering a barely-furnished apartment with a number of excitable looking men sitting round a rickety table, covered with red baize.

Their entrance did not create much impression, because a most absorbing topic was in process of discussion at the moment. They noiselessly slid into four chairs which were ranged against the wall, with their backs to the window. A tall, fine-looking man, with hazel eyes and a foxy beard, was standing up speaking, with his right arm and hand extended.

"Mr. Chairman, as ye may, perhaps, be aware, I have just returned from a thrip to Italy. I'm not one to be advocatin' lavin' yer own counthry at ivry minnit, the way the landlords do be doin'" ("hear, hear") from the other members of the board; "but I had the cough upon me, an' the docthor says, says he, thry now, may be Italy would be the mendin' av ye; an me wife she says the same thing" (here there was suppressed laughter), "and so I tuk me eldest daughther, and off we wint to Italy."

"Spindin' Oirish money among a parcel av rogin' forinners, " muttered one of the other members crossly.

"Well, whin I was there I wint to Venice, a town that's built enthirely on the sea."

"There's a good one for yer!" said the chairman, *sotto voce;* "tell another now."

"'Tis, indade, I give ye me oath upon it, there's not a strate in it, 'tis all wather."

"Well, go an, now!" exclaimed the chairman, impatiently, "time's pressin'," and he looked at his watch. "We don't want to be wastin' our time listenin' to a copious flood of what ye saw whin ye had the drop taken. All that's within easy reach of intellectual mediocrity."

"Whew, there's for yer!" exclaimed one of the other members. "'Tis the new dictionary he's been sleepin' wid his head on."

"Well, jintlemin, I was tellin' yer I wint to Venice, and there I saw gon-do-las "—he paused and waved his hand—" an' ses I to mesilf as I looked at 'em, them's the very things for the beautayful wathers of me native lakes at home, the very things." Again he paused, and brought his fist down on the table, then rubbed his lips with his thumb and first finger.

" Could I see these lovely wathers enlivened by them how happy would I be. What an inprovemint! There would then be left no peg on which to hang hostile criticism of their attractions, such as I was readin' awhile ago in a dirty London paper, which said that afthur all, there wasn't much to be seen when ye got there, meanin' here, nothin' like the English lakes, and so on."

" Yar've spoken more toime now than yer worth," said the chairman, who was suffering from indigestion, " we'll refer the matter to the treasurer."

" I won't sit down at yer tellin'."

" Ye'll have to, then, or I'll git the polaise to ye."

" Rimimber, jintlemin, there's strangers present," said another member in a would-be stage whisper.

"There's no wan stranger present than the chairman," muttered the traveller.

" Sit down," shouted the chairman.

Down sat Mr. Fagan, Venetian traveller, and up stood the treasurer. He was the very beau ideal of all a treasurer should be, simple, innocent, trustworthy, unsuspicious. "I entirely agrees wid what Mr. Fagan's bin sayin'. 'Twould be fine, an' no mistake, to have thim gon-do-las. 'Tis no doubt after that, that manny pairsons would come and winter here instead av goin' to Italy. 'Tis all a matter of sightseeing that takes 'em there. Import the sights over here, an' they won't go there, ses I."

" Thrue for ye," exclaimed the Venetian traveller, looking much pleased.

" But there is wan consideration of great importance, which my peculiar position as treasurer forces me to pondhur over, and that is, pounds, shillins and pince."

He paused, and looked at a well thumbed paper he held in his hand.

"But I have a suggestion to make, which I think will answer all purposis; an' it is this jintlemin : that we import one fine male gond-*o*-la, and one fine female gond-*o*-la, and with the singular advantages for breedin' possessed by our mild and charming climate, no doubt the waters of Killarney would soon be covered with innumerable little gond-*o*-las."

Captain Shiel folded his arms and leaned them on the back of a chair in front of him.　Massinger stuffed a red silk handkerchief almost entirely down his throat, then polished the top of his black silk hat vigourously with his coat sleeve, and looked at it as if it was the only object of interest on earth to him.　Sydney was so perfectly certain that the treasurer had spoken in satire, that he laughed out loud innocently, in the guilelessness of the ingenuous Saxon nature.　But he soon found his mistake.　Black looks were fixed upon him by the treasurer and his friends.　The Venetian traveller, however, kept him in company, and laughed loud and long while he stood up to explain matters.　But Captain Shiel could not return to a decent state of gravity. So, at a sign from him, they soon all slid away as noiselessly as a row of gondolas.

CHAPTER IX.

IT was the day before the grand Elizabethan pageant at Shiel Castle. It was to take place in the dining room, Captain Shiel having kindly consented to allow the library to be turned into a temporary dining room. This was distinctly inconvenient, as already several parties of guests had arrived, and more were expected, and the library was not a large room. Bridget had caused to be erected at the end of the room a singular structure, which she called a stage, and which had bright green chintz curtains to it, in honour of its country, no doubt. The dining room was long and very airy, capitally suited to be an amateur theatre. Behind it was a commodious pantry, which opened into it with a door just at the back of the stage. This made a first-rate green room. At the present moment it was full of paint pots, saucers of rouge, plates of sticking plaster and white lead, wigs, moustaches and beards, and various marvellous garments, which Bridget had actually gone to the expense and trouble of getting all the way over from a celebrated theatrical shop in the Haymarket.

There was to be a dress rehearsal this afternoon, and already the actors were beginning to arrive. Bridget was—well, busy is not the word for it. Like Figaro—and also like a celebrated modern statesman, she seemed to be here, there and everywhere all at the same time, and to be talking all the time at the top of her voice.

Bridget wore an enormous top ruff with several small ones under it ; a huge farthingale with a bushel of mock pearls—mere glass beads of the commonest description, but which showed up very well at a distance. Her hair was curled, frizzled and crisped, laid out in borders from one ear to the other, and for fear it should fall down, it was under-propped with forks and wires. To her flaxeny, chestnut locks, thus wreathed and crested, she had hung bugles, ouches, rings, gold, silver, glasses, etc. After the first scene with the meeting of the queens, she retired for a minute or two and came back with a high velvet hat and a close cap of gold and silver tissue. She had a jewelled stomacher, and small wings at the back of her jerkin. "Though," as she then remarked, "the Virgin Queen never having yielded to Cupid, the wings appeared somewhat *de trop*." In the green room there was such a fussing with looking glasses, pinning, such a bustle with sticks, combs, castanets, puffs, ruffs, pusels, fusles, fardingales, kirtles and busk points, that any less comprehensive intellect than Bridget's would have been driven wild.

Terence O'Flynn, the head boatman, as "Duke of Buckingham," had a suit of white uncut velvet, with an imitation of the richest embroidery that lace, silk and gold could contribute, and set, both suit and cloak, with huge, glittering glass imitation diamonds, besides a giant feather from his hat, stuck all over with mock diamonds, as were also his sword, girdle, hat-band and spurs. How he wished they were real!

The continual fault-finding would not have suited some dispositions, but it sat lightly upon Bridget.

Patrick Flyn was dressed up as "Lord Burghley." When "undressed" he was the under gardener. He had been told on no account to speak, but only to nod. Surely, so great a call had never been put upon any actor as for an Irishman to personate Lord Burghley!

As Bridget was flying past him, with her satin train over her arm, she exclaimed, "What are you doing nodding now? No one is speaking to you."

He shook his head.

"You're not to shake your head either. What are

you doing?" and she stood still and glared indignantly at him. "What *are* you doing?"

At last, Celtic human nature could bear it no longer, and he burst out in a piteous tone with—"Shure there's a buckle in the middle av me back hurtin' me in the most awfil manner."

"Tiresome, to be sure!" exclaimed Bridget, impatiently. "I suppose you will have to go and be undressed all over again, delaying the play so! Irish skins and smart clothes never have agreed."

"Plase your honour," said Tim Dolen, a boatman, who, even in his gorgeous attire as "Sir Edward Coke," smelt rather tarry and tarpauliny—"Plase yer honour," and his voice sank to that startlingly decent whisper with which the extreme refinement of the Irish lower orders always induces them to approach such subjects, "the 'Quane av Scottishe's' petticoats is all comin' off."

"Dear, dear!" said Bridget, stamping her foot, "what a dreadful bother!" She bent her brow for an instant. "She must get some kind of string, or ribbon, or tape, or something to sling them over her shoulder with, under her white satin body. Tell her, will you, nothing else will be safe."

"I will, yer honour," and he was off like a dart, with a business-like expression of countenance.

Meantime, Bridget hurried round a group of actors, and came suddenly face to face with Michael Hegarty, attired as Marquis of Dorset, in a suit of blue velvet, while from his hat waved a plume of silver and azure feathers. Now, Michael was at all times rather a bumptious man. He had often been told of the fault by father, mother, brothers and sisters, and by the parish priest. But he always declared he was not more bumptious than other men, and his mother, at any rate, took his word for it.

"Michael, do, for goodness sake, put your hat straight upon your head."

Moyrah had considerately placed a long cheval glass at one end of the pantry. Michael was standing opposite this now, with his head in an affected position, admiring himself.

" Faith, I'm thinkin' it looks more iligint a wan side," he said ruminatingly. sucking the knuckle of his thumb.

Bridget carried a stick with a gold head in her hand. She banged this sharply on the floor. " Obey me this moment, or I'll have your head off."

" The Lord save us ! " he exclaimed, crossing himself.

" Don't do that," she exclaimed irritably. " Queen Elizabeth's courtiers never did that."

" I will yer honour," he said submissively, rubbing his thumb dry on his blue velvet knickerbockers.

" You should say you won't, you old muddle head."

" I won't yer honour."

" You won't say you won't ? "

" I will yer honour, I will."

At this instant Dolen came up and said, " Plase yer honour, they can't find anny sort av thing that 'ill go over the Quane av Scottishe's showlders, they're a long way up enthirely, and all the strings is too short."

" Then the Countess of Salisbury must take off one of those garters I gave her a while ago, and give it to her; I gave her two beautiful bits of broad red ribbon, full a yard long each, to garter with ; she must manage to give her stocking a little pull up, from time to time, when no one is looking : she has such fat legs that I don't expect it will come down at all."

" I will yer honour," he said hurrying away.

" I dare say," muttered Bridget, consolingly to herself, " that the real Lady Salisbury's often came down. I don't think they wore garters in those days ; at least, I don't remember hearing of them. They seem to have come in with that French fellow, and his honey soir and mallie ponsing thing." Though good at physics and botany, she had not gone in for the history chair at college.

When Bridget was not looking pretty sharply
after him, Michael Hegarty was a little inclined to
order the others about, and to introduce innovations in
costumes and conduct, which he considered improve-
ments.

" Shure that's not the way to use a fan " he exclaimed
to the Countess of Nottingham, while he snapped the
fan out of the poor bewildered lady's trembling fingers.
" Look now ! watch me now ! now watch *me,* and I'll
show yer," and he began to fan himself, with his head
on one side and a ridiculous air of coquetry on his cleanly
shaven mouth and dancing blue eyes. Though nothing
to be compared to his sister for beauty, he was decidedly
a well looking man ; and he held his head up, and gave
you the impression that he was well worth looking at,
while too many of the others slouched along with a
down-trodden air, and their heads poked out.

. The poor Countess of Nottingham now stood staring
at him, with her eyes very wide open. " Ye are a
poor ignorant crathure," he remarked eyeing her with
patronising condescension, as he handed her back her
fan, " but if ye only watch me, that'll lerrun ye how to
behave."

" Peace, Master Marquis, you are malapert. Your
fire-new stamp of honour is scarce current," said
Bridget, who had stolen up, unobserved, behind, and
stood watching the scene for a moment in silence. Queen
Margaret's words to the real Dorset in Richard III.
had irresistibly flashed through her mind.

Hegarty looked a little ashamed, and slunk away.

" Come back, Mick," she said, imperiously. " You
must put your hat straight upon your head," and she
snapped it off his head and re-adjusted it more in
accordance with the rules of the perpendicular.

At that moment Jimmy Flanagan came up. He
was Sir Walter Raleigh, and was dressed in armour,
with helmet, to represent a knight.

" You ought to have something to ride on," said

Bridget. "You are are a knight, and books never represent knights walking except on their tombs." She knit her brow. "If I could only get that old donkey, that white donkey, don't you know, of Mulcahy's, to come in and behave herself walking across the stage."

Now, Jimmy had been told that a knight was not nearly so grand a thing as an earl or a marquis; and, besides, being exceedingly hot and uncomfortable in the armour, he felt he had been unfairly treated in being given, without any fault of his own, a lower position than his comrades.

"Faith, it's not aisy to find assis in these parts, now-a-days," he remarked, bitterly; "they're all made into erruls or markisses."

"Don't be cross now, 'Sir Walter,'" said Bridget, pacifyingly. "Remember, you first introduced the potatoe into Ireland, and that is honour enough for anyone." She turned away with a smile towards 'Lord Bacon.' "Remember, 'Bacon,' you present me with a white satin petticoat." "Bacon" blushed and looked modest at the bold introduction of this questionable garment into ordinary conversation. "It is in that card-board box there in the corner—you kneel on one knee, and hold it up to me on a cushion!"

"Blazes! but shure yer honour's nivir going to put on your petticoat, an' all the quality sittin' there lookin' at ye?" His most proper countenance wore an expression of horror.

"Il faut le dire qu'il n'est pas blasé celui la," muttered Bridget with a slight smile. Then, sucking the top of her little finger, she continued, meditatively: "He did not present it to her on his knees, it is true—no doubt he sent it by parcels post—but that is just one of those little alterations which I, in common with most historians, like to make in history." She continued to suck her finger. "It would not be history without them."

At that instant Moyrah, as Mary, Queen of Scots, walking with Cormac as Darnley, passed, keeping somewhat in the back ground and apparently absorbed in conversation. His arm was round her and his head bent down towards her. Bridget could not help thinking "what a pretty picture!" She gave a little sigh. "Ah, yes!" she said, "the sleeves of ladies dresses are worn of many different fashions now-a-days, but the coat sleeve still continues the favourite.

Suddenly she looked round and was fairly exasperated at the spectacle which met her gaze. The Countess of Salisbury was hobbling along, holding up her stocking by one hand. In order to do this, she had to drag up her petticoats, and cruelly crush her handsome pink satin train. Bridget's indignant eye fell on creases in that garment which she knew were fatal.

"Put down your dress!" she shouted, banging her gold-headed cane on the floor. "I'd like to know what your skirt will be like after this!"

Tears came into poor Lady Salisbury's eyes.

"I declare I'm at my wits' end to know how to manage you all!" sighed Bridget; "and if I'm at that, I've gone a long way, and no mistake. But, though I am at that bourne from which few travellers return, I can't find anything there to help me out of my dilemma. I have it! I know what I'll do. I'll box them. Queen Bess always did when she was at her wits' end. Capital!" She ran back into the green room out of which she had just come. There every person was trying to push every other person away from the front of the cheval glass, in order that they might see themselves in it. Michael Hegarty was still flourishing and bowing and scraping before it.

"Now, just listen. Just you listen, now," said Bridget, banging her cane on the floor. "Do you know what I shall do if you don't conduct yourselves? What do you think, eh?"

Staring eyes and open mouths were turned towards her.

"Box you!" An expression of astonishment,

followed by one of laughing submission, was the
response.

" Odds bodkins ! but I will," she continued, giving
her head a little decided wobble to the left side, so as
not to crush her ruff.

" ' Lord Leicester,' do, for goodness' sake, hold your
head up !   I implore of you, try to remember you are a
handsome English nobleman.   There you are again,
strealing along with your head poked out as if you
were a persecuted school-boy hunting for sparrows in a
hedge with a pop-gun.   Throw back your neck, man ;
dash down your feet before you so as to make the
boards rattle ; fling your head between your shoulder
blades, and try to look as if you had just ordered fifty
of your enemies' heads to be stuck on Temple Bar !"

" Lord Leicester " held up his head, but some of his
clothes gave an ominous crack as he did so.   He looked
with a roguish twinkle at Hegarty, who looked back
at him with good humoured contempt.   Michael had
studied his illustrious countryman, Sir Bernard Burke,
to some effect, and knew, to his own great consolation,
that a marquis was considerably above an earl.

" Here, ' Lord Cobham ' !" said Bridget, seizing Bill,
the under boatman ; " hold up your head—remember,
you are a bitter enemy of ' Lord Essex's ; '   Mick
Dogherty, there," and she pointed to Dogherty, looking
sheepish and shy.

" Shure he's going to get married to me sisthur ! he's
wan av the only dacint boys in Boreen ! "

" That doesn't matter ; he's a deadl!y enemy !   He's
got the wardenship of the Cinque Ports away from you ;
and you are very jealous of him, because you think I
like him better than you."

" Do I now ? " he said, with a puzzled expression.

" Here now, Peggy Maguire, you are Lady William
Hatton, a widow, young, handsome, and with a good
fortune, and Bacon wants to marry you.   Here, Lord
Bacon, you want to marry her."

" Bedad, an' I wouldn't take her if she had six cows an' tin acres of land to her back!" he exclaimed impetuously. "Don't I know what sort av a tongue she's got! Why ye can hear her half way down the street on a Sunday morning, scoldin' her old sister like blazes; de ye think I'd take her into me house to blow the roof off over me head?"

" Well, she won't have you, so it doesn't matter," said Bridget, pacifyingly, putting her hand over Peggy's mouth to stop an outburst. But the instant she removed it, out it came.

" Ye mean, contimptible gomeral! Ye baste ye! De ye think I'd marry ye iv ye wint on ye four knees to me? Did'nt ye let yer poor ould uncle die av starvation, an' you wid twinty pound nailed up in the chimney in an ould stockin'? A nice husbin' for a daycint girril!"

" Remember, Peggy you are a gentlewoman; that is what respectable females were called in those days."

Bridget bit her lips to hide a smile as she turned to look for Moyrah.

" Come, now, the acting is going to begin," and Bridget raised a small silver whistle which she wore attached to a little gold chain at her waist, to her lips and gave a long piercing whistle with it. " You know, actors, I whistle when a scene is going to begin; and when any one has got to speak I give a little, low, tiny whistle and look them full in the face. Pray, remember this!"

They all adjourned to the stage, and Bridget seated herself on a splendid throne somewhat in the background while she ranged her courtiers in groups round her.

Then, after a few moment's pause, from a door at the opposite side of the stage was to enter Mary, Queen of Scots, leaning upon Darnley. She was to advance slowly, with her head bent slightly forward, and her eyes on the ground. The programme was that she should advance in this position until she was just opposite to Bridget; then she was to look up suddenly and for the first time become aware of her presence, whereupon she was to start violently, and retreat at least a whole step backwards, while Darnley raised his right arm between her and her hated rival. Meanwhile, Elizabeth started to her feet, and remained glaring— a part of the programme which, to tell the truth, was not uncongenial to Bridget—at her hapless victim, with right arm stretched out to its full length and first finger pointed. This was a grand tableau. They were to remain in their respective positions for three minutes, while complete silence, so that you could hear a pin fall, was expected to reign around amongst the audience. A few yards behind her Eileen, as Mary Seaton, in electric blue satin was to stand.

Seated with much dignity on her throne, Bridget now awaited the entrance of her too lovely relative.

There was a pause. The Tudor Queen became impatient, and was on the point of sending the Earl of Leicester to enquire the reason of the delay, when the door opened and in came Mary and Darnley.

They advanced with slow and not altogether unstately steps. Moyrah, in a rich and handsome Marie Stuart cap and dress, looked beautiful beyond description. Even Bridget, accustomed as she was to her face, was startled into momentary self-forgetfulness by the vision.

"Don't walk too fast! Take care! Take care!" she called in a stage whisper.

On came the devoted couple, keeping exact time with each other's steps.

Suddenly just as they were in the very centre of the stage, and almost touching the footlights, by some extraordinary movement of the body on which it was pinned, Moyrah's regal handsome skirt came off; at first, with a slight struggle, and then with a sudden flop.

Poor Moyrah! It was more than her excited and overtaxed Celtic nervous system could stand. Gathering her face up into a pucker, she began to cry, just as she had been in the habit of doing, from the age of five minutes and upwards, when anything went very much against her.

Bridget started forward in a whirlwind of irritation and excitement, stumbled over the crimson velvet and gold-legged stool in front of her, caught her foot in her long, rich satin robe, and fell headlong on the somewhat rickety stage.

Alas! for the meeting of the two queens!

Though rather shaken and hurt, when Bridget was on her legs again, she tried with her usual fortitude to carry the unfortunate occurrence off with a high hand.

"What's the use of a Lord Keeper, I should like to know," she exclaimed, turning to Bacon, "if he cannot keep me from such a fall as that?"

Poor Bacon hung his head.

"By-the-bye I don't think you ever were Lord Keeper. You wanted to be, and your father was ; but I knew better than to make you," and she nodded at him, saucily.

"Ye silly crature!" exclaimed Michael, angrily, to his sister, "why in the name av all the saints couldn't ye kape yer clothes about ye? Bedad, I'll quarril wid ye now directly."

"No malice, sir : no more than well becomes so good a quarrel and so bad a peer," said Bridget, recalling Suffolk's famous words. This stroke of wit restored good humour to the company.

After a time Moyrah's tears were dried : Cormac— holding up the ill-behaved skirt—took her into a retired corner of the green room, and kissed them all away.

Would that the tears she was to be called upon to shed in days to come could have been dried so easily!

With her body and skirt united by at least as secure a tie as England and Ireland, Moyrah re-appeared. She advanced until she stood before Elizabeth; then the tableau took place; after this she retired to a throne, much inferior in size and poorer in decoration than the English Queen's, at the opposite side of the stage. The throne was hung about with tartan plaids, and a wreath of real thistles and heather encircled the tinsel crown over it. After this a play, supposed to be acted in the presence of the two queens, took place.

The play consisted of one scene out of "Twelfth Night." Bridget found that just as much as they could manage. Sally Louray and Nora Corrigan took the two principal female parts. Now, when Sally was told that in her part as "Olivia" she was in love with Nora, she burst into an explosion of repudiation.

"Shure I alwis hatid her!" she exclaimed. "Hasn't she gone repatin' the most awdayshis tales about me all over the neighbourhood? In love wid her! It's her eyes I'll tear out if I'm put opposite to her at anny toime! Didn't I swear I'd take a stick at her at the next Maragahmore?"

"Hush! Hush!" Bridget had said. "None of your sticks for me, but plenty of mine for you." She had reduced her to amiability by making Dairmuid O'Duiblhne, a young man whom she wished to marry, take the part of "Orsino," and profess to be much in love with her. She called him a little bit of a kippeen, and pretended to turn a deaf ear to his wooing; but, in reality, she was completely pacified

They all learned their parts with aptitude, and repeated the words with energy and spirit. Whether the courtiers of Queen Bess's time would have recognised Shakspere's English in its Celtic colouring is another question, though it is said that the Irish brogue is the old English of Elizabeth's time, which came to Ireland. It is said so by the lips which never told a lie, viz., historian's lips.

Tyrone, who stood looking sweet and amiable, bland and somewhat waggish in the press of nobles round

Elizabeth—very unlike the accounts of his illustrious
namesake—would probably have considered it spoken
properly for the first time.   He was the village postman.

" But let consaylemint "—

" No ! " shouted Bridget, " you *must* say con-ceal-
ment."

" Let the consaylemints," said poor Nora, becoming
nervous and flurried, " feede like a snail in a rose bush."

" Tush ! tush ! tush ! " called Bridget, furiously
banging her stick on the floor, " and here's the last
night of rehearsal !   Prompter, read it out."

" Let consayelmint," began Rourke, the prompter,
whose brogue was as marked as Miss Corrigan's.

" Tut, tut, tut ! " exclaimed Bridget, waxing terribly
wroth. " Say now, after me—con "—

" Con "

" Seal "

" Seal "

" Ment "

" Ment "

" Now then ! "

" Let consayelmint "—

Bridget rose and made two hasty steps towards the
trembling Nora."

" Shure, yer honour," said Rourke, pacifyingly ;
" couldn't we lave it out altogether, and put in interior
parts if its consayelmints they're afthur describin'."

Bridget fell back a step or two, with a hopeless stare
from one to the other.

" Shure, Nora Corrigan alwis had a fearful brogue ! "
soliloquised Sally, contemptuously.

" Go on ! " said Bridget, shortly, a whole world of
suppressed fury in her suddenly self-controlled voice.

" And wid a grave and yaller melincholy," said poor
Nora, who, by this time had quite lost her head, " sittin'
on a monimint."

" Here, listen to me now, Nora Corrigan," said
Michael Hegarty, stepping forward.   " I'll tache ye in

two minnits how to say it." He snapped the book
from Rourke—"'But let consayel-mint, like a worrum
i' the bud, fade on her dam-misk chake'—she poined
in thought, poor crathure," he soliloquised, compas-
sionately—"'an' wid a grane an' yaller melincholy, she
sat, loike Payshiense on a moniment, smoilin' at grafe.'
Was not this love indade? We min may say more,
sware more—ah! that's thrue indade," and he shook
his head with a sigh, and stopped short for a minute
as if ruminating: "'tis very unfortinit min are loike
that."

"Go on!" shouted Bridget, in perfect despair. But
he still seemed lost in contemplation.

"'But, indeed our shows are more than will—'"
continued Bridget herself, at the top of her voice;
"'for still we prove much in our vows, but little in our
love.'"

"Bedad, English or not, he spoke the thruth thin,"
said Rourke, shaking his head again, more sadly than
before. He had now had drawn from him an open
avowal of sentiments with regard to his own sex which
had long been immured in his bosom, and which he had
certainly found it safer to keep so immured, mixing, as
he did, principally in male society.

"The only thing for you to do, Nora," said Bridget,
with the utmost despondency of tone, "is to hurry over
the word as fast as ever you can—con-s-mint—something of that sort. Do you see what I mean?"

"I do, yer honour," said Nora, in a deeply humiliated
tone.

At that moment the "Countess of Salisbury"—who
had partaken somewhat freely of the good things,
especially the porter, which Bridget always provided
for her faithful amateurs before they plunged into the
toils of rehearsing—got a fit of giddiness, and began
to cry

"Hush! hush!" exclaimed Bridget, "that will never
do. Good gracious me! Suppose you begin like that

on the night of the performance! What is to become
of us all? Run quick, "Tyrone," and fetch her a glass
of water. Remember, for the future, you must eat
nothing but dry bread and water before coming on the
stage."

"I will, yer honour," said the poor Countess, submissively, with tears in her eyes.

" Troth an' wasn't she alwis the greedy girril!" said
Sally Louray, roguishly. "She'd ate the heads off
a herd av sheep as soon as she'd look at yer!"

" Shure she's daughter of a gombeen man, what
could ye expect av her?" said Nora, who resented the
interruption to the play.

Just then, the "Countess of Salisbury" got a fit of
sneezing, which made her drop her rosary, which she
habitually wore tucked into her breast: it was a large
wooden rosary, and made a great clatter. For an
instant Bridget's eyes flashed.

Then, after a minute's silence, she said gently and
kindly, "pick it up."

As she turned away she muttered, "little Poperies
everywhere."

She was a strong Protestant; though she knew Latin.

CHAPTER X.

THE evening of the theatrical performance arrived. The neighbouring families drove over armed, as they would have to return late along lonely roads. The gentlemen put their pistols down in a pile in the outer hall. They had refreshments in a small boudoir of Bridget's, as the supper was laid in the library. Then they adjourned to the dining room. They entirely filled the upper half, so much so that numbers of gentlemen had to stand.

The lower half of the room was reserved for the farmers and villagers. It was divided by a thin red cord. Near this cord, dressed in full evening dress, of the most fashionable Parisian cut, leaning gracefully against the old stone work round one of the windows stood Lenoir.

An awful pause took place before the curtain rose. The very flames of the candles seemed to bend towards the stage in breathles suspense. It was an experiment; and the élite prophesied failure. The very audacity of the scheme, many thought, was sufficient to ensure its breaking down with a fiasco. Suppressed smiles, cross glances, with little shakes of the head, and other signs of the sort, passed freely amongst the company in the front rows of chairs. Captain Sheil went about amongst his guests with true Irish geniality, trying to make everyone talk to everyone, and all to feel at home. The Irish county families, who all knew each other, chattered away fast enough, but the English visitors were more silent and shy, though their faces wore an expression of placid contentment, as if they expected a nice little bit of fun.

Up went the curtain with a jerk, and a little hitch and grizzly noise half way up.

Queen Elizabeth walked in, surrounded by her courtiers, and conducted to her throne by Lord Leicester. The remarkable phenomenon of a Union Jack waved over the throne. A murmur of applause greeted the correctness and richness of the dresses, and the general and most unexpected air of smartness about the actors.

Once seated on her throne, and the heavy folds of her regal dress arranged gracefully, and so as to show off the material to the best advantage, Elizabeth turned her eyes with some anxiety towards the door by which her hated rival was to enter.

A pause of expectation, which extended to a nervous length, took place. A pin could have been heard to fall. On these occasions it is to be observed a pin never does fall, so there is no way of testing the assertion.

The spectators all leaned eagerly forward as a door somewhat timidly opened opposite to Her Majesty's throne. The " Great Eliza," the " Sacred Queen," the " Bright Sun which gave light to sense and soul," was visibly trembling ; for, to tell the truth, she felt far more anxious about Moyrah's entrance, considering the persistent elasticity of her garments, than about any other part of the performance. She felt that her protégé would be either a great success or a great failure. It was rather like some celebrated maestro bringing out a new soprano at St. James's Hall.

The door by which the hapless Mary entered was rather in the shade, and at least a minute elapsed before she summoned courage to advance into the full light.

It was a perfect blaze of candle light which fell upon her as she did so. There was no need for Bridget to feel any anxiety about the success of her scheme after two minutes had passed. Leaning on Cormac's arm, with her long, dark eye-lashes and beautifully veined eye-lids, trembling and downcast from humility, and an exquisite deep blush of shyness and modesty on her shell-like cheeks, the vision of the most beautiful woman recorded in history seemed completely realised.

For an instant the audience's breath was taken away; then the applause broke out, no longer in a subdued murmur, but led by Mr. Lucas, who was fairly bewitched, into a regular unmistakable storm of delight. This made Moyrah blush more and more, and so look more and more lovely. The Marie Stuart cap and dress suited that sweet, soft, yielding, rather coaxing manner under which she hid the fire of her Celtic nature. There was something exceedingly pretty in the way, when the clapping was at its height, that she looked up just for one instant into Cormae's face to see what he was feeling. Then she advanced slowly, followed by Eileen, as Mary Seaton, looking very simple and sweet and childish, and conducted by Darnley until she stood opposite to the Virgin Queen.

Then the rich folds of Bridget's satin were disturbed as she rose hurriedly, or it might be more correct to say, sprang to her feet, and with outstretched arm pointed at her rival.

This was the grand tableau; but the stupid audience, composed mainly of the excitable Celtic element, would not sit in breathless silence, as Bridget had arranged they should do. From the first moment that the tableau took place they clapped and applauded in a deafening manner.

Bridget's gimlet eyes could see that Moyrah's petticoats, though slewed a little to one side, were secure, as she stood before her; and she breathed a sigh of relief. This was, indeed, a load removed from a breast already too heavily weighted with cares for one evening.

The stockings of the " Countess of Salisbury," who stood at the side of her throne, had also been made gratifyingly secure with two stout pieces of twine. Bridget's reddish hair and fair, somewhat freckled skin, suited the popular ideal of " Queen Bess " admirably.

As the rulers of the divided kingdom stood face to face, the courtiers formed in a semi-circle round the English throne, and stood in a sort of mosaic of colour previously arranged by Bridget, with a view to showing off the different dresses. The effect was exceedingly pretty and striking. At the same moment the band, consisting of a piano, a cornet, two fiddles and a flute, struck up a bit of bravura music, composed by Bridget, called "The Good Old Days." Cormac's conduct was admirable all through, for he was so completely wrapped up in Moyrah, and hoping all would go well with regard to her, that he forgot to think about himself at all, and therefore made the very perfection of an actor and a lover. When the applause had somewhat subsided, at a sign from Bridget, Moyrah turned away, and walked to her more modest throne; then came the critical moment when the play was to begin.

It consisted of one short scene out of "Twelfth Night." When it came to "Let concealment," there was an instant's agonized pause. Bridget's eyes, almost starting from her head with anxiety, were fixed on the trembling "Viola."

"'But let, ——— '" a pause, in which Rourke's voice was audible, "'Con-sayle-mint.'" Bridget's brow wrinkled up in torture. Another pause, during which the front rows of the audience looked at each other with amused but restrained smiles.

"'But let consmint, loike a worrum i' the bud, fade on her dammisk chake,'" came all rattled out in one breath, like an alarum clock going off at midnight. A sigh of relief broke from Bridget as she bit her under lip vigorously.

In two or three minutes more the play was successfully over without any fiasco whatever, and the curtain fell amid prolonged applause. It fell, but only for a few minutes. With a rapidity which might—can we say, perhaps may, in days to come—be imitated at some of our best London theatres, it rose again upon a final tableau arranged, at the last minute, by Bridget. This represented Queen Mary on her way to the scaffold. Her dress had been rapidly changed, and was now of black velvet, her cap of black velvet, with the pointed pearl row round her face. A string of beads hung at her side. An *Agnus Dei* was round her throat, and a crucifix was clasped in her hand. So far, history was followed. But now came a divergence. Cormac, dressed as a jailer, with his head bent down, walked a few feet in front of her. How that scene came before Bridget in after days! Half way across the stage she met her brother Michael, dressed as an old man, in deep mourning, with grey wig and beard, to represent " Melville." He flung himself on his knees before her, apparently overcome with grief.

Stooping with great dignity she raised and embraced and kissed him, saying as she did so, " ' Good Melville, sayse to lemint; this day thou shalt see the ind av Mary Stewart's thrials.' "

There was something very soft and touching in Moyrah's voice at all times; and now she had thrown herself so thoroughly into the part that it took a deeply melancholy cadence which brought tears into the spectators' eyes. Lucas fairly hid his face in his hands, and the tears trickled down between his fingers. Sydney, too, was much moved, and carried away altogether out of himself to three hundred years ago. It seemed as if the scene on that cold February morning, three centuries ago, was being enacted over again before the spectators' eyes. Moyrah's beauty was of that touching, pensive sort, with the half-veiled suspicion of southern fire about it, which vividly recalled most people's ideal of Mary Stuart.

For some reason Cormac became nervous, and totally forgot a nice little speech of consolation, about four lines long, which Bridget had composed for him.

Melville held up the heavy folds of the black velvet train, and slowly followed the ill-fated Queen's faltering footsteps. Arrived at the door off the stage, Moyrah turned round and gave one last look at the assembled company. In that one instant her eye caught Lenoir's. There is a mysterious magic in some looks which thrills through the person who first catches that look. So it was with Moyrah. She felt a something come over her, such as she had never experienced before, as those dark eyes rested on her for an instant.

As she stood in the half-shadow by the door, with a sort of farewell expression on her face, Sydney could not help thinking of the spathe which a lily throws off before it bursts into the beauty of its flower. Her bodily beauty appeared like that. The beauty which was within her body, and which would live after her head was cut off, seemed to shine out like the snowy petals gleaming through their commoner binding.

" Who is that young lady who is acting " Queen Mary ? " asked Lenior of the Sheil's housekeeper, who, in her best bib and tucker, with her fat, rosy face wreathed in smiles, was sitting near him.

" Moyrah Hegarty ; mind what you're sayin'," she added in a whisper, " for that's her ould father not five feet away from ye."

Lenior waited a little, and then quietly edged his way up to old Mr. Hegarty. In one minute Lenior had seen what he was ; a bettermost farmer by position, a good simple man in character ; a little nut brown wrinkled old man, with thin iron grey locks, in outward appearance.

" Been a pretty good harvest Mr. Hegarty, eh ? " he said, with that insinuating manner which enabled him to make his way amongst all sorts and conditions of men.

Instantly old Hegarty's face lighted up. The harvest was the one thought which, at this time, was never absent from his mind. " Faith, sir, not very good. A power av moisture ! "

So strange ! because in England and France they were calling out for rain."

" Oirelan' is altogithur a diffrint place ! " he responded gloomily, shaking his head again. " There's no nagerly spirit in the hivins wid regard to wathur."

" You have a nice little farm, I believe. I should like greatly to see it."

" Shure an' ye're welkim, sirr, whiniver ye loike to come. 'Tis but poor hospitality we can be offerin' strangers now-a-days, but such as it is, ye'll get it wid all heartiness."

" A thousand thanks, I am sure," said Lenior, with empressement. " The country's a good deal upset just now," he continued, pretending to look indifferent, but keeping the corner of his eye fixed on Hegarty.

" 'Tis so," said Hegarty, shortly.

" I suppose you're in favour of Home Rule ? "

There was a silence for a minute.

" If it 'ud give us good crops," he said, shortly, and keeping his eyes fixed straight before him.

" Ha ! ha ! very good ! " laughed Lenior. " You Irish have so much wit that you ought to be allowed to rule yourselves, really you ought."

" There's not much wit in the potato blight," said Hegarty, with a little toss of his head.

" But why should Ireland be condemned to grow nothing but the potato ? " said Lenoir, insinuatingly. " If each man had, as he ought to have, a little plot of ground of his own, he could grow wheat and barley, and cereals of all kinds, and so compete with England and foreign markets."

" Bedad, I'd loike to see him ! How is he going to buy all thim new jim-crackery tools an' maysheenes for his farming ? an' he wid naythur bread nor milk to put into his childer's mouths the while. Shure an' iv it wasn't for his honour, the captin there, givin' me all thim new stame ingins for threshin' and the loikes, I'd nivir make a haypinnie at all ! "

" But why should you be beholden to anyone for what you have a right to yourself? "

"Faix, I don't clearly see how I have a right to another man's threshin' machine."

"If every man had an equal amount of property, then no one would possess one threshing machine, or one-half a threshing machine more than another."

"Hum!"

"Everything everyone has should be equally at the service of everyone else."

A sensible looking man, sitting just in front of Lenoir, turned round and fixed his eyes on him for a moment.

A slightly cynical curve came in the thin lines round Lenoir's mouth. He turned the conversation back again to the crops.

After the conclusion of the theatricals, the chairs were cleared away, and a dance began amongst the village people. The quality stayed a short time, and watched the jigs and country dances, and then retired to supper in the library, much delighted with their entertainment.

"Most lovely girl girl I evaw saw in my life," said Lucas to Sydney, as he helped himself to champagne cup. "By Jove! talk of pwofesshnal beauties! not one of them could hold a candle to her!"

Sydney was helping some blanc mange on to a plate for a lady. He nodded.

"Doesn't seem to have impressed yoaw unsusceptible hawt."

Sydney smiled. "On the contrary," he said, in a thoughtful voice. "I was much struck with her. There is something more in her face than the mere outward beauty of its form."

"Well, I was quite satisfied with that, I confess. Confoundedly good champagne cup! Didn't think they could brew such a beverage in this benighted land."

"Indeed, sir, didn't you?" said Captain Sheil good-humouredly, who happened to be passing at that moment; "I fear England will wake up to learn we have brewed such a cup as she may find it difficult to drink."

In the meantime, the actors, having changed their costumes to their ordinary Sunday best, had come out from behind the scenes and mingled with the dancers.

The moment Moyrah appeared she went towards her father, who was still sitting by Lenoir talking about the crops. Lenoir stood up as she approached, and when she was close to them he made a fashionable bow.

" I must congratulate your Majesty upon still having your head on your shoulders."

Moyrah smiled, blushed, and looked down.

" We who saw you are not all so fortunate," he added, in a low voice of deep meaning.

Moyrah did not understand the drift of his remark.

" I have seldom seen such acting, Miss Hegarty, and I have attended some of the best theatres in every country in Europe."

" Ye're very kind sur, I'm shure," said Moyrah, a bright blush of gratified vanity flying to her cheeks.

" Not kind, surely, for merely speaking the truth," he said, with an insinuation of manner which would have disgusted Bridget, but which to Moyrah appeared irresistible.

" Do you know, Miss Moyrah, that, though you, perhaps, take me for a foreigner, I can dance an Irish jig? and I claim you for my partner."

Again there was a double meaning in his tone.

" Moyrah looked up into her father's face. " Farthur, darlin', will ye be lonesim loike iv I lave ye agin, wid all these strange people about?"

He looked at her with a slight smile. Her affection for her father was something quite out of the ordinary. She fulfilled Shakspere's injunction, and he " was to her as a god." Five minutes spent with him was greater happiness, and she felt always would be, than hours spent with Cormac. Yet she loved Cormac, too. She knew she loved him. It was strange! Let faith beat our hearts out on the anvil of common sense, and see what

remains of the pure gold. Her faith in her love for
Cormac was doing that now.

"Acushla agus asthore machree," said Hegarty,
looking with deep tenderness at his daughter's blushing,
beautiful face, "shure, I'm nivir so happy as whin ye're
enjoyin' of yersilf."

So Moyrah went off, for the first time leaning upon
Alphonse Lenoir's arm.

The windows of the dining room opened on to a
terrace. They were open down to the ground.

"Let us take one turn on the terrace before our jig,
Miss Moyrah," said Lenoir, who privately had no
attrait for bouncing and jigging about, like a crazy
acrobat, amongst all the peasants, whom he despised.

Once out in the calm moonlight everything took a
romantic turn. But it was a misty moon—a moon with
a halo of tears round it. A moon that did not bode
well for those who first made friends under its light.

"You had a sad part to act to-night, Miss Moyrah.
Do you know much of the ill-fated queen's history?"

"She perished on the scaffold," said Moyrah, in a
low, mysterious voice

"She did." He paused. "But before she died she
had lived, because she had loved."

Moyrah was silent.

"There is no real life until we love." He paused for
a minute and looked at her. "I fear you do not agree
with that. Perhaps you think with my countryman—

> "'Le premier soupir de l'amour
> Est le dernier de la sagesse.'"

Moyrah looked fairly puzzled now, though she much
admired the grandeur of a man who could speak a
foreign language in so elegant a manner.

"You don't, then, know the history of Mary Stuart's
life?"

"I know she was married to Darnley—that's Cormac,
poor boy!" she added, in a low, kind tone, as if thinking of some one not present.

“ But she did not love Darnley,” he said, looking at her intently.

“ Didn’t she?” said Moyrah, with an air of great surprise, almost incredulity.

“ No,” and he bent over her while he spoke very low ; “ she loved another.”

“ She was wrong, then,” said Moyrah, in a very low, half hesitating voice.

“ Love takes no account of right and wrong, Miss Moyrah,” he replied, with so deep an emphasis on his words that Moyrah was startled.

“ But love is right in itsilf.” She looked puzzled. ’Tis, sartin shure, for the Church taches that.”

“ Whatever the Church teaches is right, of course.” Moyrah’s unsophisticated ears detected no shade of satire in the tone.

“ I can fancy only living, just as you do, within the narrow scope of a little village like this, that you”—he paused, a certain dignity in Moyrah’s manner, in spite of its soft yieldingness, prevented him from finishing the sentence as he had intended.

Fungi, unlike most plants, are to a great extent insensible to the influence of light. Lenoir’s mind was like a fungus. But there was a light in Moyrah’s conscience which could influence even that toadstool. After a few minutes’ silence he said: “ I should think, Miss Moyrah, your face expresses all you feel. You keep no store of masks in your green-room, like so many of those who consider themselves above you in position.”

Moyrah did not quite follow this.

“ Not, however,” he continued, looking at her intently, “ that any mask can long conceal love where it exists, or feign it where it does not.”

“ Faith, I think that’s thrue enough,” she said, in a low, half shy, half doubtful, half pondering, wholly bewitching voice.

“ It is, indeed,” he said, fervently, looking much

pleased at having elicited such an assent. " Love is not a fire which can be confined within the breast. Everything betrays us ; the voice, silence, the eyes."

Moyrah's beautiful dark eyes, looking larger, darker, and softer than ever in the pale moonlight, were raised to his for one instant. There was surely a magic in that glance ; a vision of joy beyond anything she had imagined possible rose for an instant before Moyrah's mind.

" Just then came the low co-o-e of the wood pigeons, in the large old trees round the house, awakened and annoyed, no doubt, by the revelling, the lighting up, the noise, the dancing in a house usually so quiet.

" And when once we are betrayed, our whole life seems to hang on whether we get a response to our feelings or not."

At that moment Bridget and Sydney came out of the drawing room window, which was also wide open, and began to walk down the terrace towards where Moyrah and Lenoir were walking. Instantly Lenoir suggested they should return to the dining room, and join in the dance ; she assented. Bridget was perfectly happy in having Sydney for her companion in a moonlight stroll.

OYRAH had danced oftener than a careful mother would have sanctioned—I mean a Mayfair mother—with Alphonse Lenoir. He continually hung about the place where she was, even when he was not dancing with her.

But Mrs. Hegarty was too busy attending to her own libations, and to a gossip, Mrs. Downey (who was always out about the village picking up stray bits of news), was having with her, to think much of Moyrah. Besides, she was not accustomed to going out to balls; and her duties as a chaperon were as vague to her, and, in fact, as little within her comprehension as the eighth commandment appears to be to some political people. Hegarty, meantime, was much taken up by a neighbouring farmer, who began about the crops, went on to boast of some fishing he had enjoyed off a landlord's bit of a river, and ended by wanting to swop horses. A man who can tell you about his own fishing exploits and swop horses with you without lying is as fit for the canonization of biography as men ever become. But Hegarty had no intention of swopping horses. The horse which he drove to his jaunting car, on the rare occasions when he used that vehicle, was not his at all. It was Moyrah's, and had been given to her by Bridget when it was a little foal. With it Bridget had also given a tiny silver whistle, and had told Moyrah she must teach the foal to come to her at the sound of the whistle. Nothing loth, Moyrah had quickly set about fulfilling these instructions

Presently the jigs became fast and furious. The band had been treated with true hospitality. So, indeed, had the guests. The captain was a man who followed the precept—" Don't despise your poor friends : they may become suddenly rich, and then it will be awkward to explain things to them." Therefore, whisky had flowed like water in London milk. Mrs. Hegarty, who was overworked at home, and always wanted a little bracing, had taken rather more than her husband. She began to feel very sleepy. Eileen was scudding about, here, there, and everywhere, with a pack of girls of her own age. Sometimes they joined the jigs ; sometimes they got tired of them. People were beginning to go home—trooping off in threes, fours, and fives in the moonlight. Blue cloaks were drawn over heads. Farewell slaps on the back were given. Hegarty, who had been yawning tremendously for some time, began to look about for his spouse.

" There ye are, idlin' about," he said, good humouredly, coming up to her. " The divil goes into an idle man's house widout knockin'," he added, with a sly wink in the corner of his eye.

" Shure, ye ought to be a good judge av that, since the house is yer own."

" Where are the childer ?"

" 'Tis ye ought to know that, kickin' yer seventy-three-year-old heels, as I seen yer, along wid 'em in the jig a while ago."

Presently the Hegarty party were all gathered in the yard climbing up on the jaunting car.

Lenoir was there, seeing the last of Moyrah. Mrs. Hegarty was highly flattered and pleased with his attentions, as she looked upon him as quite the gentleman, and when she was by he took care to be more polite to her than to Moyrah. She was not accustomed to much attention from the sterner sex, or indeed, from any sex, and this struck her as charming conduct. She was only too ready to give a hearty response to his humble request that he might be allowed to visit the farm. He declared he took the greatest interest in farming. He loathed it in reality. His adieu to Moyrah was not spoken. It consisted of a long pressure of the hand, made under the flap of the well of the car, so that no one could see it.

They bowled quickly along through the moonlight, and it was the strangest feeling drive on the strangest feeling evening Moyrah had ever experienced.

When they had driven through the ever hospitably open gate of the yard at the Blue House, Moyrah was the first to jump down, and she, with her own hands, helped Michael to unharness her adored horse—her adored one, as she called him—then she walked on, first towards the loose box in which he was kept, and, as she went, gave a little low whistle with her silver whistle which hung round her neck.

The animal gave his ears a prick forward, stretched out his nose towards her shoulder, and walked proudly after her of his own accord into his stable. Moyrah gave him a gentle rub down all over, kissed him several times, and then went into the house, and stole up the creaky old stairs, to the little bed room she shared with Eileen.

The room, though low in the ceiling, was not, relatively to the rest of the house, small. There was room for an old, dark, wooden chest of drawers, with all the handles off the drawers, and the middle drawer habitually open at an angle; also a little round deal table, a good bit scratched and cut about; also a long narrow table in the window, on which some straggling geraniums stood; also the bed in which Moyrah and Eileen slept. This was a curious article. It consisted of an old black oak chest of huge dimensions, in which Mrs. Hegarty had brought all her wedding garments, and general contributions to the household linen, when she arrived as a bride. The lid had been taken off this. Mrs. Hegarty had all but died when Moyrah was born, and in thanksgiving for her recovery, she presented this lid to the church. It now hung, by a somewhat creaky iron chain, over the pulpit, and acted as such a capital sounding board, that the most nervous, timid, and retiring curate Maynooth ever sent out could completely fill the entire building. This was a great reward for her charity ; and Mrs. Hegarty sat with an allowable feeling of triumph every Sunday at last mass. on her little wooden bench, close under the pulpit, and gazed aloft at her charitable donation. Many persons who go to different churches gaze aloft at their past charitable donations, for their good deeds do follow them wherever they go. One's virtues do come before one in church in a way they do not at any other time.

It may be that the enforced close proximity to so many people whose failings we are acquainted with brings out their faults into more startling prominence than they assume when a wider distance divides us; and then the human mind, always in want of the relief of a background, seeks one in the luxuriant foliage of personal virtues.

Be that as it may ; the lid was gone off the chest we are speaking about, and it was just as well for Moyrah and Eileen that it was fulfilling a nobler function than possibly smothering them. This chest was pulled up close to the little lattice window, which, with that hatred of fresh air which is one of the most salient characteristics of that old-fashioned race to which Moyrah belonged, was tight shut, though the thermometer had stood at eighty in the shade all day. There was no blind to it, and the moonlight streamed, and fell in little three-cornered patches on the snow-white pillow, partly covered by Eileen's golden curls, which mingled with Moyrah's glossy, but darker, locks.

Eileen's nervous system was not highly strung. She was well worn out with the fatigues of the past evening, and she slept the dull, dreamless sleep of perfect repose. Not so Moyrah. The strain which had been put upon her had been too much. That strange antipathy which she had to deeds of violence, and which, in her case, amounted to an idiosyncrasy, like the sight of a drawn sword to James I., or the rattling of a carriage on a bridge to Peter the Great, had been cruelly outraged. Her mind had been fixed consecutively for hours upon herself as the principal figure in one of the most thrilling tragedies recorded in history. What wonder, then, if the round white arm which lay outside the blanket moved about from side to side, and if the fingers clutched convulsively, first at empty air, then at the side of the old chest, as though they were seeking the straw which should save the drowning man. There was no rest for the brain in her sleep.

The little oval shadows of the leaves of the ash tree outside the window, like bunches of waving almonds, moved up and down over her pale face and marble-like throat. She muttered something, rather loud, too, but Eileen slept on. Suddenly, Moyrah started bolt upright, with a piercing shriek, and seized her own throat, screaming: "Me head is gone enthirely. 'Tis gone enthirely!"

"Sure, what are ye afthur now? May the saints protict us!" exclaimed Eileen, half frightened, half sleepy, as she sat up and crossed herself devoutly.

"A massacray! a massacray!" continued Moyrah, only half awake, "an' it's the fardorougha (the dark man) that's done it."

"The hivins presarve us, Moyrah! Whativir are ye dramin' of?" and Eileen, who was fairly exasperated, gave her sister a hearty good shaking, and one or two smart slaps on the shoulder. In a rebound Moyrah's head got a slight blow against the side of the wooden chest, and this annoyed, while it thoroughly awakened, her.

"Lave me alone, can't ye?" she said, rubbing her eyes."

"Begorra, I'll shake ye 'till ye behave yersilf," said Eileen, who had been given a great fright.

Moyrah pushed her away with her hand. "I drimt just like the life now," she said, apologetically, still rubbing her eyes, "that me head was off; but it wasn't a knife at all or an ax that cut it off, but a rope; there's a quare thing for ye!"

"'Tis a quare thing ye wakin' me up scrachin' like that, that's whut I'm thinkin'," said Eileen, grumpily, settling herself to sleep again.

"Well, I'm sorry for ye, avourneen machree." Her voice took that sweet, loving cadence those who lived with her knew so well. She slipped her arm round her sister's neck, leaned over and kissed her.

Eileen growled, and then was asleep again in half a minute.

Not so Moyrah. She had none of the salt of wisdom, the alembroth of the ancients, in her composition. She could not argue herself into quietness. The key of that art of common sense which has calmed so many excited nerves had never been committed to her keeping. We know that in some families there is one member to whom the latch-key of the house is never entrusted, generally the most worthy member, too. Thus it was, spiritually, with Moyrah.

There is an old adage of good advice which might well be followed in the race of life :—" If you want to win at a race, keep calm. Turn your head away when you see the horse you have bet against a good length ahead, and your rival helping your lady-love to champagne which you have paid for."

But Moyrah knew nothing of that secret of keeping calm. That latch-key had been stoutly withheld from her. She felt too excited to go to sleep again; so, gently, for fear of waking Eileen, she got up and throwing a ragged, old, green worsted shawl round her shoulders, went to the window, and did what was most unusual for her, or any member of the family to do. opened the lattice and leaned out. The night was very still. Not a breath was stirring just then. The breeze

had died down for the moment. A sort of awe came
over Moyrah. She was not accustomed to be up alone
in the middle of the night. Her ears strained from the
tension of the quietness. Suddenly she heard a sound.
Was it Emmett munching his oats in the stable? No;
it was more human than that.

It came again, and this time nearer. The public road
ran in a curve, not ten yards from the side of the Blue
House, out of which Moyrah was looking. A low sweet-
briar hedge divided the Hegarty's garden from the road.
Moyrah now observed three men standing at one side of
this hedge, under a chestnut tree. One she quickly
recognized as a well-known rascal in the village,
O'Leary, by name; the other she thought, as well as
she could see, for only part of his profile was towards
her, was a young miller's clerk who had recently been
dismissed for dishonesty, Flanagan, by name. The
third she could not make out at all; the collar of his
coat was turned up and his hat was dragged down over
his face. He was a head taller than either of his
companions, and had altogether a different air from them.

Moyrah now leaned forward, with intense eagerness,
to try to catch what they were saying. Her ears, like
all her other senses, were abnormally keen. They
muttered, in what probably they considered a whisper,
but still, she heard:

"The captain's put him into that farm himsilf,"
said O'Leary.

"He has so-a," and Flanagan nodded.

"And Tim Whelan evictid from it."

"That's thrue!" He scratched his head. "Whelan,
bedad, is the right name for him, for he was wheeled
out in a wheel barrer, dhrunk as a piper, as, indade, he
mostly was."

"That's naythur here nor there. He was evictid,
and Cormac O'Neil has got the farrum."

As Moyrah heard her lover's name, she started and
grew deadly pale; but still, she listened on intently.

Flanagan had evidently made good friends with the whisky bottle at the beginning of the evening, and was in one of those sociable moods which are the bugbear of conspirators.

"He was denounced at the Harvest Bug Meeting to-day. Funds have come from America. We must not betray our trust," This time, the tall mysterious man spoke. He had no Irish accent.

"He's goin' to get marrid imajatelee to Moyrah Hegarty," said Flanagan.

The tall man nodded as if he already knew.

"He'll marry in his windin' sheet," said O'Leary with a bitter sneer.

Moyrah's heart seemed to stop beating. Then the hot blood rushed over her face and the whole of her body, and a paroxysm of fury siezed her.

O'Leary and Flanagan both had guns.

Flanagan was continually moving his about all the time he was talking; cocking it, pointing it, looking down its muzzle. He was a fidgety boy.

At this juncture their voices fell; but Moyrah's ears caught the words, "losing time; Flanagan, lead the way."

Off they set, stealing and slouching slowly along, keeping as much in the shadow of the trees as they could.

Moyrah closed the window. She stood at it with her hands folded, pale and cold, in the weird moonlight. She stood about five seconds in this position. Then she went on tip-toe to a cupboard at one end of the room. She opened the door so as not to make a sound, and yet quickly. She put in her hand and took down a long, light grey cloak, made of a coarse woolly stuff, with a hood to it. It was much the colour of the moonlight. This she wrapped tightly round her, and drew the hood over her head. Opening the door very cautiously she slipped down the old wooden stairs, her bare feet not making a sound. Unfastening the front

door was the real difficulty. There were one or two
tough iron bolts which had creaked from time immemorial; a rusty old lock in which, struggle as you
might, the key would go round with a jerk. It did;
and what a jerk! She stood quite still for a minute
afterwards, to hear if the noise had awakened anyone.
But the Hegarty family were sound sleepers by nature,
and to-night they were extra sleepy, from the unwonted
excitements, not to mention actual fatigue from the
exertions of dancing. Mr. and Mrs. Hegarty's room
was just over the door; but Moyrah knew that her
mother was at no time a woman to get out of bed when
she could lawfully stay in it.

Once outside in the chill night air, Moyrah drew a
long breath of relief, and then stood still to consider.
A cold, grey mist was rising from the ground, not very
dense, but still sufficient to be of use to Moyrah.

Once really off she flew like the wind. Her long
legs and agile figure had always made her a good
runner, and there was not a boy in the village who
could approach her speed in running races. She did
not seem to touch the ground at all; and objects whirled
past her and she past them, the way they do to passengers in an express train.

She knew a short cut across the fields to Cormac's
house. It was a way not generally known. In fact,
Michael had himself pulled one or two holes in the
corners of certain hedges, so as to make a passage for
himself against his father's wishes. But she had filled
these holes up again with withered boughs, which
could be easily removed at a moment's notice by anyone who knew how they were placed. Now she
whipped them away as if they had been paper, and
flung them on one side, not stopping, as she had hitherto
done, to replace them cautiously, so as to keep Michael's
secret of the holes. She bounded through these holes
like a hunted hare.

The cows and sheep looked much surprised as she

whirled across the fields through the midst of the flocks. Soon she saw the outline of Cormac's house before her. It was a small yellow house—square, like a doll's—with three windows at top, and two at each side of the hall door.

"I've bate 'em," she muttered, as she cleared her last hedge. "Shure the divil was alwis bad on his legs, since he was made to crape in the gardin of Eden."

Up the little narrow back boreen, which led to the back door of her lover's abode, she sped. Once at the door, she stood for a minute panting, and in doubt. If she knocked loud enough to wake Cormac, she would give an alarm signal to the assassins. This was exactly what she wished to avoid. She bit the top of her first finger, bent her brows, and stared about her in anxious thought. Suddenly her eyes lighted on half-an-inch of the scullery window left inadvertently open. Without a moment's hesitation she flung it up and bounded into the room. She stole on tip toe across the floor, then up the narrow creaky wooden stairs, three steps at a time. Cormac snored, and you could hear his snores before you got half-way up stairs.

"Faith, they'd have kilt him aisy, slapin' like that," she muttered, shaking her head. "A dead man as iver was alive before the mornin'." She turned the handle of the door, and stole in.

Cormac was sleeping heavily on the outside of the bed, in all his clothes, just as he had thrown himself down, dead tired, after his unwonted festivities. He was on a red railway rug, which the captain had given him, curled up into the shape of an "S," with his arm under his head. Moyrah shook him by his collar, at first gently, but presently, as he took no notice, more violently. Suddenly he started up, and striking out wildly with his fists, shouted:

"Hullo! ye ould blackgird! how dar yer! Murther! murther!"

“ Cormac, Cormac, me boy, ’tis me, ’tis Moyrah.
Quiate, me boy, quiate.”

“ Moyrah ! ” and his tone was one of stupefied
amazement. “ Shure, my girl, ’tis no toime for ye to
be here.”

“ Get up now, like shot wid ye; shure the moon-
lighters are afther ye.” Her voice fell to a whisper.
“ Hurrie, hurrie, for the liofe of ye, don’t stop now, an
instant; follee me down stairs an’ out the back gayit,
an’ I’ll show ye the rate at which ye should cut the
short way to the Blue House across the fields. Kape
quiate, now; don’t spake as much as would make a
mouse trimble. Who knows but those divils may be
widin hearin’.”

As his faculties returned, Cormac quickly grasped
the situation, as only an Irishman, living in Ireland at
the present moment, could grasp it.

He sprang from off the bed, and shook himself like
a dog; then, without a word, but with an expression of
ghastly terror on his face, he followed Moyrah down the
stairs, and out the scullery window. As Moyrah was
closing the window after them, voices became distinctly
audible approaching up the road in front of the house.

“ Bind doun double, and crape afther me,” whispered
Moyrah.

He obeyed; but Moyrah could hear his teeth chattering, and saw he was shaking all over, as if he had
the ague.

“ Kape up yer heart, avick machree,” said the weaker
vessel, encouragingly, as she advanced, bent double,
with cat-like steps, turning her head round every few
yards, with the anxious, listening expression of a hare,
which hears the distant footstep of a man. So they
procceded until they came to the end of the lane. Here
one of Michael’s holes came into requisition. Stooping
down, still more, she crept first through it, and
Cormac followed so quickly that his head touched her
heels.

They were within one field of the Blue House when
a sudden light in the sky caused them to turn sharply
round. As they stared open mouthed, open eyed and
speechless, tongues of flame were seen shooting up above
the tops of the trees, and the sky, for a long distance
round, was illuminated with a lurid glare. The heroes
who are to bring salvation to the peasants of Ireland
were beginning their work of mercy.

"An' all me hay, me hay!" burst from Cormac's lips,
in a voice of anguish, while he flung his arms above his
head in wild despair.

A gleam of strange passion came into Moyrah's eyes
for a minute.

"May the burnin' house fall on 'em!" exclaimed
Cormac, while a look of ferocity came over his face.

"They think they've got ye inside the house, gintle
crathurs," said Moyrah.

Even at that distance, as they stood still, they could
hear the crash of the falling roof. As it fell, the flames
flew up higher and more brilliant than ever. They
looked at each other, and each knew that the other was
longing for vengeance. But vengeance at that moment
could not be taken.

Moyrah was the first to move. She walked quickly
on to the Blue House. He followed with halting steps,
looking round every minute at the devouring flames,
sighing, striking his breast, and shaking his fist
towards them. Moyrah seemed half to dread that
Cormac's feelings would turn his head, and that he
would burst away from her to rush back and avenge
his cruel wrongs. She seized the collar of his coat,
and, by main force, dragged him inside the portals of
the Blue House. Then she locked, barred, and bolted
the door; after which she made a sign to Cormac to
help her to push a heavy old deal box against it.

"Faith! 'tis as well to be ready; but they won't
come here. They're cock shure, now, they've done for
ye enthirely, an' there's only yer cinders left. They'll

git home, now, as quick as convanyent; the divil himsilf is ashamed av himsilf sometimes."

"'Tis thrue" said Cormac, "or else, why does he hide
himsilf enthirely in hell, whin thar's plinty av' places
conganeal to him in this wurruld."

"He's here more than most people are thinkin',"
said Moyrah, as she pulled an old eider-down quilt, and
a couple of pillows out of a cupboard and laid them
on the kitchen table.

"Can ye make yerself at home there, me boy, till
the mornin'?"

"The Lorrud bless ye, mavourneen!" he exclaimed,
seizing her hand, and kissing it.

"This wurruld's a dangerous place," sighed Moyrah,
as she thought of the risk they had just run.

"'Tis so then; very few get out av it alive!" he
echoed fervently: for the first time, all she had done for
him seemed to dawn upon his mind.

"'Tis me loife I owe to ye enthirely; an' shure ye
risked yer own for it; may the blessed Vargin, and all
the saints reward ye!" His voice trembled. "Faith,
I worship the ground ye walk on."

They sat by the not quite extinct embers of the fire
for half an hour listening for footsteps and talking in
whispers; but no footsteps were heard. The murderers
were careful not to go back by the road they had come.

Presently Moyrah made a suggestion, and she and
Cormac knelt down, side by side, and said the mag-
nificat, in thanksgiving for their escape. After that,
no more was said; and Moyrah stole upstairs, where
she found Eileen sleeping placidly, and soon, in spite of
her adventures, she was slumbering as calmly by her
side.

CHAPTER XII.

THE next morning Moyrah's first thought on waking was, how it would be possible to provide for Cormac's future safety.

A man who has suffered brutal wrongs, in his property or his person, from the Harvest Bug Society, is not an object of pity or consideration to the rest of the community; rather, he is looked upon as other hens look upon a sick hen, to be pecked to death, if he won't die of himself. He is fair game for the village bully to tyrannise over: for cowards, who fancy they owe him a grudge, to maim. He is not allowed, if possible, to have any property, and his person is in danger every hour.

Moyrah knew this perfectly well. She knew, moreover, that anyone who sheltered the outcast, was equally in danger. Her beloved father, who was already suspected of half-heartedness, in the Socialistic cause, would become a marked man, as soon as it was known he was sheltering Cormac. The Blue House itself would - not be safe from those devouring flames which had made her blood run cold.

"What a fearful thing!" she thought, as she laid half awake, half asleep. Those first few moments of awaking to misery which are so terrible now came over her, and for a short time were worse than any wholly waking moments can ever be. At length, she shook herself quite awake, and getting stealthily out of the side of the old chest, without waking Eileen, dressed, and went downstairs. It was nine o'clock, but no one in the house was yet astir. All were worn out with last night's gaieties, and the house was so profoundly still that Moyrah started at the little noises she accidentally made now and then; the inadvertent pushing of a chair, the creaking of one particular board in the floor, which always did creak when stood on, and which she always forgot did creak.

Cormac was in as heavy a slumber on the kitchen table as he had been in his own house.

Moyrah stood and looked at him for several minutes with a sad smile. Then she pulled her red and green plaid shawl over her head, and went out to see her beloved horse.

She always declared that she knew his heart beat for joy when he heard her footstep coming into his stable. He always turned his head, while an expression, which modern poets would have described as " luminous," came into his eyes.

Moyrah had never heard of the word "luminous," but she would have been quite ready to admit any word into her vocabulary which could have added an additional halo of glory to her favourite.

This morning she was much in need of advice, and she wished with all her heart that her idol could have given it to her. She was sure it would have been more sensible than what human beings usually gave her. As she stood with one arm round his neck, and the other stroking down his silky mane, she felt that bitter regret within her which all lovers of animals have experienced at one time or another—that two-footed animals, as a rule, cannot understand the language which four-footed ones speak.

" Shure, they're tellin' me 'tis to Punchestown ye ought to be goin', me darlin'; an' Cormac ses, iv the Prince av Waylis saw ye there, he'd bet a pint av goold upon ye immajitely! But don't ye be afeered, acushla!—don't ye be afeered!" and she stroked his silky nose, and then kissed it. " I wouldn't see thim timpistuous crathurs av jockeys a kickin' at yer wid their heels (Moyrah had been to the Mallow races), an' a slashin' an' a batin' av yer sides, as iv ye were a whisp av corn in a granary in autumn. I would not— no-a, not iv they offert me all the new bonnets in Limerick, an' I seen a power av 'em there the last time I wint marketin'," she sighed. New bonnets were things which stood much in the same place to her as the crown of Ireland appears to stand to a large number of her countrymen.

As she was leaving the stables for the little plot of ground in front of the farm-yard, she suddenly heard footsteps on the road. Her cheeks grew pale, and she stood still and held her breath.

"'Tis wake in the head I am !" she exclaimed, impatiently scolding herself. "Shure, 'tis nine o'clock, an' past, an' all the wurruld an' his wife is out walkin'; an' there am I, ketchin' me breath as iv I'd a stitch in me soide, an' dancin' on me toes iv I hear the most distant reflection av the brogues crushin' the dhry mud in the road."

But, in spite of her scolding, she shuddered as the steps came nearer. She crossed herself. "The Lorrud presarve us !" she muttered. "Shure, these are troubled toimes for poor ould Oirelan'! The horsis are the only crathurs in the counthry that can be thrusted to walk upon the roads." In spite of herself she felt compelled to go up to the little hand-gate which led on to the road.

Walking calmly along, looking so cool and easy in his light grey shooting coat, with his gun under his arm, and a matutinal cigar in his mouth, was Edgar Sydney. The moment he caught sight of Moyrah he came towards her, and, raising his hat, made as courteous a bow as if she had been a princess. He had just been thinking of her. This was strange for him, as, usually, he seldom thought of the fair sex. Sport, business and charity divided his solitary meditations. This morning he had begun by thinking of the law by

which suspected poachers may be searched by constables.
This law had been brought vividly before his mind by
seeing a number of men, in slouching hats, with the
collars of their coats turned up, standing on a by-path,
with a bag from which protruded the head of a dead
hare and two dead rabbits, while nets and stakes lay on
the ground before them. He had stopped and looked
at the men, and they had returned his gaze without any
bashfulness.

One of them, a young man with a comical twinkle in
the corner of his eye, had said : " Wanted a first class
roast cook; also two experienced kitchenmaids, accustomed to clean game. Apply, by letter only, to Brian
Boroihme's ghost, at Number One's house, one Wonner's
Row, Won County."

The other men had laughed and turned their heads
away, but Sydney had been too much occupied with his
speculations about their poaching, and poaching on his
genial host's property, too, to take any notice of the joke.

He had walked on in silence, without a smile on his
face. As he walked, he pondered on the state of the
country. He thought of last night's entertainment, and
of the love for the drama most of the peasants had
shown, and began to wonder if a number of large
theatres distributed profusely over the different counties
of Ireland, and with acting companies composed of
purely Irish peasants, would afford any solution of the
Irish difficulty. From this, his thoughts had wandered
to Moyrah, who would become a Celtic Mrs. Siddons.
Were these poachers he had just seen the sort of men
she habitually mixed with? Were they, by chance, her
own brothers or near relations? While thinking this,
he raised his eyes and saw her. Then he threw away
his cigar, and placing the butt of his gun on the ground,
leaned upon the gate.

" I see, Miss Moyrah, you are one of those who keep
their early hours in spite of evening revelries ? "

Moyrah blushed, and dropped a curtsey.

" 'Tisn't very early then, yer honour, I'm thinkin' ; six in winthur, an' four in summer, I'm out fadin' the hins mostly."

" ' Fadin' the hins,' " thought Sydney, " what does that mean, I wonder ? "

Moyrah saw his puzzled look, and said quickly ; " 'Tis the little skits av burds I mane."

" Hens ! ah ! O yes, of course ; how stupid of me ! " He paused, as he complacently but respectfully surveyed her beautiful countenance. To his surprise, as he looked more closely, he saw the marks of recent tears upon her cheeks. He was too chivalrous a knight, however, to remark upon them.

" All my companions were still asleep," he said, with a smile ; " so I determined to take my gun and see if I could get an early shot at a rabbit."

Moyrah looked at the gun, and gave a slight shudder.

" Are you afraid of fire-arms ? " he asked, gently.

" No-a," she said, in a hesitating way, " not in some hands."

There was a mysterious tone in her voice, as if she was speaking with a double meaning, which aroused his curiosity.

" There are people, then, in whose hands you are afraid to see them ? " he said, kindly, but enquiringly.

" Indade there are, an' not far from here, naythur."

Now he began to think he had some clue to the traces of her tears.

" There has not been anyone shot in the neighbourhood, I trust ? " and his tone was full of interest and anxiety.

" There has not, yer honour," and she shook her head.

Sydney's eyes were so kind and honest, his whole manner was so sympathetic, yet so respectful, that Moyrah felt, somehow, as if she could, and, indeed, must, tell him everything.

" O, yer honour, I'd be glad iv I might spake to yer honour."

" Why, to be sure you may," he exclaimed, with such earnestness, such overflowing kindness, that Moyrah's whole heart opened up towards him. There and then, without any preliminary skirmishing, without any beating about the bush, but with a simple directness which made a most favourable impression upon Sydney, she recounted the whole of the adventures of the past night. Her tones thrilled with earnestness, and her gestures, all made with perfect unconsciousness, added an impressiveness and an extraordinary interest to the story, which chained Sydney's attention. It was truly a romantic experience for him, in his first dealings with the Irish peasantry.

He grasped the whole lay of the situation, and saw, even more clearly than Moyrah did, the imperative necessity for Cormac's leaving the country at once.

" I will send him over to England, to my own country place, where my mother is, this very day," he said. " I shall soon be able to find him some useful and lucrative employment there. My cousin Lucas is going to see off a friend of his by the train which catches the North Wall steamer to day, and I will put Cormac under his care. I myself will walk up with him from your house to the Hall, and he shall not be lost sight of for a single instant, until he is safe in a land where they dare not hurt him." Then his pent-up indignation suddenly broke bounds, and he exclamed, " Good gracious ! what demons upon earth." He paused out of deference to her.

Tears rushed to Moyrah's eyes. For a minute or two there was a silence. Then she humbly endeavoured to impress upon him the necessity for not letting anyone know that she had saved Cormac's life, or that he had been at the Blue House at all.

Of course, Sydney saw this at once, and he began to devise about the best means of getting Cormac into his possession and out of hers.

At length they decided that the best way would be

for Sydney to walk up and down on the road, while she
went in and woke up Cormac, explained matters to him,
gave him a sup of breakfast, then brought him out and
put him under Sydney's care.   He would walk with
his gun loaded and cocked by his side all the way
up to the Hall, keeping Cormac touching him the
whole time.

Once at the Hall they would be in time to catch
Mr. Lucas and his friend before they started for the
train.   Protected by both of them in a shut carriage,
it was probable he would be safe enough; though it
was by no means certain; but, at any rate, it was the
best that could be done.

Before Moyrah turned to go towards the house, she
went down on her knees, and called the blessing of
God, of the Holy Virgin and of all the saints upon
Sydney's head.

He raised his hat, and stood uncovered, and with his
head bent forwards.   Then he stretched out his hand
to help her to rise.   As she did so, he pressed her hand
reverentially to his lips.   Her colour deepened as
much as it had done when first she appeared on the
stage as "Mary, Queen of Scots;"   she turned
hurriedly away and went into the house.   She quickly
made up a fire, set the kettle to boil, woke up Cormac,
got him some bread and ham and tea, and explained
the wholly unexpected course events had taken since
he had gone to sleep on the table.

"But Moyrah, mavourneen," and he leaned forward
with an expression of anguish on his honest homely
face, "that manes that I'm to lave ye enthirely."

"No-a, no-a; not enthirely me boy, no-a, no-a;"
and Moyrah's tears began to flow.   "Shure Misthur
Sydney, may the Lorrud reward him! will git ye on in
grand style; ye'll be afthur making a pile av gold as
big as the Galtees; an' thin, if the ould counthree is'nt
in a daysint con-dishin, shure I'll go over to ye, hoppin'
an' dancin', I will.   But may be by that toime there'll be

somebody who can kape this counthree fit for respectible
pour crathures to live in," and she sighed heavily.

Poor Cormac, as he thought the matter over, saw it
was his only chance. He realised that he must face
either death or a separation almost as bitter as death.
He buried his face in his folded arms and sobbed.

Moyrah threw her apron over her head, and cried
until she shook all over underneath it She felt that
she began to love Cormac then as she had never loved
him before. She thought over all the times she fancied
she might have caused him unnecessary annoyance,
and each one was a stab to her over-sensitive heart.
O, misery! when we are about to lose one we love, and
our conscience reproaches us with not having acted
always towards them as we could wish. There was no
sting in poor Cormac's tears. He knew that he had
always acted kindly and fairly to Moyrah; so, though
his tears seemed bitter enough to him, he did not know
how much more bitter they might have been.

In spite of all Moyrah's entreaties he could not eat
much breakfast; it stuck in his throat and choked him.
They said their last farewells before he left the kitchen.
They swore eternal fidelity to each other; and Cormac
said that, well or ill, waking or sleeping, dead or alive,
Moyrah's image would be ever before his eyes. They
ended by kneeling down and saying one short and
fevent "Memorare" together. That prayer seemed to
bring consolation and calmness to them both.

"Jewel o' me heart, will I iver see ye agin'?"
His voice was full of anguish.

"As shure as that flower is blue we'll mate agin."
And she stooped and picked a little bit of lupin, which
was growing in the garden, and put it in his buttonhole.
Sydney, with his usual delicacy, had turned and walked
a few steps further away, as he saw them come out to the
door with clasped hands, and knew they were taking
their last farewells. They stood together for several
minutes in silence. There was no sound but the

rustling of the leaves of the trees at each side of the road, and the low cooing of the wood pigeons.

As the lovers stood with beating hearts, hearts too full to speak, the sound of other footsteps besides Sydney's were heard approaching up the road. They quickly took a last, a long, but a really last farewell. Then Sydney strode up with his gun over his shoulder, and a grave calm look of deep compassion in his thoughtful eyes.

"I think you are safe with me," he said, in a protecting tone. He was rather more than a head above Cormac.

"Musha! och musha!" sobbed Moyrah, as she threw her arms round Cormac's neck, and hid her weeping face upon his broad shoulder. Cormac's feelings would get the better of his efforts at self command—the expressive Irish nature which shows whatever is passing within burst bounds—and he walked away sobbing, with his face buried in his hands. Poor Sydney had never as yet found himself in so uncomfortable a position. He felt something like a jailer conducting a criminal to the gallows. The footsteps turned out to belong to what Sydney felt certain was another poacher, walking along complacently in the cool of the morning, with a brace of rabbits slung over his shoulder. Sydney fixed what he considered a most penetrating gaze upon him. But it did not appear to penetrate in the least. He was a lank man, in ragged clothes, with his cheeks covered by hair half an inch long; his chin, however, was shaved. Cormac seemed to know him, and he evidently was much surprised at recognising Cormac in his present position. They looked at each other for an instant but did not speak.

When he was out of ear shot, Sydney said, "Who was that?"

"Micky O'Shea."

"What is he?"

"No good at all—no good!" and Cormac shook his

head. "I wish I was a foot taller, an' he'd 'a larnt manners off me before this."

Their way lay over a small hill, or what, perhaps, English people would call a slight elevation of the ground. The Irish considered it a distinct hill. It was bare and bleak. There were no trees on it. It was divided into a few fields of long, rank grass and yellow weeds, on which two or three donkeys were feeding; quadrupeds whose appearance brought Don Quixote's steed before the mind. The fields were divided by low stone walls, the greater part of the stones of which lay about on the ground. At the highest point on the hill there was a pillar stone, or "dallan," as it is called in the country. Here Cormac stopped and looked round, shading his eyes with his hand.

The absence of trees made the view a very extensive one. Below were the wooded valleys and rushing streams, like streaks of silver. About a mile and a quarter over to the right lay the little copse close to which the ruins of Cormac's house were still smouldering. As he looked at the coils of pale blue smoke, sleepily circling into the air, his good-humoured face became crimson with fury. He shook his fist wildly in the air while he exclaimed: "Bedad, ye lighted a foire there that won't go out whin thim ashis is dead!" He paused, then getting redder than ever, added, "ye thought to efface me, did ye, ye devils yer? Maybe ye'll foinde ye've effaced yerselvis! May the curse of a man ye have made a beggar rest on ye and yers for ivir!"

Arrived at the Hall, Sydney took Cormac up to his own room, and made him sit down there and wait while he explained matters to Lucas and the captain. The latter was dreadfully annoyed at the burning down of the farm, which was the wilful destruction, as he said, of his own property by some party or parties unknown. He wished to set off then and there to investigate the whole business. Sydney had the greatest difficulty in persuading him to wait until Cormac was safe out of the way.

Sydney wrote a letter to his mother, who was at her country place in the Midlands, Hambury Castle, telling her the whole history of Cormac's forced expatriation, and asking her to find him some employment about the place until he went over himself.

Cormac was given a hot bath, with a sprinkling of eau de Cologne in it. Bridget insisted on this. She was intensely interested and excited about the whole affair. Cormac himself did not see the necessity for this process, and was rather frightened when he found himself alone in a room, in a huge bath, for the first time in his life, surrounded on all sides by steaming hot water, and without a stitch of clothes on.

" 'Tis dangerous, I'm thinkin'!" he kept muttering every minute. "Suppose now, I was dhrowned?"

However, he scrubbed his face until it shone like the sun on the Slaney.

" 'Tis dangerous!" he kept on muttering all the time. "Shure, I was burned in the night, an' maybe I'll be dhrowned in the mornin'," and he tried to push the steam which enveloped him away with both his hands. "May the Lorrud have mursy on me sowl!" and he crossed himself devoutly. The servants had made the water much too hot, out of fun, and the unpleasantly sharp tingling on his unaccustomed skin brought a realistic vision of purgatory before his mind, such as no sermon or meditation had as yet called forth. Most people say their prayers after they get out of their bath, but Cormac said his, with great fervour, all the time he was in it.

His ablutions over, Sydney himself dressed him up in a but slightly worn suit of Poole's last cut—light trousers, cut-away coat, with bit of pocket handkerchief, scented with Jockey Club, coming out of the breast pocket. Bridget insisted on shaving off his little, fair whiskers herself, and gave him one or two cuts during the process.   She then proceeded to make a pair of very respectable, though rather too curly, moustaches out of them, by gumming the hair on to a bit of the stamp paper edge, which she first painted Naples yellow. She then cut all his fair curls off close to his head, and tried to make it look as like a wooden block for fixing bonnets in a milliner's shop as the head of the modern fashionable young man usually does.   With a jaunty chimney pot hat stuck on the side of his head, and a dainty umbrella of Bridget's swinging from his hand, the disguise was perfect.   His most intimate associate would have disowned him.

Curiously enough, from some time before Cormac's arrival until shortly after his departure from the house, Lenoir was absent.

" 'Pon my word!" exclaimed Bridget, turning him round before the pier glass, " if Moyrah saw you now, she'd worship the ground you walk on!"

Whether Bridget knew Moyrah's character may be doubted; but, at least, she had an insight into some of the deeps and shallows of the female heart.

Cormac and Lucas went to the station in a shut carriage, and no one recognized the former.   Indeed, he did not recognize himself, and appeared to be walking and talking in a dream.   The only remark he made, for the first few hours of his journey, was a muttered *sotto voce,* " Shure, mavourneen will die wantin' av me; faith, she was always the gerril to show the ' grah' " (affection), and then a suppressed sob.   After which he would catch sight of himself in one of the looking glasses in the refreshment saloons, where they went for a sandwich and a glass of Guinness's XX, and would stare for a minute or two, then exclaim, " Begorra! she wouldn't know me at all, at all!   'Twould fright her to see me!"

CHAPTER XIII.

ON the day but one after poor Cormac's expatriation, a letter came for Sydney from his mother. She said the young Irish fugitive had arrived safely; that she was much interested in him; that he was lodging with the head gardener, and was to be employed about the garden for the present. She said he seemed well, although much depressed, and she could not understand all he said, his accent was so peculiar. While he was reading this, Lucas was frowning over a huge foolscap document, which turned out to be an enlarged request for a donation to the Society for Ornamenting Public Thoroughfares of London.

"I say, what rubbish," he muttered, impatiently. "Captain, would you, or Sydney, would you like to give some money for ornamenting London?"

"Phaugh!" said the captain, crossly, breaking his egg with a blow which sent the bits of shell in all directions.

"The only ornamentation I will subscribe to, and for that I will stand to £10,000, are rows of plumbers hanging from all the cross-roads of the metropolis," said Sydney.

"I believe everyone in London would subscribe handsomely to that," said the captain. "And from the head of each should go up a long ventilating pipe full of holes, thus alone will London ever be rendered healthy."

Sydney had recently had the drains of his London house put into "perfect order" four times over, and each time by a more celebrated man than the time before, and each time a more frightful illness had broken out in the house than the time before. The last time, when the most celebrated man of all did them, and another man celebrated to a degree that it is impossible to describe, and the head inspector of every sanitary institute in the kingdom examined them, and reported they were in " perfect order," and that the house was in an " eminently sanitary condition," the cook, two days afterwards, discovered a huge piece of mortar and brick stopping up one of the most important pipes in the house.

It was in consequence of this series of sanitary adventures that Mrs. Sydney resided almost entirely at Hambury Castle, and was thus conveniently placed for assisting Cormac. So the plumbers had done one good deed, at any rate. " It is an ill wind," etc. though it be a sewer gas wind, as most of our winds are now.

Sydney took his mother's letter, and immediately after breakfast set off with it to the Blue House. As he approached up the garden, he saw Moyrah sitting at the open lattice window, which was picturesquely tangled with invading roses and Virginia creeper. The sun was shining with that soft, almost tender, warmth peculiar to Ireland. It had rained all night, and as the sun lit the lime trees and the laurels outside, it made the fresh, wet, leafy foliage glow like jewels ; it threw long powdery shafts of gold dust over Moyrah's hair, and penetrated to the shadowy recesses of her dark eyes. The soft music of the waving boughs, the lullaby of the distant streams, and the far-off lowing of the cattle, mingled in a concert of such exquisite sound as seemed to contain all the pleasures of the senses and intellect within itself.

Sydney's was one of those finely strung natures which respond to outward influences, just as a thorough-bred horse does to the delight of a gallop on soft park turf on a breezy morning. He stood still, and let the picture engrave its clear outlines on his heart ; a proof engraving, perhaps, in more ways than one. His step had been noiseless on the soft green turf, so that Moyrah's profile continued towards him, while she worked away unconsciously at a net for ferreting purposes, which she was making for her father, and the diamond panes of the shut part of the window, which were rather dusty, threw queer shaped little shadows on the extreme back of her head and shoulders. A small old stone Irish cross, with some curious carving on it, was let into the wall of the house, just above the window, a relic of now very quiet centuries, surprised perhaps, at the fierce excitement of the present one. Though there was no sign of the "leprichaun," still fairy music swelled on the listening air. Higher and higher rose a thrush's voice, till it seemed as if it must be lost in some clear heaven of endless sweetness. There it hovered and stayed, then descended, rising and falling again and again upon the pinions of melody, till at last, as if worn out with rapture at its own beauty, it sank into the harmony made by the other sounds.

Moyrah took no notice of this, but went on working with a pre-occupied air. The occasional dissonance of a hen cackling or a dog barking did not disturb her either. Suddenly a plum, which had been ripening on the warm, red wall of the old garden, fell to the ground with a flop.

Sydney thought this would have made her look up, but it did not. As he watched her it seemed to him that all the elements in his soul were entering into new combinations. Hitherto he had not cared more for one woman than another. No woman had ever impressed him with a desire to see her again, except his mother, whom he idolized. She had often tried to persuade him to marry ; but he was in the habit of shaking his head, with a smile. To encourage him, she told him of a young American who paid a clergyman the usual fee on his wedding day. A year or two afterwards the clergyman was surprised by a visit from the bridegroom, and by his offering him a handsome sum of money.

"The fact is," he said, in explanation, "she has turned out so much better than I expected."

But Sydney had not as yet been bewitched out of the charms of bachelorhood by this story. "She could not turn out worse than I expected," was his extremely ungallant commentary; and then he would begin reading about hurdles and steeplechases, two subjects which his mother strenuously endeavoured to keep from his mind

But since he had seen Moyrah his feelings towards the daughters of Eve had softened. Her simple, trusting appeal to him for help in her dire necessity had touched all the most chivalrous chords in his nature. Then, he had been much struck by what he considered her wonderful bravery, self-reliance, and quickness of resource in her rescue of Cormac.

He had never been in love in his life, and, therefore, it did not occur to him that he was in love now. He merely thought the time passed pleasantly in her society, and that was all—all for the present.

Suddenly Moyrah turned, quite of her own accord, and without any noise being made, and, looking him full in the face, started with surprise. She rose to her feet quickly, and coming out to the front door, curtsied, and asked him if he would walk in.

He accepted gladly, and found her alone in the kitchen. Her mother had gone to see a married sister of hers, who was ill in the county town, and would probably be away a day or two. Her father was out about the farm. The boys were out on what was called a fishing, but was in reality a poaching, expedition; and Eileen was dancing jigs for the edification of the public on the top of the haystack in the village, an employment for which she had a great *attrait.*

Sydney sat down on an old carved boxwood settee

in the window, and persuaded Moyrah to return to the position from which his entrance had disturbed her.

"I have come, Miss Moyrah, to read you a letter containing news of someone you are interested in," and he looked up at her with an arch smile.

The lovely blush, the soft dimpling of her cheek, the gentle, scarcely perceptible, curving of her mouth into lines of great sweetness and tenderness, enhanced her beauty, and were not lost on Sydney. There was something strangely fresh and unconventional about her, even for an Irish country girl, and withal there was a look in her eye and a tone in her voice which told, with no uncertain tongue, that there were depths of passion, for good or for evil, still in embryo, but none the less existing, hidden under her soft voice and sometimes coaxing, sometimes pensive, manner.

Sydney produced his mother's letter.

"Can you guess at all who it is I am alluding to?" he asked, as he unfolded the letter in a slow, deliberate, rather tantalising manner.

"Faith, yer honour, I'm afthur thinkin' 'tis me own poor boy who they've explained away."

This was the best attempt she could make at present at "expatriation."

Sydney bit his lip to suppress a smile.

"You are right, Miss Moyrah. This letter is from my mother, from her place in Benbooshire, Hambury Castle. Cormac has arrived quite safely, and has won golden opinions on all sides—as he was sure to do, he added, with marked emphasis—but you shall hear my mother's words for yourself."

In his deep, rich voice he proceeded to read out all the part of the letter that referred to Cormac, while Moyrah listened with a blush and downcast eyes, but a look of proud congratulation on her face.

Moyrah thought herself in love with Cormac: Sydney thought he was only doing the most ordinary act of kindness, a mere bit of common English parish charity,

like reading " Pickwick " to old Tom Jones, the hunts-
man, in his stuffy little cottage in the village of Hambury, the time he broke his leg.   Yet of all the
unhypocritical men who ever walked this earth Sydney
was the most so.

" You see, Miss Moyrah, he seems to be well, and as
happy as can be expected under his most unhappy
circumstances.   My mother will show him every kindness, and will do her best to make his unfortunate
position less intolerable."

" May the hivins be her bed ! " said Moyrah, fervently.

" I think they will be," he said, his whole face
softening, and tears coming into his eyes for a moment.
" If ever there was a person who gave you the idea of
belonging to heaven, she it is.   I should like you to
see her."   He paused for an instant.

" Ah ! but I can do the next best thing ; show you a
picture of her."   He put his hand into his breast,
inside all his clothes, and pulled out a small gold
locket.   He pressed the clasp, and as it flew open,
turned towards Moyrah a face of great sweetness,
with white hair crowning it and undisguised lines upon
it truthfully represented by the unflattering artist.

Moyrah uttered an exclamation of admiration.   She
took it carefully in the palm of her hand and looked at
it for a moment intently.   " Shure, yer honour, 'tis the
very moral of yersilf ! "

Had Sydney hated Moyrah before she said this, he
would have loved her from that moment.   No one had
as yet discovered a likeness between him and his mother,
and it was the most cherished desire of his heart that
someone should spontaneously declare they saw one.
He did not know that Moyrah had a reputation in the
village for being a " great hand " at discovering a likeness.   But, unknown to herself, Moyrah had an artist's
eye ; and just as some artists put lights and shadows
into their pictures, which no one else sees, but which, it

is to be presumed, *they* see, so she really did see resemblances which other eyes could not discover. The proof that she was not romancing was supplied by the fact that, in a kitchen full of strangers, she would point out the different children of the different parents.

" Do you really see a likeness?" Sydney's voice was actually trembling with tense anxiety.

" I do, yer honour; as great a likeness as I ivir seen in a picter to anny one." She spoke with a straightforward simplicity which was more forcible than many adjectives.

" Thank you, a thousand times, for saying that !" he exclaimed, with an intense fervour which astonished her. " I cannot, of course, lay the flattering unction to my soul that my outward features are like hers, for she was a celebrated beauty; but if only I could think my expression bore some resemblance—some faint, far off touch—" he paused, then added, very low, " which angels would recognize when I die, and so admit me into heaven."

Tears rushed to Moyrah's eyes. Angels and heaven, in those fresh days of spotless youth, were very real and very near to her unspoilt imagination.

" Shure, yer honour will have a nate little creek in hivin, yersilf, I'm thinkin', widout likeniss to annyone at all," she exclaimed, fervently, remembering his goodness to Cormac.

He shook his head.

At that moment a terrified neigh, almost like a human shriek, from Emmett, broke through the summer air, and caused Moyrah to start to her feet with an exclamation, and rush out of the door to the stable.

Sydney followed her.

Before they rounded the corner of the house, and came in sight of the yard, a crackling noise was heard, and an unwonted heat and smoke filled the air, which reminded Moyrah, for an instant, of the night when she had rescued her lover from the flames. Moyrah tore on ahead like the wind. Rounding the corner a fearful sight met her eyes.

Someone had thrown a lighted torch on to the straw roof of Emmett's stable. Dried to a cinder by the summer sun, it caught at once, and before they could reach it, half the roof was in a blaze; burning straw was falling about everywhere; little wisps of blue and orange flame carried by the wind all over the yard. The ducks cackled and rushed madly from side to side; the litter of pigs set up a noise, such as Sydney thought he would be glad to hear plumbers make, when they were being hanged, while the turkeys took wing and flew about as if demented, uttering frightful gobbling screams. But Moyrah had neither eyes nor ears for anything but her idol. Rushing forward, with her cotton gown and apron flying in the wind, she plunged boldly into the very thick of the fire, before Sydney could stop her. Scarcely two moments elapsed when her apron caught, and before she could reach the rope by which Emmett was tied it had set alight to her dress, and she was enveloped in flames.

In an instant Sydney had torn off his coat, and wrapped it tightly round her, while he dragged her from the blazing shed, now a perfect bonfire. He threw her down upon a rug, which had been taken out to be beaten in the yard, and rolled her in it until the last spark was extinguished. Thanks to his promptitude and courage, her life was saved, but she had several rather severe burns on her arm, otherwise she was unhurt.

The instant she recovered the full use of her senses she sat up, then struggled from his grasp, intending to rush to the stable again.

The shrieks and neighs from Emmett were becoming fainter, but more heartrending every instant.

"If you swear to me to stay pefectly still here, I will save him," said Sydney, looking into Moyrah's eyes, as much as to say, "can I trust you?"

"I will yer honour, faith, thin I will," she said, as she felt all her limbs tremble and give way under her when she tried to rise. She seemed to forget the danger Sydney was running in rescuing her cruelly wronged horse.

Sydney was not a minute too soon. The roof of the burning stable had already fallen in, and poor Emmett, stupefied by terror and the fumes of the smoke, had sunk on his side. With a desperate wrench of the true British athlete's power, Sydney tore the halter (by which Dan, out of mischief, had tied him, just before he started on his poaching expedition) in two; and grasping a wisp of his mane in one hand, and getting his other arm tight round his fore legs, he dragged him along on his side with a marvellous strength, such as he did not know until that moment he possessed, until he got him safely out into the open yard, singed and terrified almost to death, but otherwise unhurt.

Little did he think, as he saved the good horse's life, that one day he would save his.

He knelt by his side and rubbed him tenderly, trying by soothing words spoken in his deep voice, and by a touch which long experience with and love for horses had taught him, to calm the poor animal's terror, and restore his shattered nerves.

Moyrah, after watching this process for a minute or two with tears of gratitude, gradually raised herself on hands and knees, and crept slowly and still trembling towards him.

"Take care, Miss Moyrah! take care!" said Sydney, anxiously, "You ought to keep perfectly quiet after the shock you have had."

But Moyrah was already kneeling by the side of her beloved horse, and soothing him all over with her hands.

"My word, he has a beautiful coat!" said Sydney, as he stroked his sides. "He's a grand blood-like racer, for racer I'm convinced he is; no one could deceive me;

the one and only talent I've got is my eye for a horse. He's a grand topped fellow, and not a bit wanting in bone; I've seen only one other horse like him in my life, and that was 'The Slicer,'" he continued to himself, in an absent, muttering tone; " but, then, he had straight shoulders and stilty pasterns, and was light in the thighs."

" More power to yer honour," said Moyrah, gratefully, as she noticed the intense interest and anxiety expressed in Sydney's speaking countenance. " More power to ye."

" Well, I found I had more power to-day than I thought I possessed," he said, with a kind smile; "so if I am to have a second edition, I shall be a Samson indeed." Then his thoughts became once more concentrated on Emmett. " He'd win a dozen handicaps under welter weights with such shoulders, back and limbs, by Jove! he would, and no mistake." And he ran his hand with a skilful anatomist's delicacy of touch over his silky shoulder.

The stable stood twenty yards from the house, at the far end of the farmyard; therefore, as it was completely detached, there did not appear much likelihood of its igniting anything else.

" There's not a bit of good in trying to put it out," said Sydney, turning his head over his shoulder and gazing for a minute, with raised eyebrows and staring eyes, at the pile of blazing straw, wood, and bricks. The fire threw a warm, ruddy glow over the scene, and outlined against its crimson light the two kneeling figures and the prostrate horse.

" His hocks are just a trifle small," soliloquised Sydney. " But I am forgetting you, Miss Moyrah; I hope you feel pretty well? Let me look at those burns on your arm."

Moyrah obediently tucked up as much of her sleeve as was not burnt away, and exposed her white and smoothly rounded arm to view. There were one or two scarlet burns here and there, but they were only skin deep, and Sydney was enough of a doctor to see at a glance that no danger could be apprehended from them. He examined them, then nodded with approval.

At that moment old Hegarty himself appeared upon the scene. He stood stock still; his worn, haggard face so ghastly pale as to be blue-grey, like the chilling haze of a north-east wind. His eyes opened wider and wider under his rugged brows, and his wrinkled, limned jaw dropped in abject despair.

"O father! father! we are all safe!—all safe!— glory be to the Lorrud! And shure, 'tis Misther Sydney did it all—the blessin' av hivin upon him!"

"Shure, the horrus is did," said Hegarty, stolidly; while there was a gleam in his eyes which revealed to Sydney that there was a point beyond which it would be safer not to rouse him, meek and mild as his general disposition might be.

"'Tis not did at all!" exclaimed Moyrah, eagerly; "'tis only dhrowsy loike he is wid the smoke. Shure, his heart's batin' like dhrums."

"He is as sound as a bell, Mr. Hegarty," said Sydney, springing to his feet.

Sydney had taken the precaution to pull on his coat before he had gone in the second time to the burning stable, and there were, consequently, great brown burns, sometimes merging into black, calcined holes, on the sleeves and part of the back of it.

"Bedad! ye're burnt yersilf, ye poor divil!" said Hegarty, forgetting for the moment, in the stress of his agony, who he was speaking to. "Shure, ye're burnt! an' she's burnt! an' the horrus is burnt! an' we're all burnt! or else will be before many more moons is risin'." And he gave a low groan of mixed fury and despair.

In the meantime, Emmett, who had been slowly recovering, gave one or two kicks and shakes, and finally began to struggle all over, as a prostrate horse

K

docs in his first efforts to rise. Sydney helped him, and in another minute he was standing on his four beautifully shaped legs.

"A tiny trifle light in the body and dipped in the back," muttered Sydney, smoothing him down and walking all round him, examining him as a china-maniac does a bit of rare pottery.

"To think they should have tried to burn such an animal!" Again he stroked him.

"I wish to goodness you were all safe out of this detestable country!" he added, fervently.

"Daytastibil counthry!" said Moyrah, firing up. "Is it Oireland ye're spakin' av, sur?"

Sydney appeared much astonished. He stood looking at her for a minute or two in silence. "I meant no offence, I'm sure," he said, with that polish of manner which soothed all irritation, while he bowed slightly. "But even 'the most devoted patriot must allow that living here at present does not conduce to that calm repose which alone produces health and longevity, either for man or beast."

"There's not a counthree in the worruld to aquil it!" said Moyrah, sullenly.

Poor Sydney perceived that he had put his foot in it. But Hegarty came to the rescue in a most unexpected manner.

"What his honour says is the truth av God, ivry worrud av it." And he nodded his head emphatically. "The pathriots I obsurve, lives out av it thimsilves mostly. As soon as ivir they've bullied as much money as they wants out av the starvin' pisinthry, off they goes wid their pockets full; the divil take the lot av 'em! Bedad, I wish I cud do the same!"

This unprecedented storm of bitter words fairly took Moyrah's breath away. She knelt bolt upright, supporting herself by the handle of a pump, and looked round in a terrified manner from side to side, to see if anyone was listening.

"Divil a ha'perth do I care iv all the counthree's listinin', or not!" said the injured farmer, with intense bitterness. "Shure, 'tis plain I've not got the blood in me, or I'd have given 'em a taste av the rapin' hook before this. 'Tis there now behind the cuppel, an' they shall have it. I know who done this. I know who."

And the old man shook from head to foot in a literal frenzy of mad fury; his hands clenched, his chest heaving up and down, his eyes glaring like a hungry tiger's, and his voice taking a deep, guttural tone, so thick and jerky, that Moyrah even scarcely recognized it as her father's voice.

"'Tis into the Tubber Derg (red well) the divil shall go, he shall, ivry inch av him, as shure as me name's Michael Hegarty; troth, ahagar! 'twill be a bad day that sees me at a deshort (loss) what to do wid an inimy," and he gave a harsh grating sort of half laugh, half sob.

"Der charp agus manim (by my soul and body), I'll make him repint in tears av blood for his work this mornin'," and he shook his fist towards the south, "an' he treasurer av the local branch, too! Throth, I'll make him treasurer to the worrums under the sod." Then he turned to the pump, filled a bucket with water, and flung it on the still burning shed. But it had little or no effect beyond making a frizzle.

Sydney procured another bucket, and together they worked away for half-an-hour, Moyrah pumping the water with her left arm, as her right was rather hurt.

However, they did but little good, for the stable burnt away until the last bit was consumed.

"An' who's goin' to build me up that agin, I wondhur?" Hegarty kept on muttering, occasionally varying it with, "I don't know who did it, don't I? exkimnicate divil! throth, I'll bless him for yer!"

Meantime, Moyrah watched Sydney working away like a day labourer, and listened to her father cursing with equal amazement.

Once as Sydney was kneeling on one knee, with the bucket under the pump, he met her eye, and he saw in it a look of such intense gratitude, that it thrilled through every fibre of his being like an electric shock. He knelt on after the bucket was full and overflowing; he certainly looked pleasant enough to attract any female heart, even the most unsusceptible. His cheeks were glowing, partly with hard work, and partly with the heat of the flames; his silky hair was blown wildly round his head, as he wore no hat, and his eyes sparkled with that honest enthusiasm which labour in a good cause always excites, though, as he knew from the first, it was labour in vain.

As the still blazing embers sank they threw a rich, deep, crimson glow over the man kneeling before the pump, and the woman who, with a long, easy swing of her graceful arm, was moving the handle up and down. That lurid light, warm and tender as it was under the soft blaze of the summer sun, seemed to wrap them round in the blood-red folds of a martyr's mantle. What did it prognosticate in that land of strange prognostications? Prognostications so strange, often, that only one thing stranger exists, and that is, that everybody should believe in them.

A swift inrush of delicious feeling swept over Sydney when Moyrah spoke to him. It seemed to him as if some new and hitherto undreamt-of stimulus, containing within itself the very elixir of life, unlocked to him the gate of a yet undiscovered world of emotion at the sound of her low, sweet Irish tones. There is no voice so beautiful as the Irish voice, when not used for cursing or shrieking. There is an exquisite, mellow undernote in it which takes captive the most indifferent ear. Moyrah's voice was singularly sweet, even for one of her nation: there was in it, too, a slightly plaintive ring, which was a peculiarity not without its attractions for a joyous, healthy nature like Sydney's.

"Ye're tired now, yer honour," said Moyrah, softly.

"Come in to the kitchen, an' I'll get ye a dhrop av somethin' that'll refrish ye. Shure, it's like powerin' wathur down the Blackwater, puttin' it on that ould shed ; there's not a ha'porth av good in goin' on wid it."

"Well, it is not much use, certainly," said Sydney, as he looked round and perceived that the green field, with its nodding yellow weeds, which lay below the yard, was plainly visible between the two half-consumed end walls of the stable, the whole of the back and front of that edifice having entirely disappeared.

Emmett, meantime, had found a little heap of loose hay in one corner of the yard, and was consoling himself as best he could for all his troubles by munching it ; while his mistress looked round at him every now and then with a nod and a smile.

"Father, darlin', come into the kitchen and have a dhrop av somethin' to put the life in ye : shure, I see by the look av ye ye're dead bate enthirely," said Moyrah, laying her hand gently on her father's arm, as he put down an empty bucket with a bang and a heart-rending sigh. He wiped his forehead with his handkerchief—an old, red torn one which he took out of the front part of the crown of his battered and brown chimney-pot hat.

"Bate, indeed ! we're all bate !" he responded, bitterly. As he turned to walk towards the house he muttered, " Bait we are, too, like the worrums they put on their hooks to catch big fish wid. Arn't we trated jist like worrums to catch the big fish av their subscripshins from that blastid ould 'Meriky ? Wid two big oshins, wan at ache side av it, I don't know what the divil they mane by not washin' it off the face av the globe ! There'll be no peace for ould Oirelan' till wan av 'em rises to its duty," and he growled and fumed and mopped his head again.

Sydney heard this and was almost suffocated with laughter, which he struggled vigorously and, fortunately, successfully, to repress, for Hegarty was in terrible earnest, and would not have borne any levity just then.

As they turned the corner of the house and came in sight of the garden, they espied a ragged man, lank in his figure, and with a half-grown beard, leaning on the gate, gazing inquisitively towards the kitchen.

"Confound ye, Micky O'Shea!" roared Hegarty, like a lion with a torn paw, "what the divil do ye mane, ye ould hedgehog, loiterin' about a dacint boy's house? By yer pathron saint, who turned ye out av hivin long ago, and the divil, I suppose, won't have ye in hell, I'll smash ivry jint an' limb in yer contimptible carkas!"

Moyrah, who was utterly unaccustomed to hear such language, or anything approaching to it, from her easy going, mild, pious, little old father, stared in blank amazement, crossed herself, and muttered a prayer to the Blessed Virgin for him.

"Maybe he's waitin' till he's got hell a little hotter for ye."

Sydney recognised in the somewhat severely apostrophised individual the man whom Cormac had told him was "no good at all."

"He appears to hold an unfortunate position in the opinions of his fellow villagers," soliloquised Sydney.

O'Shea, however, did not seem to care. He turned his head towards Hegarty for a minute, then put out the least taste in life of his tongue at him. After that he nodded to Moyrah in what Sydney considered an intolerably insolent manner, and drawled out, "How's the darlin' Emmett?"

Moyrah's cheeks became flame colour, and, indeed, so did Sydney's.

"Ye foul spawn av Beelzebub!" and seizing a huge log which was lying close at hand, Hegarty aimed a terrific blow at O'Shea's head. But the latter was too quick. He gave a bound like an antelope, and, avoiding the blow, flew off down the road, carried like a race horse by his long, lank shanks, gave another bound over a low stone wall, and was lost to sight in two seconds; but so mad with rage was Hegarty that he was actually setting off after him.

Moyrah laid her hand gently but forcibly on his arm. "Aisy awhile, father! aisy awhile!" she whispered. "Sure there's more on 'em behint there where he's gone, an' they'd do for ye enthirely iv ye wint among 'em."

"Miss Moyrah is right, Mr. Hegarty. That scoundrel's got confederates, and they appear to be equal to doing anything in this part of the country," said Sydney, putting his hand on the old man's other arm.

Between them they led him, trembling with passion, his eyes glaring and his fists convulsively twitching, into the house.

Moyrah hurriedly got out a bottle of the finest old "potheen" and, with a couple of lemons, some sugar and half the kettle full of boiling water, brewed such a jorum of the immortal national beverage as Sydney had never seen before.

She served it, too, in the old family punch bowl, a fine bit of real solid old silver, with a crown embossed on one side, which had come down to its present owner through many many generations; for the Hegarty's had once been Kings of Connaught.

The present Michael (the archangel's name had been in the family from time immemorial) was living on an old farm, which had once formed part of the estates of his family, but which had since been bought by the captain's ancestors.

One of the very few surviving relics of past grandeur was the old punch bowl, which Moyrah treated Sydney to, and which she produced on the rarest possible occasions; only when some highly favoured guest was at the social board.

Curiously enough, there was a small *fleur-de-lys* engraved upon that punch bowl.

Sydney saw it at once and remarked upon it.

Hegarty explained that long ago one of his ancestors had married a French lady, of high birth, and she had brought the punch bowl into the family. In fact, Hegarty declared that through this lady he had some of the blood of St. Louis, King of France, in his veins, as she was descended from him.

"It's not ivry wan can boast of havin' a saint's blood in 'em," he finished up by remarking; "for most av 'em nivir marrid at all!'

As Sydney watched Moyrah moving about he thought he could well fancy her descended from a saint and a king; she was like the few but lovely idyllic dreams of his boyhood, merging into early manhood, before he had mixed much in ladies' society.

Meantime, Hegarty kept muttering language, which it was as well not to try to understand, to himself; language which scarcely proclaimed the grandeur of his ancestry.

Sydney insisted on binding up the burns on Moyrah's arm. He was a bit of a doctor; at least, he was a very good horse doctor, and he usually employed himself on his way to his business office, in the City, by studying, as far as the light of the underground railway would permit, books on veterinary surgery.

After all, as he argued, human beings were only inferior kinds of horses, and what applied to one applied to the other.

On this occasion, he made a very gentle and tender surgeon, and his light, supple fingers wound the linen round the wounded arm, with a skill which many a young Guy's Hospital probationary nurse might have envied. Then, Moyrah made a very good patient.

After this was done, Moyrah got out some home-made whole-meal griddle cakes, some fresh home-made butter, and a little keg of oysters, which a cousin of Hegarty's, who lived in the west, near the oyster beds, had sent him.

It is to be observed that most Irish people have cousins who live near some place where some particular kind of good food comes from.

Sydney's exertions had whetted his appetite, and he did full justice to the good things put before him so daintily. For Moyrah had laid the table with a snow-white cloth, and put out the best china plates.

"Cheer up father, cheer up!" said Moyrah, brightly, and she laid her hand on his shoulder, and looked down into his eyes, as she stood at his side.

He sat staring gloomily before him, stirring the ladle in his punch, and muttering.

"What'll Mrs. Hegarty be afther sayin' to ye, iv she sees ye lookin' like that?" continued Moyrah, playfully, alluding to her mother, whose tongue was not all a husband could desire when irritated. "There's no harrum done, glory be to God, and thanks to his honour here."

"No harrum done, an' me shed in ashes, the horse liable to fits for the rest av his loife, no doubt; me daughter's arrum burnt like toastid cheese; mesilf made the laughin' stock av that blastid weekly newspapur, that turns ivry dacint boy in the counthry into scorrun! 'Tis that papur I'm thinkin' of, laughin' at me; 'tanny rate I'll be made a fool av which iver way I look," and he groaned, and leaned his head on his hand.

Never had Hegarty been so communicative. As a rule, he was a very reserved man; and when an Irishman does take it into his head to be reserved, you might as well try to pick a Milner's safe with a quill pen as to get his secrets out of him by any ordinary method of questioning.

Moyrah was much astonished, and, to tell the truth, rather alarmed at his unwonted outburst of passionate feeling. In the first place, she feared it would not end here, but that he would give vent to it in company less safe than the present. She knew there were spies about everywhere, and people ready to draw him on and then turn upon him and betray him. The thought of this filled her with terror.

"Come, father, ye havint aitin wan oysther yit; here's a goody boy," and she put a particularly dainty looking oyster on his plate. "Toimes will get betthur: cheer up, father! cheer up, me darlin'! Shure Saint Pathrick will put his best leg forwards and give us a help now whin we've come to the worst. There's good people in ould Oireland yit, an' they'll come to the fore sooner or later."

"Ah, sure, women know nothing about it," he said; but his face assumed a pleasanter expression, and he took his oyster complacently, and then eat more.

"Perhaps, Miss Moyrah, if you sang to us it would keep our spirits up," said Sydney. "I feel certain, from the sound of your voice in speaking, that you can sing," he added, gallantly; "and when I tell you that one of the greatest desires of my heart has always been to hear an Irish melody sung by a genuine Irish voice, in a genuine Irish home, you will, I am sure, spoil me enough to grant my request."

Moyrah was sufficiently quick to see at a glance that Sydney was playing into her hands at keeping up her father's spirits, and drawing off his mind from his troubles, and the look of gratitude came into her eyes again.

When a German voice sings a love song, it sounds too often like man and wife quarrelling. When a French voice sings one, it seems to be saying all the time, with a wink, "What a fool you take me for." When an English voice sings one, it seems to be repeating, in an undertone, "This is a very important matter; it almost beats grey shirtings." When an Irish voice sings one, it melts into the tune as Cleopatra's pearl melted in the cup where she threw it. The listener forgets that there is a voice, or that there is a song, and feels only that there is some spirit drawing up his purest feelings out of the muddy water of everyday life, and making them spread into a beautiful blossom; as the sun draws up a water lily from a slimy pond, and lays its petals open.

Moyrah took a sip of punch, cleared her throat, and then began.

> "Through grief and through danger
>   Thy smile hath cheered my way,
>   Till hope seemed to blossom
>   From each thorn that round us lay."

Sydney sat leaning back in his chair looking at her, enthralled. If a man is at all inclined to fall in love with a woman, and that she sings to him charmingly, his fate is sealed.

It is, perhaps, needless to say that there was no ornate ornamentation in Moyrah's vocalization. No; her musical voice was the mirror of her soul. Simple, clear as crystal; but with a depth of passion flashing out now and then, and, as it were, flushing the song crimson, like the first gleams of a sunrise on the domes of the Alps.

It was an untaught voice, but by no means an uncultivated one. She had sung from her childhood; it came as naturally to her as to the birds.

When she finished, Sydney found himself trembling, his throat choked with tears, and his eyes blinded. For full five minutes he could not speak a word.

Moyrah did not look at him, she was busy taking away the empty oyster shells off her father's plate, and replacing them with full ones, and carefully wiping up some whiskey punch which her father's hand, still trembling with indignation, had spilt on the table cloth. Then she raked up the fire, threw on some fresh peat and logs, and swept and tidied the hearth. She moved very quickly, but so quietly, that a mouse could have slept undisturbed.

Accustomed to singing to her father constantly, she

herself thought no more of the song than if the family kettle had sung it. She merely supposed Sydney was too deep in his oysters to speak much, hence his prolonged silence.

She went to the " corrag " and stood it straight up, for it had begun to lean of its own accord, without rhyme or reason. It is the custom in some parts of Ireland to collect branches when they are green, and tie them together in a bundle about a yard round, and six feet high, and keep it at the windy side of the door, so that when the door is opened, the gale of wind which usually accompanies such a performance is mitigated. This bundle is termed the " corrag," or " old man of branches."

After some difficulty, Moyrah induced this old gentleman to stand firm : whatever way she put him, he showed a strong inclination to fall at her feet, and in this it must be owned, he was imitated by a young man also in the room, only, he did not show his inclination, but kept it discreetly to himself.

When Moyrah, at length, had fixed the unsteady patriarch satisfactorily on his beam ends, she turned to the lattice window, and standing on one toe, leaned out of it, and gazed anxiously up and down the road. But she saw nothing, and soon came in and turned to the table again.

" I'm afeered yer honour don't like the oysthers," she said, in a really grieved tone, as she saw how few Sydney had consumed.

" Indeed I do ; I do indeed," he stammered, looking down with as much surprise at his half empty plate as she had done.

" They are excellent, the best I ever tasted ; but,"— and his voice trembled " I was thinking of the song."

" Oh, shure, that's poor stuff for food," she said, with much concern, while she rapidly opened some more oysters and laid them on his plate. " Iv yer honour had bin thinkin' av songs all your loife instid av atin' yer dinner, yer wouldn't have had the strength to save me an' Emmett to day, I'm thinkin'."

He could not help smiling.

" But, then, I never heard such a song as that before, or else I might have been thinking of it all my life and not eating my dinners."

A slight blush rose to her cheeks, but the corners of her mouth dimpled with a smile.

" It's in luck yer honour is, then, that you didn't," she said, as she stirred up the punch, and ladled some hot into his glass out of the old silver bowl, which was steaming in the centre of the table.

" But in the meantime you are not taking anything yourself," he said

" Moyrah, ate yer dinner," said Hegarty, shortly and decidely.

" I don't feel jist aquil to it now," she answered, "by-and-bye, when Eileen comes in, I'll tackle to, maybe."

Somehow or other, slang did not shock out of Moyrah's mouth : it was spoken so perfectly innocently, and with such transparent ignorance of its being slang, that it rather fascinated than otherwise.

Sydney himself hated to be pressed to eat when he did not want to, so he said, " Well, if you really had rather not eat, perhaps you would do us the great kindness to sing another song."

" Afthur yer honour tellin' me it privintid ye from atin', a nice spaysimin av Oirish hospitality that 'ud be."

Sydney could not help laughing outright at the quaint roguish way this was said.

Moyrah smiled more broadly than she had hitherto done.

He looked at her with his soul beaming out through his eyes, as he said, " I'll do anything in the world for you, Miss Moyrah, if you will only sing for me once again."

" Well, yer honour, if ye'll jist thin take aff yer coat, and give it to me here, 'till I mind them burnt holes in it; 'twill nivir do for ye to be walkin' up through the village wid yer coat like that, an' they gessin' where ye've been, an' we in the black books now."

Deeply touched at her thoughtfulness, Sydney again was conscious of the choking feeling in his throat. " But—but—" he again began to stutter, an unprecedented event with him, " I cannot bear you to have the trouble-——"

" It is no throuble, yer honour, but a pleasure to do annything for ye," and she leaned forward, stretching out her hand for it.

Most reluctantly, Sydney slowly pulled off his grey shooting coat, and surveyed the burnt holes in it. But Moyrah, who had her needle and thread ready, quickly took it from him, and, feeling with instinctive delicacy that it might annoy him to see her working at it, sat rather behind him, where he could not see her without screwing his head round. After she had put the first three stitches in, she began, not without a touch of sly humour :

> " No, not more welcome the fairy numbers
>   Of music fall on the sleeper's ear,
>   When half awakening from fearful slumbers
>   He deems the full choir of heaven is near."

But again Sydney became enthralled. Nursed in the houses of the rich; luxuriously reared and bred; trained in pleasure; his ear and all his senses habituated to music and soft sounds; his brain developed by intellectual effort and rendered sensitive to the slightest touch; yet it seemed to him he had never known the meaning of the word enjoyment until now.

Moyrah finished the song before she finished the coat. Just as the last notes were dying away, Eileen walked in.

" The Lorrud be praised, ye're safe back ! " exclaimed Moyrah, fervently, betraying, unintentionally, the keen anxiety she had been suffering on her sister's account for the last hour.

"Troth, an' why not?" said Eileen. Then she advanced and dropped a curtsey to Sydney, who stood up at once and made a polished bow, which sat none the less well on his graceful figure without his coat.

Eileen was followed by a party of boys and girls from the village, who had been dancing with her on the haystack. They all seated themselves, uninvited, on the various chairs, stools, and old wooden settees in the room, and asked, in a variety of different voices, for whisky punch, with as much assurance as if it had been their own house and their own punch.

"We smelt it comin' up the road," said a very ragged tatterdemalion, slapping his knee, while he grinned from ear to ear.

"We did so-a!" echoed a chorus of delighted voices.

Moyrah laid down the coat on the back of the chair for a minute, while she signed to Eileen to come and help her to get out various basins, jugs, mugs, and glasses from the cupboard. This done, she proceeded to help the whole assembled company in the most liberal style, giving them each a hot griddle cake with the "crathur."

"Bedad! that's the liquor for me!" said one promising urchin of seven, smacking his lips.

"That's thrue for ye," said a boy of nine, with no cap, hair like an enraged door mat, and pointed, almost bare, bones coming through the knees of his trousers.

"None av yer Guinness for me, ses I," continued the first connoisseur, who smacked his lips louder than any of the rest of the party, and the others did it loud enough. "None av yer Guinness for me! thick muck, like ditch wathur—Roe's the man for me, ses I, that I do!" and he took another good pull at the small, brown smoking jug he held in his little fat hand. He was a fat boy and tolerably well dressed, and evidently very highly educated.

“ Shure, what a bauliore ye are !” (bauliore is laughing stock) exclaimed the eldest boy of the party, a fair-haired lad of fifteen. Then he continued, “ Let’s dhrink to the health av the farithee ” (man of the house).

“ Here’s to yer health, Misthur Hegarty ; an’ a long loife to ye an’ to all belongin’ to ye.”

The boys all stood up and waved their glasses, mugs, or jugs, as the case might be, high over their heads ; the girls kicked their heels and cheered, their shrill trebles piercing poor Sydney’s unaccustomed ears. Yet he was delighted with the scene. He had particularly desired to study the customs and habits of the Irish peasant on the spot, as a help to overcoming the apparently insurmountable Irish difficulty, and his desire was certainly obtaining its partial fulfilment.

Hegarty just looked up and nodded at them by way of acknowledgment, and that was all the encouragement he gave them. He appeared to take their conduct as a matter of course, and Sydney concluded that their appearance, under what seemed to him such peculiar circumstances, was an event of ordinary occurrence.

They did not take much notice of Sydney. Stared at him a little ; but with that well-bred manner which is such a charming characteristic of their nation, did not obtrude their personality upon him.

“ I seen Dan awhile ago,” said the youthful Guinness despiser, addressing Moyrah, “ wid a big bramble on to the tail av his coat, an’ his coat mostly tore away, an’ the laste taste in life av the snout av a salmon stickin’ out av his pocket.”

“ An where was he goin’, now, wid that, I’m wonderin’, the young corbogue?” said Hegarty. “ What does he mane by not bringing it home wid him ?”

“ Goin’ to blow out wid his friends in the village, I’m thinkin’ ; he thought he wouldn’t get much av it if he brought it up here.”

“ By the hoky ; that’s good,” said the boy of nine

who, unperceived, had helped himself to three oysters and taken a draught of punch after each.

All the little feet were moving backwards and forwards, as if their young owners were still dreaming they were dancing, even while they were reposing in various attitudes of ease and indolence.

This put it into Sydney's head that he would very much like to see a genuine Irish jig danced on a genuine Irish floor by genuine Irish children.

There could be no doubt that all the conditions were present at that moment.

"Miss Eileen," he said, with that suave, gracious manner which wins Irish hearts directly, and which, if more Englishmen possessed, the difficulty of governing Ireland would not have become so insurmountable as it now has. "I wonder if you would have the great kindness to lead a real Irish jig for my edification.

Eileen blushed and smiled. Moyrah went to a cupboard full of jam pots and cold baked potatoes, and from its depths produced a violin. After tuning it for a minute, while Eileen and the eldest boy pushed the chairs and tables into a corner, she struck up, with a rare "go" and "dash," a rattling mixture of "Rory O'More" and the "Rakes of Mallow," which she herself had arranged as a jig.

In an instant the whole room was alive. The floor bounding up and down, little legs going in every direction, and little arms flying about like spirit arms at a séance. Most of the children were barefoot, and therefore there was not much clatter, but occasionally, there was a sharp rat-tat of a heel on the boards.

Some of the children sang as they danced, apparently to ease the overflowing joy of their hearts at being in a state of perpetual motion.

When a boy accidently knocked against a girl, or a girl against a boy, they got a good push, or a smart smack in return. That calm repose which marks the caste of Vere de Vere was not here. Every emotion as it bubbled up in the heart found instant expression.

Some called "quicker," others "louder," as the music pleased or displeased them.

One little boy of five took the opportunity of the general commotion to creep unseen on his hands and knees round by the wall of the room, until he came to the cupboard, where he had momentarily spied the jam pots, as it was opened to let out the fiddle. Crumpled up in a ball he sat on the floor, his back studiously turned out to the assembled company, his curly, almost white haired head bent down, and one little hand going up and down with great rapidity, between his mouth and a large white jam pot, which he managed completely to cover from general observation by the adroit disposal in a highly artistic fashion of his portentous person.

Every now and then a wave or lull in the dancing made him turn his head quickly, with an anxious expression.

"Ah! ye pup, ye, what divilment are ye up to?" said sweet seven, whose frantic gyrations had gradually brought him round until he was close to the thief.

"Bee dhu husth" (hold your tongue), said the other, peremptorily, his mouth tight full of jam at the moment, and he did not lift up his head. "I'll larrun ye manners, ye weasel!" and the bigger boy dealt him such a blow on the side of his head as almost to knock that head off its very thin little throat.

The little boy did not even then look up. He waited a minute to recover from the shock, and at once continued his occupation.

Meantime, Hegarty sat dreamily sipping his punch, apparently perfectly indifferent to an uproar that would have driven most elderly gentlemen mad. Sydney sometimes looked at him and sometimes at the dancers, and could not help being filled with wonder at the whole panorama, or pandemonium, according as it was viewed, delighted as he was to witness at length a thoroughly national performance. Hegarty's face wore no semblance of a smile, although it seemed to Sydney as if there was a chemistry in the present scene sufficient to dissolve the hardest gravity.

Moyrah made a first-rate orchestra. She had the soul of music in her, and it came out in her finger tips as much as in her voice.

"Handle yer feet, Terence!" she called to the boy of fifteen, who was rather fat, and was the laziest of the party. "Shure, look at Phil, now!" and she nodded towards sweet seven; "he could dance the 'Dusty Miller' on a floor paved wid carvin' knives, he's so soople."

Sweet seven heard it, flung back his head, put his arms akimbo, and dashed out his wiry little legs with a rapidity which positively took Sydney's breath away.

"Eileen, ye're forgettin' yer steps; heel an' toe, right an' left. Bravo, Phil? ye'll win the day."

"Whish, clur-r, whirroo-o!" called the galvanised Phil, who was beginning at last to splutter and puff.

"Hold an,' now Phil, the breath's lavin' yer," said Moyrah, kindly; "Sit down awhile. De ye hear what I'm sayin' to ye, Phil? Aisy now, or I'll give ye a rap wid the fiddle on yer head." But, puffed up and supported by the puff ball of vanity, Phil would not stop, and at last fell down with a flop on the floor, dead beat.

The dance ended; loud calls for more punch came; and Moyrah and Eileen between them soon brewed a second bowl, fuller than the first.

"But, really," muttered Sydney, "they will all be perfectly tipsy."

However, they did not seem at all more tipsy when they left off than when they began. Rather less: so far, they were exhausted by the dancing, and a little quieter than on their first entry.

On looking at his watch, Sydney was horrified to see how the time had flown. He rose to say good-bye at once. Just then Moyrah finished his coat, and stood at his side to help him on with it. He turned and thanked her in a low tone, full of feeling, which he tried to repress, or, at least, not to express, but could not.

"I do not know when I have enjoyed myself so much as seeing all this fun, but, above all, in hearing you sing."

Moyrah blushed, such a pretty blush, not very pink, but just enough to double her beauty for the moment.

"Three cheers for his honour!" called sweet seven, who could not, try as he might, keep his mouth shut for many seconds.

The boys stood up, waved their glasses, jugs and mugs, and gave Sydney a ringing cheer as he walked out, bowing with amused pleased smiles, first to one side and then the other. The girls shrieked, but kept their seats, which appeared to be the etiquette.

Sweet seven flung the door open, and pulled the front lock of his hair as the guest of the day walked out, with that grand prince-like air, which came naturally to him. "That's the style av gintleman for me!" said seven.

When Sydney returned to the Hall, and related what had occurred at the Blue House, Bridget's indignation passed all bounds. She insisted on ordering the car and setting off there at once, and Captain Sheil, who was scarcely less furious, accompanied her. Sydney and Lucas occupied the opposite side of the car. Lucas was much taken with Bridget, and liked to follow her wherever she went, and Sydney wished to come to some arrangement with the captain about putting an effective guard over the persecuted farmer.

When they reached the Blue House the young guests had all departed, and with the shades of evening settling down on it, the old farm looked lonely enough. But they found that Hegarty had relapsed into his usual silentness and reserve, which now was mixed with a sort of dogged sullenness which was new to him. He was grateful to the captain for his kindness, but was hopeless with regard to the possibility of anything being done to help him. He was a marked man now.

Michael, the son, was home when the captain arrived and he seemed much depressed, and inclined to take quite as gloomy a view of the situation as his father. Moyrah was the only one who tried to keep their spirits up.

The captain declared he would send his butler down to sleep at the Hegarty's, and make him take his breech-loader with him; and Sydney said he would send Lenoir with his gun.

Moyrah thanked him earnestly; for, hide it as she might, she could not help feeling nervous.

That night, before she went to bed, she spent a long time before the little white plaster statue of the *Mater Purissima*, which stood on a low bracket in her room. She knelt, with her head bowed down. The rays of the harvest moon streamed through the tiny panes of the lattice window, and made a white mist round her head, something like the veil of a Dominican novice.

Moyrah's was not only a white soul, but it was a rich one, a well of high thoughts and deep feelings, which she herself scarcely recognised. The very shadows in her soul were like the shadows of a few great painters, almost as full of tender colour as the lights.

A deep shadow now had fallen over her life. Her lover exiled, her father broken-hearted, her favourite horse all but burnt to death, herself uncertain whether the very house she slept in might not be in flames before the morning. But under every shady avenue of troubles in this world, if we could only see them, angels walk. Moyrah saw them, and was comforted.

Her prayers to-night were all for her father, and she poured out her heart in strong entreaty that he might be comforted and consoled.

“ Oh, Vahr Dheelish ” (Sweet Mother), “ take the throuble out av his heart,” she implored passionately. “ Give me anny store av throuble there’s goin’, only kape it locked up in me, an’ don’t let it get out at him. Shure, he’s gettin’ ould now, an’ wan throuble is two throuble’s to him, but I’d take it aisy like iv I’d twinty, so lang as I knew he’d got none at all.”

A week passed away. A peaceful week as far as the Blue House was concerned. No attempts were made further to molest Hegarty or anyone belonging to him.

Sydney went down every day to see if they were safe, and to find out how they were going on. Sometimes the captain, Bridget and Lucas accompanied him, but several other guests had arrived to stay at the Hall, and few and far between were the moments Bridget could devote to her favorite visitor. She generally managed to get him to take her into dinner, but that was the utmost she could accomplish.

CHAPTER XIV.

THE sun rose one morning in, for the weeping skies of Ireland, unwonted splendour. There was to be a great Harvest Bug meeting in a large field not very far from the Blue House that day.

Sydney was determined to go; it was just such an opportunity for studying the habits and ways of the aborigines as he particularly desired. Besides, Moyrah, whose acquaintance he had been cultivating, under the, to him, perfectly genuine pretext of studying the puzzling Irish character, would be sure to be there.

Bridget declared she must go, too, just for the fun of it. But Captain Sheil declared, with equal determination, that she must not. He said her face was known all over the county; she would be recognised by everyone; it would be given out that she had joined the League, and the most invidious remarks would be made; besides, there was a house full of guests for her to entertain; and Mr. Lucas. who did not show any sign of a desire to go the meeting, was never happy if she was out of his sight for ten minutes.

Sydney was sorry for her, and told her he would give her as glowing a description as a cold-blooded and unobservant Englishman could produce of what took place.

But this did not suit Miss Bridget. It was not according to Bridgettine etiquette to submit with unquestioning obedience to those who were in authority. She said nothing, however, but kept her own counsel.

Her father did not like being contradicted any more than she did.

About half-an-hour before the time appointed for the meeting she walked off to the Blue House, without saying anything to anyone. Arrived there, she was warmly welcomed by Moyrah and Eileen. She then made Moyrah dress her in an old lilac calico skirt, very skimpy, and a long dark blue cloth cloak of the country reaching almost to her heels, and completely disguising her figure. The blue hood was drawn tightly over her head, with a clean, fluted, white cotton cap under it. She put on a pair of old spectacles of Hegarty's, which, in consequence of the *retrousse* turn of her nose, she had some difficulty in keeping in their proper position. As she adjusted and re-adjusted them, she remarked, dryly: " there is something peculiar in the Irish air which prevents anything in the country from remaining in its proper position."

How she did roar with laughing as Moyrah and Eileen, having put a few finishing touches to her, she stood in front of the cracked bit of looking-glass in Moyrah's room surveying herself.

" I'm iligint now entirely, Moyrah," she said, turning towards her. " Your grandmother, my dear," and she made her a profound Court curtsey.

Moyrah laughed until she had to bend forward double, holding both her sides. That is the Irish nature. She had lain awake crying nearly all night, thinking of Cormac, of Emmett; one houseless, homeless, an exile, the other stableless, and exposed to the vindictive fury of a section of her fellow countrymen, who found their money and their joy in tormenting dumb animals.

But now she laughed, with a clear, ringing joyousness, as if she had never shed a tear in her life; and yet she laughed till the tears rolled down her cheeks.

Bridget tried her best not to laugh, for laughing made her nose crinkle up, and then her specs. fell off.

" Mind now, Moyrah, you introduce me to all your friends as Mrs. Mulhashgary, a distant cousin of your mother's, who has come over to keep your father company while your mother's away. I'm going on for eighty." Bridget gave a series of long, low coughs, after which came great gurgles in the throat, then sighs, gradually merging into groans. " I have suffered martyrdom for many years from the rheumatics, and walk with much difficulty. Here, where's the stick ? "

Moyrah quickly handed her an old stick of her father's, full of knobs and joints.

" If I could only make my wrists and fingers like that !" she said, looking at the knobs, " I should be safe, but my skin looks horridly smooth and young. I fear—I fear—unless I can paint it with a few wrinkles it will betray me !" She looked about. " Ahi ! une idée ! " She was fond of speaking French when excited. She dipped the feather of a quill pen in the ashes in the grate, and made a series of little lines all over her forehead, round her mouth, and down each side of her nostrils. Then she tied a huge red cotton handkerchief over her head, underneath her cap, and brought it down until it concealed her forehead and her cheeks, leaving only her eyes, nose and mouth exposed. This completed the transformation and made her resemble, to a very close degree, the popular conception of the grandmother in " Little Red Ridinghood." She hunched up her shoulders, rounded her back, narrowed her chest and wheezed like a broken bellows.

Then Moyrah and Eileen had to dress. They tied a piece of bright green ribbon round their long plait of hair, another bit round their throats, and pinned a rosette of shamrocks and green ribbon on their right shoulders. Attired in their Sunday best, and with clean faces and hands, they really looked a charming couple, as even Bridget could not help thinking, occupied as she was with her own appearance.

Michael, Moyrah's eldest brother, had gone on an hour before to drive a car, which was to bring up some of the contingents from the railway. As to Jim and Dan, they had been at the scene of the meeting since daybreak. Hegarty himself was not going; he said he was busy on the farm. By the time Bridget, Moyrah and Eileen arrived at the scene of action many of the processions had already filed up; and a huge, hot, jostling crowd was pushing and elbowing round the different tables and barrels, and various attempts at platforms, which were erected here and there. At the moment of their entering the field a procession with horns, like very cracked fog horns, was entering at the other end. The noise these horns made could scarcely be believed by those who had not heard them. Bridget was fairly taken off her guard, and said quite loud in her natural voice, "What an atrocious row!" then correcting herself quickly, she gave a long, low cough, and ended by groaning, which made her position safe at once.

The arrival of these horns was the signal for a demonstration. It appeared they accompanied a popular speaker, who got great cheering as he was helped on to the small improvised platform. Waving round this platform were thin, long, green banners, with such mottoes as "God save Ireland!" "Down with alien rule." "Ireland for the Irish!" etc.

Whole strings of jaunting cars kept arriving every moment, crammed to overflowing, people sitting all along the wells, holding on by each other tight, so that if one fell off all should fall together.

Large barrels of porter (the despised Guinness' XX.) were being rolled up the hill by hundreds of willing, if dirty, hands.

Suddenly a brass band of the most *prononcé* description, consisting of ten harsh trombones, marched up at the head of a procession of men with green scarves. These men carried the effigies of a land-grabber, and a bailiff.

They were headed by a man driving what the people
called "a tandem of three." He was dressed in
brilliant green, his clothes being a cross between
Garibaldi's uniform and that of a British admiral of
Nelson's time. Moyrah and Eileen appeared to
admire him exceedingly.

As the effigy of the land-grabber was passed round
amongst the crowd and came near to Bridget, she, to
her amazement, saw that it was meant to represent her
father, a landlord who was known to be deservedly
popular and beloved by all his tenantry. Too popular
by far for the Harvest Bugs, who had dressed up this
effigy and sent it down on purpose to try and injure
him in the eyes of his own people. How could they
hope to get the money out of the tenants' pockets and
put it into their own while there was a popular
landlord in the neighbourhood? So they had devised
this piece of wit. But the wheel of wit, even if left
to itself, can seldom be long in motion without getting
into a glow, and there was no want of hostile sentiments
here to quicken the friction.

"Mornin' to ye, Moyrah Hegarty!" said an
extremely smart woman, dressed in a lilac merino,
which she held high to show a worked petticoat, and
with a mixture of colours in her ribbon that fairly took
away Bridget's breath.

"Who's yer friend?" she whispered to Moyrah,
while she acknowledged Eileen's presence by a little
bit of a nod.

"'Tis a cousin av me muther's, from the North.
She's vurry ould, and deaf too, so there's no good in
hollerin' to her."

Bridget quailed under this woman's scrutinising eye,
but she resorted to her infallible refuge of a low, heavy
cough, ending with much groaning, and moaning, and
spitting, which served her well throughout the day.

At that moment the tandem driver of three was
hoisted on to the platform, amidst much cheering, while

a lady who was with him was also successfully hauled
up. When he had recovered his breath, and taken a
draught of porter from a small blue earthenware jug,
he stood forward to make his speech—the speech of
the day. He was not tall enough to look very im-
pressive ; a spry little Ananias was he.

"Jintilmin ; and I think I may add ladies, as I see
a great many av the daughters av Eve—av Erin I
mean—present, this is a proud occashin in me loife ! "

Great cheering, and waving of jugs and mugs of
porter. Miss Sapphira, on the platform, waved hers
so vigorously that some of the porter fell over the
side, and, alas ! was lost.

" This is thruly an imposin' organizashin av a
demonstrashin which I see before me. We are met
together to protest that Oireland has a right to the
favourable geographical position which providence has
assigned to her in this wurruld av woe."

Great cheering.

" We wish all the ships which sails the Atlantic
to touch here, before takin' their wealth to England,
an' whin we've a parlimint in Collige Green, we'll
oblige 'em to do it."

Tremendous cheering.

" The thing, then, is to get a parlimint in Collige
Green. The way to get that is to exterminate all the
landlords, an' every wan belongin' to 'em ! "

Great cheering.

" Pleasant for me ! " muttered Bridget.

" The way to exterminate 'em is to prevint the
tinints payin' 'em their rint."

Great cheers.

" The way to prevint the tinints payin' them their
rint " (It's rather like ' The House that Jack Built,' "
muttered Bridget, raising her eyebrows) " is to make
an example av anny lily livered pessimist who goes
sneakin' up to the agent with his rint."

Very faint, uncertain cheers, during which a dark

look came over Moyrah's beautiful features, and she bent her eyes thoughtfully on the ground.

"Jintilmen; I niver goes to England, but I goes to Dawblin; and I'll tell ye that sometimes ye'll find the land agent like the castle flunkey, as sleek and slippery as though he had been takin' a hip-bath in a tub av soap-grease."

Much laughter.

"That's how some av the farmers gets taken in; and then they ses Ireland is going on beautifully—plenty av money, lots av food; that's what they say in England."

A voice in the crowd: "How the divil do ye know if ye niver was in England?"

At that instant Mickey O'Shea bounced on to the platform, uninvited, and shouted out: "I see a black hearted villain in our midst"—he pointed at young Michael Hegarty—"but I'll put a thorn in his carcass which will rot there till the day of judgment!" and he shook his fist fiercely.

"Get down wid ye; don't be interruptin' the speakers," shouted several voices.

"I've as good a right here as anny man."

"Ye have not; nobody asked for ye."

"I'. good an Irishman as anny of ye."

"Ye are not; toime was whin ye were bullyin' a nint av yer own for his rint."

"Didn't ye go split on Larry O'Clery to the agint? Informer that ye are," and O'Shea's yellow face became ghastly with rage, while he pointed at a man in the crowd.

"Ye dar to call me informer!" and the man in the crowd swung himself on to the platform to avenge the insult. He was a cousin of the Hegarty's.

"We'll tache ye to use yer feet! we'll tache ye to use yer feet! shouted Michael Hegarty.

"Informer! Lorrud's man."

But he was seized before he could say any more, and

pulled down, being pacified, however, by a promise to speak later on.

The green man, who had stood in open-mouthed silence during this episode, now proceeded.

" If I might be allowed to paraphrase the verse in scripture, and say, ' Seek ye first liberty, and all these things shall be added unto you.' "

At this stage a violent fight broke out between the skilled artisans and the day labourers. The two factions were rather near where Bridget and her two aides de camp were standing. Sticks and clubs were flourished in the air, and, amidst boos and hissing, a good many severe blows were given, and many sadly violent expressions used

Bridget took it all as a matter of course; and only hoped that her cloak would not be knocked off her head, and her youthful, ruddy locks displayed to view in the general *melée.*

Whack, crack, went the sticks and heads. " Whir-oo-o," went the voices.

The green man kept on with his speech all the time, not noticing the little irruption. Our trio gradually sidled round the combatants, and got nearer to the platform.

" If anny man is found payin' his rint, or desertin' the Harvest Bugs, as I said before, let that man be made an example av. It does'int mattur a pin who he is, if he's yer own father or brother, ye must go agin him."

Moyrah shuddered, and again the dark look came over her face. She muttered something very low as she crossed herself. She held on to one side of Bridget's cloak, and Eileen to the other, and thus they propelled their young mistress through the crowd.

Many curious eyes were fixed on Bridget. It was a perfectly strange face in a neighbourhood where most of the inhabitants were known to each other, and, as such, it excited a rather disagreeable amount of interest.

But the cough, and the groaning and spitting, carried the day.

Meantime, in another part of the field, young Michael Hegarty was calmly inspecting a pile of sticks and clubs, which one contingent had laid down close to the door of a tent, before entering into it to consume porter. At length, after trying many, he found one which appeared to suit him, very long and thick, and tremendously heavy; it was rather like a miniature battering ram than a stick. He swung it several times round his head, to try what sort of "go" it had in it, and was apparently well satisfied, for he walked off with it over his shoulder, composedly, to the other side of the field.

Micky O'Shea was sitting astride a small empty barrel of porter. His hat was in his hand, and he was mopping his forehead with a red handkerchief, for he was rather warm after his exertions on the platform, and the struggle which preceded his descent from it.

Suddenly, the peculiar whirring noise which a stick makes passing rapidly through the air was audible just behind him, and before he had time to look round, a terrific blow descended on the top of his head.

For just one instant he sat half stunned; then, with a yell of pain and fury, started to his feet, and turned to meet his foe. His head was not seriously affected in any way by the blow; it was not the first he had received on exactly the same spot. In fact, he had never been a favourite in the neighbourhood, being drunken, cruel, cowardly and dissipated. No one, except a few wretched subordinates who had trembled beneath him had cared two straws about him until lately. Having got the Central Committee of the Dublin Harvest Bugs to make him chairman and manager of the local village committee, he now contrived to keep the whole community in awe of his frown. Now was his grand opportunity to vent petty personal spites on victims made helpless by the reign of terror.

Seeing who his assailant was as he turned, he became purple with righteous wrath, and suddenly dragging out a huge knife, something between an overgrown razor and an Italian stiletto, he made a desperate lunge at young Hegarty's unprotected left side. So rapid were his movements, and so unexpected was the appearance of the knife on the scene, that his blow would have probably gone home, and Moyrah would have been " keening " for her eldest brother before the sun set, had not his arm been dashed upwards with such strength and energy that the knife was flung out of his hand.

" What are you two up to, eh ? " said a calm voice, speaking in a tone of quiet command, which made even O'Shea's blustering spirit quail. " What a contemptible coward you are, to use a knife on an unarmed man. You have a stick lying by you; why could you not use that and fight like a man, instead of going to knives like a midnight assassin ? "

Sydney—for he it was—looked at O'Shea with withering scorn for a moment; then running his arm through young Hegarty's, he led him forcibly from the spot.

" Michael Hegarty," he said, gravely, " take my advice, and keep as quiet as you can just now. It is true you have fearful provocations, and I sympathise with you with my whole heart," and his tone was full of that earnest sympathy which was the chief characteristic of his nature, " but you have terrible odds against you, and the law of the land does not appear to protect you, or any other respectable citizen. If you provoke these cowardly scoundrels, your life, and that of your parents and both your sisters, may be the forfeit. Wait patiently for a very little while, and if it is finally decreed by the British Government that lawlessness is to reign supreme in this unfortunate country, I will get you all over to one of my farms in England."

" The Lorrud save yer honour," said Michael, gratefully touching his hat. He was keenly alive to the horrors of the sudden death from which Sydney had just rescued him.

Strangely enough, the green man, who was still holding forth, at that moment called out, " There's too much 'yer honourin,' and touchin' yer hats amongst ye southerin' boys. Shure ye're as good as anny man, and why should ye touch yer hat to another man ? Ye're as good, anny wan man is as good as another man."

" An' I'm as good as ye," shouted a voice in the crowd.

" It's the landlords should be not only touchin' their hats, but touchin' their noses in the mud to ye."

At this instant the circulation of the crowd brought our trio face to face with a cousin of Micky O'Shea's. He recognised Moyrah and Eileen at once, and began to abuse the whole Hegarty family in the most violent and uncalled for manner.

" Suillish machree, come on," said Eileen, who was somewhat frightened, pulling Bridget by the cloak. But the dark look came over Moyrah's face, darker and stronger than ever before. There was a strange flash in the liquid depths of her violet eyes.

" That old sneak-rint, your father," said Edmund O'Shea, that was his name. " I'll black-sole his eye for him. Didn't we know well the white hen was in him ? "

Bridget's face became crimson with fury, she bit her lip until little wandering tracks of blood trickled down from it. A few more insults to her friend's father, and she felt she must betray herself, even at the risk of her life. And at the risk of her life it very probably might be under the circumstances.

" An' ye, slime of a viper, come creepin' and crawlin' to a meetin' av honest men to hear what ye can catch up, an' go an' report against 'em." And he shook his fist at Moyrah.

" If it wouldn't sully me hands to knuckle down to a woman, I've a mind to thrash ye as ye stand there."

" O you have, have you ? " said a quiet voice at his elbow, while a fist, very different to any other he had as yet felt on his skin, came flying through the air, hit him square, just between the eyes, such a blow as he had never tasted in his life, and laid him flat on his back, stunned, severely hurt, and for some time senseless.

This was the " editor's note " to Sydney's sermon on patience, submission, and peaceableness to Michael Hegarty, delivered about three minutes previously.

Bridget started violently and uttered a short, sharp, exclamation, then put her hand over her mouth in horror, for fear she had betrayed herself.

Eileen called out, " Begor, you've done for him enthirely."

" Praise the Lorrud for that," said Michael. " Shure, an' it was the finest blow I ivir seen ; 'twould have knocked the head clean off the biggest bull that ever come into Corruk markit."

When Moyrah realised who had been her defender, there came over her face a deep blush, the colour of the rose in Sydney's buttonhole, which Bridget had given him just before breakfast.　Then she turned, and kneeling down by her fallen foe, raised his head gently on her arm, wiped his forehead, and loosened the tie round his throat.

" There's not a bit av good in all that ; he's done for enthirely," said Michael, in a tone of intense excitement. " An' not a pastiah (child) in the counthry will send up a screech for him " (meaning that he was so unpopular, that there would be no one to wake him).

" Eileen, fetch a dhrop of porther out of that shebeen," said Moyrah, in a low voice, indicating with her thumb a little tent close by.

Eileen let go of Bridget's cloak, and ran off nimble as a rabbit.

" Stop, Miss Eileen, I will go," said Sydney, catching

her arm. "Don't you get separated from your sister and your aged cousin in a crowd like this, or you may never be able to fight your way back to them again."

Eileen, seeing Bridget winking violently at her to come back, returned, and again took hold of the end of her cloak.

Sydney got so many bangs coming back with his brown jug that half the porter was spilt. However, what little was left had a magical effect on the hapless scion of O'Shea. Moyrah bent his senseless head forward, and poured it carefully down his throat without spilling a drop, to Sydney's great admiration.

As the senses of Ned O'Shea (for that was his name) began to return, he looked slowly, in a dazed way, at Moyrah. What could he see so odious, so detestable, in those deep violet eyes, that he was obliged to turn away with a shudder? Hatred is like a bailiff who puts in a "bill of sale" on everything beautiful in our souls. Moyrah appeared actually loathsome to Ned O'Shea.

At that moment, the day labourers, who out-numbered their opponents by three to one, came tearing along, chasing the skilled artizans before them like chaff before the wind.

Sydney coolly placed himself at the weather side of Moyrah, so as to receive the brunt of the storm on his broad shoulders.

"Look out for the old lady," he said, indicating Bridget by a slight nod, "she is shaking all over, and looks as if a breath would upset her."

Bridget was shaking with suppressed laughter. The idea of meeting Sydney in her present disguise, and of being totally unrecognized by him, was the most delicious part of the whole day's play.

"When you come to be seventy," said Sydney, in a *sotto voce*, which, however, to Bridget's keen hearing, was perfectly audible, "you had much better keep at home by the fireside, and not come out to noisy meetings like this. Really, old ladies are getting so frisky, now-a-days, that it will give a good spin to the young ones to keep up with them."

Never in her life before had the centre of gravity in Bridget's mind received such a strain. Not being English, she had no great powers of self-command, and nothing could have saved her but a violent fit of coughing, which ended in her stuffing the greater part of her large red cotton handkerchief down her throat.

The air around them was reverberating with "boos" and "whirroos," and the ground trembling from the rush of some twenty feet flying, and some sixty feet advancing. The autumn sun flashed on clubs and neatly polished sticks waved high in the air, while every now and then a stone, a rotten egg, a raw potatoe, or a bit of broken crockery flew whistling along close to Moyrah's and Eileen's unprotected heads. Bridget's heavy folded cloak, hood and cap, made her tolerably indifferent to what she called, in a whisper to Eileen, these "areonautic dangers."

Bang came the shock of the day labourers against Sydney; but his back met them without a quiver, as the white cliffs of old Albion have met the little socialistic waves which have come dancing across from Calais these many centuries.

They were mostly slight, thin, agile little men, more like antelopes than the heavy, ponderous, plodding, bullock-like English day labourer. They had lithe springy limbs, active enough when a row was in question, though with a distinct tendency to the *dolce far niente* when no fighting was to be had.

Whack! whack! crack! crack! went the heads of the flying artizans, under the shower of blows from their merciless attackers.

There were a good many fair Amazons amongst the day labourers. Each one had taken off whichever of her stockings had the most foot to it, and had put as large and heavy a stone in it as would go; with this she laid about her in rattling style, and dealt such blows as no miserable son of Adam could defend himself from.

Eileen got a whack just between her shoulders, which made her stagger forward on her toes for a minute.

" Bad cess to ye ! " shouted Michael, who got a good blow himself from a lovely heroine, as she swept triumphantly onwards.

The moment Ned O'Shea recovered his senses entirely, he scrambled up on to his hands and knees, and crawled away, without a word of either blame or thanks to any of the party.

" Yer sowl to pardition ! " shouted Michael after him.

" Whist ! whist ! Michael ! " said Moyrah, crossing herself, while tears rushed up into her eyes, " The Lorrud have mercy on us all ! " she added in a low voice, while she bent her head.

Sydney, who, by means of muscular determination and dexterous movement, had contrived to shield Moyrah from a single blow, or even rough push, now became enthralled in watching the " Retreat of Co-run-ners," as he called the stampede of the artisans.

They had reached the low stone wall, which divided the field of meeting from a boggy morass. Over this they scrambled pell-mell, some falling backwards, others, in their terror and excitement, banging so violently against their fellow fugitives as to roll them over down the hill into the morass.

With the most magnificent bounds, clearing the wall with a foot to spare, the day labourers came after them.

" By Jove ! those day labourers would make the finest steeplechasers the world has ever seen ! " exclaimed Sydney, in enthusiastic admiration. " Such wind over a stiff country, and nailing fencers, every man of them ! " and he watched, as one after the other, gathering up their legs, flew through the air over the wall, his features glowing with the rapturous delight

of a keen sportsman. " Compact, springy blood horses,
like balls of india-rubber every one of them ! "

Begor, the bog 'll play the divil wid 'em ! " said
Michael, holding his sides and roaring with laughter,
as the combatants fell about in the morass.

The green man was still holding forth on the
platform. Men might come, and men might go—into
bogs or otherwise—but he went on for ever.

" Shure, ye've a landlord in this neighbourhood, a
brutal, bloodthirsty tyrant, Captain Sheil; a vampire
suckin' the blood av all ye tinints."

" Your old cousin is going to get a fit ! " whispered
Sydney to Moyrah, " her face is purple; the heat and
excitement have been too much for one of her advanced
years. Really, old people like her have no business
coming to places of this sort; it lays such a responsibility
on the young ones having to look after them."

Moyrah slipped her arm softly through Bridget's, and
pressed it tight, to show her sympathy, and to help her
to keep down her feelings. From her childhood,
upwards, there had always been a magic in Moyrah's
touch which strengthened every sufferer, animal or
human, to bear his pain better. It was a rare gift,
and came from the extraordinary power of quick
responsive sympathy in her heart.

" An' what are ye to do wid a landlord like that ?
Put him in Dawblin Cawstle says the British Government—put a potater in the pig's snout ses I" (this being
literally translated meant, put a bullet in the man's
head).

Had it not been for the strong, warm pressure of
Moyrah's arm on hers, Bridget must have shouted out
a torrent of fury and retort. As it was, her eyes flamed
fire, and she shook all over like a ship at sea in an
earthquake.

" I'll get her a little porter; the poor old lady's done
for, I fear," whispered Sydney to Moyrah, while he ran
off to the tent, feeling convinced that Bridget was on

the verge of a fatal apoplectic fit; he knew porter was
not the best thing for her, but water was not to be had
for love or money. Who would insult a Hibernian
gathering by bringing that mean and despicable fluid
on to the ground?

" He's wan of thim blusterin' hypercrits that thries
to throw dust in yer inercint eyes, by posin' on his
hind toe before ye as a gineris landlord, offerin' ye
tin per cint. reduction, first of all, and then, whin ye
stood out like min, twinty per cint.; fal-lal! Begor,
what he ought to offer ye is all the money he and his
villinis ansisturs have robbed ye of undher the name
of rints for hundrids av years. Ye tache him his duty
the next time he comes palaverin' down to ye; or if,
as is most likely, afthur hearin' av the success of this
magnificent meeting he's afraid, like the sneakin'
coward he and all his kind are, to come, and sends that
little spit-fire av a daughter of his."

Moyrah felt the arm and hand which hers was resting
on become as hot as a poker just taken out of a roaring
fire, but she pressed her own cool, soft, gentle one tightly
over it.

" Why, tell either one or the other of thim that
landlords will soon be heard of in the Zoological
Gardens, an' only there where they'll have stronge·
cages than has ever been made for any other wild
bastes before; and where studints of natural, or
unnatural, history can go an' stare at 'em, along wid
all the other extinct brutes of the field, to their hearts'
contint."

At that moment Sydney returned with the porter,
forcing his way, by sheer strength and size, through the
cheering, shouting, talking crowd.

" Drink this up, my good mam," said he, courteously
holding the porter to Bridget's lips. " It will do you a
world of good," he added, encouragingly.

Fortunate, indeed, was this diversion, for in another
second the pent up volcanic forces, which had continued

to shake Bridget like successive vibrations of earthquake, would have found vent in the Mount Vesuvius of her mouth ; and the stream of burning lava which would have poured out, would not only have betrayed her, and astonished the green man, but would have taxed the capabilities of the compiler of the most comprehensive dictionary in Europe. That porter saved her life, though not in the way Sydney thought it did.

She took a good drink, and nodded her thanks. She dared not speak, for she knew her voice was rather a peculiar one, and would probably betray her, however successfully she might adopt the accent of the peasants.

" She's rather hard of hearin', and her voice is wake from her great age," explained Moyrah, graciously.

" She's a very shaky old party. I should think she's getting creeping paralysis," muttered Sydney. Bridget heard him.

Sydney was wondering what he should do with the brown jug he had brought the porter in, for he did not want the trouble of taking it all the way back to the tent again. Suddenly his anxieties on this score were unexpectedly relieved by Michael's snatching it from him, and flinging it with full force at the head of Micky O'Shea, which could, at that moment, be discerned protruding cautiously round the end of the tent. It turned out a rattling good shot, and the earthenware shattered into a hundred bits on the ill-used pate of that unpopular member of society.

" Let's get home," whispered Bridget to Moyrah. She was conscious of the weak points in her harness of self command, and dreaded hearing another word from the green man.

" We're goin' to take my cousin home, yer honour," said Moyrah, respectfully, to Sydney.

" Let me give the old lady my arm," he exclaimed at once. " She's not the least bit fit to walk by herself."

" Well, she's got my arrum, thank yer honour kindly, an' she's used to the stick in her other hand."

Bridget felt intensely relieved. She certainly was not going to run the risk of exposing to view her round, young arm.

As they turned away, Sydney said, "I must be allowed to see you safe home."

"Well, I'll stay here with Michael, said Eileen," who was in no hurry to put an end to her fun. So Sydney walked at one side of Moyrah, and Bridget came hobbling along at the other.

"Ah! Miss Moyrah," said Sydney, who, like all good men, had a strong touch of sentiment about him. "How sad it is to think we must all come to this, sooner or later; tottering, with one foot in the grave, nearly stone deaf" (from her never having spoken, and from her general stolid behaviour, he considered Bridget must be this), "having lost all interest or care for the subjects which once so keenly excited us; a burden to ourselves, and an infliction to our friends."

Moyrah had a momentary struggle for gravity, but unselfishness had taught her self control. She felt Bridget's arm shaking, but she spoke calmly. "I was readin' in a pothry book, Miss Bridgit lent me, a while ago, that 'grey hairs is the dawn of another life.' "

Bridget could scarcely contain herself on finding the gravity with which Moyrah treated the situation, and at hearing what good use she had evidently made of an old copy of Longfellow she had given her some time ago. Sydney was struck with the reverence and beauty of tone with which she repeated the quotation.

"That is one of the most beautiful ideas that a poet has enriched the world with," he said, looking down for a minute; but when he raised his eyes again they retained their expression of keen pleasure. There was something so exquisite in Moyrah's voice, when she said anything pathetic, or anything which touched on chords not often struck in every day life, that it arrested even rough natures little used to care a button about spiritual influences.　To an artistic temperament like Sydney's, it was a treat which marked distinct spots in life.

"Shall you be afraid of getting old, Miss Moyrah? he asked respectfully, hoping to draw her on to speak again, with that melody of tone which so fascinated him.

She raised her violet eyes, and looked at the fleecy clouds on the horizon for a minute. "I don't know till I thry, yer honour," she said, simply, in her ordinary every day voice. "But I think 'twon't be very convanyent."

Bridget now began to be rather jealous, as she remarked with amazement the extremely easy and pleasant terms which seemed to exist between Sydney and Moyrah. Indeed, quick reader of character as she was, and connoisseur in outward signs of human faces, she saw a look on Sydney's which she knew no man's countenance ever wore, except when he was moved in a very unordinary manner. She read the heart of the man she loved better than he read it himself. He had never been in love in his life; therefore it was natural he should not recognize a feeling to which he was a stranger.

The fact is, he was not in the habit of probing into his own feelings. He was an alien in the united kingdom of his own heart. Too free, manly, breezy and open air by nature to care for introspection and self conscious hair splitting, as long as nothing startlingly wrong turned up, he allowed things inside of him very much to take their own course. He had never done a deed or thought a thought which, had his mother known it, could have brought the faintest blush upon her cheek. The worst he ever had to accuse himself of, when preparing for going to his Christmas Communion at her side, in the little old-fashioned Anglican Church of Hambury, was having betted rather too high upon the Paris races.

"Do you know," said Sydney, "I've got a horse

called Longfellow, but I doubt if he would recognize that quotation for all that, though it is his own; and some of his own hairs are beginning to turn grey," and he laughed. " Even if there should be a heaven for horses, which I am very much inclined to hope, I am afraid it is not the dawn of another life for him, for a more villainous temper I never saw on any animal. My stud groom had to exercise him every day in blinkers and a hood, and with a rearing bit. He's a raking goer when extended, and I had hoped he would do great things upon the turf; but his temper made a fool of him at Doncaster, and I have never tried him again. Your Emmett is cut a little like him, only better on every point."

Moyrah's cheek flushed with pleasure. Praise of Emmett came next to praise of her father.

" If ever you should, at any future time, want to get rid of Emmett," Moyrah winced visibly, " and will only let me know, I'll give you a longer price for him than I believe you'll get from any one else in the United Kingdom."

On looking round, he saw that she was rather upset, and hastened to change the subject.

" What an atrocious scandal it is that such speeches should be allowed as that green man's," and his eyes flashed with indignation. " Upon my word I don't wonder the people doubt whether there is a government at all or not."

A look of increasing pain came over Moyrah's speaking face.

Again Sydney changed the subject, and tried quickly to find a more cheerful one.

" He was not so far wrong about Miss Sheil's being a spit-fire," he said, with a pleasant laugh.

Moyrah again felt that burning sensation, as of a red hot poker, come over the arm resting on hers.

" Of course I don't mean anything discourteous to my fair hostess, but I pity her husband," he added, with a hearty laugh. " She will have home rule, and no mistake."

A cold shudder succeeded to the hot-pokery sensation.

" What order she does keep her old father in, and all the house, too, for the matter of that," and again he laughed, as if keenly amused.

Moyrah struggled valiantly for self command.

" She's wan av the most charitable, kind-hearted ladies in the whole av Oireland," she exclaimed, in a tone which astonished Sydney. " Iv it was'int for her goodness there'd be manny an' manny a brokin harrut an' starvin' family in this village."

" O I'm sure she's good—excellent—excellent," he said, apologetically, " most charitable I'm sure ; I only spoke of her in domestic life."

The arm now burnt again, this time like a living coal just plucked by the tongs from a furnace.

Bridget might truly have said with Voila, " Disguise, I see thou art a wickedness."

At that moment, fortunately, they came out of the field on to the road, and their attention was attracted in a practical manner to a cart which almost ran over them.   It was a long cart on two wheels, with two poles sticking out at its back.   It was open, and without sides to it, and was covered with peasants, sitting and lying all over it.   A fine jolting they were getting, too, as it had not the vestige of a spring, and the road was like the sides of Vesuvius after an eruption.

Moyrah could tell at a glance the occupants were all strangers to the neighbourhood, evidently come a long way on purpose for the meeting.

" The top av the evenin' to yer," said the driver, a handsome young man, to Moyrah.   " Would ye kindly tell us is this the road to Wexford ? "

" 'Tis not," said Moyrah, with a sly twinkle in the corner of her eye.   " 'Tis the road to Kerry ; but shure that'll do ye just as well ; faith, Killarney's a lovely spot for pleasurin' in."

There was something so irresistibly comical in Moyrah's tone, that Sydney had to turn away and smother his laughter in the hedge as well as he could.

The good looking young Jehu slewed his horse right round, and dashed off in the opposite direction.

The shadows were lengthening, and the bees, satiated with sweetness, were lazily going home, while the butterflies were folding up their wings, when our trio reached the Blue House.

" My cousin is tired, and will go to bed at once," said Moyrah, as they entered the kitchen.

" She ought never to have left it," said Sydney, heartily. " I will just have a look at Emmett, to see how he is after his troubles, and then I must set off home as fast as a shot, or I shall be late for dinner," and he glanced at his watch; " and my fair hostess is not a pleasant person to encounter if you put out her household arrangements, I can tell you."

When Sydney had inspected Emmett, and found him wonderfully well, all things considered, he came round to say good-bye to Moyrah, but she was upstairs with her aged cousin.

" How wonderfully kind and self devoted she is to be sure," he exclaimed, as he turned to walk, with hurried strides, to the Hall.

Bridget waited until the coast was well clear of him, and then, in her ordinary dress, stole quietly home by a short cut she knew of.

CHAPTER XV

LUCAS was surprised that evening, and truly enraptured to find Bridget at his side, asking him if he would take her in to dinner. He looked towards Sydney, but saw that he had been provided by his hostess with the ugliest, heaviest, and most intolerably pedantic bore of the whole female party; a woman who wore heavy gold specs., and talked of a summer picnic as if she was delivering explanatory notes on the Greek classics. Sydney was looking rather astonished and a little put out himself, but of course, he made no remark. The captain never started a subject of conversation until he had finished his soup and a glass of sherry. Having disposed of this, he said genially: " Well, Mr. Sydney, what did you think of the national character, as seen at the Harvest Bug meeting ? "

" Why, I thought the speeches were the most scandalous things I ever heard. So far from wondering the country is disturbed, while such speakers are allowed to go about unpunished, what I wonder, is—"

" That there is any country left to disturb," finished Captain Sheil, good humouredly.

" Yes, precisely."

" Did they say anything about me ? "

" O yes; a great deal."

" Mon pére, les domestiques ! " exclaimed Bridget, in a stage whisper, looking round the epergne of flowers at her father.

" True, true ! " he said, looking down and pushing

his bread crumbs into a little heap with the back of his knife.

They waited until they were alone at dessert, and then Sydney gave a glowing account of the meeting; adding, however, that he had not been able to catch everything that was said, as he was obliged to take care of an " old cousin of Miss Hegarty's."

"An old cousin of Moyrah's?" said the captain, looking puzzled, "who can she be, now? And what a bad time for them to be getting people to stay with them, when the house may be burnt over their heads any minute!"

"The most tiresome old woman you ever saw in your life!" said Sydney, vigorously; "such a bore! She would insist on going everywhere we went, and kept us in a state of terror, for fear she should be knocked over in the crowd."

No one noticed that Bridget's face was most unlady-likely red.

"Ha! I must find out who she is," said the captain. "I flattered myself I knew nearly all their relations."

Bridget's heart bounded into her mouth.

Of course, in his narration, Sydney suppressed the greater part of what had been said against Captain Sheil, and all that had been said against Bridget. A general outburst of indignation was expressed by all the guests. Many of them, however, were well accustomed to such meetings being held in their own immediate neighbourhood; and some actually had the audacity to say that the only thing that was wanting was for some celebrated English statesman himself to come over and take the chair on the platform.

It was a lovely, calm evening, and, after dinner, the ladies strolled out of the drawing-room window on to the terrace. Soon the gentlemen began to drop out of the dining-room window, one by one, with their cigars, and went sauntering along towards the ladies.

Sydney had an uncomfortable sensation that Bridget

was annoyed with him, and began racking his brains in vain to try if he could recall any speech or action by which he might have given unintentional offence. He did not care about her; but it is never pleasant to feel you are in your hostess's black books. So he approached her and asked, courteously, if she objected to smoking.

"I like it," she answered, shortly.

"You will not allow me to offer you a cigar?" he said, with the most charming gallantry, as he took out his dark red leather case, with his silver monogram on it, and held it towards her.   -

"Thanks," she said, coolly, taking one and lighting it from his. "Are there many men like you in England, Mr. Sydney?"

"Well—aw—really, I don't know," said Sydney, looking rather taken aback: "I hope, for the sake of my country, there's not," he added, humbly.

"Why? Are you a bad fellow, then?"

The hot blood rushed up under his bronzed skin. "That depends on your definition of a bad fellow, Miss Sheil."

"Perhaps you would not like to hear it," she said, with a deep meaning in her tone.

"On the contrary," he answered, in a tone of forced flippancy, which only partially concealed genuine eagerness, "I shall never rest again until you tell it to me."

"Remember what you have said."

"Of course I will; I am not in the habit of going back on my words," he answered, with that touch of English haughtiness which so fascinated Bridget's Irish nature, struggle against it as she might.

"Suppose I said I don't believe you, what would you do?"

"I have yet to learn how to act under such circumstances, I confess," he answered, bowing.

"My definition of a bad fellow, then, is a man who seeks to win the fresh affections of a girl whom the world would think beneath him in position, though in reality she is above him, and which he knows he does not intend to return; who, in order to amuse himself more easily, sends her affianced lover in her own station of life safely out of the country, under the pretence of being his true friend, and acting with the greatest possible kindness towards him, and who goes regularly to church and allows the world to consider him a model man while he is doing it."

The whole of Sydney's sunburnt face and neck and even hands got rosy red like a russet brown apple. For two or three minutes he did not speak. He was more moved than he cared Bridget should discover from his voice, which he felt he could not at once control. At length, after some time, he spoke in a low tone: " I believe I understand you, Miss Sheil; but I conclude that, in order to deserve the appellation, the ' bad fellow' must do all this with *malice prepense;* that is, with full knowledge and conscious intention of the evil he is working while he works it."

" He would be a strange man who did it otherwise," she replied, in the bitterest tone he had ever heard from any lips.

At that moment Lucas joined them; then several other members of the party came up, and soon afterwards they all adjourned to the drawing room for music and whist.

That night Sydney sat for a long time at the open window of his bed room, smoking and looking at the stars. A rich man's heart is often unsearchable, because, being at the top of human desires, there is no end which he aspires after with sufficient vehemence to make it remarkable as a poorer man does; and by the end which a man pursues, and the method in which he pursues it, alone can we discover those hidden depths which *are* the man, rather than his outward face and form, or superficial actions. How often it comes over us in moments of profound stillness, silence, and solitude

that the subtilty of our own nature is beyond the power
of our own understanding to decipher! And we think
that all the sermons we have ever heard, and all the
books of good advice we have ever read, are like
insanity, because they are the arrows of a marksman
who fires at a target behind him; so wide of the mark
have they flown in piercing the mysteries of our hearts
that we might look in upon them.

Sydney felt rather as if he had been starting for a
glorious day's hunting, when, suddenly, as he rode along,
it began to rain heavily, and the rain froze as it fell.
He could swear, and not be foresworn, by his honour
and his hopes of heaven, that no unworthy thought in
connection with Moyrah had ever come within a
thousand miles of him. Had he known that he loved
her, and had she been free, and not pledged to Cormac,
he would have come forward, without one instant's
hesitation, and asked her to be his wife with as much
courtesy and deference as if she had been, in outward
position, the highest lady in the land. But he had not
known that he had loved her until the scalpel of
Bridget's satire had laid bare his heart to him.

Now he saw : now he knew. His was not a nature
when it did love to love lightly, and the thought that
he must immediately say good bye to Moyrah for ever
gave him a pang so severe that it astounded him. As
he felt it, he knew better the truth of Bridget's words.

The first step towards safety is a knowledge of the
real source of our strength, confidence in it, and a
resolution to exert it.

Sydney laid his cigar on the window sill, and knelt
down, still looking up on those stars which he remembered
were looking down on his mother, who at that hour, on
a summer's night, constantly walked in her garden.

When he rose he was calm, though rather pale.

If, after a sharp battle, we have come to a noble resolve,
it sometimes seems to us as if we were put into immediate
and intimate communion with those high spirits who

have gone before us across the battle field of life. Their
songs of triumph echo in the stillness round us. Sydney
had taken his resolve, and he would stick to it. Like a
brave rear-admiral, he had hoisted the white ensign of
St. George, with its blood-red cross of self-sacrifice at
his mizzen, where only a rear-admiral can carry it, and
under the colours of England's patron saint, he would
trample beneath his feet that dragon which is in every
man's heart.

CHAPTER XVI.

THE next morning, when the servant brought in his hot water for his bath, Sydney desired him to ask Monsieur Lenoir to come to him at once. When he appeared, he told him to pack up his things for him as soon as possible, for he was going to Dublin by the twelve o'clock express, on his way to England.

Lenoir looked very much astonished and considerably annoyed; in fact, at first he showed signs of absolute mutiny. But Sydney was not a man to be disobeyed. He never repeated an order. If it was not attended to instantly, he merely said: " Did you hear what I said to you ?" This usually had the desired offect. Lenoir, too, was no mean artist at concealing his own feelings, few couriers are.

" Lucas, I am going to-day," said Sydney, who met Lucas in the corridor, on his way down to breakfast.

" By Jove! No! Never! What for ? " exclaimed Lucas, looking startled.

" I have my own reasons," said Sydney, who never would give an equivocal excuse. " Well, I shan't go," said Lucas, crossly.

" Stay by all means, if you think you are wanted."

" Do you think you are not ? "

" Most assuredly I do," said Sydney, with great vigour.

" You've had some tiff with Miss Sheil, I suppose. I thought you looked rather like the Kilkenny cats when I joined you on the terrace last night. But, bah ! my dear fellow, it will have blown over in half-an-hour !

She will have forgotton all about it by this morning. For heaven's sake, don't cut off your nose to spite your face."

"Bosh!" said Sydney, shortly, as he began to descend the stairs.

When Sydney announced his intention to Captain Sheil, he was very much annoyed. He had taken a great fancy to his young English guest, and had hoped to have him with him for some weeks, and to show him all the beauties and interesting sights in the surrounding counties.

Sydney much appreciated his kindness, and thanked him with real gratitude for it. In return, he invited him and his daughter to Hambury Castle, when next they should visit England.

"You must ask my daughter about that; I don't think she will let you off so easily for this extraordinary freak—there, go and explain your conduct to her, if you can."

" I think my conduct requires no explanation in that quarter," he said, in a low voice, and with a slight bow towards Bridget, who, attired in a pretty light summer muslin, was pouring out tea at the head of the table. Her colour deepened, but she did not raise her head. Captain Sheil looked astonished, and it instantly occurred to him that perhaps Sydney had proposed for Bridget, and been refused by her. This was a most fortunate delusion for he used no more arguments to endeavour to persuade Sydney to stay, but at once led the conversation as far from the subject as he possibly could, and kept it there throughout breakfast. The same delusion took possession of an elderly lady who was there, and she at once spread all over the country the authentic report that Mr. Sydney had proposed for Miss Sheil shortly after his arrival at the Hall; that she had refused him, and he had, in consequence, left at once.

"I hope, Mr. Lucas, you are not going to desert us,"

said the captain, hospitably, as the party were leaving
the dining room.

"Well, thanks very much; if you will allow me, I
should certainly immensely enjoy staying a few days
longer.   Most delightful neighbourhood I was evah in
in my life."

"That's right!" said the captain, heartily.

There had been a heavy dew in the night, and the
grass was saturated. Sydney therefore did not as usual
walk up and down at the bottom of the lawn, to smoke
his matutinal cigar. He strolled away along a broad,
winding gravel walk, which led through a wood of firs
and chestnuts. The brilliant leaves of the wood sorrel,
changing from soft deep green to scarlet, as if in protest
at its approaching death, carpeted the ground. Autumn
roses were clustering round the stems of trees. The air
was very still, no sound but the splashing of a waterfall
in the grounds, and crows cawing. Suddenly he heard
soft but hurried footsteps coming round a hydrangea
bush close to him, and before he had time to escape, he
found himself face to face with Moyrah. He got
crimson. She smiled, and dropped a respectful curtsey;
while she showed, with the most perfect ingenuousness,
that she was pleased to see him.

"Good morning, Miss Moyrah," he said a little
stiffly, as he took off his hat and made her a courteous
bow. "I hope nothing has happened at the Blue
House to bring you out so early in the morning?"

All was well at the Blue House, but Moyrah could
not easily explain her errand to him. The fact was,
Bridget, in her hurry changing her dress, had forgotten
a valuable gold and diamond locket, which she wore
round her neck, containing her mother's portrait, also
a real gold bracelet, which her father had given her.
Fearing she might be distressed at their loss, Moyrah
had set off with them to the Hall, as soon as she
thought she would be likely to find Bridget up and
about. So the only excuse she could make was, that

she wanted to see Miss Bridget about a little bit of business.

"I am going away, Miss Moyrah," he said, turning to walk up with her, "in two hours time, so I had better say good bye now, as we may not meet again."

The melancholy in his voice seemed to touch her. "I'm very sorry inthirely yer honour's goin' away; but may be ye'll come back agin to ould Oireland."

He shook his head sadly.

"Of course, one can never tell. But I wanted to say something to you before I went, so I am glad to have this opportunity. I wanted to ask you if you would promise me faithfully, if ever you are in difficulty or trouble, or in any perplexity or want, to come to me, or to my mother."

He paused for a minute. Then he continued. "I cannot tell you how I have felt for you in this infamous persecution you have had to bear, but we will hope brighter times may come. I have an uncle who is one of the leading ministers of the day, and I mean to lay my personal experiences of Ireland before him, the moment I arrive in town, which will be the day after to-morrow. Things cannot be allowed to remain as they are in this distracted country. In the meantime I must tell you I got a letter from my mother this morning. She says Cormac is doing well, and seems to give general satisfaction to all with whom he works: the head gardener hopes he may turn into a first rate horticulturalist. What do you say to that, eh?" he asked, with a good humoured smile.

"It's all thanks to yer honour! I'm shure!" she said, while tears of gratitude glistened in her eyes. "May the prayers of the Blessed Virgin and all the saints go up for ye, mornin' and night!" Again came that beautiful tone which thrilled through him.

"What message shall I give to Cormac from you?"

"Give him my love yer honour, plase, an' thank ye kindly for doin' it. Tell him not to fret about us; shure, the Lorrud cares more for us than for sparrers, an' it's the sparrers he's good to, too ! livin' up there in the air, widout anny houis to burn over their heads!"   And a dreamy look came into her eyes, as she raised them to the patches of sky visible towards the horizon, between the stems of the trees, and watched the sparrows flying backwards and forwards across them.

"I wondher what could I send him?" she said, meditatively.

"How would it be if you were to send him a lock of your hair?" he suggested, in a low voice.

Putting her hand into her pocket, she pulled out a pair of scissors, and cut a glossy curl off the end of her plait.

"I hav'int anny papur!" she said, in an embarrassed way, looking about on the ground for a bit.

Sydney took out his Russia leather purse, and from its depths produced a soft piece of silver paper.   He took the curl from Moyrah, wrapped it up carefully, and put it in the purse, which he then replaced in his pocket.

Little did they dream that Bridget was watching the whole scene from behind a hydrangea bush, out of hearing, but well—too well—within sight.

"But you have not given me your promise yet, Miss Moyrah."

"I give it to yer honour wid all my heart! An' may the blessin' av hivin folly yer honour, where ivir ye go, for 'tis ye that desarve it, ershi misha" (say I).

"I shall trust to you to keep your promise, and I'm sure I shall not trust in vain," he said, regarding her with eyes full of earnest feeling.

At that moment a light springy step was heard on the gravel, and immediately the captain joined them.

"The masthur himsilf! said Moyrah, dropping a low curtsey.

"How do ye do, Moyrah?" said the captain genially, jovially, it might be said.   "So I hear you've got an old cousin staying with you! Bad times these for visiting; I must come down and be introduced to her this afternoon."

Sydney was surprised to see the warm colour fly over the girl's face, and her eyes fall, while she appeared embarrassed.

"Come, now, Moyrah, Mr. Sydney is going away from us to-day, I am sorry to say, and I think it would be a nice way of repaying him some of the kindness he has shown to your family if you were to sing "Come back to Erin."

"What ivir yer honour wishes," said Moyrah, as accustomed to obey "the masthur," as a highlander is the chief of his clan.

She did not put on any fashionable airs of mock modesty, but standing just where she was, and just as she was, only that she put her hands under the corners of her apron, which was her habit when she sung, she began that song which has melted many valiant hearts, since first it was sung to those who were leaving Ireland's shores.

Sydney stood with his arms folded, and his eyes looking away into the shadows thrown by the tangled foliage of the wood.

Just as the last note was dying away, Bridget came forward. She had, unnoticed, been creeping gradually nearer, for some time, concealed by hydrangea bushes. She had seen the tears stealing slowly down Sydney's bronzed cheeks, and had heard the peculiar, and exquisitely pathetic, tone in Moyrah's voice. There was anything but pleasure written on her brow as she advanced. Moyrah dropped her a low curtsey, and gave her a meaning look, as much as to say she had something private to say to her.

" I'm sorry to interrupt this rural concert," she said, with a satirical, almost mocking, tone which astonished her father and Moyrah, "but O'Hagan" (the land steward,) " is waiting to see you, papa, in the library."

" Why, dear me, of course, I told him to come ! How stupid of me to forget!" exclaimed the captain, starting up, and walking rapidly towards the house.

" Thank you very much for your kindness in singing ; I hope the wish expressed in your song may some day be fulfilled ; good-bye, Miss Moyrah !"

Sydney was too visibly agitated to attempt concealment, as raising his hat he turned sharply away, and strode over the crunching underwood, and finally the wet grass towards the house. Little did they think under what circumstances they would meet next.

CHAPTER XVII

A HIGH gig, with large attenuated looking wheels, and an immense horse, met Sydney at the station at Hambury. Conversation with the groom about the horse, which had been put to the gig for the first time that day, occupied the whole of the way home.

Mrs. Sydney was standing on the old grey stone steps of the hall door to receive her son, and soon was clasped in his arms.

"My darling mother!" he murmured, feeling somehow quite a new delight just now in the support to the noblest part of his inner nature which her presence had always afforded him.

My darling boy! welcome home." Then as they turned to walk arm-in-arm towards the cosy morning room, where Mrs. Sydney usually sat when there were no visitors in the house, she said: "You have come back sooner than you intended."

"I know I have," he said, with a little awkwardness in his manner. "The fact is, for one thing, I wanted to see Uncle Charles at once about the state of Ireland. It is beyond anything you can imagine. Unless I had seen it, I could not possibly have believed it! But I can speak now with the assurance of an eye witness. I expect I shall tell Uncle Charles a few things that will open his eyes!"

His Uncle Charles was Lord Gargoyle, a brother of his mother's, a conscientious, but somewhat stick-in-the-mud, old English Baron.

"I intend to go up to town by the eleven o'clock

train to-morrow morning. By-the-bye, mother dear, do tell me about Cormac; could I see him now, I wonder? How is he? I have a message for him, of importance— at least, which he himself will think important."

" He is doing very well; a nice pleasant face—only I find it rather difficult to understand him. Shall we stroll out and look for him in the garden? It is a lovely evening." He gave his arm to his mother: her head reached just to his shoulder, and they went out together, he giving a thrilling description of Ireland's wrongs as they walked.

Cormac, without hat or coat, and with waistcoat unbuttoned, shirt sleeves and trousers tucked up high, was digging in the garden. As Sydney and his mother had walked past the English gardeners, they had touched their hats with a distant, formal manner, and had looked stolidly at their spades, or else into space before them.

The moment Cormac saw Sydney, he flung his spade flat down on the earth and stepped eagerly forward, his head raised and his little round eyes glowing with delight.

"The Lorrud save yer honour!" he exclaimed, enthusiastically, taking off his hat entirely, giving it a little wave in the air, and then holding it by his side.

" Such very odd manners for a gardener ! " Mrs. Sydney mentally soliloquised. To her astonishment, her son seized the young man's begrimed hand and shook it heartily.

" Welcome to England, my poor fellow ! We'll see if we can't do something for you here, better than they managed in your own country ! " and he smiled. " They are all well at home, and I have messages for you, and something more than messages ! " he added, in a low voice.

Then turning to his mother, he whispered, " I have some messages to give to the poor fellow, which I think he had rather hear alone."

She withdrew her arm, and walked on with a smile and a nod.

" Cormac ! " he exclaimed, the moment they were alone, " she sent you her love—and this," and Sydney slowly produced the precious lock, and laid it glistening in the evening sunshine on the palm of Cormac's hand. The young Irish man pressed it passionately to his lips.

" May the Lorrud save yer honour ! An' did she think av sindin' me this ? Shure. I'll kape it like me scapular, to the ind av me loife, an' die wid it round me thro-at !" and he kissed it again and again.

Sydney himself was more agitated than he cared to show. He would rather have parted with a thousand pounds than with that one little lock of hair. Yet he had not kept it an instant after it was in his power to give it up.

" She says you are not to fret about her ; the Lord takes great care of the sparrows, and—" he stopped, emotion choked his voice.

Cormac, too, was overcome, and wiped his eyes with his huge, red, earthy, bare fist.

" I went to the Harvest Bug meeting with them," said Sydney, quickly recovering himself. " They had an old cousin staying there, and she would come too ; and was such an awful bore ! and finally Miss Moyrah had to go away early, on purpose to drag her home !"

" Bless me soul ! Who the divil can she be ? A cousin av Moyrah's as ould as that !" and he scratched his head and ruminated.

" She'd a fearful cough ; I don't think she'll live very long. Miss Moyrah seemed to think of no one else."

" 'Tis a quare thing, now, I nivir heerd tell on her," exclaimed Cormac, looking more and more surprised.

Just then Mrs. Sydney approached, and the tête-à-tête broke up.

The next morning Sydney found a letter from the captain in the pile of business letters by his breakfast plate. Mrs. Sydney was pouring out tea, and suddenly

she was startled by a sharp exclamation, and by
Sydney's bringing down his first on the breakfast table
with a violence which made the knives and forks jump.

" I beg your pardon, mother!" he said, apologetically,
" but really, when you hear what this letter contains, you
will not be surprised at anything I do."

" My dear boy, since you have been to Ireland I *have*
ceased to be surprised at much that you do ! "

He smiled, and proceeded quickly to explain. It
seemed that on the very evening of the day Sydney
left the neighbourhood, as Eileen was coming home from
her usual diversion of dancing on a hay rick, she had
been set upon by a contingent of the Harvest Bug
League, acting under the direction of the O'Sheas.
They had tarred her all over, even her lovely fair hair,
and soft white face, had stuck crows feathers behind her
ears and in her hair, and had sent her home like a
Fiji islander. She had been very ill ever since, and
the dispensary doctor had been threatened he would be
shot if he attended her, so he would not go near her.

Mrs. Sydney had never seen him in anything
approaching to the state this letter produced. His face
grew crimson, the veins stood out on his forehead, and
on his clenched fists. Horrified as she was at the
account of the barbarities in the letter, she was far too
anxious about him for anything else to occupy much
of her attention. Not so Sydney, who seemed almost
beside himself with indignation. The dispensary doctor
came in for the largest portion of his ire, and under his
breath he used some language, with regard to that
cautious saw-bones, better suited to a race course than
the dining room of a lady.

The moment breakfast was finished, and he bolted
his in a dangerous hurry, he ordered a young
thorough-bred he was training to be saddled, and tore
off at full speed to the nearest telegraph station.

First of all he sent a long and most expensive
telegram to the leading doctor in Dublin, begging him

to go down at once to Mr. Hegarty's farm, and at whatever expense, and see what he could do for Miss Hegarty. The name of Edgar Sydney was too well known, too widely respected wherever England's commerce had penetrated, to require him to give any references, but he informed the doctor that he had telegraphed to a banker in Dublin, who transacted much business for his firm, and had a good deal of his money in his hands at present, to send him whatever fee he might demand. Then he telegraphed to Mr. Hegarty, to tell him what he had done, and to express his deep sympathy; and then to the captain, to ask him if he would give the doctor a bed, and beg him not to return until Eileen was out of danger. Then he rode home, said good bye to his mother, and set off for London for a couple of nights.

CHAPTER XVIII.

LORD GARGOYLE was sitting quietly in his ground floor library in Mayfair when his excited nephew burst in upon him. The old gentleman had just finished a long political conversation with a veteran statesman, aged ninety-five, a humanitarian, a vegetarian, a teetotaller, a philanthropist, and an anti-disciplinarian, who had left about five minutes before Sydney arrived. Both the old gentlemen had urgently impressed on each other the desirability of excessive caution and moderation in dealing with the Irish question. Stringent measures were at all times to be avoided. The agitators were to be consulted as much as possible upon how they would like to be kept in order. It is not the milk of human kindness which we want in our statesmen of the present day, it is a trustworthy lacto-meter for discovering the quality of that milk. Anyone who discovers this lactometer should make a fortune—that is, if he takes out a patent at once—larger than undertakers do by getting agitators to worry respectable statesmen. After putting the lactometer into the cushion on which any given statesman sits, it should be constructed to register infallibly whether the milk of human kindness in his heart is of the quality which would throw open all the jails, and allow the criminals to sport themselves to their hearts' content amongst the respectable portion of the community; or whether it is of the quality that makes good whipped cream for garotters, incendiaries, burglars, in all ranks of life; traitors, sedition mongers, cut throats, dyna-miters, assassins, socialists, communists, and other wheel

barrows for conveying new forms of selfishness into
the light of modern society.

Lord Gargoyle received his nephew most cordially.
He was proud of his undeniable talents, of his high
character, and of the universal affection which he
inspired. Little, indeed, was the mild and placid old
nobleman prepared for the outburst that followed. He
was treated to the whole history of the Hegarty family;
of the Harvest Bug meeting; of all that was said at it;
of the direct instigations to murder and maim which
the principal speaker from Dublin, unchecked, had used.
Nothing could be more graphic than Sydney's language,
and his manner was absolutely enthralling. He wound
up by reading the letter he had received that morning.

"Well, what do you think of that, I wonder?" he
exclaimed, as he threw the letter on the table, and
looked up into his uncle's eyes.

"Most serious! Very serious! Hem! Shocking!
Really, quite shocking!"

A long and earnest conversation followed. Sydney
found, as he had often done before, that his uncle's
heart was ever active to exert itself for the benefit of
his fellow men. It is true, his mind was somewhat
inclined to deal in the abstract, but a few syllogistic
exhibitions soon brought him down to the concrete.
He was not quick to follow a logical formula, and this
was probably the reason he had never been placed in a
prominent position by his party. Once, however, that
you brought before him the real intrinsic connection
of part with part in an argument, he showed that
spontaneous power of the reception of truth which is
probably only granted to a man who has honestly
followed the guiding of his conscience from early
years. True, he had not individual genius; neither
had he talent enough to substitute scientific methods
for it, as so many of our modern statesmen have. He
did not possess the smartness of some of our political
zoologists, who can build up an intricate body of

statesmanship from the sight of the smallest bone of popular clamour.

Ilis English common sense was opposed to remedying the ills of society by emptying the jails and the public houses into the drawing rooms. But, though the reverse of an extremist, he did more than refuse his consent to such a process. He was not content, like some of his compeers, to " sit tight and laugh " while it went on. He spoke out, like a man, when he thought that by so doing he could benefit the England of the future. Sometimes he got a good snubbing for his pains.

There was a necessary incompatibility between him and the tribunes who make politics an arithmetic book for paying their weekly bills; a handle for getting invited to showy parties; a draught to gratify a thirst for notoriety. All his mental associations, indeed, all his idiosyncracies, took the form of an honest desire to serve his country, apart from any personal advantage. Of the delirium of the born orator, or the zephyr breath of the genuine diplomatist, he knew nothing. But of the tangible gifts of an upright conscience, a straight-forward tongue, and a polished and gentle manner, he knew and exhibited much.

It was late when Sydney parted with him, but he left him in a consoled and calmed state of mind. As he walked away down Park Lane, he wondered why his uncle did not marry again. " Lords ought to marry, and present the world with numerous editions of them-selves," he soliloquised. " The peerage destroys the infection of unworthy ambitions in modern society," his lip curled slightly, which made him look unlike himself, for satire with him was not usual. " Therefore, it is the duty of every true patriot to multiply those lumps of aristocratic camphor, which alone clear and purify the social atmosphere in the present day." Little did he guess the surprise in the matrimonial line his excellent uncle would, one day, make him shudder with.

Sydney did not see his uncle again. He was obliged to leave town hurriedly, as he received a telegram informing him that there was to be an important meeting of a committee of which he was a member.

When Sydney sat on a committee a new element was introduced.

Most men who sit on committees regard the matter in this light. First, what a great man I am to be asked to sit on this committee, what a greater one to sit, what a greatest of all to sit as I do. Or else, what a confounded bore to be asked to sit on this committee; shall get out of it if I can; if I cannot, shall take care to do it so as never to be asked again.

But when Sydney sat, he remembered, even then, in the black depth of his unromantic position, Nelson's romantic words—becoming every day, more and more romantic—signalled at Trafalgar.

When Sydney reached Hambury it was sunset time, and he found Mrs. Sydney walking on the terrace of the garden with the rector of the parish, talking over the wants, wishes and tastes of the villagers. Framed in the gold of the setting sun, they made a beautiful pair; though the hair of both was snow-white, and many wrinkles were on their skin. In that somewhat stiff, quaint garden they looked like an old-world picture, come to life out of the old picture gallery. She, with her well drawn-up, dignified figure, dressed in soft silks, her stately bearing, and her soft, grey eyes full of interest, now, and, indeed, usually, about the wants of others. He, with his long, wavy, silver locks; his well-worn umbrella, which he used as a stick, his legs not being what they had been when he was the first cricketer in the parish; his rugged brow and clear cut features with their sweet benign expression—that expression of gentle toleration and heavenly good temper which the faces of the old people—the faces which are leaving us, do wear, now-a-days—that expression which the much tried nerves, and literally *tattered* tempers of the modern young will never allow their faces to be beautified by.   He had been in the parish, first as curate, and afterwards as rector, for fifty years, and was beloved by everyone.   He had been as a father to Sydney, advising him on many points on which his mother did not like to interfere.

Sydney got a cordial greeting, indeed, from them, and then, with his mother leaning on him, joined them in their walk, giving, in his eager, eloquent way, a full account of the result of his visit to his uncle.

CHAPTER XIX.

EVERAL months have elapsed since the events narrated in the last chapter. None of the perpetrators of the outrages on the Hegartys had been found, but, with the tarring of Eileen, those outrages had ceased for some mysterious reason.

Hegarty was getting on pretty well. He had, in common with all the tenants, received an absurdly large reduction of rent; but his pocket had been none the better for it, as it had all been drained off him by an enforced subscription to the Harvest Bugs.

Cormac either had taken a dislike to garden work, or, what Sydney more than half suspected, was afraid he might be followed, and vengeance taken on him even in England. At any rate, he had begged Sydney to obtain for him a post as warder in an English gaol. Sydney was very much amazed; but he found the young exile was quite determined about the matter; therefore, yielding to his wishes, he procured him a place in the county gaol of a Devonshire sea-side town, as under warder. This appeared a secure haven from molestation—perhaps the only absolutely secure one he could have found. He had refused a farm Sydney had offered him at low rent. He wrote at intervals to Moyrah, but he sent his letters through a third person, as he did not wish it to be known where he was.

Mrs. Sydney had given up the idea of going abroad. And, almost immediately after Sydney's return to Hambury Castle from Ireland, he had dismissed Lenoir.

Truth to say, he was glad to get rid of him. There was something about him inexplicable and intangible, but which made Sydney look after his diamond studs and his despatch box as he had never done before.

After leaving him, Lenoir went to Paris; from there to Chicago; then on to San Francisco, and home to Paris again by New York. Those nine months had been a brilliant epoch in his career. He had accomplished, with astonishing success, a difficult mission which had been trusted to his care, and had risen considerably in the estimation of the heads of the foreign secret society of which he was rapidly becoming a distinguished member.

It was the time of the Dublin Cattle Show. Hegarty had brought up a good deal of butter to the show, and some fine, fat beasts. He had a cousin who kept a grocer's shop in Leeson Street. This cousin had invited him to stay at his house during the time he remained in Dublin. Strange enough, for an Irishman, this grocer was an old bachelor. There was, in consequence, plenty of room in the house, and Mr. Mahony—for that was his name—had invited Hegarty to bring all his family if he wished. But Mrs. Hegarty was laid up with rheumatic gout in her knee, and Eileen stayed to nurse her. Michael could not leave the farm while his father was away, and as for the two youngsters, Dublin was certainly not the place for them. Therefore, Moyrah was selected to accompany her father, for his sight was getting rather bad now, and it was not safe for him to walk about the crowded streets of a large city alone.

This was Moyrah's *début* into the *beau monde*, as she had never been more than four or five miles from her own hall door before. Everything was delightfully new and charming to her. As they drove along the quays she was impressed with the grandeur of the dome of the Four Courts.

Hegarty only intended to remain two days, so

Moyrah had to make the most of her chances of sightseeing. The morning after her arrival she accompanied her father and cousin to the show. They were
leaning over the side of a pen : Hegarty was remarking
that the bulls were well fleshed, well brought out,
broad backed, "iligant" cattle, when, suddenly, Moyrah
felt someone leaning over at her side, a hand clasped
hers, and a voice of the most unctuous politeness said—

"*So delighted* to meet you again, Ma'm'selle Hégarty!"

She looked up, and recognised Lenoir

A thrill passed over her. For an instant she was
thrown off her guard by surprise, and gave a low
exclamation, which caused her father to turn round.

When he saw Lenoir, he too, expressed astonishment,
even while he greeted him.

Lenoir explained matters by saying that he had
been touring for his amusement in the States, and had
decided to see the Dublin show on his way home from
New York, so had landed at Queenstown, instead of
going on to Liverpool.

Hegarty introduced him to his cousin, Mr. Mahony,
and they all talked over the cattle, and sauntered slowly
round the show.

Lenoir knew a good deal about the best foods for
fattening cattle on, and could discourse very learnedly
about the reason of the present fall in prices besides
affording valuable information about the prices, at
present being given in New York, Philadelphia,
Chicago, and San Francisco. He discussed the
political, financial and commercial horizon with all
the acumen of a finished agriculturalist, and pleased
Hegarty and Mahony. He made himself all things,
to all men.

Moyrah could not tell why, but the most strange
sensations came over her while she listened to him
speaking. Not such calm, happy, ennobling feelings, as
when she listened to Sydney, and felt drawn up by the
influence of his brave, ingenuous heart, sparkling

intellect, and pure manly soul, to a higher and larger world. No; tempestuous emotions, which she could not comprehend, and which brought no peace along with them, swept over her. It had always been so when Lenoir spoke. And yet, the fascination of his conversation was such that she hung on every word of his with the most unaccountable, almost breathless, interest.

He did not address himself directly to her until later on in the day, when the two elderly men had met some common friends, and were engaged talking to them. Then, indeed, he addressed himself solely to her, and, for almost an hour held her spellbound. She did not see her danger; some powerful opiate seemed to lull every whisper of suspicion which could rise in her mind. There was no one near to warn her, no hand stretched out to save her.

Lenoir remained with the Hegartys the whole of that day, and came early again the next morning to Mr. Mahony's, to escort them out, for they were going to the Four Courts to hear a case tried which interested Hegarty. It was that of a farmer from his own neighbourhood who had brought an action against his landlord for " trespass:" the landlord having followed the hounds after a fox across the corner of one of his most boggy fields. When he tried to seize the reins of the landlord's horse, the landlord had raised his hunting whip in a menacing attitude, which was an attempt at " battery," and, therefore, constituted an assault. Trespass and assault, therefore, were the crimes of which the landlord stood accused. Lenoir, by some means, best known to himself, managed to secure admirable places both for seeing and hearing in the court house. The landlord was a friend of the Sheils, and a near neighbour, and was a fine, good tempered looking man, who seemed more amused than annoyed at the whole proceeding. The farmer himself did not seem to like it at all. The leading Harvest Bugs of Dublin had got up the trial, paid for it, and were virtually conducting it. The farmer was acting under strong compulsion from them. They all appeared to know Lenoir, and many were the nods, winks and friendly greetings exchanged between them.

The trial lasted nearly all day; and when the jury came back into court, they unhesitatingly returned a verdict against the landlord. It was received with rounds of stunning cheers, and the triumphant farmer was carried out of court on the shoulders of two tall men, and chaired up and down the quays, while the heavy, smoky air was rent by the vociferations of a madly excited crowd. The unfortunate landlord had to escape by a side door, enveloped in mufflers to avoid recognition, or he would have been torn to pieces.

After the trial, as soon as they could cleave a way through the crowd, the Hegartys and Lenoir, for Mahony, having been gadding all yesterday, was obliged to remain in his shop and attend to business to-day, went off for a last view of the cattle show. Hegarty soon met friends amongst the crowd of farmers, and became absorbed, talking to them, and Moyrah was left once more to her fate. She was like a child playing upon the sea sands, with his back towards the ocean, while a tidal wave is sweeping towards him. But he does not see it until its shadow falls over the little sand castle he has built. Then he looks, to see it—too late.

The next morning, by an early train, the Hegartys returned home. Lenoir accompanied them to the station, saw them safely into their modest third class carriage, and, as he raised his hat and made a bow, with his feet together, and his toes turned out, he muttered, "au revoir."

CHAPTER XX.

IT was a sultry day in the beginning of June at the Blue House. Heavy clouds hung about in the distance, and there was that oppression in the air which usually precedes a thunderstorm.

It was just a fortnight since the Dublin cattle show.

Hegarty was out looking at his ripening crops with some satisfaction. There was every prospect of a good harvest, if only the weather should prove propitious. In consequence of the heavy rains, which had come late, last autumn's fodder had been inferior through all the winter, and had not even borne up well as litter. The beasts had gone through rather a bad time, but were beginning to fatten up well now. At the last fair Hegarty had disposed of some prime milch cows at a price which had fully satisfied him. Pigs, however, had been two-pence per 8lb. lower than usual. Therefore, he did not feel in a very good temper with the old sow and her litter.

He was leaning on the low half door of the pig stye now, surveying her ladyship with a critical eye, when, suddenly, a voice at his side said: "She is safe to bring you in a nice little sum next market day."

Hegarty started, turned round, and saw Lenoir touching him. He greeted him cordially. They had always got on very well together.

"I did'nt know ye were in these parts, misthur," he said, in some surprise.

"I only arrived yesterday evening," said Lenoir graciously adding, " and I made it my first business, as I may add, it is my first pleasure, to come down and pay my compliments to my old friends, *le* Hégarty family."

Hegarty was pleased with compliments. He had not received many in his life, and he considered them the sign of very good manners.

He now took Lenoir all over the farm, showed him everything, and became more and more impressed with his amiability. He, however, did not talk much himself, for he was a shy, reserved man, but he listened with great interest to Lenoir, who descanted learnedly upon the relative values of different sorts of French oil-cakes for cattle.

After a time, low rumbles of distant thunder broke the stillness of the air. Gradually these came nearer. The storm stole up dead against the wind. The old Blue House, with its thick clusters of honeysuckle, jessamine and myrtle, climbing up its sides, and surrounding its windows, loomed out quite light-coloured, from the inky background of approaching clouds. Heaped upon heap, they came rolling up. Slowly, huge drops of rain began to splash down, and then came the lightning.

Hegarty, who—like all Irishmen—had a strong dislike to anything phenomenal in the elements, suggested they should go into the house. In the kitchen they found Mrs. Hegarty washing the dresser.

She received Lenoir most cordially. His manners, more than satisfied the highest requirements of her taste. He asked for Moyrah. She had gone down into the village with Eileen, but would, probably, soon be home, on account of the storm.

The long, rolling, booming peals grew louder every moment, and the flashes more startlingly brilliant. All conversation was at a standstill, because Mrs. Hegarty interrupted every sentence with invocations to the saints and the blessed Virgin Mary; and Hegarty became gloomy and silent, and crossed himself frequently, while he muttered murmurs about the

harvest. Suddenly, there came a flash which was so
dazzling that it seemed as if a ball of fire had burst in
the kitchen of the Blue House. The crash which
followed, or rather accompanied it, was so appalling
that Mrs. Hegarty screamed and almost fainted, and a
number of the plates were dashed off the dresser on to
the floor, and broken to atoms. At that instant the
door opened and Moyrah walked in alone.

"An' wher's Eileen?" shrieked Mrs. Hegarty, starting
up.

" Wid the widder Flanagan," said Moyrah, shaking
the rain out of her masses of hair.

It seemed Eileen had grown frightened and would
not face the storm, but Moyrah had dreaded that her
father and mother might be anxious about their safety,
and so had determined, at all risks, to come home. She
now picked up the " coorag " which had fallen as she
entered, and then, for the first time, noticed Lenoir.
She started with surprise. Then a deep blush and a
slightly amused look came over her face at his foreign,
and almost fulsomely polite, greeting. Yet she did not
seem displeased. Notwithstanding the discoveries which
have enriched science during the last twenty years, no
genius has, as yet, found the key to the bi-literal alphabet
of the female heart. Woman has ever at hand some
new and useful invention to elude the examination of
the cypher. She can transform the two letters, which
serve simple man so well, A and B—I love; I do not
love—into a thousand significations, which baffle the
most erudite male reader of hieroglyphics.

Moyrah could not imagine why it was that, ever
since she had come under Lenoir's influence, he had
exerted such a strange power over her. She did not
know it, but he was an accomplished mesmerist, and
she was, in fact, an admirable subject for mesmeric
experiments: the subjectiveness and receptiveness of
her mind exposed her to this danger.

Lenoir could, and often did, mesmerise simply by his

eye, without using any passes of the hand whatever. But when once he did use hand passes, and, by that means, sent a subject off into a mesmeric coma, that person was his slave for ever. It need scarcely be said this power had proved of marketable value to him at many epochs in his life.

As for Moyrah, she had never heard the word mesmerism, and was, of course, absolutely ignorant of its meaning and of everything connected with it. But there certainly is in us all a secret electricity which attracts us towards some people and repels us from others; hence the satisfactory feeling of being in sympathy with a pretty woman, and the misery experienced by non-conductors.

There was something, too, in the extremely smart style of Lenoir's attire which, being unlike anything she had ever seen before, attracted Moyrah much. He told her himself that it was "ultra-chic;" but she did not altogether understand the meaning of that word. He also remarked that she ought to see him dressed for a masked ball, the Bois, or the races, or even for the Casino Vivienne, Bulliers, or the Elysée Montmartre. In fact, he liked arraying himself in fantastic habiliments, almost as much as he liked sipping vermouth and reading the *Intransigeant* in the boulevards. He hated being, even for one moment, an ordinary man of no importance—an inconspicuous figure in life— almost as he hated Ireland and the greater part of its inhabitants.

He was staying at a small inn on the outskirts of the neighbouring town, and he came over every day to the Blue House. He said he liked the walk: he had no objection to the open air in summer. In fact, he told Moyrah he was a regular "boulevardier" during the warm months in Paris. She thought it sounded something like "bombardment," and possibly had reference to warlike feats he had performed in his native city, in which he had probably distinguished himself.

One morning Lenoir found Moyrah hemming a kitchen apron, as she sat on a log of wood in the garden under a lime tree. After his usual absurdly elaborate bow, he coolly sat down at her side. When he had been talking fluently, and she listening attentively, for some time, he told her she was looking pale. She confessed to having a headache. He told her to shut her eyes and lean back against the stem of the tree, and that, without touching her, or giving her any medicine, he would cure her completely. In perfect simplicity and innocence of heart she obeyed. There and then he made the mesmeric passes in the air, and soon had mesmerised her completely.

Just as she had become insensible her father's footsteps were heard approaching, and Lenoir quickly brought her back to life again. But Hegarty did not see the couple, and passed on up the garden path into the house.

When Moyrah had recovered she sat up, looking dazed and bewildered, but confessed, when she was questioned, that her headache was cured. She seemed much astonished, and asked Lenoir what he had done. He laughed, and said he had prayed to his French patron saint, whose peculiar *métier* it was to cure headaches—St. Bon Marché.

Moyrah was very much touched, though she had never heard of this saint before.

Lenoir turned away to conceal a smile, while he bit his under lip. Then he began to converse on general subjects in a pleasant, off-hand, agreeable, if distinctly bumptious, manner. More than ever now did Moyrah become enthralled—literally magnetized by the charm of his society.

Presently, as he was talking, he asked her if she often heard from Cormac?

She confessed she had not heard for a long time now.

Lenoir, who, by some unknown means, appeared to

have discovered where Cormac was, told Moyrah that he had seen him when he was in England, during the fortnight which had elapsed since the cattle show, and that he was quite well, but had ceased to care for her. He assured her, on his sacred word of honour as a French gentleman and a good Christian, that Cormac had declared to him that he would give anything to be able to break off his engagement with her, as he was deeply in love with a charming English girl, the accomplished daughter of a harness maker, who lived near the gaol.

At first Moyrah was thunderstruck, and absolutely incredulous.

But Lenoir produced a letter written unmistakeably in Cormac's own hand and addressed to Lenoir. In this he declared how he had grown tired of the chains of his engagement to Moyrah, and how anxious he was to break them. He set forth the charms of the harness maker's daughter, and implored Lenoir to let him know, when he returned to Ireland, whether there was any chance of Moyrah's releasing him.

Lenoir handed the letter to Moyrah to read for herself. There it was, in black and white, as plain as a pike-staff.

Moyrah had read but few letters in her life, and was no adept at detecting differences in handwriting. She could have sworn in a court of justice that the hand was Cormac's. Cut to the heart, wounded in all the tenderest fibres of her woman's nature, she leaned her burning head upon her trembling hand, while large tears ran slowly down her cheeks. She muttered low to herself, and, for a short time, passionate sobs, kept down by a violent effort, seemed to choke her. At length, she buried her face in her hands and cried outright. All dignity of self-control, for a moment, seemed lost in the agony of her shame. Well would it have been for her had that been the deepest measure of her humiliation in this world.

A gleam of satisfaction, very revolting in its lurid light, shot over Lenoir's features, as he listened to her sobs.

"Des larmes d'orgueil!" he muttered, satirically, to himself. Then he added, still lower: "Nous avons une belle épousée; nous voulons un époux aussi beau."

Presently, as Moyrah's sobs subsided, Lenoir began to speak in a gentle, insidious tone.

"I feel for your sad position, Mademoiselle Hégarty, with my whole heart. The conduct of Monsieur Cormac is indeed cruel and indelicate, and shows that he can never have really cared for you, but only deceived you for his own amusement. Such, alas! is too often the conduct of men! Of *some* men, I should say—*not* of all!" and he came closer to her.

Moyrah listened to this, and to a great deal more, in the same Parisian high falutin' style. High, indeed. High as the Eiffel tower. She listened intently, that day and many succeeding days. Listened while he told her wonderful stories of his travels, and the brave deeds he had done, and felt stirred within her that wild Irish love of adventure and admiration of the adventurous which makes the Irish character so kin to the American. She listened, and did not know that a prairie fire was being lighted, which no resources at her command would be able to extinguish, until it had swept over her whole future life and calcined every flower. For a fortnight Lenoir came daily, and always managed to see Moyrah alone, during part, generally a great part, of his visit.

One day, as they were sitting out in the garden, on the stem of a felled tree, talking over Cormac's conduct, Lenoir suddenly exclaimed:

"While I cannot help execrating the baseness of one who could so behave to the loveliest and most amiable of her sex, I cannot but feel that his betrayal has been my opportunity." Rising suddenly, he dashed his hat at his side, and flung himself on his knees before her.

"My own beloved, adored and idolized one! I love you with the true and fervent love and worship of my whole heart, such as I never felt for anyone before, and such as absence for years, or death itself, could not efface or change! I feel that every moment I exist separated from you is misery, and should you now refuse me, I declare before Heaven I will take my life with my own hand before an hour has passed!"

His voice trembled, his eyes flashed, his whole face and form, seemed to Moyrah's enthralled vision to be transformed into that of an angel of light.

"You may wander from pole to pole, but you will find none ever again to love you as I do now! If you but trust to me, and become truly my own for ever, the whole of my future life will be devoted to making you as happy as it is given to man to be on this side the grave. O, my darling! my idol! say but the one little word which will make known that I am the proudest and happiest man the world contains to-day!"

As Moyrah listened, a strange rapture, almost a delirium of joy, unlike anything she had ever conceived before to be possible, came over her at the thought that he loved her. She said the one little word which can never be unsaid; and the next hour passed in that dream which is more dreamt of than any reality. Dreamt forward to up to nineteen; dreamt back upon up to ninety.

Even to a fastidious person Lenoir made a not un-romantic lover. His height, his personal appearance, and his *savoir faire*, to a certain extent, brocaded over his innate vulgarity. To Moyrah's unsophisticated view he appeared the most perfect specimen of humanity which had ever existed.

As they sat there, side by side, they looked, to a certain extent, not unlike two orchids. Of all flowers, and almost of all animals, orchids most impress upon us the idea that they have spirits in them. Those hideous, bright yellow ones, with great splotches of angry looking, odious, muddy brown, sometimes seem to live and move as if a demon incarnate of cruelty and treachery was inside. Then the beautiful snow-white ones, just tipped here and there with the softest, most exquisite shades of mauve and violet, make us feel as though they must be the tabernacle of a spirit from a better world.

CHAPTER XXI.

THREE weeks after the events narrated in the
last chapter, the little Catholic church of the
parish in which the Blue House stood was
decorated for a wedding. Eileen's deft fingers had
stuck white hedge roses everywhere ; in some places
she had mixed them with lime blossoms, and there was
a good deal of jessamine, which she had pulled off the
house, wound round the alter rails.

After Moyrah had consented to marry Lenoir she
had to meet the bitter reproaches of her father and
mother for having so basely deserted Cormac. But
Lenoir quickly showed them Cormac's letter, and told
them just what he had told Moyrah. Then all their
indignation was turned against Cormac, and they were
ready to further Lenoir's suit in every way.

Lenoir declared he was very well off, and would settle
five hundred pounds on his *fiancée* the day they were
married. As a sort of guarantee of his solvency, he
presented Hegarty with a cheque for twenty pounds, and
assured him that whenever he wanted money he would
only have to apply to him, as he had many wealthy
relations, and was doing a good business in the wine
trade with them in Paris. He showed him numerous
orders for more wine from people with titles.

When he saw how terribly Moyrah felt leaving her
father, he vowed to her on his solemn word of honour
that, after a few weeks' honeymoon in Paris, they should
return to the neighbourhood of the Blue House and
take a farm, which happened to be unlet, called Kintore.

He explained his having come to Ireland as valet, by

saying that he wished to see some friends in Dublin, and that, being anxious to settle down in life, and on the look out for a wife, he wanted to save money, and preferred coming at some one else's expense. Such economy promised a frugal husband, and greatly gratified his future father and mother-in-law. He acknowledged that he had been to Ireland several times before, in his business capacity, as travelling agent for the wine firm to which he belonged. He said his health being occasionally rather precarious, he had long thought of retiring, at any rate, for a time, and trying how farming would agree with him. He had realised sufficient capital to stock a farm, and give him a good start.

Lenoir declared to Hegarty that he felt convinced farming in Ireland could be made a most profitable business, if the butter and egg department was properly worked. At any rate, he asserted that he intended to try.

Moyrah was delighted at this prospect; and the terrible nightmare of separation from her darling father was robbed of many of its horrors.

The Sheils were away in London, and knew nothing of what was going on at the Blue House. Bridget was playing a game of her own which occupied her whole attention. At the same time, had the faintest shadow of a conception of what was occurring to her favourite become known to her, she would, at all expense and trouble, have gone home, even had she to return in a week, and though it was the height of one of the most delightful London seasons on record. But Moyrah found great difficulty in writing letters; and, moreover, she was of a shy, modest disposition, like her father, and could not bear to obtrude her private affairs at such a time as the London season, when she knew, from Bridget's own lips, how every moment was taken up with such important business during that whirligig of pleasure. Besides, Lenoir had particularly begged her not to write to Bridget, suggesting that it would be tantamount to asking Bridget for a handsome wedding present, and from this, he said, his pride revolted. Moyrah's pride revolted from it also, once the idea was put into her head. It would not have come there of itself.

Moyrah had made a little retreat for a day or two before her marriage, to prepare herself for her new life, as is the habit with devout Catholics. Lenoir excused himself from doing the same, by saying he had made one only a short time ago, in Paris. He, however, readily consented to accompany her, when she went up to chapel to make her general confession, on her wedding eve. He said he also would make his. He was so very short a time in the confessional, that Moyrah rejoiced to think what a spotless career his had been, and thanked God for giving her so devout and holy a husband.

The morning of Moyrah's wedding day dawned dark and cloudy. Rain fell in torrents, and the wind moaned drearily round the house. The old furniture creaked and sighed, and made strange noises, as if something was weighing on its mind. The clouds swept low down, and seemed to be passing close to the house in weird, fantastic shapes, the way they do on a thoroughly wet day in Ireland. The rain beat in sheets and sluices against the lattice windows till it seemed as if the house would be washed into every moment. When the bridal party assembled in chapel, it seemed as if the roof of the little white-washed edifice would be blown away, so violently did it sway with the gale, which had increased to a hurricane.

Moyrah looked entranced with happiness, but as innocent and sweet as one of the white jessamine flowers Lenoir's scented hand crushed, as he leaned on the altar rails. He was covered with scent. Rimmel's shop, with the stoppers out of all the bottles, was nothing to him. His hair was brushed in every sort of extraordinary and fantastic shape; he had studied the fundamental laws of capillary attraction. He wore a white waistcoat, a scarlet geranium in his buttonhole, and a brilliant scarlet tie. He carried a pair of white kid gloves in his left hand. Moyrah thought he looked something too beautiful for words. He always smiled most benignly, when he looked at her, and showed his long rows of snow-white teeth to perfection. As he took his vows, there was a lambent flame in his eyes for an instant, a strange movement in those heavy lips, shaded, but not hidden by his black moustache.

When the feasting was over, and the jaunting car at the door, waiting to take them to the station, and Moyrah turned to say good-bye to her father, she broke down entirely. He pressed her to his heart, and showered fervent Irish blessings upon her. His poor, old, wrinkled face was covered with tears, and his now bent and rapidly aging form trembled. Moyrah flung her arms round his neck, and seemed as if she could not tear herself away, while her sobs unmanned all who heard them, except her husband. He helped her gracefully on to the car, and went off bowing and smiling, and making pretty speeches all round, especially to Mrs. Hegarty, who thought him perfectly charming, and her fortunate daughter greatly to be congratulated.

Through a mist of driving rain and blinding tears, Moyrah gazed at the old red walls of the house she so long had called her home, as they gradually disappeared in the distance.

Ah! Moyrah, gaze long! gaze well! Who knows when you may see that sight again, and when you do, with what feelings?

When they reached the station, there were more sobs, more tears, as farewell was said to Emmett. But it was only, as she told him when she gave him her parting kiss, for a very, very short time; soon she would see him again, and he would come to be hers, at Kintore farm.

CHAPTER XXII.

MEANTIME, Bridget, in London, had been making hay while the sun shone. Through the instrumentality of Lucas, she had contrived to get introduced to Lord Gargoyle. Lucas was acquainted, more or less intimately, with most of Sydney's relations.

From the moment he first took her down to dinner, she set her cap at him in a manner which, to those acquainted with women, caps and widowers, could leave but one view of the issue.

The old peer was a childless widower, and had been so for many years. He had quite made up his mind not to marry again. But alas! for the mind of man when made up contrary to the mind of woman!

Bridget used every art known to her designing and unholy sex, since long before the days of the Irish lady who went out on the lake in a row boat after the saint on his island. The poor amateur defendant was no match for the professional besieger. Bridget used her stiletto of attack like an accomplished duellist, while Lord Gargoyle was as awkward with his sword of defence as a Leicestershire deputy lieutenant at his first levee.

The end of it all was that either he proposed for her, or she proposed for him, it was never quite known which; society said the latter, and Bridget attained her object, and had the supreme satisfaction, the unspeakable triumph of writing herself to claim Sydney's congratulations on the announcement that in a short time she would be his aunt.

Certainly, she had succeeded; there were few things that could have caused him greater annoyance. But soon it seemed as if judgment overtook her. The very day after her engagement to Lord Gargoyle was publicly announced came the news, through one of the servants in Ireland, that Moyrah was married and gone.

Bridget was literally thunderstruck. She could not believe her ears. That Moyrah had been engaged, had married, and had gone away without telling her a word about it, seemed like a fairy tale. It could not be true. For the time being, herself and her own engagement, and all her prospective splendours, were completely forgotten. She sat down at once to write to Mrs. Hegarty, to beg to be informed of the whole matter; quite forgetting that Mrs. Hegarty, who had been educated in an earlier generation, could not read writing, though she could read print.

In Bridget's indignation and misery about the one friend she had, whom she really loved better than herself, she was ready to accuse Sydney of having connived at the whole plan, out of spite to her. Spite was a disposition she knew the alphabet of well. She attributed more actions in life to spite than to any other cause. A man who could call her a spitfire was capable of any crime. Spite must with him be the ruling motive of life.

Meantime, Sydney was fishing in Devonshire, totally unconscious alike of Moyrah's fate or of the infamies that were being laid to his charge by his fair aunt-elect.

He had not in the least forgotten Moyrah. His was not a nature which lightly forgot any deep feeling, much less the deepest it had ever experienced. He loved Moyrah with a noble and lasting love, such as is felt once only in a lifetime. But she had been engaged to Cormac, who was his protegé, and who had in his defenceless misery thrown himself on his mercy.

The path of duty had lain straight before him, and
he had followed it without a swerve. But that had
not altered the fact of his feeling for Moyrah as he had
never felt for anyone before. He could only say with
Angels,

> "Ever till now,
> When men were fond,
> I smiled, and wondered how."

But not now. He had placed her where a man only
places one woman once in his life. Yet he had decided
that if Cormac steadily continued to refuse to take a
farm, or to live anywhere out of jail, that he would
use all his influence in the county, and with the
governor of the jail, to get him raised to such a
position as might enable him to offer a wife a comfortable home.

Imagine, then, his feelings when, one morning, as he
was overhauling his tackle, assisted by a tankard of
cider and a short briarwood pipe, in the bay window
of a little primitive inn near the Exe, he was handed
a newspaper, which had been forwarded on from
Hambury Castle, and which had originally been
sent there by Cormac, with a red cross marking
a short account of Moyrah's marriage with Lenoir.
It was a local paper, published at irregular intervals
in the small town near which the Blue House was
situated.

Sydney sat as if stunned for full ten minutes, deadly
pale, and trembling all over. Then he rose, packed up
his things, started for Bristol; there took a packet which
was just starting for Ireland, and in twenty-nine hours
was walking into the Blue House.

Mr. and Mrs. Hegarty were very much pleased to see
him, but were surprised and somewhat awed at the
sternness of his countenance.

He said he knew his position did not entitle him to
make any such request, but yet he begged they would
afford him some explanation of Moyrah's conduct in

jilting Cormac, for whom he had done so much, and in marrying a man with whom she was so very slightly acquainted as Lenoir.

They at once told him of Cormac's letter, which they had seen with their own eyes, and of what he had said about Moyrah to Lenoir.

Sydney became crimson with fury. The whole scheme of trickery flashed before him; he saw it all in a glance. To the amazement of the old Hegartys, he let his head drop on his folded arms with a groan of despair. Too late, too late!

When he could steady his voice sufficiently to speak, he told them there was not a word of truth in what Lenoir had said. Cormac had been ill with the small-pox, and had not written for fear of conveying the infection. Sydney had been to see him several times, as he was not a bit afraid of infection, and had taken down with him one of the leading physicians in London; he had also procured for him two first-rate nurses from a celebrated nursing institute. He had sent him the most expensive fruits, jellies and wines. All that money could obtain had been lavished upon him, and he was making a very good recovery. The one thing, however, which he had looked forward to as the reward for his steady good conduct, and the compensation for all his troubles, was the prospect of being able to make Moyrah his wife as soon as he was completely convalescent. The cheerfulness and hope inspired by this consideration had aided his recovery more than any medicine, good nursing, or luxurious feeding.

When Mrs. Hegarty heard this, she burst into a wild storm of sobs and groans, threw her apron over her head, and rocked herself backwards and forwards on her wooden arm chair.

Hegarty's thin, lined face became ashen. He said nothing, but looked as he had done the day Emmett's stable was burnt.

Eileen shrieked, flung her arms over her head, then

threw the top half of her body across the kitchen table and sobbed.

"How you could believe him I can't conceive! Why you did not question him further; especially when you saw how much his own self-interest was involved in the whole story," exclaimed Sydney, in a voice of terrible anguish.

"Shure, we all thought him an iligint man, an' trustid him intirely," sobbed Mrs. Hegarty. "I'd have sworn to him from wan blue moon to another."

Sydney was now experiencing, for the first time, that strange and almost boundless credulity which, while it is one of the most beautiful characteristics, has also been one of the greatest curses, of the Irish race.

Soon, with that love of talking which distinguishes their sex and nation, Mrs. Hegarty and Eileen began to give some account of Lenoir's courtship, and let out plainly how much attached Moyrah was to him. Eileen incidentally described how one day, the day she had seen Moyrah lean back against the lime tree in the garden—she had been watching from the corner of the haystack in the yard, on which she had a habit of sitting—and how he had moved his hands up and down in the air in a strange and extraordinary manner in front of Moyrah's face.

"How? how?" exclaimed Sydney, eagerly, leaning forward.

Eileen imitated the mesmeric passes exactly.

"The devil!" muttered Sydney, under his breath; while the blue veins stood out on his forehead as if he was undergoing some sharp pain.

Eileen then continued to explain that Moyrah had a headache, and she said Lenoir had cured it.

"It would have been better if it had ached till it burst!" exclaimed Sydney, passionately.

The longer Sydney pondered over things the more plainly he saw that there was now nothing to be done, and the more utterly depressed and despairing did he become.

As he looked round at that house, and saw little things every instant which reminded him of Moyrah, he felt he could not bear it, so he rose and said he would go out and look at Emmett. Hegarty accompanied him.

Emmett turned his head as they entered his new stall, and Sydney noticed at once that his soft, expressive eyes were full of a wistful enquiring look, as if he was in momentary expectation of hearing a voice and feeling a hand he had been accustomed to, and which now, to his surprise, came no more.

From the very first moment Sydney had heard the story he felt certain Moyrah would never return.

"They tried to fire this stable agin last night," said Hegarty, with a strange flash from under his shaggy brows; " an' I've had a letter tellin' me they'll hamstring him the firrest toime he goes out in the field."

There and then Sydney offered three hundred pounds down for him.

After a very little consideration, and a short consultation with his better half, Hegarty accepted it; though he protested that it was infinitely too much, and seemed perfectly overcome at the munificence of the offer. Mrs. Hegarty, however, though overcome to a certain extent, was quite sufficiently master of herself to strongly recommend her spouse to close with the offer as quickly as possible.

Under the new threats of persecution, Emmett's life was not worth a week's purchase. Had Hegarty tried to sell him anywhere in the neighbourhood, he would not have got twenty-five pounds for him.

Now he decided to bank the three hundred pounds for Moyrah, in case the time should come when she had need of it; for Emmett was hers. Mrs. Hegarty said she would see about doing that.

So, when Sydney returned to Hambury Castle, which

he did in the course of a day or two, he took Emmett with him, and introduced him to his mother.

She could not see any such very great beauty in the horse. All her son's horses were handsome; and to her there appeared to be nothing extraordinary about this one to account for the feelings with which Sydney regarded it.

As to the grooms, they all declared their master had " gone perfectly daft about the new 'oss. E's a hin and hout of the stables a 'undred times a day, a looking at 'im, and a strokin' of 'im down."

It was an odd thing, but everyone who knew Sydney thought they understood him. " A very transparent character," they said.

How blinded acute observers sometimes are about character. There are times when we all exhibit a muddled vision on the subject. We set ourselves to argue and prove by certain flagrant outward appearances; and as a result, we fail to reason correctly, because we have built our argument upon a bundle of straw floating on the top of the water. As well might we deduce that the cooking in a certain house was good, because the outside of the house pleased our architectural taste. If our reasoning powers are weak, using argumentative forms will not make them stronger. And in judging of other people's characters, it sometimes seems as if everyone's reasoning powers were weak.

There is a certain superficial sparkle, it might almost be called effervescence, in some men's manner which leads the observer to conclude that the man is easily understood. " He is transparent;" they really mean, in other words, that he is all on the surface. You can see him as you sit on the bank, without taking the trouble to dive for his peculiar and cultured virtues. Now, this process of diving for peculiar and cultured virtues is what your modern observer of character expects and enjoys.

Men who draw you on, by dark hints and ambiguous inuendoes, to think that there are some marvellous pearls of sentiments down, down—far down—in the mud, which is all you see of their characters; some wondrous wounds which have caused these pearls to exist, and even write poetry on those pearls and those wounds. These are pets whose characters are worth modern psychological investigation; though one would imagine a wound must be well skinned over before we begin to beat a rhythm on it.

Well, this was not Sydney's sort of character. He had wounds, but no living being knew of them. He had a depth of feeling and a power of affection such as poets have written about, but not always experienced. Pearls there were, and abundance; but he did not go about like an auctioneer calling out their value. No human instruction, no school board, no competitive examination, could have organized the hearing ear of Mozart; and no psychological investigator could have pulled it to pieces so as to be able to tell other people how to get one like it.

Thus with Sydney's character, all the most minute probing into that feeling, and pulling out this, hanging up such a sentiment on the clothes line in the psychological investigator's darkened study, and putting such another under his microscope, would not have shown his real character, or even conveyed a glimmer of light with regard to it to an interested observer.

Sometimes, indeed, on rare occasions, when touched by another character, which had some answering strain in it to his own, the deeps were broken up. It is permitted to men's hand to strike the rock; but the fountain which sparkles out comes from waters which are above the heavens of even the greatest man's genius.

A few simple words from Moyrah had done more to bring to light the hidden depths within him than whole years of systematic investigation could have accomplished.

CHAPTER XXIII.

THE first week or two that Moyrah was in Paris she was too much bewildered by the novelty of everything round her to form any just idea of the city. She had never been in a large town of any sort before. Now, to find herself in one where she could not speak the language, or understand it; one where all the modes of life seemed different from anything she had ever heard or dreamt of, coupled with her thoughts of home, and of what her father and Eileen were suffering from her absence, sometimes almost upset her self-command. Alphonse was kindness and politeness itself, and every evening took her to a grand restaurant, where he gave her a first-rate dinner. But she had lost her appetite, and did so little justice to the food that he was sometimes quite irritated. After dinner they sat out on the pavement, under a red striped awning, at a little round table, while he smoked and sipped, sometimes absinthe, and sometimes vermouth, and amused himself by ridiculing and making comments on the passing crowd.

They generally went somewhere between the Place de l'Opera, and the Rue Montmatre; usually to the Boulevard Poissonnière. He bought a little newspaper, cocked his hat very much on one side of his head, stuck the polished toes of his boots straight out before him, and translated scraps of news or witty—he considered them witty—remarks for her edification.

One thing struck Moyrah very much, and that was the large proportion of women of the lower middle class in white caps, with, what she considered, rather bold faces; who hurried and bustled along, looking as if the whole government of the nation rested on their shoulders; while, for the most part, the men sauntered lazily about, with hands in pockets, cigar in mouth, and hat much on one side, as if indifferent, for the time being, to politics, business, or anything but the enjoyment of the present moment.

The way the foot passengers walked out in the middle of the street also surprised her; and at first she expected, every moment, to see them run over.

Anyone who has been much in France must have come to the conclusion that the deity that most of the men worship is god scrubbing brush, and the only place they worship him is on the outside of their heads. Their mode of worship consists merely in the most servile imitation, not in his application to their skins.

Now, Irishmen generally grow their hair rather long, so the change in the style of coiffure struck Moyrah forcibly.

For the first week or two, Alphonse stayed with her nearly all day, and took her out sight-seeing, and tried to amuse her in every possible way. But it was being with him that she really enjoyed, and not the sights they saw.

Still, the fish market at the Halles Centrales did interest her greatly; and though she could not understand what they said, she stood listening, with keen attention, to the sharp passages of arms between the *petites bourgeoises*, and their invariable *bonnes*, and the *dames de la Halle.* The frogs and the snails which were sold in large quantities also caused her considerable amazement. She soon yielded to Alphonse's desire that she should taste some. She was ill afterwards, and did not repeat the experiment.

Alphonse appeared to have an unlimited supply of money, and they took a drive in the Bois de Boulogne every afternoon, he smoking all the time; and when he could summon up self-sacrifice enough to take his cigar out of his mouth, making pretty speeches to her, or telling her the names and private histories of the occupants of the different little open Victorias they passed.

The fresh, balmy air, the rustle of the trees, the fashionable carriages, and the smart dresses—smart beyond anything she had ever dreamt of—pleased her greatly. But all was as nothing to the fact that she was in the society of the person whom she loved with an idolatrous worship, such as only a nature like hers was capable of feeling.

She had that unfortunate construction of mind, for a woman, which obliges its possessor to be always looking up to something. Such people, too often, end like the philosopher who, in staring at the stars, fell into the water. But this passion for looking up was the predominant passion of Moyrah's nature, and twined itself like ivy round every action and resolution of her mind. It was the dark line in the solar spectrum of an otherwise warm and sun-like heart. A heart so warm and tender to every phase of suffering in another, that like the sun, it shed warmth wherever its influence was felt.

But still, there was in it this stupid love for looking up. Like a raphide or crystalline substance in the cell of a leaf, this accumulated to such an extent, as she gave free vent to it, that it blocked up and impeded the healthy action of her nature. Like the granules, it became the ashes which the fire of life deposited as it burnt, and which, at last, turned traitor and extinguished the life it once had fed. To Moyrah it was actually rapture to sit at Lenoir's feet and worship him, as a Chinese might worship one of his hideous little brass images. Every word he uttered was as the laws of the Medes and Persians to her; everything he did, even to the swagger with which he walked into a café and ordered *déjeuner*, was perfect in her eyes.

But, insane as she was about Lenoir, and bewildered and dazzled by the complete and extraordinary change of her present life, she had not forgotten her father and Eileen, or her beloved home. She wrote straggling letters, wandering all over the paper, the words sometimes immense and sometimes tiny, to her father, with long postscripts to Eileen. She sent messages, with blots for kisses, to her mother and brothers. She bought bright silk ties for the boys, and brilliant neckerchiefs for Eileen, and greatly enjoyed making them up into parcels and sending them off, while she pictured the faces of those who would unpack them.

Her father's image was never absent from her heart. It always seemed to double her delight in sightseeing to realise how she would tell him of it when she went home. That she should go home again, and at no distant date, she never doubted for a moment. Alphonse had promised she should. They were both to go back after a month or two, taking with them stores of wonderful things from the Paris shops as presents to those loved ones at home. Yes, Moyrah's heart was one which could never forget, or ever cease to love, or diminish in love where once it had loved. Her apparently all-absorbing affection for Lenoir seemed only to have increased her love for those at home. "O how darlin' father would like to see this! How Eileen would enjoy this!" was constantly on her lips when sightseeing. There is an idea in Ireland that whenever you enter a church for the first time whatever you pray for is granted. Moyrah took full advantage of this idea to pray for her father at every altar in each church the first time she entered it. As she went into a new church almost every day, this occupied a considerable portion of her time. Alphonse always behaved with great devotion in the churches, which much pleased Moyrah. She rather wondered why one or two curés, who appeared to know him, stared so hard at him when they saw him kneeling, hat in hand, before some saint's shrine, with an air of cherub-like simplicity on his perfumed countenance. Certainly, they did stare; and once two curés stopped and whispered together, and looked so very hard at him that Moyrah thought they must be going to speak to him; but after a few minutes they passed on.

Moyrah got a good deal stared at during their drives in the Bois: indeed, wherever she went people looked at and looked after her. Paris, jaded and painted, was not accustomed to beauty such as hers. Lenoir gave her most ravishing bonnets, mantles and dresses, and in these, arranged by herself with considerable taste, her loveliness shone like a jewel in a fair setting. No wonder that gentlemen stood up in their carriages and looked back as she drove past. This pleased Lenoir, and he puffed away at his inevitable cigar with much complacency.

It did not please Moyrah, however, at all. She hated it, and always looked down, or looked quickly away, with a blush on her cheeks. Such unusual conduct in a Paris belle caused more surprise than her beauty.

The first evening that Lenoir took her to a theatre of his own selecting she was not altogether pleased. The heroine of the play exhibited her graceful form under the undulating lines of a gauzy costume, consisting of a *robe décolletée de gros de Naples*, with lace trimming, *à la Maradan*. Her external form, like that of Sappho, appeared to conceal a volcano; sometimes pouring forth from the crater of her lips the lava of hatred, envy, jealousy and murderous malice, and sometimes of affection, or, at least, what she was pleased emphatically to term affection. That affection, which follows love in this world, as shadows pursue substance.

Lenoir translated for Moyrah as the play proceeded; and many brilliant blushes he brought to her fair Irish cheeks as he did so. The heroine appeared to think that " light are the bonds of Cupid," the only chains which the captive rejoices to rivet for himself.

True, she had as difficult a part to play as a pilot in a South Sea hurricane. She had to steer through breakers of black eyes, which we all know even the craft of woman seldom weathers successfully.

Lenoir assured Moyrah that she was at that moment the great theatrical star of Paris. Be that as it might, her extraneous effect upon male meteorology appeared to be deplorable. She met adversity—for there was plenty of adversity in the play—in such a strange spirit that Moyrah was puzzled and fairly astounded. She did not give a hint that there could be anything elevating in sorrow. On the contrary; she appeared to carry in herself an antidote to whatever could ennoble human nature in external circumstances. In her mental construction she was like an armadillo, an animal peculiar to America, but which, no doubt, might be acclimatized in France, mostly covered with a scaly and hard shell formed of compartments resembling little paving stones.

At those sharp corners in the weary road of life, when the softness of a woman's nature should have come out, these paving stones were waved in the face of the audience. The whole play, in fact, appeared to be modelled on the pattern of a revolutionary administration, that is to say: Satan, a tyrant, who can bear no freedom, had united to form a constitution, or a plot, with passions which can bear no government. The magistrate of conscience was badly wanted to read the riot act; but he was far from the scene, and as yet, science has not discovered a telephone which can be securely run to him.

They had been lucky enough to get the two front places in a box, and Alphonse, who could be most charmingly polite, had got her a *petite banc*. He was very much interested in watching a fine straightforward-looking fair-haired young Englishman, who was sitting,

with a somewhat severe and proud expression on his
face, in the front of the theatre. At length, after
repeatedly directing Moyrah's attention to him, in order
that she might laugh at him, he exclaimed, " I declare,
every Englishman in France looks as if he was always
thinking of his grandfather, and saying, ' Je dois
quelque chose á la fierté du sang qu' il m'a transmis.' "
But his wife's thoughts were on the play and she
only looked at the Englishman to admire him for
a moment, and then her attention returned to the
stage.

Moyrah had never argued the question out, either
internally or externally, but she had a sort of floating
feeling in her mind that womanhood was like a
diamond. That when cut by affliction, it exhibited a
play of transparent colours in the sunbeam of a holy
love; and all true love, she thought, must be holy.
Now she saw that diamond torn from its golden setting
of family and faith, flung upon a muddy road and
crushed to useless bits. Finally, its light was extinguished, and it became all of that soot which, at the
outset, had only been one of its ingredients. At first,
it seemed as if the darkest blot upon the picture was
that the diamond threw itself there. But as the play
went on, a darker one showed out ; the diamond rejoiced
in its own obliteration ; and so the girl from the wild
west of Ireland sat and watched womanhood in the
hands of Communism, and required no physiological
investigator to amplify upon the subject before she
could draw her own conclusions.

Moyrah leaned back in her seat, and stared at the
heroine with an amazement which every moment
merged into deeper and deeper repulsion.

Lenoir had told her that her ideas on many subjects
were fossils, which the hammer of modern advancement
would soon break. There are hammers, and hammers.
This heroine was a very tolerable sort of a hammer.
She appeared to consider the commandments as useless

for a guide in ordinary life, as a general map of the
world to show the bridle-path from Cork to Kinsale.

Lenoir leaned his chin on his fist, and watched the
surprised and parted lips, the large wide open dark blue
eyes at his side, with a smile of great amusement.

"Sacré bleu!" he muttered, "un de ces enthousiastes
sublimes qu'il faut enfermer comme des fous, ou adorer
comme des dieux."

Moyrah was so absorbed in following the play that
she did not see he was looking at her; or, indeed, that
other people were looking at her. She was unconscious
of the opera glassses which were focussing her from
many parts of the house, unconscious of the bold
insolent stares of two prominent members of the
government, who were sitting near them.

But Lenoir saw them, and was pleased; it gratified
him that he should possess what others admired.
Moyrah's charming impulsive spontaneity, and beautiful
ingenuousness he did not consider of any value; but
that she should attract the marked attention of two
prominent members of the government made her worth
being civil to. As he watched her face, he said, with
a slightly satirical accent: "Je sais que tu as vécu
jusqu' ici comme la fille enchanteé dans son globe de
cristal," and then he laughed, while she continued to
remain absorbed in the stage. And yet, hardened as
he was, there were moments when unexpected aspects
of her character affected him to a slight degree; but
only moments. This was one, and as he continued to
look at her, he muttered: "Fraîche comme les fleurs,
belle comme les anges, vive comme un oiseau, gaie,
vermeille, élégante!" then he smiled as he thought of
her future, and added cynically, as if speaking to her:
"Vous avez fait la folie, il faut la boire!" and he
smiled again, and twirled up the end of his black
moustache, and pictured, in his fancy, what her face
would be when she learned the truth.

One of Lenoir's accomplishments was that of

designing ladies' dresses, and he turned most of his few honest pennies by providing costumes for some of the leading milliners.

Moyrah dressed in clothes he brought her, and it amused him to watch her face of delight as he laid a new pretty dress on the chair before her.

To-night she wore a dress of rich green silk, with the bodice of silk and velvet to match, exquisitely fitting; on her left breast a bunch of lilies of the valley, with the smaller leaves of that flower; a green bonnet, to match, with lilies of the valley in it. Set in such a framework, and her cheeks glowing with health and happiness, her beauty looked dazzling; her colouring was so brilliant and still so soft, that it puzzled many of the connoisseurs of beauty, whose opera glasses were fixed on her. In its richness, yet delicacy, it was scarcely that of the western countries, but more like a Circassian girl's.

The ladies who looked at her declared it could not be natural, but must be obtained by consummate art, though what art they would much have liked to know; for they had, most of them, tried all known arts without arriving at the same results.

The gentlemen, however, saw the colour come and go as Lenoir spoke to her every now and then, and directed her attention first to one thing and then to another; and the most ingenious prejudice could not produce an array of evidences sufficient to convince an independent male intellect that this was art.

"You do not, apparently, like the star?" he said.

"But does anybody?" she asked.

"Does anybody!" he echoed, in almost a mocking tone. "Why everyone who is a judge of acting says she is the most rising young actress of the day. Paris is not peculiar on that point, I can assure you," and he put up his opera glasses and inspected the object of their discussion minutely.

Moyrah said no more; but when next he looked at

ner he saw her long dark eyelashes sparkling in the glare of the gas lights, as if they had been fringed with diamonds.

When she saw him look at her, she returned his gaze with a gentle, confiding expression that would have touched most men. She shrank up closer to him, as if for protection from some external, invisible, evil principle in the air.

Had she but known, she might have said with Isabella,

" You bid me seek redemption of the devil."

But she did not know. He had been really kind to her; though she was the first person he ever had been kind to.

Why is there nothing to prevent the grafting together of two such dissimilar natures? Trees are endowed with many degrees of difficulty in being grafted together in order to prevent their becoming inarched in our forests. But two characters, without the slightest capacity for understanding each the depths of the other, without any systematic infinity in their modes of thought, suddenly, by some despotic authority, become engrafted together. We must all have seen it.

CHAPTER XXIV.

ONE evening they went to the Buttes Montmartre, and he showed her St. Cloud, and Meudon. "That," he said, with a sarcastic smile, pointing to Meudon, "was Rabelais' cure of souls."

"Rabelais; was he a praste?" she asked.

"He was a genius, which is, perhaps, more to the point; however, he *was* a Benedict monk originally."

"Holy man!" she ejaculated, devoutly. Lenoir all but burst into a shout of laughter, but just checked himself in time.

"I will lend you a translation of his books, some day, when you are less occupied with sightseeing, and have more time for reading. Come, let us get up to the north end, and see the Carrefour des Cascades; we shall get a capital view of the lower lake from there."

They left the carriage and its impatient stamping horse to wait for them; and entering the ferry boat, were conveyed to the long islands. Hearing them talking English, the man demanded three francs. For the first time, Moyrah saw a flash in Alphonse's eye, which startled her. He burst into some very rapidly spoken French, which the boatman apparently perfectly understood, and ended by flinging him, contemptuously, ten centimes, his legitimate fare. He took it, sullenly, and looked up out of the corners of his eyes with an unpleasant expression at the honeymooners as they walked off.

"Tell me your idea of a holy man, Moyrah."

She paused in thoughtful silence.

He waited several minutes. Then, as she did not reply, said : " Do I fulfil your idea of a holy man ? "

" Indade, and indade ye do ! " she said, fervently ; while she slipped her arm into his with a shy tenderness which was very touching.

He looked away, and knocked the ashes off his cigar. " That is right, my beauty ; wives ought always to think their husbands holy ; the church teaches that."

" Shure enough, an' it does," she said, earnestly.

" Most men are holy, I have observed, especially Frenchmen," and he raised his eyebrows, and puffed clouds of blue smoke round his mouth.

" Faith, I think they are," said Moyrah, thoughtfully.

" You have had a large experience, so you are a good judge," he said, with a patronizing smile. " Bien, ma belle ; tell me now what you would do if the church was suddenly to teach wives to disobey their husbands ? "

She looked puzzled. " But it couldn't do that same."

" Oh, hey ! I'm not so sure of that. Suppose, for a minute, that a husband wanted his wife to disobey some command of the church, what then ? "

She paused. Then said, low, " Shure, the church is the voice o' God." Her words took an awe-struck tone and trembled slightly ; while her eyes were down, and she looked almost as if she was saying her prayers.

" Mais, mon Dieu ! " and he kicked his foot impatiently. " But if you loved your husband, would it not be more natural to obey him, rather than an invisible power which is altogether removed from you ? "

Moyrah did not speak. There was a very pained look on her face.

" Amour tu perdis Troie ! " muttered Alphonse. " More natural I say. Would it not be more natural, Moyrah ? "

" God is our masthur," said that sweet low voice, every tone of which was like the dreamy organ music at St. Roch.

"Chassez le naturel, il revient au galop!" muttered Alphonse, sarcastically. "I thought your husband was your master."

Tears were in Moyrah's eyes now; her lip trembled, and a blush was on her cheeks.

"Come, come, ma petite, this will never do. Beautiful and charming as your tears are, I cannot allow them to be shed during the honeymoon."

Moyrah brushed her tears hastily away.

"Come," he said, good humouredly, "we will follow the route de Longchamps, and go to the lake of the skating club and see if I can have a shot or two at a pigeon."

"O me darlin' boy, ye wont be afthur doin' that, will ye?

"Doing what, shooting the pigeons? What is there to object to in that, eh? Fine sport, quite a l'Anglais."

"Ah! the power little crathures," she said, tenderly. "Shure, it 'ud kill me enthirely to see thim slaughthered."

"Well, I dont want to get rid of you just yet, ma jolie, so I'll give it up for to-day. Well, then, we'll go to Pré Catalan and drink 'Viva il Papa' instead."

On their way home, westward of the large lake, they went therefore to the restaurant, Pré Catalan, for some refreshment. Alphonse declared that, in order to counteract the pernicious effects of the Paris drinking water, it was necessary to have constant recourse to absinthe or vermouth. Moyrah having once tasted these liquids could not be induced to repeat the experiment. She now had a 'petit noir,' only that she did not touch the brandy which was supplied with it; but passed it over to Alphonse, who soon disposed of it. Her 'carafe frappée' she greatly enjoyed; indeed, the unlimited supply of iced water she was able to obtain, was the only gastronomic indulgence she appreciated in Paris.

Alphonse took a sup of coffee out of her cup, to see

what it was like he said. In returning the cup to its
saucer he spilt some on his knee; he took out his
handkerchief to wipe it off, and in doing so he pulled
out two cards, apparently from a pack of playing cards.
He glanced sharply up at Moyrah to see if she had
noticed them, while he returned them hastily to his
pocket. She had noticed them, but their appearance
made no impression on her, because it conveyed nothing
to her mind.

For a minute or two afterwards he seemed extremely
nervous, and looked round over his shoulder once or
twice, apparently to see if anyone had observed him
from the other little round tables. But no one had
been taking the slightest notice of him.

Just at that moment, however, a blasé, rakish-looking,
man stepped forward, and slapping his hand on Lenoir's
shoulder, said, in a strong American accent: " Why
you look in a state of collapsity. Flat broke, me
boy, eh ? "

Lenoir started to his feet, stared at him for an instant,
and then wrung his hand.

" So you have arrived; heard you were coming next
week. News, eh ? " The stranger winked one eye
towards Moyrah, as much as to say he could not speak
in her presence.

Lenoir nodded his head. Approaching Moyrah he
said : " My dear, I want to speak to this gentleman; I
shall not be away more than two or three minutes.
Will you wait here for me ? "

She looked not altogether satisfied at being left alone,
surrounded by strange people who stared at her. Her
face was charged with a meaning and a pathos greater
than the occasion seemed to require. She had not liked
the look of the man who had come up to speak to
Alphonse at all. Though simple and innocent, in
consequence of her bringing up, she had, where not
blinded by love, a sharpness of intuition which compensated for the want of more elaborate intellectual training.

Besides, the moment Alphonse was gone, the gentlemen who were sitting at the tables near her began to stare more disagreeably than before. In the village at home no one had stared at her; everyone knew who she was, and beyond a friendly nod and a pious wish or blessing, no one took any notice of her.

In the meantime, Lenoir linked his arm in that of his new found friend, and was soon deep in confabulation. He called him Bitty Tit.

"You see," said Lenoir, "I'm on the look out for that fire-Zouave; he's at the bottom of all the mischief; you know who I mean? The other day I could have sworn I saw him just as I was going into the Morgue, but when I came up close, I saw it was his double."

"His tail must be put out of curl," said Bitty Tit. "You see, I'm on the fence just now."

"I see you are, I saw it at once. What the deuce is the meaning of that?"

"Wull, ye see—wull—I'll explain presently, I've got other fish to fry just now."

"Sacré bleu! you and your fish," said Lenoir, contemptuously. "What's the London press saying?"

"Howling and squeaking, as usual, because of something Jackety said in his election speech."

"Hem!" said Lenoir, biting his under lip.

"Hormy's come the gum game over me, but I guess I'll be quits with him yet."

"How? where?"

"Why, last few days I was in Dublin he worrited like blazes. Wull, ses I, I hav'n't bin here such a despud while without having larnt my bisnis; and farzino (a contraction of far as I know), I'll do it."

He twirled his short pointed beard. "I calculate he was always too full of notions to be any good to us."

"Bien, oui," said Alphonse, thoughtfully.

"Wull, I told him we must have another go at funkyfying the Saxon; dollars beginning to run short. On that, he shied off like a skittish mare; not set eyes on him since. Trotty swears he's suttin he'll run athwart our hawse yet."

" He'd better. You've no tin, then ? "

" Devil a rap."

" Hum ! " Lenoir fumbled in the inside pocket of his coat, took out a pocket-book, opened it, and after turning over a few papers, selected a note, which he handed to Bitty Tit. He examined it ; nodded, and put it into his pocket. His eyes glistened. " Hum, I can cut didoes with that."

Bitty Tit lived in suspense. He was not sure from day to day whether he would have money enough to cut a dash upon—which was what he really enjoyed—or whether he would have to crawl about in some miserable back purlieus of whatever large town he was temporarily honouring by his presence. He was like the sloth, which moves suspended, sleeps, eats suspended, underneath the branches of trees, in fact, passes his life in suspense, like a young attaché distantly related to an ambassador. At this moment Bitty Tit was gratified and satisfied. " I'm regular out of whack now," he said, looking down at his travel-soiled clothes. " I'll go and get a fixin' up, I guess." He paused. " What are you going to do this evening? I saw the cards. Been making a good thing lately ? "

Lenoir shook his head. " I want to ' have at ' the Préfecture ; plenty of capitalists on the hooks, if I can get the authorisation of a new club," he said.

" Old ones played out ? "

" Just about."

" Pidoux is the new croupier," continued Alphonse, twirling his moustache, " la gloire n'est jamais où la vertu n'est pas," he added, with keen enjoyment in his tone. " In half an hour we shall have a hundred louis in the cagnotte."

Bitty Tit rubbed his hand gleefully.

This drew Lenoir's notice to fingers not as much at home with soap as with other people's money.

" When other trades fail, I advise you to qualify as an agent for Pears' soap," he exclaimed, contemptuously, while he eyed his own white and rather effeminate hands.

An angry look came into Bitty Tit's eyes.

Just then Lenoir heard a rustling, and looking round, saw Moyrah approaching. He hastily made an appointment with Bitty Tit, whom he peremptorily dismissed, and then turned to receive his wife with a patronising smile.

" Who was that boy?" she asked, with an anxious look in her face, as she watched Bitty Tit slouching off in the distance.

" No one in particular," replied Alphonse, raising his eyebrows in a nonchalant manner; " a dilettante enquirer after religious truth," he added.

" Do ye know, I think I've sane him before," she said, with a puzzled expression, as if trying to recall something to her memory. " Yes, faith; I remimbur now, enthirely!" she exclaimed. " He was spakin'—as loud as a thrumpet—at that big matin' av Harvest Bugs at Clonagarry, an' I axed Cormac who was he, an' he tould me, ses he, he's an ' American boss ' ses he, for thim's the very wurruds he used."

" O, you must be mistaken, mon enfant, he's never been in Ireland in his life. Bien! have you finished your coffee? We must be getting home." He assumed a very off-hand manner, and talked incessantly on other subjects all the way back to the flat in the noisy, dusty street for which Moyrah had exchanged the Blue House. Whenever she showed the slightest sign of recurring to the subject, he turned the conversation with a determination of manner which at last made her see that it was hopeless to try to get anything out of him about it.

That evening, for the first time since they had been married, Alphonse told her he must go out and leave her alone, as he had a business appointment of

importance. Her face fell very much, and for a
moment she was inclined to cry.

"Come! come!" he said, pleasantly, "I'll make up
to you for it by taking you to the theatre to-morrow
evening. There, there now, I promise you."

But tears seemed determined to come into her eyes,
and her forehead to pucker up, preparatory, apparently,
to a good cry.

"Ah! bah," he muttered, impatiently. "Regardez! I
bought you a nice little ring in the Palais Royal a while
ago. I meant to give it to you to-morrow, but I think
it will console you to have it now, maybe. Here is the
key of my dressing-table drawer; you will find it in the
left-hand corner, lying right on the top. Don't disturb
any of the papers."

He unbuttoned a thin, light grey overcoat he wore,
when Moyrah saw, to her astonishment, that he was in
full evening dress, with white waistcoat, and a white
gardenia in his buttonhole, a shirt front covered with
highly starched frills and diamond studs. He saw her
look of surprise, as he took a small key out of his waistcoat pocket and handed it to her. Hastily buttoning
up his grey coat, he said: "I'm to meet an old married
lady of some importance in the political world, and she
is very particular about one's get up."

Moyrah said nothing; and in another minute he was
gone.

CHAPTER XXV.

OUR heroine went to mass every morning, sometimes very early, and heard two or three massses. Alphonse did not accompany her. He said he had had an illness about six months ago, and that the doctor had forbidden him, at the risk of his life, to go out before breakfast, while the air was raw and cold.

The churches were, indeed, a source of unfailing delight and amazement to Moyrah. Accustomed to the little simple erection, with yellow-washed walls and slate floor, of her own village, she had no idea what the functions of her religion could be, when performed in such a building as the Madeleine. The pomp and splendour impressed her so much, that her whole face would change, and Alphonse would watch her with amused interest. One evening he took her to a grand benediction at Notre Dame. The rare organ music reached the furthest corner of the immense church. Wreaths of incense, coloured by the mosaic lights from the windows, curled round the pillars, as high aspirations cling round those noble natures which are the true pillars of the Christian church. High over the altar, brilliant with a hundred lights, rang the voices of the choristers, and penetrated by their distinct articulation the remotest corners of the church.

Moyrah knew so little of architecture that she did not even know there was such a thing; but yet, for all that, the delicacy of the stone tracery, the symmetry of proportion, and the exquisite designs of the rose windows, and the lights thrown by the splendid old glass in them, all acted upon her inborn sense of art. She liked trying to count the small pillars in the triforium, but she always grew puzzled and bewildered before she had reached seventy-three. Art is the witness of what really exists behind the theatre of this world, and as such, it speaks most strongly to those natures which are the least tied in to the scene-shifting of this life; and Irish natures, as a rule, though much influenced by what they see, are not enslaved to it, but live a good bit in the invisible world. So it was with Moyrah. As she knelt there, in the moment of her highest earthly happiness, a feeling came over her which told her that for her, too, an hour would come when this life, which was coursing so freshly and strongly through her, which seemed so to surround and envelope her now, would be but a speck on the ocean of another. This life, which held her in so vigorous a grasp now, would be weakly, letting her fall from it into the great "for ever." The shadow of eternity came over her, like the shadow of a gigantic mountain towering over a tunnel which a train is entering. All the little sanctities of her past life stood out as distinctly as each little one of the wild flowers in Doré's picture of the prairie; and she let this feeling have its sway.

With Moyrah, when she went into a church, her first idea was not to criticise, or even admire, but to pray in it. La Chapelle Expiatoire interested her greatly. Alphonse told her the history of Marie Antoinette. At the conclusion of it she said, meditatively: "Faith, it seems to me all the best wimin perishid on the scaffold."

"Not such a bad place, after all," said Lenoir; adding low, "for one's enemies."

She was much interested by the portrait of Madame Elizabeth as religion; and in the group by Bosio, where the angel is saying to Louis XVI, "Fils de St. Louis montez au ciel," Alphonse translated for her. She was a long time looking at this. " Blessed wurruds," she muttered to herself. " Rise to hivin. The Lorrud grant it!" and she crossed herself devoutly.

" But if you have found one heaven, which you say you have since you loved me, what should you wish to rise to another heaven for? Surely, one heaven is enough for one person at a time," said Lenoir, looking at her enquiringly. It was a sort of half patronizing, half good humoured, slightly contemptuous, and slightly cynical look he turned upon her on these occasions. She thought it all kindness, for her eyes were blinded, and she saw nothing of the other ingredients.

Like some few of his countrymen, Alphonse was vain. He could never stir hand or foot without making it clear he was thinking of himself, and laying little traps for approbation. In his conversation there was always a reference to himself, as in the above remark.

Moyrah looked perplexed and pained. The old guardian who was showing them over the ' chapelle,' had, from the first, seemed greatly pleased with Moyrah's devotion, and at the way she crossed herself, and knelt at all the most sacred spots. He saw, though he did not understand the words, that Lenoir had said something which pained her. He looked at Lenoir. As he looked more and more intently, his face changed, a look of strong suspicion and of recognition came over him. Lenoir did not see it; he was admiring the reflection of his own head and face in a piece of highly polished, very dark marble. But Moyrah saw it, and it puzzled and rather alarmed her. Did the guardian know Alphonse? If so, why did he not speak to him. If he did not know him, why did he look at him like that?"

" Bien, mon enfant, you have not answered my question," said Lenoir, arranging his neck-tie, and running his finger through his hair as he continued to admire himself in the marble.

Moyrah saw the guardian looking more and more suspiciously at him. "Come on, Alphonse," she said in a whisper, giving a little pull to his coat.

He looked round quickly, and caught the guardian's eye. He had not noticed him at all before. "Come, we've had enough of this gloomy place," he said, hurriedly. He fumbled in his trouser pocket for a minute, drew out a franc and handed it to the guardian.

He pulled himself up to his full height, made a short bow, and declined it.

Lenoir's face got crimson. He left the church as fast as possible. Once safe out in the open his usual nonchalant manner returned to him.

"Well, how did you like that, ma petite?"

"Faith, thin, I liked it greatly," she answered, with fervour. "Power crathure; to think av thim cuttin' aff her head, an' she a quane."

"But why is it worse for a queen to have her head cut off than for anyone else?"

"'Feare God, honour the king.' Sure, I read that out av the Douay manny a time."

"Yes, I should think it's very probable the two go together," he said. For the hundredth time Moyrah failed to detect the satire in his tone. "But that's no answer to my objection. Why is all this fuss to be made when a queen loses her head? A chapel built, and everyone pitying her. Phaugh! the sooner it's pulled down the better. Allons, let us go to the Porte St. Martin."

They took an omnibus to the Place de la Republique. After they got out he lighted his cigar, and they walked along in the sunshine.

"I have an ambition to show you the place where the Communists defended the barricade against the government in 1871. Some of the grandest deeds of the Commune were done just about here.

Moyrah shuddered. She had heard her father talking about the French Communists.

He looked at her with his patronising smile. "I

suppose you think I ought to have but one ambition, 'un soupir, un regard, un mot de votre bouche, voila l'ambition d'un cœur comme le mien, eh?

Poor Moyrah looked puzzled.

"Ah! I forgot. You must really try to pick up a little French." He marched up to a particular point on the road and put the polished toe of his boot on it.

" Here, observe. This is where the principal barricade was. Here they loaded and re-loaded their guns, and mowed the people down like rats."

Again Moyrah shuddered visibly. She had a horror of bloodshed; even legitimate war she looked upon as something too terrible to think about. She turned away and began to look at the buildings.

Lenoir, holding his cigar in his fingers, said, not loud enough for her to hear: " Vive les Communes de France, fédérées avec celles de Paris. They have blotted out God." A most extraordinary expression came over his face, as proudly folding his arms he walked up and down on the spot where the greatest excesses of the Commune were committed. As he looked towards Moyrah, he could see only a part of her side face, just the oval of her cheek, which was flushed and had a tear on it.

" Aye, " he muttered, while there came into his eyes a gleam almost diabolical in its sneering scorn, a gleam which Moyrah had never seen. " Aye, my fine Irish- woman; and we will teach your bigoted sots of countrymen to do the same." He looked after her with a leer, which is was indeed well she did not see. " Indeed!" and he took another turn. " Did I not walk on the spot where Irish tyrants were executed, as I am doing on this? Both spots consecrated to the sacred cause of liberty. Vive la République Uni- verselle!" He took another turn. " Have I not got a bit of earth from it in my pocket?" He put his first finger into his waistcoat pocket and pulled out a bit of silver paper, unwrapped it, and looked with hungry eyes at a few grains of earth in it. After he put them back into his pocket, he passed his hand round his waist until it touched the hilt of a dagger which he wore concealed there. As it did so a new expression came into his face. He muttered between his teeth: "With that we will cut down the three heads of the serpent, the crown, the altar, and the family."

That strange frenzy of cruelty which comes over some natures at certain undefined times, without rhyme or reason, and carries them forward like a flood, was strong upon him. Adept at deception, master of the art of looking the opposite of what he felt as he was, he could not wholly change his face when he saw Moyrah walking towards him.

She gave a slight start as she looked at him. "Ah, shure, me darlin' boy, ye're ailin'" she said, anxiously, as she observed his whitened cheeks, and the almost livid look which passion had left round his mouth.

Fearing he had betrayed himself he put on a forced smile. As she slipped her arm tenderly into his, he patted her hand and said, kindly: "On est aisément dupé par ce qu' on aime," and he looked at her and laughed.

"Shure I'm muddled about it," she said, looking puzzled at the French.

"One is easily humbugged by those one loves," he translated, softly. He looked down into her face with one of those would-be arch smiles which to her were so bewitching.

"Allons! We will go to the Buttes Chaumont."

He called a fiacre and off they set. Arrived at the park, he threw away the strong black cigar which had consoled him on his way there, and grew rather excited as he began to act as showman to her.

"This was once a chalk pit," he said. "It was used as the spot where the classes revenged themselves on the masses, and called it 'The Place of Execution.'"

She shuddered.

"The gibbet was made of stone pillars joined by

beams, from which hung chains, and these hanged those who would now be at the head of the government." A gleam came into his eyes.

A look of horror came over Moyrah's face. She crossed herself. He saw her out of the sides of his eyes, and made a movement with his lips as if he was spitting on the cross she had made in the air. She did not see this. He was in a dangerously aggressive mood that day; but, fortunately, she was in an equally trusting and unsuspicious one.

"Here were spoken those memorable words, 'the body of a dead enemy always smells sweet.'"

He ran his finger up and down over the bit of silver paper with the earth in it in his waistcoat pocket, as he muttered, "Parbleu! but it does!"

Horrified out of the power of speech, Moyrah turned and walked away towards where the stone quarries have been turned into rock-work, with a little lake in their middle. For the first time since she had seen Alphonse she was anxious to get away from him, to hear no more words just at present from his lips. But he followed her, and made her go across the suspension bridge to the island in the middle of the lake and up to the Belvedere.

She was fairly enchanted with the view, and forgot the disagreeable impression of the last few minutes, as her eyes roamed over the countless spires of Paris, the heights of Montmartre, and the cemetery of Père La Chaise. It was an exceptionally clear day, and he pointed out the large flat plain and straggling town of St. Denis, and afterwards St. Cloud and St. Germain.

"Shure, thim's three av the blessid I nivir heered tell on before," she said, looking devout and interested. "Saint Denis; 'tis afthur him, no doubt, Denis O'Flagharty's called. The poor bhoy! I wondhur how is he now." and her thoughts wandered back to an old admirer, a young farmer, who, on finding his suit unfavourably received, had offered his services to Her Majesty in a cavalry regiment.

"And who was Denis Flagharty, I'd like to know?" he said, in a bantering tone, "some deadly rival of mine, like the saintly Cormac?"

The hot blood flew into Moyrah's face. For the first time, he saw the flash of the Celtic fire in her eye; this amused and pleased him. He liked "getting a rise" out of people immensely; it was one way of making others suffer, an amusement which afforded him keener gratification than a cigar and absinthe; in fact, he never obtained solid satisfaction out of any enjoyment, unless it was purchased at the expense of pain to some-one else.

"What's the matter, Moyrah? Look up at me," he said, putting his hand on her arm.

She turned away her head.

"Can't you look round?" he said, with the first touch of roughness she had ever heard from him, "I am afraid you've got a crick in your neck from thinking so much about the people who were hung, eh?"

Moyrah did look round, and he was satisfied that he had inflicted sharp pain upon her. Relieved by this certainty, he became more good humoured.

"Why should you grieve over so many people having died in an exalted position?" he said, satirically. "A drop too much is not so very uncommon amongst your countrymen, I should have thought." He gave a little whistle.

Moyrah said nothing; her feelings were deep and keen, and a wound with her did not heal rapidly.

Finding that, apparently, Moyrah took no more interest in the view or in the park, he suggested a pilgrimage to the grave of Théophile Gauthier, who, he announced, had been a friend of his, and whose poems he said he would lend her when they went home.

Moyrah had never heard of him. As they drove

along towards the cemetery of Montmartre, Moyrah gradually softened, and recovered her usual bright temper, under the influence of Lenoir's smiles; for such was his curious disposition that, strange as it may appear, he liked to make up by being extra agreeable, after any time when he had been extra unkind to any-one. Not that his agreeability usually lasted long, or was more than palpably skin deep.

"When I introduce you to my friends, you must try and talk more, ma belle; it is not 'pschutt' to be glumpy."

"Shut? What's that, now?" and she looked puzzled.

"It's the new word for 'chic.'"

She evidently was still unenlightened. He looked at her, and then burst into a loud laugh. She coloured and turned her head away; she appeared the reverse of amused.

"Well, you English call it 'good form,'" he said, more pleasantly, "I should like you to be a pschutteuse, that is a young woman 'tres á la mode,'" and he looked into her face with a smile, "plenty of spirit and ' go ' about you. You must not be a veritable fille de marbre," and a curious gleam came into the corner of his eyes.

"Feel day marbur?" and she looked pleased at her skill in repeating the French, "what's that now, Alphonse?"

He laughed again in a tone which jarred on her like the old-fashioned drag at home, under the wheel going over stones. "It means a girl so cold and stiff and sulky that people say she is made of marble." He watched her closely to see how she would take it.

She returned his gaze with one of those peculiar bright beamy looks which were especially characteristic of her. "It's a very quare sort av marble I'm made av."

He laughed heartily, and seemed much pleased her

good humour had returned. “ Belleek pottery, more likely,” he added, “ eh ? ”

He took her home by the Jockey Club, and they feasted their eyes for some time on the diamonds at Otterbourg’s. He guessed their different prices, and wished aloud several times that they were his. He parted his moustache down the middle with his finger and thumb, and licked his lips as he looked at them.

“ I ought to have those,” he muttered, so low, she only caught a word here and there, “ who has them ? Who, but those cursed rastagoères, who have no right here at all.”

When they reached their rooms, he threw off his coat, kicked off his boots, put his feet on the table, lounged in an easy chair, smoked and began to read a newspaper which had arrived for him by post during his absence.

Moyrah laughingly leaned over the back of his chair, and tried to decipher the heading of the paper.

“ La rec—re—volte, la revolte ! ” she exclaimed, “ there, I’m gettin’ an wid me French.”

“ More than you are with your English,” he muttered, puffing away, without looking round.

Proud of her progress, she proceeded to attack the paragraph on which his eyes were fixed.

“ Anar—chiste, a—morphiste. What a long name ! What is it, Alphonse ? ”

“ It’s a new religious order, which is just being established,” he said, gravely.

She crossed herself devoutly.

“ Praise the Lorrud for that,” she exclaimed, with touching fervour.

“ It’s just the order for doing that,” he replied, complacently sucking his cigar. “ I do not see my way to joining the order as yet ; I am a rational anarchist, that answers to the third order of St. Francis.”

“ Ah ! that’s the order I love,” she exclaimed,

eagerly. " Will there be a scapular wid this new order ? "

" Why, of course ! Cieux et terre ! an order without a scapular ! It will be made of white satin, embroidered with tiny little gold bombshells. Whenever you put it on, it will transport you suddenly wherever you want to go. I should think when females put it on it will always be to a heavenly ball. La danse est un remède pour la spleen, and I'm sure they want a remedy for it badly."

" O, Alphonse ! ye are takin' yer fun aff me."

" No, my darling; I never would do that," he.said, pleasantly.

She smiled a laughing, joyous smile, while she twisted her finger round one after the other of his black curls, drew them out to full length, and then let them fall back on his head again, while she continued to lean over the back of his chair.

" Mon mari," she said. She had mastered that word, and also " oui," which she thought a most sensible, English-sounding word—a word particularly captivating to bridal ears.

" Votre mari ! Bien, oui !" responded Lenoir, with a peculiar intonation.

" I like ' oui,' " she said. " There's no wurrud which sounds so nice to me now as ' we.' I do like the French people for sayin' it so aften."

" Ah, yes. You see, we are such a thoroughly domestic nation that we cannot help repeating we, we, we incessantly."

She smiled pleasantly, and tickled the top of his forehead with one of his curls.

" Now, in England you use the word ' we ' to define any number of persons, but in French we employ it only for young married couples; comprenez bien cette distinction ?"

" But it means ' yes,' and not ' we,' " she answered, laughing, and she pulled down one of his curls until it tickled the corner of his eye. "Only I like the sound, Alphonse; don't ye see, 'tis the sound I like, because it makes me be thinkin' av ye an' me."

"A charming subject for contemplation. You'll have to brush my hair, my young lady, if you pull it about in that fashion."

"Bien, oui," she said, imitating Alphonse's tone exactly.

She was busy tying two locks of his hair. "I'm makin' a thrue lover's knot," she announced.

"And in the meantime I am supposed not to turn a hair, but to read my paper in perfect contentment."

CHAPTER XXVI.

OME weeks have passed since the last chapter.
Lenoir continued kind, in a certain sort of
way, to Moyrah, when he was with her, but he
was now out a great deal. He said he was tremendously busy just now, but would soon be able to devote
more time to her. So she was very much alone in the
gaudy, but somewhat tawdry, little apartment which he
had taken for her.

It had, indeed, become to her like Monsieur Gustave
Guillaumet's famous picture, "A Habitation Saha-
rienne." Sometimes she ventured out alone for a little
stroll on the boulevards, and brushed shoulders with
the *bourgeoisie*, hated by Lenoir; but she was always
veiled, so that but little fresh air could get down her
mouth. The Avenue du Bois de Boulogne and the
Allée des Acacias were the ones she liked the best.
Sometimes she got as far as the Champs Elysées, but
not often. When strolling in the Allée des Acacias,
one sunny day, she met Lenoir, very much muffled up,
and walking with two strange looking men, also muffled
so as to be absolutely disguised.

Lenoir stopped, took off his hat, made a circle with
it in the air, then brought its top into contact with the
pavement, while he bent double before her. Then he
burst out laughing.

"You should wrap yourself up more, ma belle," he
said; "you will get fluxions de poitrine. Remember,
you are not a brasserie nymph!" and again he laughed
as, with a nod, he looked at his two companions. He

was always greatly amused at anything satirical he said
of other people. Then, seeing the hot blood fly to her
cheek, and the flash in her eye, he said, in his most
engaging manner, while he took her hand and spoke
low, " I am very busy just now, but I will come home
soon," and, with as kind a smile on his handsome face
as he was capable of assuming, he turned away.

Moyrah had, by dint of constantly poring over dic-
tionaries and grammars, in union with a quick ear,
sufficiently mastered French to understand much of
what was said in ordinary conversation ; and she caught
the remarks his companions made, and comprehended
them too well for her peace of mind.

Soon after she parted from Lenoir this day she came
across a man speaking to a small crowd in one of the
bye streets. He was apparently delivering a lecture on
politics. Moyrah recognized him at once as an intimate
acquaintance of Lenoir's. She, therefore, stopped a
moment to hear what he was saying, though she did
not much like the look of the men who were standing
round. Their faces were inflamed with alcohol; and
so, indeed, was that of the speaker. Truly, it is the
only element in which the principles he was uttering
freely dissolve. His words poured out like polygalic
acid—an acid constituting the peculiar principle of the
rattlesnake root; it dissolves abundantly in boiling
alcohol, but is insoluble in pure ether and the fixed oils.
So it was with the principles Moyrah heard then for the
first time in her life. They could not dissolve in her
heart, so full of the oil of human kindness and of the
pure ether of Irish innocence. As she listened, her face
became inflamed too, but with a shame and horror
which seemed to make her blood run like fire in her
veins. Blasphemy was heaped upon blasphemy, ribald
jest on ribald jest. Fierce defiance was hurled at all
that is above the lowest depths in the lowest human
heart. Socialism, plain, naked, and unclothed with the
sophisms invented to mystify refined minds—minds *en*

grande toilette—was held up before her eyes. Socialism as it really is, not as it appears coloured to the taste of the cultivated dabblers in intellectual licence of the nineteenth century.

Socialism, which she was too horrified to have the coolness to see, was merely an abnormally great inflation of the always inflated puff-ball of human vanity, nowhere so inflated, at all times, as in France. French Socialism, which may be called physalia, which is an animal swimming on the sea in *calm* weather, resembling an extremely large oblong bladder, and stinging and burning all it touches. This sort of orators usually prefer calm weather; in a time of war, they disappear in a mysterious manner. "Just behind the battle mother," that sort of thing.

And so he squalled on and on, in a voice like the hippopotamus, at the Zoo., when his keeper pokes him, while he balanced himself on tip-toe on half an empty barrel, so as to get a bird's-eye view of his audience.

And the crowd listened with that peculiar mixture of sudden, impetuous attention, followed instantly by a self-conscious inattention, which marks a French street mob, they stare round as much as to say, "what did I look like when I was attending; and now, what do I look like when I'm not attending." The men in their greasy, blue, cotton blouses, with their short, cropped hair, and hats on the sides of their heads, pouted their moustached lips, and puffed out their bronzed cheeks, and looked as if they, sometimes, a great deal more than agreed with him, and at others, thought him a confounded fool. They shrugged shoulders already high enough, said "Ciel!" and puffed clouds of smoke from their old brûle-gueules. The soubrettes, with their white, frilly caps, and baskets on their arms, looked about to see if there was any chance of getting a chat with their male friends in the crowd, and, if there was not, passed on, humming a selection of operatic airs.

The way in which he spoke of the religious aspects of modern social life puzzled and dazed her. She simply could not understand him. How could she, reared in the heart of a small and unconventional Irish community, under the care of pious Irish parents, and the guidance of a pious Irish priest, and surrounded on all sides by the unquestioning devotion of Irish peasants, understand a man who used his temptations as stirrups for blasphemy, rather than spurs to faith, who made himself the "generalissimo" of this world and the world to come; and, having proceeded to "reckon up" his Creator, declared the results of the sum to be eminently unsatisfactory?

Some of the listeners near Moyrah said, "He is a great man; a great man!"

"A great man!" she repeated to herself, in puzzled amazement.

Poor Moyrah! She had yet to learn that some men, and out of France, too, who persistently stand with their backs to the sun, think themselves great men because they cast great shadows across life. Moyrah was not well read enough in history to see that he was only an *avant courier*; a sort of first gust of one of those little temporary hurricanes of insubordination which, from time to time, sweep over different parts of the globe.

If we could only find it out, surely there must be some law which governs these little "we won't have anything over us" whirlwinds, which make such a commotion every now and then in the moral atmosphere. This law once discovered, quiet folks' facilities of protection would be pleasantly increased.

The law which governs storms in the physical world is beginning to be clearly understood. For instance, it was stated in the London *Globe* newspaper, of June 16, 1881, by Mr. Jinnan, that the Tay Bridge storm was again due on December 20, 1886, (five and a half years in advance) and it came true to its date. Where a law exists, time is no hindrance to forecasting. May it not be possible some such law governs the social atmosphere?   What a consolation to statesmen the discovery and the accurate explanation of such a law would be.

Once, when this little French advance gust was going to utter an atrocious sentiment, so vile that it seemed extraordinary it did not paralyse the lips which framed it, the orator did pause for an instant, and asked, " Est-ce disable? " then shouted, " Ici tout se dit! " and went on, with the usual modern medley of the arrogance of the persecutor, and the despair of the sceptic, served up in the strongest acids of Parisian scum slang, to say things which made Moyrah's heart stand still with horror.   The grisettes in the crowd nodded at him, laughed and applauded.

Moyrah looked at them, and wondered if they were really women, or if in foreign countries there was another sex. She had seen so many strange things since she came abroad that it would scarcely have surprised her to find there was.

By this time, the orator had worked himself up to boiling point. He threw his arms about like flails in a granary, over his head, behind him, in front of him, shrieked, foamed at the mouth, and flung denunciations in such a manner, that some came dangerously near to fitting themselves into comfortable caps on to the listeners' heads.

One sensible looking, middle-aged woman, with a basket on her arm, did turn away with what appeared to be disgust, but might not have been, for the French have so many outside signs for what is going on in their insides that a stranger gets puzzled. However, as she passed her, Moyrah heard her mutter, " Il est dans un état horrible, hâve, livide et presque fou! " It was, then, his appearance, and not his politics, which turned the balance against the speaker in this Gallic mind.

Suddenly, Moyrah started at hearing English spoken close to her.

" He's made a fizzle, and almost a flunk, of it," said Bitty Tit, in a loose shovel hat, turning, with a laugh, and sauntering away with his hands in his pockets.

Just as the little gust was making his *coup d'état*—giving a final rattle to the windows in the house of the state—a gendàrme was seen round the corner.

" Je m'en vais d'ici," concluded the valiant Cicero, and immediately disappeared amidst the laughter and jeers and cheers of the crowd.

As Moyrah reflected on his speech, she muttered, " And this from a friend of Alphonse's!" Her lips trembled, and she seemed dazed for an instant. " He cannot know what he is like!" she thought. " He has been deceived in him! Alphonse is truly religious; he would be horrified! But I will tell him," and she turned and hurried away.

She felt humiliated at the reflection that a man who could utter such sentiments had ever been, for a short time even, a friend of her husband's. Sentiments which made her tremble when she compared them with all that lay near her own deepest and most sacred feelings. She, fortunately, did not even guess at the meaning of much which had passed his lips.

When Alphonse came home to supper, she told him what she had heard—at least some of what she had heard, for not for hundreds of pounds would she have polluted her lips with a great part of it. She told him also who the speaker was, and expected him to look amazed.

He did, indeed, raise his eyebrows as if surprised, gave a little whistle, said, " Mon Dieu !" looked puzzled for an instant; then, as if a happy idea had struck him, said that his friend had a twin brother who was the image of him, and who, he knew, was a great socialist, and no doubt it was he whom Moyrah had heard. ·He declared the twins were constantly being mistaken for each other.

This satisfied her to a certain extent; but the horror that such principles at all existed in any human mind did not wear off for many a long day. There was in her character an innate tendency towards respect for the authority of religion, which seemed bound up with her passionate love for, and continual thought of, her home and family. Her heart was like a forget-me-not, in which flower the cyme is rolled round in the form of a crozier. Before she came to Paris she had never imagined it possible to attack either home or faith—to crush the flower, or break the crozier.

CHAPTER XXVII.

THAT evening, after Lenoir had, as usual, gone out, Moyrah went where she spent a great part of her time now, to St. Roch. To her it seemed the most devotional of all the churches she had been in. She would spend hours before the beautiful statue of the Blessed Virgin there. In the perplexities and heartachings which were gathering round her, the thought of that mother was like the shadow of a rock in a weary land. She liked the feeling that she had been a mortal as she was, a creature as she was, and that her ear was ever open to the sufferings of her children, which she understood by intuition and experience. She could tell her of more beautiful things than poets who have not known her have ever dreamt of; and she could bring those beautiful things out of the very deformities of life which depressed Moyrah.

As she knelt there she used to dream that she was far away from the noisy, dusty city, with so much in it that perplexed and pained her; and that she was standing at the door of a lowly cottage in a hill country. Here were no advanced thinkers, advancing thinkers, or thinkers of advanced thinkers' thoughts—people whom Alphonse was constantly alluding to, and who worried her. Here was a little room, simply furnished. It was morning, and the early sun shone into the open window; and the song of the birds came borne on the wings of a fresh breeze from the hills. The hills were bathed in a soft, pink glow, like the glow she had so often seen from her lattice window at the Blue House,

making the valley, with its river, look warm and love-
able. Inside the room there was a character and tone
of repose so great that even her most troubled moods
were calmed by it. A mother sat there, and in her
arms a little child, while the morning sunshine came in
through the half open window and twined itself into a
soft wave of light round their heads. The beauty of
that mother, exceeding what was ever known in a
human face or form before, the softness of her manner,
and tenderness of her voice when she addressed her
child, the dignity and gentleness of her smallest movement, came before Moyrah, not as if seen in a picture,
not even as if a mirror had leaned against the wall and
been told miraculously to keep for ever the reflection
flashed upon it, but with a reality so intense, that it
seemed as if she was actually living and moving in the
scene herself.

Round that mother clustered all the highest visions
of a perfect womanhood which had passed over her
passionate, but innocent, Irish nature. A secret holiness
in the air here seemed to stamp the dross out of those
wanderings of her fancy which of late often pained her.

And, as she pondered, she saw, in direct contradiction
to what the Socialist had said, that there was no second
place for woman in dignity and self-control; when she
ceased to be first she was nothing. And as again she
looked up into that mother's face, she saw she was the
crown of that true womanhood which is the one unswerving foe that bars the progress of those principles the
street orator had crowed forth in their rush to subjugate
mankind. And then, it seemed, she knelt down on the
threshold, and bent her head in adoration; and the mist
of her frailties cleared away in the sunshine of the love
which seemed to be in the very air, and she felt able to
raise her head, and dare to look into that mother's face.
As she did so, she saw those pensive eyes, full of that
mother's yearning, which is the most perfect expression
of a higher love, bringing close to us the highest love

of all to be found on earth, fixed on her; while a voice, which thrilled through her, said: " Come in my child. All who are in sorrow or perplexity are welcome here. The least little trouble of your heart is known to us, and we sympathise with it with such a sympathy as will rob it of all its sting."   And then Moyrah poured out her whole heart. She told, in simple and touching language, each inmost feeling, every one of those wild fancies and difficult windings, which, if left unchecked, too often, like autumn reapers, put the sickle to the loveliest flowers in the garden of our soul. She laid down at that mother's feet every trouble about the present, every misgiving about the future.   There is an old Chaldean proverb which says: " God could not be everywhere, so he made mothers." In spite of its theological unsoundness, it has an undertone which appeals to our deepest feelings. What heart is like a mother's? And just then Moyrah stood in great need of a mother to guide and help her. So she told all to that Holy Mother on the model of whose heart all the holiest earthly mother's hearts are made. Troubles grew light, and peace came. In that scene of calm loveliness she learned the language spoken by those who have passed into eternal peace.

CHAPTER XXVIII.

WHEN she returned to her apartment, to her surprise, she found Lenoir. For the last two weeks he had been out every evening, until quite late into the night. He was gathering together his papers, and his open portmanteau lay on the floor.

In answer to Moyrah's gesture of surprise, he told her that he had been summoned to the death bed of an uncle. He gave her his address: it was a street in Bayonne, and told her he should be away about a week. He said he was very sorry he could not take her with him, but it would be a doleful mission, and there was nowhere she could be put up in the house he was going to.

Struggle as she might, Moyrah could not repress her tears. The sense of misery and desolation which came over her, at the prospect of being left all alone in Paris for a whole long week, overpowered her self control, and she sobbed aloud. Oh, Alphonse!" she cried, " a week! a whole week!"

He smiled. To witness suffering had always afforded him pleasure.

" Bah!" he said, at length, with a slight intonation of contempt. "Eve charmante!" And he went on packing his portmanteau. Then, he added, to himself, in rapidly spoken French, with a leer, "The time will come when you won't cry at my departure!"

" Oh, Alphonse!" she exclaimed, between her sobs. "How long will this dreadful 'business,' which is always takin' ye away, last?"

“ Parbleu ! ” and he gave a little whistle. “ Only till it’s finished ! ”

He was standing by an escritoire which was pushed into a niche in the wall. This escritoire was an object of great curiosity to Moyrah. She had never seen its inside. It was always locked, and she had noticed that Lenior carried the key on a small gold chain, round his neck, inside all his clothes. She had also noticed that he never opened the escritoire when she was in the room. Once or twice she had come in and found him with it open, but he had shut it instantly. Now he looked at her furtively, to see where her eyes were turned. They were buried in her hands, while tears trickled between her fingers. He seemed satisfied. Going hurriedly to the escritoire he unlocked it, took out a paper and slipped another in, then glanced over his shoulder to see where her eyes were again. Still buried in her hands, while her slight figure heaved slowly with half suppressed sobs. He opened the lid again, and bending his head down, ran his hands quickly over some papers, put two into the breast pocket of his coat, then, with a click, closed the lid, locked it, and turned to Moyrah.

“ I leave you in charge of everything in this apartment,” he said. “ See that no none comes in here but yourself.” He paused, then added, as if much depended on it; “ You will see to this, will you, please ? ”

“ I will, indade ! Shure, I don’t want anny wan in here when ye’re wantin’.”

“ Bien ! ” he exclaimed, as if satisfied. Suddenly he approached her, and clasped a strong leather belt round her waist. From it hung an American bowie clasp knife.

“ I wish you to wear this while I am away, in case, which is not the least likely, but just in case anyone should come in and try to get at that escritoire, which contains many valuable things.”

She turned deadly pale.

"There, don't look as if you were going to faint. Nobody will come, I'd bet a thousand francs; but it is better to be prepared for every contingency," and he laughed to re-assure her. Then he put his hat on one side of his head, ran his fingers through his silky locks, looked at himself in the glass, and whistled. " Bien! au revoir, ma belle," he kissed his hand to her, and, in another minute was at the door, which he held open. " You dont seem a bit sorry for me having to leave joy and go off into gloom and stupidity," he said, in a bantering tone. " It's only yourself you are thinking of," and he nodded his black curls impudently at her, as he added, satirically, "Of poor me it may be truly said, ' Mais aussi quelle chute, quel cataclysme épouvantable dans tout son être, quand, à l'accès de joie et de tendresse, succédait l'accès de douleur, de soupçon et de dépit!'" he laughed. " It's only yourself you are thinking of, like all women, they never think of anyone else."

" O, but I do think of ye, Alphonse, indade an' indade I do, an' I'm greatly sorry for ye, goin' off alone. But thin ye need not go, an' I can't help mesilf bein' left behind."

" Need I not go, indeed! There's a dévote's sense of duty for you. You would have me neglect a solemn religious duty, going to the bedside of the dying," and he pulled that long face, and put on that sanctimonious manner which always hoodwinked her entirely.

"Adieu, grosse dormeuse!" and he went out in roars of laughing at her puzzled face, for she did not even understand the literal meaning of his words, much less any other.

When he reached the street he was joined by a short, powerful-looking man, much muffled up about the throat and mouth, and with his hat slouched over his eyes, and a loose cloak flung over his shoulders. He had evidently been waiting for him, and spoke hurriedly : " You are late, damn you, we shall miss the appointment."

"Damn you!" was the concise reply, and on they

strode, side by side, for some reason best known to themselves not choosing to call a fly.

At last they arrived at one of the most luxurious and expensive cafés in the town. As they entered, three men rose to meet them. They were dressed in those loud, slangy garments which make one instinctively think their tailor must have been coached by the upholsterer of an American liner. Nevertheless, their wearers looked as if they had not studied the advertisements of Pear's soap upon the sides of the cabin. They all had flowers in their buttonholes. One of them had a rose bud and a bit of thyme in the top buttonhole of his waistcoat.

"We're regular dragged out, waiting for you. What the deuce has kept you?" said one of them, nicknamed "Bangs."

An angry flash darted from Lenoir's yellowy black eyes. It was extraordinary the terror his anger inspired in his associates.

One of the other men, nicknamed "Crispy," saw the look, and gave Bangs a nudge. "Draw a straight furrow, and don't poke yer nose into another chap's tater patch," he said.

Bangs gave a short whistle.

Then the third man spoke, nicknamed, and with judicious discrimination, the "Blusterer." He was as stout as the Claimant. "We've ordered dinner this ever so long, it'll be spoilt, damn it; come on, let's pitch in."

They ranged themselves round the table. As the good dishes were handed to them, good humour began to return.

Lenoir was a greedy man. Indeed, they were all greedy men. The dinner was such as to put the greediest men into the sublimest temper. Every luxury that the most refined Parisian *gourmet* could desire, or genius of a *chef* devise, was there. A Lyons duck being the most appreciated by Crispy, Bangs and the Blusterer. They did make a fool

of the poor bird, but it must have been a bit of a
fool, to begin with, to have got itself into such a
position.

The menu was as follows: clear gravy soup, salmon
cutlets, and fillets of sole à la reine, duck and lamb's
fry, saddle of mutton, asparagus, eggs, and potatoes a
l'Italienne, stewed pigeon, French beans sautès, roulade
of veal, and spinach à la reine, almond cream, and
cheese fondu, followed up by ices, curaçoa, coffee, etc.

" Well, how's 'the Plan' been doing these last few
weeks, eh?" asked Lenoir, who, by this distance in the
dinner, had reached a state of mind which might almost
be described as cordial

Bangs, Crispy and the Blusterer were three American-
Irish agitators, who had only arrived from Ireland the
night before, where they had been stumping the country,
and collecting the sinews of war for dinners such as
the present one. Now Bangs and Crispy were still
filling their mouths, and munching with a rapidity
which rendered prolonged conversation inconvenient.
It was only during the last year or two they were
accustomed to meals with such menus as the one I have
copied. The Blusterer, on the contrary, was the son
of a pawnbroker, money lender and dealer—successful
dealer—in left off clothes. Therefore his youth had
been passed in affluence, and he was so far accustomed
to disposing of enormous quantities of food in a limited
time that the process required no exceptional effort on
his part. His gastronomic genius had burst forth full
fledged, like Athene from the head of Zeus. From the
age of two upwards it had been in complete working
order. Though he had already put into him as much
food as would have made a dinner for two or three
starving Irish tenants, and meant to put into him as
much more again, he was capable of conversing agree-
ably upon any subject. He laid down his knife and
fork, with the points resting on the edge of his plate,
and the handles spread out latitudinally. He took a

good pull at his champagne, wiped his mouth with the
back of his hand, then wiped the back of his hand on
the side of his trouser; then hic-coughed, and then said,
" Tol-lol well, latterly.　At first I thought we'd get
nary red," (no money), " and I was peskily narvous, I
can tell yer, but the Kildrowninaholey election settled
it all.　We'd some fine pipe-laying there, I can tell yer!
Blow me tight, but we had! and he dashed his fist on
the table and laughed.　(Pipe-laying is bringing up
electors not legally qualified).

Crispy and Bangs laughed, too, but did not stop
eating for an instant.

" Now ' the Plan ' is in full swing, there's a lot of
spry chaps down there, and they put the screw on recal-
citrant farmers pretty tight, I can tell yer!　We had
the *little* devils undher our thumbs from the first; a few
of the big chaps cut up rusty at starting, but we got
some spunky boys down from Daublin, to head the
League, and the bumptious rapscalions soon caved in.
Divil a landlord's got a haperth in that whole country
side this year, nor nivir will agin!　If we cud only kape
the shopkeepers up to the level we'd do well enough.
But they're like staky horsis, they gibbs the minit you
put 'em into harniss."

" You're right, begor!" exclaimed Crispy, though
his mind was evidently more with his food than with
his country's wrongs.

" And the tenants have funded the money? " asked
Lenoir, raising his eye-brows in a nonchalant way, as
he helped himself to a fresh dainty, carefully scooping
up the gravy and pouring it in a stream over his
meat.

" Yas!" and the Blusterer winked the corner of his
somewhat bloodshot eye knowingly at Lenoir.　" Yas!
they've funded the money!" And he looked at Crispy
and Bangs, who nodded, and suppressed a smile.
" Yas! they've funded it, and a smart sprinkle of tin
they've funded!" And he took another drink of

champagne, and complacently flopped the glass down
on the table, with a sort of satisfied bang.

"Banks full I suppose?" asked Lenoir, with an air
of child-like innocence.

"Just about!" said Bangs, who was beginning to
feel slightly uncomfortably stuffed, though he would
not have owned it for many dollars.

"Which bank is most favoured?" asked Lenoir, who
liked to gain all the useful local information he could.

The Blusterer gave a knowing look out of the corner
of his eyes. Then he slapped his portly person just
below where his rosebud and thyme were stuck in his
waistcoat buttonhole.

"'I know a bank whereon the wild thyme grows!'"

"We are not a bad bank," said Crispy, complacently.
"Eh monsieur? Look at us and say what you think."

Lenoir ran his dark eyes over the trio. Then he
twirled the corner of his moustache and said: "Un
charmant panorama."

The tone in which he uttered this flattering reflection
made the Blusterer frown. Lenoir saw that ruby brow
contracting, and at once became polite to punctilious-
ness, positively velvety. If the Blusterer's humility
left a margin to be desired; if his sentiments were
"louches," and his manners not, as yet, Parisian, still,
his firm adherence to his party was of incalculable
importance. He was a burning speaker who could
make a whole hall full of dull people bristle with attention. He was an *esprit fort*, and he had the knack of
collecting round him, and imbuing with his own spirit,
everyone in the phantasmagoria of peasant life, whose
glimmer of a conscience was on the point of expiring,
and who, therefore, could be easily turned into *esprits
forts.*

The Blusterer knew his own social worth, and saw
through Lenoir's assumed civility with a keenness of
spiritual vision peculiar to the man who lives by his

wits. " You're plaguy apt to talk, Turkey, when you wants to get sociable a bit, eh?" and he laughed, with a slight jeer in his manner. He was a different character from Lenoir. There was nothing silky about him. He spoke out just what suited him in a rough, loud, auctioneering tone, and meant only the words he used. But Lenoir's vocabulary was charged with subtle allusions; almost every syllable had a double meaning. He was more than a match in speech, thought, and action for the boasting, bragging, though distinctly eloquent, swaggerer. " Well, talk as you may, I reckon I'm a whole team and a horse to spare!" and he drew himself up and stuck his thumbs in his waistcoat arm-holes.

Eloquent he was He had the true orator's fluency and fire. He could rouse the fiercest passions of an innocent and unsuspecting peasantry until they were maddened like herds of cattle in a prairie fire. With the ease and rapidity of a conjurer he could plunge guiltless souls from the secret sins of hatred, malice, and envenomed spite, to the overt and less safe ones of murdering, maiming, assassinating, robbing, and torturing. In one week he could turn the quietest village in a county into a pandemonium that the shapes on the Brocken would have been ashamed to be found in. Lies flowed to his lips in as continuous a stream as the poison of a wasp's sting to its tail. A reputation which had stood unblemished in a neighbourhood for twenty years he could grasp in his octopus-like fangs and crush to death in ten minutes. He was not a man to quarrel with.

At that moment a hungry-looking woman was peering nervously round the open door. As she stood in the street she leaned her head against the door-post, and just her eyes and her forehead could be seen coming round in front of it. She could not see the Blusterer plainly, for his quarter side face was towards her, and he kept his head continually turned away, looking at

Lenoir, whom he was addressing. The five diners had broken up the rolls by their plates; most of them had pulled the crumb out and pushed the crust away. On these crusts her eyes were fixed with an intensity which seemed to strain them as though they would start from her head and burn through the air.

O fearful eyes! the eyes of a starving woman looking at food she cannot get. Eyes once seen never to be forgotten.

Lenoir could see the eyes from where he was sitting, but, being himself rather too full of food for comfort, it never occurred to him she was starving. We are slow to realise a state of mind or body opposed to our own. He wondered what on earth she was staring at. After a moment's consideration it struck him it must be at the extraordinary figures of his foreign friends. "They certainly are like very ·odd shaped houses," he soliloquised, as he looked at them. " Public men built like public houses. It might be said of this café, elle renferme un certain nombre d' edifices publics qui sans être remarquables par leur architecture, attirent cependant les regards des étrangers." He smiled to himself at his wit, and called for a fresh bottle of champagne. The uneven shoulders and ungainly arms and legs of his associates flattered his pride in his own well-proportioned limbs. He could see those limbs in a mirror nearly opposite to him, and, when repletion forced him to pause for a moment, he ran his fingers through his silky locks and surveyed himself with profound satisfaction.

In the meantime, the woman continued to stare, and always at the crusts.

Presently a French waiter, with his napkin under his arm, lounged close to the door.

She spoke hurriedly, in an eager, trembling whisper, and in tolerably good, though by no means perfect, French, "O! for the love of God, could you manage to slip me over a few of those crusts? Nothing has passed my lips for two days. If you could slip them into your napkin, and give them to me as you pass, no one would notice it."

He turned. "Fah!" he said, impatiently, tapping down his toe as if he was crushing a black beetle, " be off with you! We allow no beggars here."

She was a peculiarly shy, proud woman, but still, she did not go, she could not go; there were so many crusts, and they were so near the door. She clung on to the door posts with her white, wasted, trembling hands. Her eyes, though now dimmed with tears, were still glued to those crusts.

"We had some of the finest meetings you ever saw down at Bullybluhash, a fortnight ago. Two bloated English M.P.'s came over to help us; we must have had twenty thousand at the last meeting," said the Blusterer, who, occasionally, like all orators and poets, drew the long bow.

"Come, that bangs Bannagher," exclaimed Crispy, who had been at the meeting, and knew that the attendance numbered a little under five hundred. "Cut off nineteen thou——"

"Hold your jaw!" said the Blusterer, peremptorily.

"These mistakes frequently occur at overgrown meetings," said Lenoir, with gracious suavity.

"Speshully in Oireland," said Bangs, laughing, and winking at Lenoir.

"I stood on a gate to make my speech," continued the Blusterer.

"Are ye shure ye did not fall undher it?" asked Crispy. The champagne had made him, what he himself would have called, "coxy."

"No, nor ovur it, aithur," replied the Blusterer, shortly. "There was an emergency blaigard down from Daublin, who tried to cross my track; but I soon got some chaps to settle his hash, and then I had a full swing." He smacked his lips as he recalled his oratorical triumph. "The peelers came at the end, having cut up rough with the jarvies in the town because they wouldn't bring 'em. But I soon bluffed 'em off. After I'm havin' a series of them meetin's in a neighbourhood, I reckon that for fifty mile round there ain't a landlord's house which isn't like a barracoon " (slave house). He laughed. " They're obliged to keep 'emselves shut up there like niggers, or else only poke their noses out undher protection, as if they war afraid of 'emselves runnin' away across the swamps."

The others roared laughing at this.

Just then a young, fair-haired English waiter, who had come over to learn French in Paris, passed close to the door.

The starving woman stretched out one lean hand towards him, and whispered in so piteous a tone, and with such despair on her face—a face which, had it not been so haggard, would have been handsome—that it seemed as if it must have touched a heart of even Parisian asphalte. " Will *you* have pity on me? I am fainting with hunger; could you manage to slip one or two of those crusts into your pocket, and pass them on to me as you go by—no one would see you."

He stopped. After a moment he advanced a step closer to her, and peered into her ghastly face. Then he drew back, and said in the Queen's English, " You are not French? You are English, are you not? "

" Irish."

Her name was Peggy Donovan. She was from Bridget's and Moyrah's village, and had received a good education at a local convent, for she had thought of being a governess. Her parents were bettermost sort of people, but she had married a small shopkeeper, in a village in another county, the year she came home from the convent. Donovan, her husband, had died of consumption, after some years of married life, leaving her with six children, but, as he thought, well provided for. He owned a good many cottages in the neighbourhood, and the rents they brought in made a fair

competency. For the last two years not one farthing
of rent had been paid her. She had struggled for some
time to support her six children and her aged mother
of eighty, who lived with them, by her needlework, but
she could not do it, and latterly she had lain awake for
nights trying to decide whether she should send her
children or her mother to the workhouse. While still
working out this problem, she had seen an advertisement
in a paper, an Irish paper, taken very largely by the
peasants, from a lady in Paris, with children, who
wanted, apparently, a sort of a mixture of a nurse and
a governess, a good English scholar. After a short
correspondence with the advertiser, she decided to take
the situation, on promise of her passage and journey
being paid there, and, if she returned, back again.
The advertiser promised everything, and a salary of a
hundred a year besides. She did not, however, send
her the money, as she explained there was so much
difficulty with foreign post office orders, and letters
containing orders so often miscarried; but she said, if
she could manage to borrow enough to come out, she
would refund it to her on her arrival. This she
contrived to do. Arrived in Paris, she found the
advertiser was not a lady, but a firm of low class
auctioneers, in a disreputable part of the town. They
had a good deal of business to transact with foreign
money lenders, and were in want of a good linguist,
who, apparently, was to work for nothing. For she
was to provide her own lodging and board, work eight
hours a day, and get a hundred francs four times a year.
The hundred pounds a year turned out altogether a
myth. Bad as the terms were, she would have accepted
them, at any rate, temporarily, as she had come so far.
But she, unfortunately, knew no language but her own
and a little French. As she would not engage with
them, the firm refused to pay her journey; and she
found herself alone in Paris, with no friends there, no
means of returning home, and five francs in her pocket.

She had not the heart to write the terrible tidings back to her loved ones, and beg for what she knew they had not got—money to return. She determined to try if she could find any other employment. Day after day she roamed the streets in search of work of any sort. But there were many thousands bent on the same errand, and nearly all with superior qualifications to what she possessed, for they all had some knowledge of a trade or a profession, or of domestic service.

Her five francs were soon exhausted, scrape and screw as she might. For some days she lived on begging. She applied to several well known and wealthy leaders of the Communistic movement. But, though possessing, besides many thousands of francs, a knowledge of the laws which govern the operations of digestion and nutrition in their own persons, they did not apply that knowledge to the persons of their neighbours. Like mongrels, they could wag the stumpy tails of their eloquent universal brotherhood at public dinners, and bite bare feet in private.

For the last three days she had wandered from pillar to post—that is, from one human pillar to another flesh and blood post—without getting a sou or a crust of bread from any of them. Yet they were pillars and posts who could so touchingly speak at public meetings on the enthusiasm of humanity, that they filled some Christians with strange apprehensions lest the new creed should beat the old one. The new pillars support the church best.

"O, for the love of God, don't keep me waiting any longer, or I shall faint. Look! look! he is giving them fresh bread; he is going to sweep those crusts away into the basket. Quick! quick! get them for me—quick!"

The young man turned, snapped up a brush off a side table, took a plate in his left hand, swept the crusts into it, then slipped them into his napkin, and, unobserved by the other waiters, brought them to her and slid them into the front of her dress, which she held up. She turned away, walked a few steps from the door, and then began a scene absolutely tragic in its horror. With her wasted, trembling hands, with the blue veins standing out on them, and the joints looking as if they were swelled from the flesh having fallen off between, she seized the gnawed and broken crusts and devoured them like a savage wild beast.

The waiter watched her for an instant in amazement; he thought she would certainly choke, so frightful was her hurry. Before one lump of crust had been a moment in her mouth, another was stuffed in. He followed her, first looking round over his shoulder to see that he was not observed from within.

"Tell me your address, and I'll come to you as soon as ever we close to-night, and bring you some proper food. It's awful to see you like this! It's awful m'am, I say! Perfectly awful!"

"I have no address," she stuttered, between her mouthfuls. "Go! They're calling for you; may God reward you, and may you never know what it is to be starving. I'll come here again, I will, if I may. There must always be crusts here."

At that moment she looked up, and through the open window saw the Blusterer's full face. She at once recognised an agitator who had been sent down from Dublin to hold a number of meetings in her village. He had established a Harvest Bug depôt, and had made himself temporarily the head of it. From that moment disturbance and distress began. Hitherto the village had been a singularly peaceful and happy one. There was not a poor person who did not feel they had in their old parish priest a true friend. In every sickness he visited, in every sorrow consoled them. Morning after morning he was to be seen walking along the narrow roads, from cottage to cottage, carrying food to his sick parishioners. Everyone who fell into misfortune at once went to him, and poured out their troubles, certain of sympathy and assistance. He had taught them lace making, and many of the girls were earning a good bit by it. All was quiet and comfortable; no fussing, no rowing, no political bullying, storming, and bear fighting. He had been educated in France, and declined to cut off the bough he was sitting on.

Suddenly, with his fret-work apparatus for carving into domestic peace, appeared the Blusterer, to the horror, and disgust, and infinite annoyance of the good priest, who had hitherto managed to keep even the saw well out of sight. Soon the most quiet, easy going, pious peasants were transformed. Gentle, brave Irish boys, who had been full of high dreams of self-sacrifice, of the priesthood, even of monastic life, suddenly veered right round, and turned into disorderly sort of kangaroos, ready to tear down their nearest and dearest, unless they would go along with them in their dance after the devil's tail. That little blazing bit, which, having lighted in Paris, he has cocked so high in Ireland. Money which had been saved against sickness or old age was drawn out of the bank and given to agitators. The harvest was neglected, the lace work was given up. No one would do anything but curse and damn his neighbour.

With that delight in a new toy which marks all susceptible, witty people, the peasants seized on the principles of Communism to give them " a try." Revolution was a matter of experiment. You could take it up or lay it down for a frolic. That repacious Gulliver, holding high in his hand the dagger barbed to stab the altar, the throne, and the home, was a coquette to flirt an idle half hour away with. They took him so, and drew him so close that he changed their nature into his.

Soon no rents were paid at all, except to the agitators, in whose houses the peasants were not living; the fact being that the agitators were living in the peasants' houses. But they took good care not to pay them any rent. And so the poor peasants sank from one degree of poverty to another.

Peggy staggered away round a corner, out of sight, and the head waiter called the English one peremptorily back. As he re-entered the café, the Blusterer was alluding to future history.

" Dash my buttons ! If before manny months we're not in the seats of them damn landlords. Then if we don't make a clean sweep of them as opposed us—begor, new brooms sweep clean ! "

" They do so ! " assented Crispy, scratching the top of his head. " An' bedad, 'tis mighty comfortable to be on the side of the handle."

Lenoir laughed at this, as he sipped his champagne.

" Handles have been known to break off before now, and run into the hands which held 'em," remarked Bangs, dryly.

" Shut up, you half-baked idiot ! " said the Blusterer.

Bangs went into roars of laughing at this.

" What a clatternhocking ! " exclaimed the Blusterer. " Faix, it is hot ! " and he unfastened his waistcoat and flung it wide open, while he fanned himself with his napkin.

Just at that instant a waiter handed round strawberry cream, ices, and glasses of curaçoa.

" We have had a square meal, and no mistake ! " ejaculated Bangs, complacently.

Lenoir looked at his watch. " Remember, gentlemen, we have not much time to lose, we are going to a reception at Monsieur———" (naming one of the leading politicians of the day). " And I have to catch the night train for the South."

" Ah ! Monsieur——— , I don't know that I quite swear by him," said the Blusterer, tossing off his curaçoa. " He's one of those slicked-up, squirtish kind of fellars, as ain't partiklar hard baked, and always goes in for aristocracy noshins ; talk as they may of the people."

Lenoir's lip curled, but he said nothing.

Peggy had tottered on, devouring her crusts, tearing

at them, scarcely chewing them, almost swallowing
them whole. Once, in her violent hurry, she dropped
one on a tin can which was floating in the running,
oozing mud of the gutter, snapping it up out of this
curious *batterie de cuisine*, without stopping to wipe it,
she forced it into her mouth, though already there was
a large bit there. Soon she dropped another piece,
which she knelt down to hunt for, as she did not find it
directly. Some of the more advanced thinking dare-
devils of the Sorbonne and the Maison Dieu, were
swaggering along, arm in arm. They kicked her out
of their way, while one of them turned his head over
his shoulder, and shouted, jeeringly, "Church is the
place for prayers, ma belle; we don't worship gutters
here," blind to the fact that the reverse was the case.
She took no notice; too intent on finding her lost bit of
crust, which she did, presently. When she got up, she
crept nervously along, sometimes taking two or three
hurried steps, to get out of sight of passing strangers,
then stopping altogether, the more readily to devour
her crusts.

The day was frightfully hot, and the stones burnt
into her feet as if the streets were the bars of a furnace.
Presently she came to an archway, leading to some
narrow alleys in a low part of the town. Faint and
exhausted, she sank down in a sort of crushed bundle
in the shadow of the arch. Her head fell sideways,
pressed against the wall. Her eyes shut, and her mouth
slightly opened. Many people passed by, but no one
took the slightest notice of her. Such a sight was too
common in the great city of pleasure.

CHAPTER XXIX.

OUR friends at the café, at last, really could eat no more, so they lighted their cigars, and started out on to the boulevards. Though it was getting late in the afternoon the sun was still unpleasantly hot, and they sat down for a few moments to rest under the shelter of a tree. They took off their hats, and let the delicious, cooling breeze which was springing up blow through their hair.

Another half hour found them entering the hotel of Monsieur Savon, one of the leading politicians and foremost *libres penseurs* of the day. Here were all the diplomatic pluralists, themselves in comfortable possession of five different offices, who in public, vehemently denounced the enormity of one man holding two offices, and drawing two salaries, while doing an infinitesimal amount of renumerative hard work. Here were denouncers of royalist parsimony, who would not themselves spend sixpence on a new piece of soap. Here was all that dignity of manner which might be expected from men who had risen to power by robbery, and kept themselves in it by sacrilege. Here every one was welcome who could make a mock of his God and a deity of his stomach.

The room was large, and picked out in white and gold. There were Sèvres cups and saucers standing about on little rickety looking, gilded tables, a few bibelots, bonbon boxes, and perfume caskets. There was distinctly no cachet of good style about the company, though the hotel had once been a royalist abode where the bluest blood had congregated. There was much floral ornamentation about the plaster cornices and doorheads. In one of the small inner salons was a showy grand piano, on which a crazy looking man, with mud coloured hair, which reached to his shoulders, was pounding the Marsellaise.

No one was in evening dress, and the costumes were as diversified as the characters they shrouded. There was a good deal of loud laughter and joking; for the black cloak of the assassin sits easily on the round shoulders of the satyr. Lenoir knew everyone, and, from the first moment, was quite at home. Everyone knew him, but, strange to say, everyone gave a slight start when they saw him, as if they did not exactly expect to see him there then. He introduced his friends to anyone they did not know, but they already knew a good many of the distinguished guests.

There was one very short, fat man, with eyes too large for their sockets, and a tongue too big for his mouth, and his black hair cut close to his head, who would talk away at the top of his voice so as to drown everyone who was near him. He incessantly touched the tops of his fingers, spread out with a space between each finger, to his arm sockets, then flung out his whole arms full length, straight in front of him. He was declaring that the present governors of his nation were assertors of prerogative independent of law, and announced that the present Chamber of Deputies was a pretty kettle of fish, or rather kennel of dogs. Considering that he was one of the deputies in the chamber this was distinctly impartial. Indeed, it might be called humility carried to its finest point. Some civility shewn to Germany had irritated his patriotic sensibilities beyond endurance. As the Blusterer lounged gracefully, with his hands under his coattails, listening to him, he shouted out in burning accents: "The treachery of a friend may become a virtue compared to the loathsome, fawning baseness which grovels before a declared enemy." He went on to enquire, in fiercely impassioned tones, where "la gloire" had gone to if such conduct as this was to be the order for the day?   One minister seemed peculiarly obnoxious to him : he declared that, while the other deputies were going on in their usual dull round of senseless stupidity, this one appeared to have marked out, by a deliberate choice, "the means to precipitate our destruction."   Finally, he declared the unfortunate deputy in question was possessed with the devil.   Most Frenchmen believe in possession by the devil of their enemies.   No doubt internal evidence on the point is too strong to be resisted.   "He has risen," he said, "like his arch-type, on the steam of his own self-praise; and, like him, the vapour will desert him, and he will fall plump to the lowest abyss, dragging a great part of the glory of France after him."   He ended up with—"We are betrayed!   We are betrayed!   We are betrayed !"

"Who is the little chap?" enquired the Blusterer of Lenoir, for the speaker's face was strange to him.

"He was originally a trolleur—a fellow who does his own work and sells it to the dealers.   But he seems to have got a pot of money lately, how, no one can tell."

"He's in a jolly wax with the members of his own parlimint, anny way.   He's bully-ragged 'em all round me hat," and he laughed.   "Not one, except himself, got off."

Lenoir's brow clouded.   "You will find that to be the case with most of the members of the Chamber of Deputies," he said, quietly.

The little deputy went on in tones which impelled attention.   "Whatever the Chamber desires the Senate denies.   The Chamber wants progress; the Senate has no more idea of it than one of the oaks at Fontainbleau of getting up by its roots and dancing the can-can. We all want progress.   We want the army and navy strengthened.   We want to teach our foes that France is mistress and will be mistress.   We wish to put a few of our enemies *hors de combat*."   These last sentiments met with excited approval from his audience. "A few of the bullies shall be made to sing small—England first." A burst of applause greeted these words from the group immediately round him. "She can easily be managed. Her army are boys of the lycée: her navy is beneath contempt; to every three of our working iron-clads she has one and a half."

The Blusterer understood French well enough to follow accurately what he was saying.

There was a laugh at this, and much complacent shrugging of the shoulders and rubbing of the hands. "That nation of shopkeepers will not pay to put up iron shutters to the shop."

"That's good, begor!" exclaimed the Blusterer, laughing.

"We can get at her through Ireland. She will join us to a man, and rise *en masse* the moment we land." This met with hearty assent. "With Ireland under our thumb we can soon bring England on her knees before us. Once down, we have a good bit to revenge."

Here, however, he paused. He did not see fit to enter into particulars with regard to Waterloo, or any other combats of a similar character, such references not being congenial to the Gallic mind, however useful to point a moral.

After a minute, he continued, in eloquent periods— "Ireland is the flag-staff to which we shall nail our tricolour. She will carry it to victory, while we tear the union jack to her recruiting ribbons and trample the British lion in the dust."

"Hear, hear," called the Blusterer.

"There are plenty of Irishmen here to corroborate what I say," and he looked round, with a consequential air, on the fair sprinkling of Irish-American agitators which adorned the apartment.

"Bien, oui," assented a Philistine, an *épicier*, who was standing near.

"Yes," he exclaimed, flinging out his arms again,

and letting the tip of his large tongue appear beyond his lips, while his eyes almost started from his head with excitement.

" We will plant the shamrock in the top of the bonnet rouge———"

" Que diable," muttered a grey-haired Parisian.

" Bedad," muttered Crispy, " 'twon't know itself along wid such gorgeous millenery."

" And may it live to take root there until it becomes indigenous in the soil," added the French orator.

" The trifoil *above* the tricolour, me boy," muttered Crispy, with a sly chuckle; " but ye're right for all that; 'tis through yer nashin that we'll be revenged on the Saxon."

Soon after this refreshments were brought in and carried round on trays, and Bangs, Crispy and the Blusterer, who had had time to digest, went at it again. But the little man with the big tongue would not stop to eat.

" Listen, gentlemen," he exclaimed, trying to wean the attention of his audience from gastronomic attractions. " Listen. Russia will attack India all along her northern frontier; England will concentrate her resources there; then will be our moment. We land in the south and the west of Ireland. The population rise *en masse* to meet us. By means of our navy we intercept their merchant ships bringing them food. They have just enough provisions in their own country to last one week. See, messieurs? Attend! We starve them out! The channel will be ours. What few ironclads they have will be in the Baltic and the Black Sea, or defending Malta, Gibraltar, and their other possessions. We shall make an easy business of it. Mark my word, the tricolour will wave from Windsor Castle, and the bonnet rouge crown the Albert Memorial before another year is out."

The audience forgot their food for a moment to applaud these sentiments. Indeed, for a short time everyone round the speaker was carried away by that sort of self-congratulating, self-conscious pleasure which is the utmost tribute of approbation which can be won from a French audience.

Lenoir looked ill at ease. He kept moving about from one spot to another. He looked as fidgety as a *greffier* who has lost his register, and is hunting for it, first in one corner, and then in another. He kept glancing behind him constantly, and turned his head first over one shoulder, and then over the other. He seemed as if he was walking over prickly pears with bare feet. A fidgety man of any sort is a wonderful medicine to an impatient character, but a fidgety Frenchman is like certain well known pills worth a guinea a box. He moves about with the short, sharp snappish pertness of a very impudent cur puppy expressing his displeasure at a cat on a wall. Lenoir was not always in this state. He was often quiet and silky enough. But, like one of the most irregular verbs of his own language, he had many moods. The mood he was in now betokened physical fear to anyone acquainted with the workings of his character.

That hurried look over his shoulder, that quick change of position, that discomfort in each new posture he assumed, was an evidence—though one not discerned by most of his acquaintance—that his nerves were in a state of tension which made him almost insensible of his own movements. Everyone else in the room was enjoying himself to a greater or less extent. He alone could fix his attention to nothing.

He started at every little noise, and in a room filled for the greater part with excited Frenchmen, the noises were neither few nor small. If anyone addressed him suddenly, he turned round with a wild, astonished look, as if a bamboo had struck him across the face. He recovered himself, however, immediately, and assumed an exaggerated imitation of his ordinary cynical swagger. He evidently did not attempt to follow any of the speakers into their ramifications of politics. He only listened to a word here and there, then turned away, frowned, listened to outside sounds, started when the clock struck, and constantly fixed his eyes on the door, scanning everyone who entered it.

It seemed odd that no one noticed a way of going on that was unlike his ordinary manner. It is not lack of innate power of observation in Frenchmen that prevents them from discerning sudden changes in each other's deportment; it is because there is a prior object of attention in each Frenchman's heart which occupies even his large powers of observation—and a Frenchman's powers of observation are very large— and that is himself. No. 1 stops the way. In those rare instances where No. 1 can be induced to take a back seat, then the national quickness of sight and keenness of suspicion shine forth in all their unapproachable radiance, and we have the finest detectives in the world.

But though his singular conduct escaped observation, it could not have been exactly a pleasant party to Lenoir. When the hour came for him to go, the first look of relief which had visited his handsome face that evening passed over it. He said good-bye to one or two of his intimates, and slipped away unobserved.

Meantime Peggy was still crouched in a bundle under the archway. Towards sundown a gendarme passed. He stopped, and leaning forward, examined her carefully. Then he caught her shoulder and shook it, saying: "Get up! get up! We can't have tramps stopping up the public way."

Now, the archway was very private, for only a few rag pickers stole under it now and then.

But she did not move. Again he shook her, more violently than before, and bawled into her ear with that peculiar grating bawl of the French lower orders: "Wake up, I say! Get up, will you!"

But still she did not move.

She never got up again. The food had come too
late. She had made her last move on. Her difficulty
about whether she should send her mother or her
children to the workhouse was solved by their being
both sent.

Her soul went before the Judge Who gave the
commandment: " Thou shalt not steal ;" and her body,
which she had tended all her life with such modest
care and reverence, was—with the delicacy unique
to the nation where she died—stripped naked and laid
in the public morgue to await identification, but it
never was identified ; so, when it was beginning to
decay, it was carelessly thrown into a nameless pauper's
grave. There, without any mark over it, it waited the
resurrection to judgment, face to face, of those who
have stolen and of those who have been stolen from.

CHAPTER XXX.

OYRAH sat sobbing for a long time; desolation seemed to sink into her heart. Everything was so different from what she had expected. She thought of her old, free, happy life at the Blue House, of the kindly faces and cheery voices all round her, of her idolized father, who somehow was so totally different a kind of being from Lenoir, that she could scarcely believe they were both men, and actually belonged to the same race. Yet she loved Lenoir with a love very different to what she felt for her father, or for anyone else on earth.

The next day she spent almost entirely in St. Roch. She got her luncheon, which consisted of some coffee, an egg and roll, at a little café close by, then went back again to its peaceful shades, and the comfort and companionship of the holy presences of angels, saints, martyrs and virgins, who seemed to people its dim aisles to her as if they were really walking about them.

She was beginning to understand French comfortably; and the Suisse kindly explained the different objects of interest to her. But she did not go to stare about and sight-see, rather to worship and to hold friendly intercourse with those who had trodden the thorny path which was now bruising her feet; but who, having exchanged the cross for the crown, looked back on the troubles of time as a dust mote in the sunshine of the long day they had begun.

The statues and the pictures whispered their own tale in a language which many failures of Babel cannot defeat. Each saint had his own story to tell, and his own distinctive kind of sympathy to give, different from any other saint. And yet there was a unity of design through their lives and underlying the sympathy of each, which imparted to Moyrah a comforting sense of companionship, a sort of *esprit de corps*. She had a feeling of being in one large family where all were working together for the good of each other; which in her present isolation consoled her, as the poor wanderer is consoled when all the family come out to meet him at the cottage door, and pull him in between them until he stands surrounded by them close to the kitchen fire: each one expressing their joy at having him back, in different tones, with a different manner; and yet united in the one overpowering feeling of pleasure at his being amongst them again.

Moyrah was experiencing sharply just now the vicissitudes of life's weather. So sharply that she could fully appreciate the comfort of a shelter like this. She felt that sense of full consolation, combined with elevation, which comes over us when we are listening to Mozart's Twelfth Mass. It is as if the greatest musical genius who ever lived had seen the human heart as much before his mind when he composed his great work as that divine vision which is the crown of all supreme musical imagination. At any rate, he has united that vision and the human heart as they have never been united before or since. He has not tried to refute false musical ideas by wearisome arguments, as some more recent classical composers have; but he has expelled them by substituting the true ones. This was how Moyrah acted with the false teachings which had lately fallen on her ears.

Some one had put a bunch of white water lilies at the foot of the statue of the Blessed Virgin. Moyrah smiled with pleasure as she saw it. While she was looking at it, she saw a boy of four years old going round the church putting a single water lily at the

foot of each statue, and then looking up into the face
with confiding recognition, and giving a little smile and
nod as much as to say "are not you pleased at that,
now?"

It is improbable the flaxen curls shrouded any knowledge of botany, but perhaps some day their owner
would find out the significance of his act. Though in
the water lily the whorls are made up of a great number
of parts with complicated relations to each other, still
in no flower is the unity of design more conspicuous.
The final result being here, as in the lives of the
saints, the white blossom of innocence floating on
and beautifying the muddy water of the passions
and ambitions of ordinary life.

When he had bestowed the last water lily, he hunted
on the floor for his cap, which had rolled away, and
which Moyrah eventually found for him ; then he
marched out of church, stump, stump, stump, with
his head erect, and somewhat the air Napoleon I.
must have assumed immediately after he had been
crowned emperor.

Moyrah thought of Tim, and with the vision of home
and all its sweet sanctities, the value of which she had
not realised when she lived amongst them, tears came
into her eyes. To day, she could not tell why, she felt
a strange presentiment of coming evil. As the shadows
deepened in the church this feeling gathered round her
heart with a darker and darker foreboding. When
something dreadful is going to happen to us, it seems
often as if the castastrophe was drawing its shadowy
outline in the air for hours beforehand. We do not
think of this at the time, but remember it afterwards.

When she came out of St. Roch, she found the air
in the street extraordinarily oppressive and sultry.
Paris, after a long, broiling, hot, dusty day, can be about
the most stuffy and stifling place in Europe. Talk of
the breathed-out atmosphere of London in midsummer,
it is like the breezes of Exmoor compared to the air of

Paris after one of those roasting days when the asphalte is melting; when everyone is pushing and jostling on the shady side of the street, while only one British tourist is to be seen striding along on the sunny side, with his " Hare's Walks " under one arm, and his field glasses slung at his back, filled with confidence in his national integrity and indifference to the violent attentions of a sun distinctly not his national one.

The heaviness told upon Moyrah, and she walked slowly with her head bent down, and a sense of strange depression pulling her feet after her; she did not know why, but she felt more exhausted than after she had been working hard, and walking for miles and miles over the hills, or even over the bogs at home, in Ireland. She felt lonely, too, dreadfully lonely. The bustle and gaiety of the streets jarred on her. Had she been walking over the graves of some dry-as-dust old politicians, her nerves could not have been more out of touch with her surroundings. It is this which forms the kernel of all painful loneliness, for there is a loneliness which is not painful. As she passed down one thronged and fashionable boulevard, the crowd of gaily dressed pleasure seekers increased her isolation. The jiggy look of the women, the bold stare of the men, who have but one recipe for manners in Paris, produced in her a sensation of aloofness which, to a nature with keen sympathies, was full of pain.

Every now and then she turned away from the people towards the shops; but some print met her eye with the outline of the cloven hoof done in better drawing than its artistic outline, or little red stucco statuette, heaping ribald mockery on that religion which was the life of her life. Then she crossed herself, looked down, and walked on with a heart heavier than before, and a yearning for the village at home. She felt, somehow or other, as if the substance of things was leaving her, and only shadows remained. Everything was getting so unreal that she was obliged to be making perpetual concessions to her reason, to make sure she was really herself, really the old Moyrah she had known all her life at all.

When she reached her apartment, she went very slowly and quietly upstairs. She let herself in with a key, lazily and so gently as not to make a sound, while she raised her thick veil. To her amazement, as she walked in she saw a man, not Lenoir, leaning over the mysterious escritoire. The lid was thrown back and the papers were disordered. The man had, apparently, gone to sleep, for his arms were folded across the front of the desk, his head, a very unkempt, untidy one, lay on them, and he was snoring loudly.

Moyrah advanced on tip-toe and leaned over him ; as she did so, the smell of brandy nearly poisoned her. She persevered, however, and read the heading of a paper which lay open before him. "Scheme of Retribution," it was called ; as she proceeded, she grew white with a death-like pallor. It was written in plain, straightforward English, and she could understand every word of it. It was neither more nor less than a dynamite plot to blow up a meeting of royalists which was to take place that very evening in the Rue —— The names and addresses of the intended victims were given in full. Moyrah read the names of two or three French noblemen, who were unknown to her, when suddenly she gave a slight exclamation and staggered back a step, as if struck by a dagger.

In her quick movement, she unintentionally brushed against the man ; and awakened, either by her cry or her touch, he started to his feet.

But she was too quick for him, and had snatched the paper up and retreated with it several steps towards the window, before, in his half maudlin, half awake state, he could get on to his, so to speak, "working feet." As he stood up she saw, to her amazement, that it was Bitty Tit.

With a howl of fury, like a maddened wild beast, he

rushed towards her, his hand outstretched to catch the paper. Like lightning Moyrah wheeled a table round between her and him. In his hurry, he fell with his body right across it, then rolled off on to the floor. Moyrah stuffed the paper into her breast, and was turning to leave the room, when he shouted out: "If you peach, your husband will be guillotined; he's at the bottom of it all!"

For an instant these words seemed to overcome her; she staggered as she tried to reach the door. Bitty Tit saw his opportunity, bounded to his feet, and flew at her, seizing her wrist with the fierceness of a tiger.

"This is the best way to close your cursed lips!" and he dragged a pistol out of his breast, and aimed it full at her face.

But he had forgotten that his foe was a sturdy country girl, with hands and arms strengthened by good, hard, honest work, sometimes in the fields, sometimes at the mangle, sometimes scrubbing the floor, sometimes digging potatoes. In Africa the bold secretary bird is complete master of the dreaded poisonous snakes. The buzzard makes short work of the common viper. There are other things in Europe like Africa besides the slave trade.

She seized his wrist in her other hand, wrenched the deadly weapon from him, and put it into her own breast, while she gave him a tremendous swing backwards.

He fell, his brain still half stupefied by the fumes of brandy, and lay speechless and dizzy on the floor; having knocked over and broken a table covered with little ornaments in his descent.

In another moment she was in the open street, had taken a fiacre, and was driving to the Gare St. Lazare. She was just in the nick of time to catch a train going to St. Cloud.

CHAPTER XXXI.

THE Vicomte de Laboulaye had a pleasantly situated, but somewhat out of repair château, built in a sheltered nook in the wooded range of hills which inclose the valley of the Seine. The château was situated more than two miles from the station of St. Cloud.

The last rays of the setting sun were shining on the bright clean outsides of the spick and span new houses, raised since the conclusion of the late war, which left the town a mere heap of ruins. The rays lit up the now tottering but picturesque remains of the once famous and magnificent palace of St. Cloud.

There it lay bathed in the rich crimson glow, which wrapped it round in a blood red mantle as if it were the corpse of an emperor on a battle field.

The bell of the modern romanesque church was ringing for vespers. The Vicomte and his two guests had been dining, and were now, in full evening dress, walking up and down the terrace in front of his château. There was a birdseye view of Paris from the terrace; all the chief buildings could be distinguished, crowned now with floods of sunset glory, until a romantic gazer might imagine the distant city was about to ascend bodily into heaven; though frank criticism would oblige one of the initiated to confess it was more likely to pursue the reverse course.

Presently the sun set a crimson ball in a sea of fire; there seemed no limit to the tones of colour represented in that evening sky; then a cold, grey mist

came on for a few minutes; and then, in her calm
beauty, the moon rose, and shed her beams over the
spires and domes of Paris, over the snake-like windings
of the Seine, over the rippling leaves of the old trees
round the château.

The Vicomte had, by this time, mastered the English
language thoroughly, and spoke it with remarkable
fluency. Nevertheless, the conversation was being
carried on in French. One of his guests was a
Frenchman, the other, an Englishman.

"Yes," he said; "it is one large society." He held his
cigarette between the extreme tops of his first and
second finger; "it has its roots in Italy, but its
branches in every country."

"Yes," responded one of the other guests, "it is the
laboratory of the revolution." He sighed.

"France is certainly in the van; yet how calm, how
peaceful it is out here," said one of the men.

"Because," said Laboulaye, "no socialistic scorpions
are allowed to wander out here and cock their tails
against their Creator, their family, and their king."

At that moment, they strolled off the terrace on to
the grass. After walking a short distance, they came
to an ant hill, the top of which Laboulaye kicked off
with his foot. They stood and watched the commotion
for some moments; they saw the queen mother going
off into as speedy seclusion as under the circumstances
she could obtain, surrounded by her faithful body
guard.

"Behold!" said the Vicomte, "a monarchical constitution, which has never changed since the Pleistocene,
and which is the best governed kingdom in the visible
universe."

His two guests, two men almost as young as himself,
laughed. After they had watched the ants for some
time, and seen one obstreperous one, Laboulaye said:
"An individual who supports Communism and
revolution in the state will be certain, sooner or later,

to have, perhaps, without his support, and against his will, Communism and revolution in his own soul."

"True," said one of the guests, with a deep earnestness, which encouraged Laboulaye to proceed.

"And a nation which encourages Communism is certain to fall under the sword of the dictator, or the dagger of the anarchist." He took his cigar out again, and puffed a cloud of scented smoke away.

The Vicomte had deeper feelings than his manner or the ordinary tone of his voice would have led an acquaintance to suspect. Presently he spoke with admiration of an old royalist friend of his, who had attended the hospitals with great self-devotion when they were filled with wounded rioters, at the time of the insurrection of the "Ateliers Nationaux;" when, by republicans, Paris was made to swim with the blood of her republican sons, in the gentle month of June. He spoke, with a shudder, of the typical republican manners of the wounded insurgents. How they sprang from their beds to bite their suffering fellow citizens, and when reproved for this strange disregard of the rules of propriety, flew at their nurses. He declared that, had Cavaignac not promptly crushed the rebellion, it would have ended in the destruction of the few monuments of past greatness her children have left to France.

"Les architectes mettront leur gloire a atteindre la plus grande élévation possibles, pyramides, flèches des cathedrales, tour de Washington, tour Eiffel; les explorateurs a poser le pied sur les plus hauts sommets des montagnes; les aéronautes á monter au plus haut de l'atmosphère." He paused, evidently somewhat moved.

"But the modern Parisian chooses for his object of ambition, what?" exclaimed the Englishman, so carried away by excitement as to burst out suddenly into his own language.

"La chute au plus profond des abîmes!" exclaimed Laboulaye, with deep emotion.

They were all impressed, and remained silent for several minutes. Presently Laboulaye continued:

"The pivot on which republicanism turns is destruction; never creation."

"True," assented one of his friends.

"It seems strange," he added, meditatively, "that Englishmen, who are so distinctly creative, should be found at any time to admire it; but I am bound to say that when they come nearer, their admiration evaporates. When Dr. Priestly sent his son, William, here, he said in what, you will excuse my remarking, is the somewhat grandiose style common to the more learned members of the English nation: "Go, my son, to that land of hospitality, and learn to detest tyranny." The Vicomte paused, while his guests smiled. "When the massacres of September took place, however, he changed his tune, got into a fine fuss, and said if such goings on were not stopped, there would be no hope for liberty."

"While there is a single country left which upholds monarchy, there will be hope for liberty," broke in one of the other gentlemen, emphatically.

"True, true, mon ami," assented Laboulaye, heartily.

After a moment's pause, during which all the three young politicians seemed deep in thought, the Vicomte continued:

"Wordsworth came in 1791, brimful of enthusiasm, like all poets" (the Vicomte was a bit of a poet himself). "The massacres turned his admiration into loathing. For years he dreamt he was pleading for his life before that pocket edition of the devil and the demagogue—synonymous terms—Maillard."

The two gentlemen smiled, looked at each other and smiled again.

The Vicomte was just a little bit fond of airing his learning.

"Sir John Stanley, of Alderley, bitten like so many Englishmen of 1790 with the hydrophobia of republicanism, was quickly cured when he came to Paris, and the Pasteur of that day inoculated him with the genuine disease in its full malignancy. This opened the eyes of all Englishmen and of some Irishmen. Even le Monsieur Daniel O'Connell was so ' boulversé' at what he saw at St. Omer and Douai that he became for the time a strong Tory."

" Is it possible?" exclaimed one of the gentlemen. " I never knew that before! "

"I have read it," affirmed the Vicomte, nodding. He was a great reader, and if missing, was usually to be found concealed in the boughs of a tree with a book.

" Well," exclaimed his friend, " he went afterwards and straightway forgot what manner of man he was."

Again there were several moments of silent thought while the three young men puffed at their cigars and, with knitted brows, stared absently at the plants in the garden.

Presently Laboulaye spoke again. " After all," he said, " the revolutionists, at their best, are like Mofind Mendes, the mad-cap shepherdess, in Gil Vicente's Christmas auto. They say the revolution is their god, and they are its mother."

The other two young men smiled.

The Vicomte, without being in any degree a genius, had a quaint, it might be said, almost grotesque, way of putting things which made him an entertaining companion.

So they strolled on, talking with that strange mixture of depth and flippancy which distinguishes almost all interesting French conversationalists; men, perhaps, more than women, for the latter have the flippancy without the depth.

CHAPTER XXXII

MOYRAH hired a fiacre when she reached St. Cloud, and implored the cocher to drive very quick. He said he would, but he did not; and she was almost beside herself with impatience as they crawled along like an undecided elector tardily creeping to the poll. When, at length, they reached the gilt, child's toy looking lodge gate, she jumped out and asked the cocher to wait for her; but he refused point blank. He said his horse was dead tired, and he was going home as fast as he could.

Remonstrance was useless, so Moyrah resigned herself to her fate; she must only walk back she supposed.

With trembling hands she opened the smart gate, let herself in, and walked rapidly up the short, thickly gravelled avenue.

By this time, on the terrace in front of the château (the lodge gate and hall door were at the back) the young royalists' conversation had become intensely earnest. The Vicomte was giving an account of a terrible death bed scene which had once taken place in the very château under whose walls they were then walking. How the members of a secret society collected round the bed, and prevented the invalid from seeing a priest. The young Vicomte, a devout Catholic, grew pale as he described it. The dead man's ghost haunted the château, and, it seemed, preferred promenading on summer to winter nights. In that he showed the taste for which his nation is famous.

"It is just such a night as this he walks," he said,

scarcely above a whisper, looking round from side to side. The night wind rustled through the leaves which were hanging close to them. Then came a ghostly stillness.

At that moment a tall footman in livery, brilliant with gold lace, bowed before his master.

" A lady wishes to speak to monsieur in the portico."

He started.

" Pray ask her to walk in," he exclaimed. " Take her into the salon ; I'll come at once."

Apologising to his guests for leaving them, he hurried away.

" Let us hope it is not a ghost," they said.

He was absent about five minutes.

During that time the Vicomte's carriage drove up to the door. It was to convey them to an express train to Paris, which was to take them in time for an important meeting in the Rue ——

The footman hurried round from the front door to the terrace at the back of the house to inform them that the coachman said there was not an instant to lose, as they had barely time to catch the train as it was.

At that moment the Vicomte returned accompanied by a lady.

In an instant she was standing face to face with the two guests. One of them gave a loud exclamation and turned deadly pale, while he started back a step.

" Moyrah ! " he exclaimed.

" The Lorrud save ye, Mr. Sydney."

" Moyrah ! " he repeated.

" 'Tis me, indade, yer honour," she said, with the pretty little curtsey which was so linked in his mind with the Blue House.

From being deadly pale, Sydney's face got crimson, then paler than ever again.

The Vicomte looked from one to the other.

Moyrah's fashionable attire was somewhat dis-arranged, her lovely face was full of the most earnest purpose, her deep, dark, violet eyes were fixed on Sydney with a look of intense interest.

Sydney was trembling like a girl, and apparently unable to speak. What did it all mean?

But she did not leave them long in doubt. Speaking with a calmness and self control which, considering her Celtic blood, and wild bringing up, did her credit, she said: "Ye are goin' to a meetin' to-night, yer honour, in the Rue —— Numero ——?

"Yes, we are," said the Vicomte, starting forward quickly. "What of that?"

"Ye must not go," she exclaimed with the most strange and passionate eagerness.

"Not go!" echoed all the three gentlemen.

"No!" and there was something in her tone which startled them.

"But why?" exclaimed Laboulaye, looking amazed and puzzled, his fair eyebrows almost dissappearing under his opera hat.

"I cannot tell ye why," she said, getting crimson, "but ye must not."

"Impossible, madame," said Laboulaye, who had seen the wedding ring on her gloveless and trembling hand. "We are absolutely bound to go; our presence is of the utmost importance, especially that of Monsieur Sydney; the whole meeting is expecting him."

At that moment the footman re-appeared with a pressing request from the coachman that they would come at once.

"O, Mr. Sydney, for the love o' God," and she clasped her hands and advanced towards him, "don't go."

Once more those soft eyes, as they seemed to pierce him, struck the key note which made the deepest passions of his soul reverberate.

"But," he said in a tone of terrible agitation. "Moyrah, tell us why. What is your reason?"

"O, God help us all, but I can't, I can't!" she

answered, in a tone of fearful agony, while she pressed her hand across her brow as if distracted.

For an instant the thought flashed through Sydney's mind that trouble had temporarily upset her reason. From that moment his determination to go was taken.

"Moyrah," he said, gently, and with great tenderness and reverence, taking her hands in both of his. "The heat of the weather has been too much for you, you will get better presently. You must give me your address, and I will come and see you early to-morrow morning. Now you must try to be calm; there is a place in the carriage, we will take you with us to the station and see you safe into Paris.

All this time they had been walking slowly across the hall lobby and vestibule towards the hall door.

"Monsieur," said the footman, meeting them, "the coachman says it will be as much as ever he can do to catch the train now."

"And if we miss this, there is not another for two hours," said Laboulaye; "the meeting will be over."

They had reached the hall door and stepped out on to the gravelly front into the moonlight, under the waving trees. The carriage was a one-horse brougham, with an apology for four places inside.

"I am not ill, yer honour. But ye must not go; ye shall not go!" and she drew her hands from out of Sydney's and clasped both his wrists tightly.

Suddenly, as the horse heard the sound of her voice, he turned his head and gave a wild neigh of delight.

"Emmett!" shrieked Moyrah, startling the whole party as she rushed forward to greet her lost idol.

It was, indeed, Emmett. The fact was, there was to be a horse show in Paris, and so proud was Sydney of his purchase that he had determined to bring him over and exhibit him.

Now, the Vicomte, at that moment, had only one horse. He had been taken ill this morning, therefore Sydney's permission had been asked to allow Emmett

to be harnessed to the brougham to take them to the
station that evening.

Sydney had, however, intended to drive himself, for
he had no notion of trusting Emmett's mouth to the
pulling and dragging of a Parisian Jehu.

" It is Emmett, Moyrah," said Sydney, with the
deepest tenderness. " They had fired the stable and
threatened his life again, and I bought him from your
father there and then. He was harnessed to the carriage
to-night because the only other horse in the place is too
ill to go."

Moyrah kissed the horse's face again and again, and
stroked it with passionate affection ; while the coachman
stared until his eyes seemed starting out of his head.

' Come, Allons. Will you step in madame? We
really cannot wait another moment,' and Laboulaye
held the door open, and put out his hand to assist
Moyrah, amazement giving place to extreme impatience
in his voice and manner.

" No, No !" she answered, the look of wild agony
coming over her face again as she recollected the
position they were in. " You *must* not, *shall* not go."
She left Emmett quickly, and came close to Sydney.

" Impossible, madame; we must go, and go this very
moment, too." Laboulaye held out his hand. " Pray
allow me to hand you in, otherwise we must go without
you."

With an exclamation of heartrending anguish, she
flung herself on her knees before Sydney, and clasped
his ankles with her arms until they were held so tightly
that he could not move.

" O, Misthur Sydney, for the love o' God don't go.
See; I'll hold ye an' ye can't."

" Quick, send for the housekeeper," said Laboulaye
to the footman. We must put her under her care until
we return. Quick, quick !" and he waved his hand
impatiently.

Sydney bent down, and with the superior strength of

his masculine muscles, by sheer force, unwound her
arms and raised her up.

"Moyrah," he said, with a veneration such as he
might have used to his mother, united to a tenderness
which made her tremble, while he looked intently into
her deep dark eyes, "you know what," he paused,
emotion choked his voice for a moment, "what duty
means, for you have done yours nobly all your life;
why, then, try to prevent us from doing ours? We
have promised to be at this meeting; we are bound by
every rule of honour and duty to go. Under such
circumstances, you would be the first to go yourself,
would you not? Tell me, Moyrah; would you not?"
and he looked intently into her eyes.

At that moment, the housekeeper, a tall stout person,
evidently of great bodily strength, appeared, and seemed
inclined to advance towards Moyrah and take her away
by sheer force.

With the extraordinarily quick intuition of her race,
Moyrah felt they looked on her as mad. She saw
that in another moment she would have her arms
pinioned and be held down by the might of the
strongest.

There was one awful moment of dead stillness, as
there so often is before something terrible happens;
then a low, soft whistle was heard, the sound of the
silver whistle.

Emmett turned his kingly head and fixed his loving
eyes full upon his mistress, as much as so say, "I know
it well. Blessed am I to hear it again!"

Sydney started, as he saw the moonshine flash upon
some bright instrument Moyrah had dragged from her
bosom; but in an instant, a more brilliant flash, and
this time from no celestial orb, dazzled him. A sharp,
cracking report whizzed through the evening air;
followed, or it seemed accompanied by a terrific piercing
neigh, or rather shriek from Emmett. He reared bolt
upright for an instant, pawed the air wildly with his

front legs, as if he did not know what he was doing; then, with an appalling crash fell over on his side, smashing the shafts to atoms, overturning the carriage, and entirely shattering the glass windows.

When first Emmett reared, the valiant Jehu had incontinently flung the reins to the wind, sprung off the box, giving the whole concern a wide berth, and so saved himself from a scratch

Emmett gave a few gasping, sob-like snorts, a few feeble struggles with his poor fore legs, and then all was still.

CHAPTER XXXIII.

MOYRAH fell back senseless into the arms of the old housekeeper, who was advancing to take her by force alive.

As soon as Sydney could collect himself after the fearful shock, he went towards the housekeeper, and taking her burden from her, carried the lithe, graceful figure, now apparently dead, into the library of the château, which stood immediately on the left of the hall door. He chose a soft-looking blue velvet sofa for its resting place. As he laid her down, he leaned his head over her heart and heard that it was beating.

The Vicomte, looking terrified out of his senses, went in and stared at her, and so did the other gentleman, Monsieur Lupin.

Sydney called for sal volatile, eau de Cologne, and cold water, and the housekeeper fetched them as fast as she could; but nothing seemed to have the slightest effect on her, though Sydney could tell she was still alive, because her heart was beating, and there was a vapour on the pocket mirror he held before her mouth. As he knelt by the sofa chafing her cold hands and bathing her forehead with eau de Cologne, he kept muttering: "What villainy has that fiend been up to by which he has unhinged her reason? Demon! Scoundrel! Would the shot had gone through his head!"

An hour passed away and Moyrah had not recovered. In the meantime the Vicomte had sent for a celebrated doctor, who kept a small private *maison de santé* about a mile and a half from the château. He arrived; said Moyrah was well and healthy, and would soon recover her senses. He took out some strong medicine he had with him and poured it down her mouth. Almost directly afterwards she regained consciousness, sat up and looked about in a bewildered manner.

"Where am I?" she asked, looking round in a dazed way, as she laid the palm of her hand across her forehead.

"You are amongst friends, Moyrah, avourneen," said Sydney, using the Irish word to try and give her a home-like feeling. The sound of it stirred some strange, or, rather, some familiar chord in her heart, and she burst into tears.

"Don't fret, Moyrah; you are amongst friends, and the truest, though the most unworthy you have, is kneeling at your side."

"You must take her home to your house, doctor, as soon as ever you think she can walk. I fear it is a hopeless case," said the Vicomte, in a confidential whisper. He was dying to get her out of the house, not knowing who or what she might shoot next.

"My good madame, pray be composed," said the doctor, who was a polished blade; "there is nothing which so impairs the beauty of youth as immoderate weeping," he added, with true French instinct as to the logic best calculated to affect the female brain. It had not, however, the slightest influence on Moyrah; in fact, she neither heard nor heeded it.

"I fear it is a hopeless case," repeated the nervous young Vicomte. "I implore of you to get her away, my good sir, as quickly as ever you can," he added, in a whisper so loud as to be very " stage " indeed.

"Bien, monsieur, bien," said the doctor, a little impatiently.

"Madame," said the doctor, gracefully bowing to his fair patient, " those charms which must fascinate all hearts will be completely effaced if you continue to weep thus." He approached and took her hand. "Compose yourself, my dear madame, and all will be well. You are about to accompany me to my house."

"Sir!" she said, looking hard at him, and then at Sydney.

Sydney trembled as her eyes rested on him. There was something so perfectly sane in the quiet dignity of her manner, that he felt a reasonable excuse must be given to her.

She drew her hand away from the doctor, and came close to Sydney, as if for protection.

"Moyrah," he said, with a deep, extraordinary tenderness in his voice, which contrasted strangely with the flippant tones of the doctor, "I will go with you and see that you are made comfortable."

· "Consider, madame," said the doctor, "there are no ladies in this house; only three young bachelors."

"Mais oui!" exclaimed the Vicomte, in enchantment, catching quickly at the idea. "It is true, madame, you are as safe here as in the palace of a king; but you must consider what the Parisian world would say. We have our reputations to maintain, madame; mine has ever stood high amongst the party to which I have the honour to belong; the drapeau blanc has more than one meaning for its followers," and he bowed towards Moyrah, while he rubbed his hands, too exuberantly pleased for any disguise of politeness to conceal his joy.

A painfully brilliant blush came over Moyrah's face and neck. She looked down and stood quite still and silent; but Sydney could hear the beating of her heart. She clasped her hands tightly together in front of her; so tightly, that Sydney felt certain she must be causing herself great pain; but then, mercifully, mad people did not suffer physically to the same extent as sane ones, he recollected.

He laid his hand on her arm, and with his head slightly thrown back, glanced indignantly from the doctor to Laboulaye. There was something in his eyes they did not care to meet, and gladly turned their own in another direction.

At that moment, there was a sharp ring at the hall door. They all started; started almost like guilty people disturbed in some crime.

Immediately afterwards a footman appeared with a telegram, which he handed to Laboulaye. He tore it open with a trembling hand, and flung the envelope on the floor. It was of an official nature, and of that charmingly useful character which usually distinguishes official communications.

" Do not go to meeting ; there has been a dynamite explosion ; all present wounded."

Laboulaye let the paper drop from his hand, and sank on to a blue velvet chair, while his knees knocked together, his teeth chattered, and a cold perspiration stood out on his forehead.

The doctor picked it up and read it out in a loud voice.

Had the explosion occurred in that room it could scarcely have produced a greater effect. Monsieur Lupin fell back against a table with a terrible exclamation. The doctor's eyes grew rounder and more like doll's saucers every moment.

The housekeeper shrieked four or five times, and fell back on to the sofa, with her arms flung wide, like the sails of a windmill, at each side.

Moyrah's and Sydney's eyes met in one long, silent look

To Sydney, the recollection of that look made the darkness of his future life more beautiful than the brightest light of his past. It was like the ancyle, or shield, which fell from heaven in the reign of Numa Pompilius. It shielded him from those foes within the fortress which we all have to fight. The voice that spoke in it did not, indeed, say: " Rome shall be mistress of the world ; " but it gave him strength to become for ever master of that, to him, far greater world, his own heart.

The first person to speak was Laboulaye. He rose, and advancing towards Moyrah, said, with the utmost courtesy: "Madame, I fear I must have seemed impolite to you; pardon me. We owe to you, madame, our lives," he paused in visible agitation. "It is impossible for us ever to repay you, madame; quite impossible; perfectly impossible! But if there is anything in the world I can do for you, or give to you, you have but to command me." He stopped again for a moment, overcome. "Always, at all times, madame, I shall be entirely bound to you." He bowed very low.

He ordered the grandest room in the house to be prepared for her, one which had not been used since the uncrowned King of France had slept there. All his prejudices in favour of his own reputation vanished like the evening mist.

The idea of her, to whom they all owed their lives, going off with a " mad " doctor to a lunatic asylum was not to be thought of for a moment. Every Frenchman has a perfect horror of even the mention of a *maison de santé.*

The doctor was very much thanked, and dismissed with a magnificent fee from Sydney.

The transformed host ordered up supper in the *salle à manger,* and sent for the best wines his cellars contained, to do honour to Moyrah. But she would not touch them; indeed, no one seemed inclined to eat much.

Moyrah sat silent, deadly pale, with a tremble on her lip, and a soft dew welling up into her eyes, the sight of which cut into Sydney's heart like the stab of a dagger. He was also silent, and sipped his wine as if in a dream.

Soon, the Vicomte, perceiving that Moyrah was eating nothing, and was silent from the force of a strong will keeping down her emotion, asked her, with great courtesy, if she would like to retire; and upon her giving a pleased assent, ordered the housekeeper to come at once and accompany her to her room. Rising himself, he, with the greatest deference, conducted her to the door, and again thanked her with the most profuse and sincere gratitude.

Once alone in the magnificent apartment devoted to her, Moyrah threw herself on her knees and sobbed in the most terrible manner, as if all the foundations of her nature were giving way.

For a whole hour she sobbed on, until at last, worn out with the fearful excitement, the awful scenes, the terrible disclosures she had gone through, she actually fell asleep, still sobbing. Gradually she sank on to the floor, and there she lay all night.

CHAPTER XXXIV.

IT was a strange scene the early morning sun broke
in upon through the slits in the jalousies. The
walls of the room were padded with blue satin on
which was embossed elaborate *fleurs-de-lys*; the chairs
of the same; the curtains of the bed of the same; the
material being so thick that it stood out almost like a
metal, gathered up finally into a gold crown at the top,
representing the crown of France. Girandoles and
mirrors were arranged about everywhere, and reflected
couches, easy chairs, and little velvet tables innumerable.
There were two small pictures let into the wall; one
was of Saint Louis, King of France; the other, of
Marie Antoinette. The housekeeper had filled a vase
full of white lilies, and put it on the dressing table, and
another on a little bracket under the picture of the
queen.

In the midst of this gorgeous setting lay Moyrah,
full length on the rich carpet of blue pile, her arm under
her head, her brown hair tossed off her forehead, her
long, dark, silky lashes resting on a cheek whiter than
the whitest of the lily flowers.

The calm face of the martyred queen smiled down
upon her; one of the first victims to that storm of
revolution, the waves of which were now buffeting
her.

In consequence of the great heat of the day, the
housekeeper, when preparing the room the night before,
had left a bit of the window, which opened down the
middle, open. The songs of the birds, and the gentle

waving of the boughs in the fresh morning breeze, came in, making a music which appealed to all the most secret and loveliest faculties of our nature. The air seemed full of pensive, pathetic stories, mingling weeping and smiles in some of the sweetest melodies of thought imagination can suggest. The thrush's song united with the deep coos of the wood pigeon and the distant humming of the bees. There was the smell of countless flowers from the garden. All external nature under its present aspect in and around that royalist home seemed to trace that golden path of life which lies before all who will tread it, and leads to a crown no revolution can shatter. Yes; the air was rich with the scent of the living *fleurs-de-lys* adorning the beds in the old-fashioned garden of the château under the window; and so the spiritual air was rich with the living—living with a higher life—*fleurs-de-lys* of innocence and holiness, kept through all trials, which adorned the beautiful, but, in these days, distinctly old-fashioned garden of Moyrah's soul.

The sun was rising in such splendours of gold and crimson that the dyes upon the sky could scarcely be called colours, but were like a sheet of flame. Each leaf upon the grand old trees was like an Irish diamond cut with many facings, flashing its crowd of colours towards the room where Moyrah was sleeping.

On the long beams of the morning sun, down the pathway of ages, there seemed to come in triumphant procession all the noble spirits who made France so beautiful and glorious in the days gone by; made her the chosen home of chivalry, the garden of romance, when she had a few other beliefs besides the one that everybody is betraying her. St. Louis, Bernard of Clairvaux, Charlemagne, Joan of Arc, Godfrey de Bouillon, St. Regimus of Rheims, Clodowald, son of Chlodomir, the goldsmith, St. Eloi, minister to Dagobert, Louis VII. and his wife Eleanor, who both took the cross for the crusades, Anne of France, married to

Pierre de Beauju, of whom Louis said: "She is the least silly woman I know, for of wise women there are none," St. Denis, St. Roch, St. Hubert, St. Cloud himself, and many thousands more.

On they came in unswerving ranks, just as they marched on earth. Here was no malicious hatred of all that was above them, no ghoulish delight in exhuming the crimes of heathendom, and forcing them down the throats of Christians, no envenomed trampling on the rights of others. Here there was no imitation of Limulus, the Molucca crab, which progesses backwards at such a rate as to astonish all beholders. Here were no fierce unbridled hatreds, no vindictive jealousy of all that is better than self, no deification of all that destroys the deepest sanctities of life. There were countless great men in this glorious throng taken from all ranks of life, many from the official classes, but there was no *juge d'instruction* to teach the young idea that virtue is an *émigré*, who has been banished because she carried a slip knot in her hand with which she throttled progress. Nothing to bring before the mind an image of the modern condition of the town in whose suburbs Moyrah was lying, and which had once been the glorious capital of their glorious country.

Here all was calm, peaceful, just, and yet brilliantly pure and beautiful, like the exquisite crystallized octaëdrite found so richly in veins in Dauphiny, and which formed the vase holding the lilies under the picture of Marie Antoinette.

They held swords in their hands which were twined with laurels. On they came, many of them in royal robes and with kingly crowns upon their heads, representing that true principle of monarchy on whose pattern the church in heaven and the church on earth is founded.

As each majestic form passed Moyrah's girlish figure in that haunted room they bent their heads, recognising in her a friend and ally, one who was fighting on the same side of the battle field of life as that on which their swords had waved when here below. A descendant worthy of the name.

And so they left her and passed on and away to that unfading palace of the king, the road to which she was so bravely treading. They left her still sleeping, but with a flush of returning happiness and peace on that soft cheek, which had been all night as white as a lily, and the lines of sorrow round her mouth smoothed away.

At six o'clock she awoke; she had been used to get up at four at the Blue House. She awoke from the repose, not of recruited, but of exhausted nature. At first, she stared round her in a dazed, bewildered way; then she made her habitual sign of the cross, which she always made on waking, and even while her eyes became dazzled by the regal splendours round her, remembered, as she always did the first thing in the morning, that she was in the presence of the King of Kings. She used visible things, not to hide, but to remind her of things invisible. She laid quite still for some time, staring at the marvels of sumptuousness which surrounded her on every side; she had never been in a room the least like this before and felt awed.

But soon terrible thoughts and recollections came back to her mind, and tears rushed up to her eyes. Waking to sorrow on a bright summer morning is like a skeleton sitting at a wedding breakfast. As she lay there, she formed her resolution; she sat up, took a pencil and a bit of paper out of her pocket, and wrote a few lines to Sydney.

She begged him to thank the Vicomte for his great kindness to her, and she said she had gone away so early, and without saying good bye, because she had been obliged to for reasons which she could not at that moment explain. She begged Sydney and the Vicomte to forgive her.

She folded up this little note, and having arranged her dress to a certain extent, she stole softly on her tip-

toes down stairs, laid the note on the table in the centre
vestibule, then tried the hall door. It had been opened,
some of the under servants were up and about; but she
did not meet any.

Once out in the open air she walked quickly. She
let herself out at the gilded gates as she had let herself
in the night before. She had an admirable memory for
locality, fortunately, and, with the assistance of a few
questions, easily found her way to the *gare*.

But she was tired with the long walk, fasting, and her
head ached badly by the time she reached her apartment
in Paris. There she washed and dressed herself, took
a cup of coffee and a roll, replenished her coffers, and
started for the *gare*. Once in the train, obliged to
sit still, and unable to stifle reflection by exertion, her
mind wandered to the pedestrian journey she had taken
to save Cormac from his burning house; and then came
a vision of her girlhood. Old thoughts, old feelings
came over her. Those characters which are woven of
the finest web are the most natural, that is, the most
like nature. Season after season nature ushers the
same daisies and roses on the scene. She says the same
thing in the note of the wood pigeon; the rustling of
the breeze in the young mountain ash leaves; and so
the noblest natures are most fond of passing and
re-passing through the best feelings of their youth.

Packed into that stifling railway carriage, filled as
full as it would hold, and with both the windows tight
shut, after the fashion of French carriages going south,
Moyrah stared absently at the flat level of country and
the tall poplar trees which shot in the window and out
again. The other passengers were occupied fighting
about politics, or eating and drinking. Almost unknown
to herself she sank into a reverie. She saw again the
Blue House, her father and mother, Eileen and the
boys. She recalled their pranks and jokes, and merry
laughter; then she compared her life there with her
present existence. Though to a certain extent un-

cultured, her mind was reflective and capable of indefinite expansion under proper training. It was a plant which would well have repaid care and attention; now, though terribly restless and feverish, some of the loveliest flowers blossomed in it, in the shape of ideas of patience and self-devotion towards the husband whose real character was beginning to dawn upon her.

It is thought an odd thing (though why it should be thought so is the really odd thing; only that everything nature does is thought odd by some minds) that there should be one genus of plants, the Aristolochia, which is as widely distributed as the poisonous snake whose bite it heals.

Under the form of what, to her, was an angel of light, the snake of Communism had bitten Moyrah, and tried to kill her soul; but she had quickly found the true Aristolochia. Those plants of the heart which are as widely spread as true womanhood, had provided an antidote ready to hand; an antidote which, in her Irish soul, had lost none of its power, and which made the poison of the most malignant viper as contemptible as an earwig's pinch.

Patience, at least, she could have. What an insignificant place moralists appoint to patience; but the authors of the new translation of the Bible have given a striking version, and one which raises patience to a kingly throne. " In patience ye shall win your souls." In the battle for our salvation it is, then, what the sword is in a light cavalry charge. It is remarkable, too, that Goethe, who knew a good deal of the external relative value of virtues (and often virtues are most correctly judged of from the outside) gives patience a position of supreme importance. When Mephistopheles is mocking Faust, until he maddens him, Faust curses everything holy; but he curses patience with a fury greater than that with which he curses faith or hope.

Moyrah had never thought much about patience;

Irish natures as a rule do not. But it was a flower she would cultivate. Flowering is always accompanied by an evolution of heat considerably over the normal temperature of the plant; and the very fever of her pain may have brought those flowers to light. The lessons of unselfishness she had learned, as she knelt by her father in the little chapel, were, no doubt, the parent stock from which the blossoms sprang; but, still they required the sufferings of the present hour to bring them to perfection.

As the train rattled on, and the sun rose higher and higher in the sky, the heat became overpowering. Moyrah was obliged to put up her thick veil, or it would have been a case of suffocation.

For a moment the enchanting excitement of political squabbling was forgotten, and that prodigy witnessed, a carriage full of silent Frenchmen. After staring for some time, however, and giving one or two low whistles, they soon began to fight again. Fight, fight, fight in words, the whole employment of the modern descendants of Bayard, Charlemagne, King Louis, and many thousands like them fight, fight, fight about every-thing natural and un-natural; while the only intercourse with the supernatural they appear to have is like what Balaam had when taking his ride.

CHAPTER XXXV.

HOWEVER enigmatical the complicated problem of a man's mind may be, even to himself, and much more to a woman, this much is certain : that he has in it depths of power and heights of majesty, a capability of conceiving glorious visions, of putting into practice noble dreams and high purposes, such as no woman's mind can ever approach to, or even guess at. It is useless for women to deny, or to grumble and be cross at this. No amount of wounded vanity or spiteful words will alter facts ; it is an ordinance of nature. They might as well expect to make the halfpenny dip they carry about the house turn suddenly into the sun by nagging at the sun, as to make their little, but, nevertheless, useful, as far as they go, intellects turn into the mighty minds which have produced the greatest works the world has ever seen. Within themselves, men are constantly surrounded by a splendid pageant of imagery, which, if it leaves them for a time, when engaged in business, etc., they can whistle back in a moment.

This, perhaps, is what separates them most from women, and makes the simile of the sun and a halfpenny dip not an exaggerated one. For, of this imagery women know nothing, except what they read in the poetry of men, or in what often seems to be their almost divinely inspired poetic prose. It is disagreeable for women to have to own this ; but there is no use in running your head against a stone wall; contradicting a fact will not alter it.

Every man at his outset into life, has a beautiful building, a temple, in his heart. In those earliest days, his happiest times are when he can go out for a long dreamy walk or ride in lovely scenery, alone; then he enters by himself into this temple, and explores its wonders. It is like the Taj Mahal at Agra.

To bring it a little before those carping, criticising women-puffers and men-condemners, who are trying to give an object lesson to society by proving white is black in the present day, I would like to describe the Taj Mahal. I will do so by a quotation from one of the most brilliant writers of our time, whose words will portray it more graphically than any language I can command.

" I had recently been in India, where my eye had been educated, and my taste chastened by wrapt contemplation of the fairest masterpiece fashioned by human hands, conceived by human brain, in all the world. Few who can appreciate the divine simplicity of true beauty can gaze on the Taj Mahal at Agra without tears. There is no single flaw to be found in its unique completeness. It is approached by a massive and noble archway of highly decorated—purposely over-decorated—red sandstone, and as you stand on the steps under its shadow, your heart-beats seem to be stilled by the poetic languor of the scene. Fine trees, a wealth of trailing creepers and flowering shrubs; in the centre a long, white, straight line of tank, in whose pellucid water is mirrored the most elegant and fairy-like building conceivable, of warm white marble, crowned by an exquisite cupola. The delicate and refined grace of its shape is sharply cut out against a cloudless sky of purest turquoise; its pale hue becomes visionary by contrast with the full green of the foliage. It combines the acme of lightness with solidity and dignity; is essentially lady-like in the best acceptation of the word; fit resting place for a lady who has been handed down through admiring

ages as the best and fairest of her sex. Closer inspection
leads to greater admiration, for walls which might at
close quarters seem too severely simple, are relieved
by a delicate tracery in pietra dura, an inlaid pattern,
composed of jasper, cornelian and lapis lazuli. The
cunning architect has to throw up the mellow beauty
of the white, juxtaposed at fitting distances, buildings
of warm red sandstone peeping through the green.
As one sits and looks and marvels, one is smitten with
awe in that a mind should have existed so highly
cultured as to conceive such a combination of perfections."*

A man built the Taj Mahal, and this is what is in
every man's heart at his outset in life. This is what
makes a young man's face, just as he is standing on the
threshold of the world of action, the most beautiful
sight that is ever seen. It is the glory of the temple
shining out through his eyes. Later on he may let an
earthquake in his lower nature dash the building down,
and shatter it. If he does so, he soon finds it cannot be
re-built; it lies a heap of ruins for the rest of life. But
the stones have voices, and they tell him always of what
they once made. The vision of the temple as first he
saw it haunts him to the last; it has a persistent vitality
which sometimes he wishes it had not. But my
argument is, that it existed in a man's mind, and it
never existed in a woman's, and there's the difference;
as great as between a halfpenny dip and the sun. The
simile is *not* exaggerated; I insist on that. Men's
writings, men's paintings, men's buildings, men's
musical compositions prove its truth. That temple
as it stands at dawning manhood is meant, is built
entirely, expressly, and only, whether he knows it
or not, to hold the image of the Madonna. Many
men who do not know it, acting up to what they
do know, keep that temple without a rift to the end.

---

* " Wanderings of a Globe Trotter," by Hon. Lewis Wingfield.

And then at the last, let us hope—who can say?—
they have the exceedingly great reward, when the
sight of all earthly buildings is growing faint, of
knowing what it was built for. A Catholic young
man does know it from the first; with him, when
it falls, the ruin is complete.

Henri de St. Cyr knew it well enough; he had
learned it at his mother's knee.

In a house in a narrow street in Bayonne, a young
man lay dying. Round his bed were gathered a number
of other men, mostly middle aged, but one or two young
ones.

The dying man's face had the most terrible expression
on it. Had a model been wanted for one of the men
only just arrived in Dante's " Inferno," he would have
supplied it. The bewilderment, the horror, the amazement, the repulsion, the terror, the longing to get away,
and the not knowing where to go; the " I *must* get out
of this," and then the baffled look on finding he could
not, were all there.

A clever-looking, smartly-dressed man, with his hair
already considerably tinged with grey, held before him
a dagger, and said: " Renew your vow."

" Yes, yes; I do! " said the dying man, in a tone of
agony, hurriedly, while he turned his eyes towards the
door with a hungry, eager look.

" That won't do," said the man. " You must say ' I
renew it,' and kiss the dagger."

" I renew my vow," repeated Henri St. Cyr, for
that was the name of the victim, and he kissed the
dagger.

" You know," said the eldest man present, " you
joined the society when you were in full health and
strength, of your own free will, and now you must
remain true to the end."

" Yes, yes ; I know," gasped Henri. " But if I might
see my brother for only, only "—a fearful gasp—" one
minute."

"But your brother is a priest; you know what he would do."

"I would do nothing; I swear to you I would do nothing. I only want to say one word on family business."

"But whatever family business you have to arrange you can tell me. I will repeat it to him later on. Remember, I am a lawyer. You know you are not dying intestate. We have your will and your letters of administration, and I am the administrator."

"Yes, yes; I know," said the sick man, with a frown and another hunted, hungry look at the door.

"The trustees will see that all the legacies are duly paid, especially those to the propagators of the society."

A look of hideous torment came over the young man's face. He clenched his white blue-veined fist and dashed it down on the coverlet.

"I give you my word of honour I don't want to recant. I give you my word of honour of it. I only want to speak to my brother about something he and I know about, and nobody else knows. I will leave all my money to you, every single farthing. I swear to you not a penny shall go to my own family, if you will only let me see him for five minutes by the clock!"

He fixed his terrified, bloodshot eyes, full of the most agonizing entreaty, on the administrator's face.

At that instant an old lady, with a sad face and snow-white hair, and a young priest, were standing on the steps knocking at the hall door.

A man put his head out of a window near the door. "It is useless for you to knock," he said, "I have my orders, and you cannot come in. How often do you require to be told?"

"But I am *his mother!* O, have pity on me! I will pay you anything you like to ask! Have pity on me; you must have had a mother!"

" Allez vous en ! " said the man, fiercely, slamming the window.

The lady and the priest—who was Henri's twin brother Louis—beat upon the door with all their might. Louis kicked it until he hurt his toes well, but it resisted every assault.

Suddenly a thought struck Louis. He smashed in a window on the ground floor, undid the fastening, flung up the sash and bounded in. Like a greyhound he sprang across the floor, and was soon up the first flight of stairs. He had taken three steps at a time of the second, when two men seized him from behind, and dragged him down. They were immediately reinforced by two others, and in the desperate struggle which ensued the young priest's smooth black coat was torn from top to bottom, his head was dashed against the bannister and cut, until blood streamed over his face, and his left wrist was dislocated ; but he fought on like a man.

In the meantime, in the sick man's room the conversation continued.

" Bah ! You wish to be a renegade at the last ! " said the eldest man, contemptuously.

" No ! no ! I swear to you it is only something connected with my boyhood—something I once did that only my brother knows about—that I wish to speak to him of. Oh, I beg of you ! " and he stretched out his hand, while a look of piteous entreaty, which seemed as if it must move any human heart, came over him.

" Enough of this ! Silence ! " said Lenoir, who was standing by a small table near the bed.

" Are you ready, gentlemen ? "

" Bein, oui."

Henri trembled so that the bed shook under him. He knew what was coming.

Alphonse quickly took a parcel out of a cardboard box, unwound the paper and held a statue of the *Mater Purissima* before him.

" Say she was not a virgin and curse her ! "

Henri turned his head away.

" Come ! come ! " said Lenoir, " Make haste ! "

Henri turned his face towards the pillow.

" Come ! come ! " said Lenoir, stamping his foot. " What the devil are you maundering about now ? "

Still Henri did not look round.

" Damn you ; you weak-kneed, lukewarm turncoat ! " and Lenoir struck his fist angrily on the bed. " We're not going to stand any snivelling or drivelling now, I can tell you."

" Don't frighten him," said the elder man, cautiously, " or we shan't get him to do anything."

" Bah ! " said Lenoir, fiercely, " we'll soon see what he'll do."

Lenoir was in no mood to be crossed or worried just now. He had arrived from Paris thoroughly out of temper, and his present employment was not calculated to restore him.

" Come, come ; make haste ! " Lenoir felt his pulse. " I would'nt give you five minutes more ; come ! " and he held the statue close up to his face.

" Say you curse her," said the oldish man, in a much gentler, quieter manner than Lenoir spoke in.

Henri's ashy lips trembled so that they could scarcely close and open, his hands clutched at the bedclothes, and his eyes wandered from one of his persecutors to the other, with a half piteous and imploring, and a half hating and loathing look.

Lenoir seized his shaking, wiry wrist, with the dew of death upon it, and exclaimed furiously, " We'll stand no more trifling, young cub ; curse her this instant ! "

The bloodless lips moved up and down, and the faltering words came out : " I curse her ! "

Lenoir fixed his piercing, yellowy black eyes intently on him.

" Say she was a vile woman, and you hope her name may be trampled off the earth."

"I do!" said Henri. Then he gave a shriek, his head fell back, and in another instant he was gone. That frightful shriek penetrated the thin glass of the windows and reached his mother's ears as she stood on the doorstep. It seemed to freeze her blood to ice. It never again left her ears.

Lenoir gave his shoulders a contemptuous shrug, and, turning away, sat down at a table in the window to finish a letter he had begun some time before. It was a letter full of advice to one of the Irish-American agitators in New York—advice which was followed. He had scarcely stamped and sealed it when a telegram was put into his hand. He tore it open, and read:

"Fly for your life. Your *cocotte* has peached and flown to a royalist lover at St. Cloud. England safest."

The telegram was in hieroglyphics, but this was its translation.

Crushing it in his hand, he uttered a frightful curse on Moyrah. Then he said a few words to one or two of the men. They stood in a sort of conclave for a short time. After that he left the room hurriedly.

CHAPTER XXXVI.

WHEN Moyrah reached Bayonne, the sun was setting; another brilliant sunset like the last night's. It made the broad winding river a sheet of gold, and lighted up the rigging of the countless ships lying along the quays. It fell upon the trees scattered here and there on its banks, and transformed them until it seemed as if they were clothed already in their autumn robe of many colours; last of all it lighted up the low spire, with the large cross, the flying buttresses, and the pointed windows of the cathedral. It shone in long, slanting rays upon the Place du Marché, and lit up the door to the south transept of the Cathedral, the only part where the ancient statues are preserved. Those old stone saints have seen strange things in their day, but surely the events of these later times surpass all. In the days when they lived, sin existed in France, certainly, but it was a foe, and when you fell you went down under the blows of an open enemy. Now, it is the god at whose shrine you are to worship, and when you have the misfortune to fall into goodness, hundreds of willing hands are ready to drag you out of the scrape, thousands of racy books to tell you how to avoid getting into it again. This is what makes those poor old stone saints stare with such wide open eyes as they do, so that the lids in many cases are crumbling away.

Moyrah thought of none of these things as she hurried along with her head bent down. She got confused by the labyrinth of streets, and lost her way, and strayed

round by the Château de Marrac, where Napoleon
dethroned the Bourbons of Spain, and put his own
brother Joseph in their place ; and at the same time,
with his usual unique liberality, bestowed on Spain
a new constitution.　As the Americans say : " Conceit
grows as natural as the hair on one's head, but
it is longer coming out."　Where the strange,
extraordinary scene was enacted between Charles IV.,
Ferdinand VII., and Napoleon ; each one simulating
passion, and telling lies in hopes of deceiving the other,
a veil which, however, was too thin to wash.　Like men
pretending to play chess blindfold, but each detecting
the other peeping from under the bandage, they soon
burst into that noble contempt which such circumstances
command, and the house is chiefly commemorated by the
row they had there.

Moyrah had the bit of paper, with the address on it,
which Lenoir had given her ; but she could not find the
street.　She wandered on and passed without noticing
it that symbol of the *libre penseur*, the high column
of vapour, which marks the hot fountain in the middle
of the town.　Suddenly she came upon an old lady
sitting on the doorstep of a house, sobbing bitterly.
Moyrah *never* could see suffering without the most
strange passionate longing to alleviate it.　Hurried and
miserable as she was she stopped ; bending down towards
the lady, she said : " Will ye forgi' me for spakin' to yer
honour, but could I do anythin' to help ye ? "

The lady looked up in astonishment.　It was some
years since she had heard English spoken, but she had
known it well when youug.　The sweet, pale, lovely
face looking down at her, full of the most intense
compassion, touched her heart.

" My son is dying," she said, taking Moyrah's hand
in an agitated, trembling grasp, " and I cannot go to
him."

" But why not ? " exclaimed Moyrah, with breathless
eagerness.

“They will not let me in. It is in this house, this
very house,” and again her sobs burst forth.”

“ I’ll knock wid a rale slatherin’ row,” she exclaimed,
seizing the knocker, and giving such a rat-tat-tat as
nearly broke the door in.

“ It is useless,” she said, in a tone which pierced
Moyrah’s heart. “ My son, the vicaire, has gone in
through the window. God grant,” and she clasped her
hands, and raised her eyes to heaven, “they will not
kill him ! ”

“ But who are they ?   What are they ? ” exclaimed
Moyrah, furiously.

“ They are the leading members of a secret society,
who wish to prevent him from seeing a priest on his
death bed, for fear he should save his soul.”

“ God help us ! ” said Moyrah, crossing herself. Then,
seeing the need of comfort the poor old lady stood in,
she added : “ But, maybe they’ll give in whin they see
him sit upon it inthirely.”

“ If you know anything of my unhappy country, you
will know how much chance there is of that, when I tell
you Alphonse Lenoir is leading them.”

Moyrah uttered a piercing exclamation, and recoiled
backwards.

“ What ! ” she exclaimed, “ *what* did ye say ? ”

“ Do you know Alphonse Lenoir ? ” asked the old
lady, looking up in surprise.

“ I do, I do.”

The old lady looked at her ; then repeated low :
“ May God have mercy on you if he is a friend of
yours ! ”

“ A *friend* of mine ! ” exclaimed Moyrah. “ He is
my husband ! ”

“ No, *that* he is not, and never can be as long as my
most miserable daughter is alive,” said the old lady,
starting to her feet.

Moyrah uttered a cry of terror.

“ *What ?* What did ye say ? ”

" Alphonse Lenoir married my unfortunate daughter some years ago, when they were both very young ; she has been obliged to separate from him ; his conduct was too infamous for it to be possible for her to remain with him. She now gives him an allowance to live away from her. He is always teasing her to get a divorce ; but, of course, she is a good Catholic, c'est impossible."

Moyrah leaned against the projecting corner of the house, while a pallor, positively death-like, spread over her.

At that instant a man sprang out of the window Louis St. Cyr had broken to get in at.

As he turned to hurry away, the lady stretched out her hand and said : " Le voila ! "

Moyrah looked and recognized Lenoir's figure, though he was very much muffled up.

He did not see them, apparently. He never turned round, but walked so fast as to be almost running, only evidently he did not wish to create suspicion by running actually.

As Lenoir hurried along he muttered : " I wish I could get hold of Moyrah, I'd teach her a lesson she would not forget in a hurry. This comes of being kind to people. I never was so kind to anyone in my life as I was to her. She must have broken open my escritoire ; the little devil. If so, she has all my secrets, and a good many other people's, too, in her possession. She is too dangerous to be at large ; I must get hold of her by hook or by crook ; besides, I had intended, when I had initiated her, to make her of great use with the Irish contingent. This comes of showing kindness to people. She shan't have much of that to complain of when we meet again."

At that moment the door opened and a man came out whom Moyrah instantly recognised as the man whom she had heard making the socialistic speech in the bye street in Paris.

He recognised Madame St. Cyr at once. " Well,
old macaques," he exclaimed, jeeringly ; " your cub
is dead ! He died true to his principles, and cursed
your Virgin with his last breath, led by Alphonse
Lenoir."

Moyrah uttered a low exclamation of agony, and
put her hand to her forehead for a moment.

" *What* did you say Alphonse Lenoir did ?" she
asked, in the best French she could command.

" He —y, ma femme galante," he exclaimed, turning
and looking at her lovely face with the utmost inso-
lence. " What do you know of Alphonse Lenoir?
What did he do? Why ——" and he repeated his
former words, only this time so clearly and distinctly
that there was no possibility of mistaking their meaning.

The most terrible emotions passed over Moyrah's
face. Even the chartered libertine who was staring at
her, and who had a fresh insult on his lips, shrunk
back abashed at the sight of such agony.

At that moment the young priest, a most noble
looking young man, came out, his clothes all torn, his
hair dishevelled and his face cut and bleeding.

" You are safe, my son! You are safe! Thank
God!" exclaimed his mother, embracing him. He
offered her his arm, and with one glance of contempt
at the man who was on the door step, was walking
away when Madame St. Cyr stopped, and putting her
hand on Moyrah's arm said : " Come home with us ;
this is no fit place for you."

Moyrah gladly followed the old lady and her son ;
but she walked as if in a dream; there was a dazed
look in her face, and a stamp as if some horrible actual
bodily torture had passed over her on her brow, which
it would have wrung the hardest heart to see, while
there was an expression in her eyes which the old lady,
in all her long life of seventy-eight years, had never
seen in any human eyes before. When she reached
Madame St. Cyr's house she both felt and looked so

terribly ill that she willingly assented to the kind old lady's entreaties that she would go to bed, and soon found herself in a pretty primitive apartment, hung with white dimity curtains, and a polished wood floor.

The fact was, the heavy town air of Paris and the long close confinement to the house, so different to her usual life, had already begun to tell on her, while the events of the last few days seemed likely to bring matters to a crisis with a regular bad illness.

For the first day or two, she was too stunned, too paralysed in mind to speak or act at all; and it seemed to those watching her as if her brain must give way; so great was the trial her mind was undergoing, that substantial things appeared to express no meaning to her. And this is the most terrible sign of all mental phenomena, when the doctrine of union, or the common tie of soul and body seems to be shattered while both are living.

But, gentle nursing and tender care, combined with the feeling of safety, calmness and security, which came over her insensibly in Madame St. Cyr's house, acted as powerful restoratives. The kind old lady, who spent her whole time in good works, had taken an immense fancy to her; broken hearted herself at the appalling death of her son, she seemed to find a comfort in soothing Moyrah's grief. After a time; and by dint of some cautious French questioning, always the cleverest questioning in the world, Moyrah told her a little about the history of her life; and Madame St. Cyr listened, her face quivering with interest, her eyes full of tears of sympathy.

In return she told her how, almost immediately after her daugher had left her convent school, Lenoir, who was then occupying what appeared to be a good commercial position at Bayonne, had won her affections and been legally married to her in the cathedral of the town, obtaining with her a handsome *dot*. She was then proceeding to give an account of her daughter's married life; but there was an expression on Moyrah's face which obliged her to stop; the cruellest person on earth could not have gone on, and Madame St. Cyr was far from being that. She had, however, said enough to show what would probably have been the fate of anyone who remained with Lenoir. As the Latin verses on the walls of Pompeii are to Christians, so were her words to Moyrah; a scarecrow to prove the horrors from which their creed has saved them. She merely added, therefore, that she had been obliged to leave him; and that she now feared she was sinking into a consumption, and had gone to spend the winter with a cousin at Granada, in hopes that the change of climate might restore her health.

When she returned to her son in the drawing room, she said, at they sat over their tea, after she had explained the whole story to him, " What words can tell the misery that one man without principles can work? "

" No; *not* without principles," said the young priest, emphatically, "but with clear, definite and decided principles, and who *acts up to them*," he put down his tea and leaned forward. " This, mother, is what I want you to explain to the Irish young lady, for it is necessary for the good of her country that it should be distinctly understood there." Like all men his interest quickly went from the individual to the general, from persons to politics. " Entreat of her to tell all the people round her what results *must* follow from the principles of Communism, which I see from the papers are being preached to the less learned part of her people just now. We, in France, have put those principles into practice, and can speak with the authority of experience; tell her this; persuade her to become an apostle when she goes home, so as to avert the ruin of her nation." His fair young face flushed as he leaned forward in eager excitement. " Tell her to do this, unless she wishes to see her brothers die as I have just seen mine; her sisters become as she is."

His mother turned away with a sob, and shook her head.

"O, *do* tell her mother," he reiterated, with intense earnestness. "The laity might do so much if they only knew; people pay ten times as much attention to them as to the clergy."

"I cannot," said Madame St. Cyr.

"At least, mother; *at least* explain to her that he is *not* a man without principles, for this is the gist of the whole matter. A man without principles does little harm, weathercocks don't influence the wind; but a man with villainous principles, who persuades men they are right, acts up to them, and spreads them, he is the real devastator. It is the principles, mother, which I dread, not the individuals; this is what I want you to make clear to her, to impress upon her."

She shook her head, buried her face in her hands, and sobbed: "I cannot speak to her again upon the subject."

"O mother, do, do!" and he laid his hand on her shoulder.

"Louis," and looking up, she fixed her eyes steadily on him, "do you really expect a girl in her position to go about lecturing her countrymen on politics?"

"Not politics! Religion, faith, home, her own soul, the souls of her countrymen! Surely for these, she might forget herself for the sake of her nation" (and all the large manliness and grandeur of his man's nature shone out through his eyes), "personal feelings are so small and contemptible when duty calls; *pro patria*, one can do anything."

But his mother had only the small woman's nature, in which the individual evermore obscures the general; and she knew Moyrah had it, too. So she shook her head again more decidedly than before.

CHAPTER XXXVII.

A S soon as Moyrah's physical strength was sufficiently improved to enable her to get out of bed and stand without support, which it was after a few days, she decided to start directly for home.

She would go at once to Cormac, and ask him if what Lenoir had said of him was true ; for she now began to doubt every word he had uttered. If it was not, she would humbly beg his pardon for having believed such a charge against him ; then she would go back to the Blue House ; once more see her father ; then lie down quietly and die, she hoped, and be buried under the shadow of the old Irish cross in the church-yard, with its many mystical meanings worked out in the lives of those who knelt round its foot.

Madame St. Cyr endeavoured, in vain, to persuade her to stay on with her until her health was entirely restored, and promised, if she would do so, that she should have the most perfect quiet, and as much seclusion as she could desire ; and that when she was obliged to go, she would herself accompany her as far as Paris. But Moyrah was firm, and the first day that she was able to go out, she decided to take the evening mail to Paris.

In the interval between her *café noir* and roll, and the large *déjeuner* at eleven o'clock, she stole out unobserved, and for the first and last time entered the old cathedral.

She did not stare about her ; she did not even ask to see the *chasse* of St. Leon, patron and bishop of the cathedral; nor the *crosse* of St. François de Sales, though Madame St. Cyr had told her she must be sure to see them when she went. She stole up one of the side aisles with her head bent down and her eyes on the ground.

The dominant impulse in her mind at that moment was to creep away into some dark corner where no one could see her, and there remain unnoticed by men or angels or any living or discerning creature for ever. Her one desire was that her name, her personality, the fact she had ever existed, might be blotted from the history of mankind.

The only pain human nature is called upon to bear, which seems absolutely intolerable, and as if it must end in death unless relief quickly comes, is the pain of shame. What is so terrible is, that when that shadow strikes even the most sturdy intellect, the dial of conscience appears useless; and this is, perhaps, because the sunshine of that heavenly love, which, falling on our conscience, alone enables us to keep time with the march of the church militant, seems to be darkened with a darkness which, in our then state of mind, we imagine will never be removed.

When we are in great shame we do not think we shall ever come out of it. Our reason forgets itself, and gives an impulsive assent to the dictum of our imagination, which says it is for ever.

This is what Moyrah felt; the sun was never to shine on her again. It seemed as if the whole world had its eye fixed upon her in the accumulated scorn of all scorners put together; and this eye, she thought, would be there for ever, following her on into an eternity of ever deepening disgrace. There was no cave in the centre of some far off and entirely lonely mountain where that eye of scorn would not follow her. Nowhere on earth! And heaven seemed a long way off and, so to speak, entirely out of her beat, now. It was the sense of its endlessness, of the impossibility of its ever being removed, which was, perhaps, the bitterest drop in the dregs of the cup which was now held to her lips.

There was, however, another very bitter drop, and that was that she felt as if she were prevented from asking for compassion. She thought she was the only person who ever was in shame, and she dared not claim sympathy in so unnatural a trouble. She realized from the first that there are some wounds of the soul so deep, that the dearest and most intimate earthly friend cannot sympathise with them; so deep, that we do not put them into words even to our own secret thoughts. It is this hiddenness which acts like such a strong narcotic over the rebound of hope, even in extreme youth.

Too often, also, acute shame so dulls the intellectual faculties, that we turn away from all light, even divine light, to hide ourselves where, as we hope, light of any sort can never come.

In such moments we forget that heavenly light shining on the tear of worthy shame—and certainly there is such a thing—is like a beam of solar light falling obliquely on a rain drop. It is refracted on entering the drop, is in part reflected at the back of the drop, and on coming out from the drop is again refracted, so that the dazzling blaze is softened to our weak eyes, and still enriched with many warm, beautiful prismatic colours; and is ten times more lovely when it comes out than when it went in. But all this is hidden from us at the time. It was all hidden from Moyrah; and what in part hid it was the shadow which shut out human sympathy from her. No kind eyes could be won to look with pity into hers, as they had hitherto done in the smallest home troubles. No warm, strong human hand could clasp hers, and give her that indescribable sensation of support which such a grasp imparts.

Fragments of scenes in her future life rose before her; no longer haunting and evanescent, but taking a

scorching reality and nearness of colouring from her
quickened imagination—an imagination always vivid,
and now terribly sharpened. Everyone turning away
from her, and pretending not to see her. Kind old
village friends, who were wont to stop her when she
was busy and in a hurry just for the pleasure of a chat,
now crossing to the other side of the road, and striding
or bustling along with their heads down; as she had
seen happening to other girls in the village before.
Black looks on all sides, even from people she used to
think small things of. No sympathy anywhere.

She had always been deficient in mastering the cold,
hard, unsympathetic side of human nature; but now it
came before her, not as a shadow seen from a distance,
but as a present and very close reality. It came in
that horribly real way suffering has got of coming to
us when we are most defenceless. It came, and she
felt, indeed, a prisoner, with the torturer standing near
at hand.

Like all natures which are themselves full of
sympathy, and with affections so quickly in touch with
those around her that sometimes her intuition seemed
like magic, she was morbidly sensitive to want of
sympathy in others. One glance of coldness, one word
of indifference, in the old days, would upset her entirely,
and would dwell in her mind for months, seeming to
destroy the springs of buoyancy, and make her unable
to laugh, even at her father's best jokes.

Then, though she felt what was coming and tried to
ward it off, there rose before her her father's face. Oh,
awful thought! His face when he came out to meet her,
as she walked up through the garden of the Blue House;
the look of suffering with her suffering that would be
on it. She could not bear that greatest of all pains,
seeing one we love suffering for us, and we unable to
comfort them. She could not bear it! No! she could not
bear it. She drove the image almost passionately away.
Then her mother's bitter disappointment, which she

knew would, after a time, take the form of reproach.
Then Eileen's face, and the boys' faces. Then again,
in spite of all her efforts, her father's face. No! she
could not bear it. She trembled from head to foot,
while she buried her face in her hands and shuddered.
And ever as she tried, almost fiercely, to drive away the
thought of her father, of that rugged brow, and those
soft grey eyes, of the load of suffering and humiliation
she would add to his closing years, it came back over
her again and again, and stabbed blow after blow down
deep into her heart. Could she have borne her troubles
alone, hard as that might seem at first, it was almost
happiness compared to the thought of the expression
with which his eyes would meet hers evermore for the
rest of her life.

But while struggling with the thoughts of her father,
a hitherto undreamed of agony slowly crept up towards
her. Its shadow, getting closer and closer, seemed to
paralyse her efforts to keep it at a distance. Up to this
moment the tortures she had suffered had not been one,
but broken into numberless partial aspects, independent
each of each, and so unable, because baffled by division,
to reach the utmost depth of pain. But now, one, one
only, was coming. Not the combination of many
torments, scattering their darts in many places, but
one, only one, all by itself. Closer and closer it stole
up, as some awful figure seems to be coming near us
sometimes in the depth of a dark night. She struggled
so fearfully to escape, that even her body moved as if a
corporeal danger was at hand. But her last shield of
self-defence was broken.

It came, and, in one instant, all other thoughts were
swept away—as they must be in such a character as
hers—like a number of little ripples before a tidal wave,
when the thought of Lenoir rushed over her. She had
loved him with a love which was perfectly dispropor-
tionate, according to the judgment of reason—a love
which had magnified itself as it grew until it became

almost dangerous to the dignity of her nature. Every day she had loved him more and more, and each hour she had, as it were, put stone upon stone, until the edifice of her prison was complete, and she found herself surrounded by walls thicker than those of the Bastille. The walls of love for an object which was worthy only of hatred and scorn. But she was as little at home with hatred and scorn as Lenoir with thoughts of true love.

She had loved—*had* loved—*had!* And now, in one moment, she was asked to tear that love out of her heart entirely and for ever. She was asked with a small human hand to tear down the walls of the Bastille. And no one would sympathise with her for having to do so. On the contrary, she would meet only with blame and reproach for ever having felt that love. But what did she care for contempt, or reproach, or anything else, if that love must go? It seemed as if agony, in a concrete, personal form, was taking the measure of her capability to bear agony. For the shadow had come up to her now, and was worse than anything her worst fears had imagined. She was bewildered, almost stunned. Certainly, we need a clue to the labyrinth of unaccustomed visions which twine round us at all the great crises of life.

She knelt down on the cold stones, behind a pillar, close to an altar of the Blessed Virgin, but from where she could catch a glimpse of the statue. She did not dare to go any nearer, or even to kneel on the little *prie-Dieu* chair close by. She knelt on those cold, hard stones, which were like the face the world would turn to her for the rest of her life. But she had forgotten that; forgotten home and family; forgotten shame; forgotten her mother's reproaches, even, for the moment, her father's suffering. Forgotten all in the whole world except Lenoir, and felt that if she might still love him she would be content—aye, and happy—to be trampled under the feet of all men. If, though the world divided them, she might still think of him as hers; still work for him; still slave to procure him the smallest happiness, and feel when she did it that he was hers, her own; she would not care if even inanimate things turned away from her in scorn.

If she might! If only she might! Like all of us when we are in suffering, she craved for a versatile rule. That is, a law that would change according to individual character. A law that would not cause such infinite agony, because she was so peculiarly capable of feeling that agony. It sometimes seems to us as if it might be urged, that the variety of different dispositions in human nature, was a reason for expecting a variety of different laws. Not the one unalterable inexorable fixed rule for hard characters and soft, loving natures, and loveless ones.

In junctures of such awful moment as had now come to Moyrah, our intellect is not left alone, but strange impressions come over it, and words are spoken to it it hears at no other time. Suggestions are made which no antecedent reasoning in our minds has at all either prepared us for, or justified our being tortured by. Where do those words come from? Who suggests these suggestions? That imposture too often accompanies the most subtle working of our brain all will allow; but imposture is not personal enough to offer a suggestion. It can obscure, it cannot reverse those true findings of our higher nature of which it is but the mockery. Therefore there must be some personal being at work behind the imposture trying to destroy those findings; those findings which in most natures of the finer sort have worked for years, and moulded the character before the imposture tries its hand. They had so worked with Moyrah.

But sometimes the imposture is dominant and tyrannical; and though it may only be for a few moments, those moments are a time of crucial peril. Having crept in disguise into the sanctuary of our heart, it puts

its back against the door and will not be turned out.
Without a note of warning to herald its approach,
without a preliminary skirmish of any sort, suddenly it
seemed to have gained a foot-hold in Moyrah, for the
first time in her life.

Theologians might have used severe language concerning the doubts, the questionings, which came to her
just then. The leaders of the modern revolt against
theologians would have used other language. This is
ever the way men act concerning the arguments of
others. In reality, they dissent from their *first principles*, which puzzle them, and which they never clearly
understand. If we could all get at each other's *first
principles*, and thoroughly understand them, what a
reign of peace would descend on earth! We should
know then it was useless to discuss some subjects at
all. But life goes by in superficial arguments, which
answer no purpose but to inflame the minds of all
parties. Many good people are really agreed about
first principles, though their mode of expressing their
views is so contradictory, involved, and extraordinary,
that they come at last to think they differ on every
point and must be sworn foes.

Moyrah's first principles were just now being shaken
to their foundations. Her first principles—her very
first principles, not her mode of expressing them. It
seemed, for a few seconds, as if her soul had become
like a pagan city, with the hierarchy all in dispute
amongst themselves about signs of bad augury in the
heavens. What insubordination, what a tumult was
within her! A riot of revolt, like the riot which ran
in the Parisian socialist's words which had so horrified
her. How new to her! How utterly unheard of in
her past life, where she had never taught herself to look
on disbelief as a privilege, God as behind the age on
important points, and man as His teacher; the moral
law as a tyranny, and self-will the only freedom; doubt,
the highest religious duty! All her deepest feelings

hitherto had been like "Antrustions," who were personal vassals, subservient and extraordinarily obedient
to the kings and counts amongst the Franks, in that
land where she now was.   But now they were in open
rebellion.   The inborn dislike of rule, the wildness, the
love of doing what it was told not, of the Irish nature,
defied every barrier of past self-restraint.   What that
wildness, that delight in insubordination, is, only those
most intimately acquainted with that nature can form a
correct conception.   Her soul was now in a sort of
murky, unnatural twilight.   Light and darkness are
the eternal principles in which our souls live ; not equal
principles, but one the negation of the other.   Sometimes, in a soul like Moyrah's, in which there has been
true light all its life, the noble system of light will sink,
as it did with the magicians of old, into a petty char-
latanism.   The darkness is bad enough, but this is
worse.   These false lights, so well at home in modern
society, were struggling desperately to illuminate her.
Fashionable will-o'-the wisps wandering from Paris and
London west-end drawing rooms to the Irish girl's
heart in the Basque land of faith.   Here was a new
happy hunting ground for them.   A landscape of
unspotted snow on which their rays had never shone
before.   Would she be dazzled and bewildered into
following them ?   Would they be powerful enough to
melt her Irish faith, child-like earnestness of belief, and
innate innocence ?

An argument with characters of such perfect veracity
that it becomes almost personal, may be presented before
the mind, but, notwithstanding, there may be no external
reality corresponding to it, though it may be so vivid as
to appear absolutely faithful to nature.   Arguments and
images, undreamt of before, crowded over Moyrah's
mind ; and they were followed by propositions on propositions of the most daringly sceptical and rebellious
colour.   And words, actual words, seemed to ring in
her ears, as if some one was speaking to her.   But,

though puzzled, baffled, bewildered, she retained enough sense to see that she ought to have some more logical reason for assenting to a proposition than the powerfulness of the image of which it was the expression.

But still it was a hard, a desperate, a hand-to-hand fight. So tremendous was the assault that, for a short—a very short—time principles, and even feelings, of long standing reeled before it, and appeared as if they must go down. The enemy seemed rushing in from every side, equipped with the deadliest weapons. Aye, with the deadliest of all, the worship of her whole nature, the love of her whole heart. The solid square of the ten commandments quivered, quivered terribly, but remained unbroken, so far. They stood shoulder to shoulder, with their feet set on the rock of that church of which Moyrah had, hitherto, been the happy and faithful child.

But Lucifer had raised his standard with consummate skill and daring, knowing the weak points to an ace on which to concentrate his forces—that standard with the old, old motto ; and the powers of her soul seemed to rally round it with a fierce determination to stay there and not to budge a jot, which appalled her judgment.

Once again the ten commandments quivered, as they so often do when acting, so to speak, in their private capacity. They stand firm enough on the walls of the church, or in the printed pages of the Bible, but once they quit their official position and enter everyday life, it is there the rebel from the beginning " has at them."

It appeared to her that in one deafening shout, which stunned her altogether, her own voice, her own very voice, Moyrah's voice, echoed the burning words written in letters of flame on that well worn flag, 'now as ever, *non serviam.* Words which rang through heaven once, followed by a quick reply; words which rang through her now, and to which she did not seem able to give any reply; words which sound so fascinating, but hide such wells of bitterness. The motto which has led the first revolutionist to victory so often, over so many broken hearts and ruined lives.

That motto now seemed to take entire possession of Moyrah. The attack was too sudden for her to protest, or, it seemed to her, even to oscillate. Her judgment appeared like a general looking on from a hill in horror, while he sees his whole army go over bodily to the enemy. But this was the exaggerated impression which a bird's-eye view so often gives, and which our judgment, necessarily being bird's-eye, constantly deceives us with. There was no real desertion of the true colours; only amongst one corps of the army a conspiracy, which might lead to disastrous results, unless treated with rapid decision. Suddenly, while the battle was at its height, she raised her eyes, as of old Constantine raised his, and before her, standing on the side altar near which she was kneeling, was the sign he saw. She looked at it intently. In one instant the exorcism was complete. *Now* there was truly no oscillation. In one blow the day was won. But the battle over, it left her lonely and desolate. It had taken away her breath with horror and amazement while it lasted; but it had occupied her. Once over, that fearful desolation took possession of her again. As she knelt, with her head bent low, a longing for sympathy came over her, so terrible in its passionate thirst that it seemed harder to bear even than the pain which caused it. This, she thought, could never be satisfied. For that tender mother to whom she had gone for comfort in all her other troubles had never known the one she was now called upon to bear. Shame had no place in the burdens of her sinless soul.

While she was thinking this, the low, deep notes of the organ began to swell through the gothic arches. With a soft, gradually increasing glow of tone, full of richness and splendour, rolling on in one glorious flood of mellow harmony, pealed forth the strains of Rossini's

"Stabat Mater." A few soft, southern, tenor voices and one boy's soprano united in concord with the tones of the organ. A grand volume of melody rolled round and round the pillars, and seemed wafted, like the clouds of the incense, into the furthest corners of the church. It lingered round the heads of the old grey saints in their niches; and some of them, fonder of music than the rest, clasped the roving notes in passing, and took from them that softened expression which some of those old, grey cathedral saints have so much more than others.

It was Friday, and a rich châtelaine of the neighbourhood was having a requiem mass said at the high altar for the repose of the soul of her only son, who had been killed in the Franco-German war.

Moyrah had sometimes helped in the village choir at home. She knew the music well, and she had learned the English translation of the words by heart out of her prayer book, the Golden Manual. Those sublime words, which have brought consolation to so many thousands of sufferers since first Jacopo di Todi, himself a sufferer and in shame, wrote them, came like balm over that pain which had been so great because it was not known to any one.

It seemed as if the very abyss of her misery had spoken to the abyss of peace, and that, all in one moment, the answer had come. As she listened she meditated as she had done in Paris. But the scene was changed now.

It was a cold, grey morning in Jerusalem, the morning of the first Good Friday. Moyrah had so often read about this in her "Douai," and in a few rather musty old "Lives of the Saints," which her mother kept in a tin biscuit box in her bed room, that the scene seemed to come before her as if she were there.

The inhabitants of the densely populated city, and all the strangers who had collected for the festival, were hurrying about fearing an insurrection. As they went they remarked :

" The disciples of that impostor will now not know where to hide their heads."

" He will find no one now to cut olive branches and strew their garments before his feet."

" Yes, and of all his disciples, one has betrayed him, one has denied him, and the rest have all run away."

The Blessed Virgin was there, but not so as to be recognized, but she overheard all that was passing.

Moyrah went with her in spirit, step by step, throughout the whole of that day. And in the evening she was standing alone in the small, eastern room of her now desolate home. Moyrah knelt at the door. She saw her, and turned. She held out her hand, with a sort of light on her face, which was scarcely a smile, breaking through her tears. Moyrah looked up, and as she did so, felt she had never known the meaning of the word sympathy before.

The rich, beautiful, southern voice had finished the *Cujus Animam,* and the hymn was drawing to its close. The choir were singing with such harmony and modulation that no single strain could have been taken away without injury to the whole. Now and again a boy's voice flew with that peculiar Basque lightness—for some of the choir were Basques—up to heaven, as though tipped by an arrow plume. Then the rich, deep baritones rolled round the arches, full of the colour of tone, and imparting such an ideal of the strength the words give to bear suffering, that the listeners wondered if any bribing would coax those deep notes to linger on for ever, to be at their side, to heal each future wound in life. As they repeated—

> " Eia mater fons amoris
>
> Me sentire vim doloris
>
> Fac ut tecum lugeam."

Moyrah did, indeed, mingle tears with that compassionate mother, and as she did so, felt that there was one, at least, who loved her better in her shame than in her joy. One face of her own sex that never would be turned away from her, one entirely human heart which beat, even in her deepest humiliation, side by side, pulse for pulse, with hers; one mother's breast on which she could lay her tired head, and learn all that " a mother " means.

END OF VOL I.